THE

CW01619874

Ali Roberts

DEDICATION

To my husband Dominic. You are the funniest person alive and luckily for you, I'm the second funniest. Thank you for laughing all the way through this book with me.

CONTENTS

The Unseen
Copyright © 2025 by Ali Roberts

All rights reserved.

No part of this book may be reproduced, stored in a retrieval system, or transmitted in any form or by any means—electronic, mechanical, photocopying, recording, or otherwise—without prior written permission from the publisher, except for the use of brief quotations in a book review.

This is a work of fiction. Names, characters, businesses, places, events, and incidents are either the products of the author's imagination or used fictitiously. Any resemblance to actual persons, living or dead, or actual events is purely coincidental.

CONTENT WARNINGS

This is a romantic comedy that dabbles in the dark. Our MMC has a significantly violent past and mentions of events that involved violent acts are included. This has been used to advance the plot and character progression and is not used in excessive detail.

Trigger warnings:

- Violence
- Murder
- Tasering
- Stalking
- Abduction
- Therapy/mental health
- Childhood trauma
- Mentions of parental death
- Light breath play/impact play

Reader discretion is advised.

PROLOGUE

Two Years Ago

There's nothing more embarrassing than a thirty-something year old man speed walking between pedestrians. I mean sure, I could be wearing lycra with a funny headband on but I'm not. I'm in a tailored suit with split knuckles and an expression of pure panic, which only confirms I hadn't *planned* to speed-walk through the streets of Seattle this morning.

I barge into a man who despite scrunching his brow and opening his mouth to give me a good telling-off, takes one look at me and smartly closes his mouth and scurries away.

I know why too. I have a hideous purple bruise on my left cheek that has swollen so extensively, I can't open my eye more than half way. My knuckles are red and scabbed, threatening to split every time I clench my fist in frustration, which, spoiler alert, is quite often.

But here I am, burning my calves to escape one of my father's associates who'd propositioned me two months ago. His wife had been curling her stilettoed shoe up and down the inside of my leg for an hour before I felt him do the same. She wasn't asking for a risky romp in the bathroom right under her husband's nose. They were asking for a threeway.

Something, in all honesty, I wouldn't normally hate. Who doesn't take their business with a little pleasure? But the text my father sent me earlier that day made a lot more sense as I felt the unsaid proposition between my legs.

Do what it takes to close this deal.

The realization that my father had pimped me out was a hard pill to swallow. I do a lot for my father as his enforcer. I'm the six-foot-four brawn that will politely encourage you to do what is in your best interest. If not, there'll be consequences.

Hint, it's me. I'm the consequence.

But I'd never been asked to sleep with an associate and his wife before. Sure… I've done it. Not under the orders of my father, but of my own volition. Is this my life now? Even my sex life was at his command. The sting was measured equally between embarrassment and the sense that I had been a dutiful lap dog my entire adult life. Had my other encounters been orchestrated like this one? Had my father had a hand in all of it?

So for the first time in my life, I politely refused, settled the bill and high-tailed it out of there. Two months later and I am fleeing a mid fifties, hair-thinning man, like a scared little boy. Which, I'm not ashamed to admit. I am. I'm fucking terrified.

I had told my father that I was done working for him a few weeks after that dinner. The evening with Mr and Mrs Winter, a.k.a. Mr. and Mrs. Proposition had been a catalyst for me to make some changes in my life. It took a few weeks, but I'd finally told Dad I wasn't doing it anymore. And now, despite the changes I've been making to become a better person, flashes of screams, blood, and smacks of metal on flesh cloud my vision before I push them back down. As if the very sight of Mr. Winter brought them bubbling back up to the surface.

The final straw came when I did something unforgivable. On paper it might not be worse than anything I've done before, but it cut deeper this time. The shame rose high and I felt my face redden for the first time in years, just from the thought of it.

Given that I'd quit a job that doesn't accept resignations unless they're in the form of obituaries, I'd spent the last few months attempting to build something legitimate for my life. Something secret that my father couldn't know about. Something that sounded scary enough to keep people at bay. But by the time night rolled around, the memories of my previous life came swooping back in. The only way I could get through them was to get black-out drunk at a local bar. It always seemed to end with me vomiting most of what I'd drunk on my hands and knees in an adjacent alleyway. It was that, or fighting. And last night, I apparently felt the need to over-achieve, so I did both. Therefore when I say that speed-walking through Seattle wasn't on my list of things to do today, I meant it.

I duck into a lime green colored café and hide behind the largest person I can find and pretend to tie my shoe. I'm watching through the throngs of morning café dwellers waiting for their coffees or smoothies as it seems everyone in here is drinking. I spot Mr Winter's head through the window popping up and down like a meerkat as he scans the street. I stay hidden despite the cluck of a tongue and a scowl from a woman attempting to give me away. I give her my best sheepish smile but that still seems to terrify her so I decide to keep my face neutral going forward.

As Mr Winter's moves along, I dare to stand, ordering a black coffee at the counter.

"Olivia," the worker calls out and that's where I see her. Long blonde hair braided into two plaits, her workout gear hugging her body tightly in a way that makes me jealous. Two round cheeks outlined by the high pull of her shorts. Fucking spectacular. She turns so I can see her face, reaching out to take the smoothie.

I freeze. I know this girl. But surely it can't be her? I'd just watched her video this morning. She's a fitness influencer and I had somewhat guessed she was local to me given her accent but it hadn't occurred to me I could bump into her.

My lips part as I'm about to tell her I know her but the café worker slips and her body throws forward. Her hand grips the plastic cup housing the bright green smoothie and it spurts out all over Olivia's pink lycra clothing, slowly oozing between her hiked up breasts and dripping down to reach the sliver of stomach she has exposed.

I expect her to be furious. Hell, I'm furious for her. She's covered in green sludge which will never come out of that fabric. I step forward to help, but Olivia promptly throws her head back in a deep cackle. She takes the napkins that multiple patrons have offered and starts to dab herself.

"Oh my god, I'm so sorry. I slipped and I-" the café worker practically screams so the whole place is watching with rapt attention.

"Hey, it's okay." Olivia reassures her. "Come here for a second, you're shaking."

She sits her down, most of the green smoothie wiped clean from her body, the rest I have the strong urge to lick up myself and given the way the other men in this room are gawking, I'd say I wasn't the only one.

"I'm so sor-" she starts again.

"I told you. None of that. We all do embarrassing things. One time, I went on a run with a client and made him do burpees in this field. It turned out, a lot of dog owners went to that field and he was covered in dog poop by the end. It was absolutely disgusting. This is not nearly as bad as that, Jenny."

Jenny hiccups and laughs, the red in her cheeks lessening, "Thank you."

"I will need another smoothie though. And a cup of tea for yourself."

She nods, smiling before heading back behind the counter.

I stare for a moment, bewildered that she didn't scream in her face for being so clumsy. But she didn't. She laughed. *Laughed*. And then proceeded to make her feel better about the situation despite being the one covered in smoothie.

Looking around the café, everyone has mostly gone about their day. They're sipping on their drinks, pulling on their jackets, like they hadn't just witnessed something so life-altering.

People are genuinely nice to each other.

This isn't something out of a cheesy movie. People genuinely don't go round starting fights with people and screaming in their faces for perceived slights and minor altercations.

I stumble back into a free chair against the wall and I watch Olivia settle into the worn armchair by the window. She pulls out a book, dabbing herself a few more times with some napkins Jenny brings over.

I decide there and then I have to talk to her. She's squinting a little, blinded by the light shining through the window, but she looks happy. I have to know how she does it. I have to find out if it's real or not. Maybe she's masking her anger and she'll go home and stuff pins into a doll with Jenny's face on it. My gut tells me no. My gut tells me she might be a genuinely kind person.

The video that had popped up on my suggested feed this morning had been on mindfulness. And I won't lie, the only reason I clicked on it was because it showed the most beautiful girl sitting cross legged, barefoot on a brightly colored yoga mat. As I watched her complete the video, I scoffed at the notion of tricking your mind into calming down. Following none of her instructions I watched as her breasts heaved as she took deep breaths in and out.

Her warm smile at the end of the video left me with a strange tingling in my chest that seems to travel around my body. Despite only watching, I had felt calmer. My shoulders had relaxed, which was a feat given that I haven't felt a sense of peace in years. I frown as I touch my bruised cheek, before attempting to shake off the pain that was seeping in now that I was due some more painkillers.

"Austin, coffee." The barrister calls out.

Olivia's head whips up from her book and her eyes widen, a small squeak escaping her parted lips as her eyes meet mine. I frown as fear flashes across her face. She looks like she knows me. But I'd only just watched her video this morning, so there's no way. I'm only certain because I wouldn't forget her face. It's too perfect, too pretty. She looks like she's got one of those filters on her face, but in real life. It would be annoying if she wasn't so lovely.

But her serene self is gone as she quickly dips her head back into her book holding it so close to her face it looks like she's trying to hide.

I grab my coffee, trying out a small smile to the barrister that didn't bare any teeth. She smiles back and a warmth floods my chest.

I turn around to make good on the promise I made to introduce myself but the armchair is empty. The ding of the bell rings through the juice bar. She's gone.

CHAPTER ONE

Austin

It's ironic, really. None of the crazy shit that I've done in my life has prepared me for this moment. In my arrogance—or perhaps naivety—I don't see this coming. But I'm getting ahead of myself. The day starts like many life-changing days: a little off. I wake up as furious as I was yesterday and the day before that, if I'm being honest. And as if trying to mock my internal struggle, Seattle blazes with a burst of glorious sunshine so unfamiliar to the typical cloud coverage that it just pisses me off even more. Truthfully, I could do with a gray day and a light drizzle that clings to my clothes for hours, but the universe chooses otherwise. For many, it would be a lucky day. However, my foul mood singes, seeping through my fingertips, so everything I touch bears the brunt of my frustration. The stomach acid burning its way up my throat for the last few days has been attempting to spray out like venom, and I know just the person I want to aim at.

But then, like a cruel trick, I realize why the sun has been shining, the universe's pathetic fallacy incarnate. Olivia Daniels sways over to me, smiling—no, *beaming* down at me—as I dribble god-awful coffee from my gaping mouth. Not the image I want her to keep. As I dab the coffee stain on my shirt, the girl I've been watching for two long, long years asks me for help, and of course, I don't suspect her.

This must be why the sun is shining. The universe is

providing me with a perfect backdrop for my fantasy coming to life. One door closes, and another one opens, if you believe in that kind of thing.

So now that I'm handed a cloth with the sickly, sweet smell of chloroform and instructed to hold it to my mouth, I pause and wonder how I could have been so stupid.

You know those docuseries that women seem to be fascinated with? The ones with the serial killers? And despite women being their primary victims, they can't seem to stop watching with some morbid fascination. They're the shows that are as much a warning as they are informative.

Watch out, these bad men will get you, and you'll let them. Because before you know you're in any real danger, it'll be too late. You're trapped, caught, *snared.*

This is that moment.

Except, I'm not a damsel in distress. I am a six-foot-four man, lift weights four times a week, and have the muscle memory of a man who used to do terrible things. The onus on *used to do terrible things.* I'm a good boy now. And being good when you're so used to being bad is tricky. If you start letting the bad in certain aspects of your life, it becomes very easy to justify it in others. So, despite being a good-looking boy, I've never made a move on Olivia Daniels. Although, even if I had, it wouldn't have worked on this goddess. Up until her swaying hips this morning, she's been completely uninterested in the likes of me.

Again, I'm getting ahead of myself. I'm still confused about how I'm in this situation. Still unsure of what it is I'm doing here. All I can think is: do you know what doesn't happen to six-foot-four ex-Enforcers? They don't get Ted Bundy'd. They don't get outmaneuvered by women in crop tops and matching leggings with a fake sling.

There's no warning for men. No warning against sweet eyes and full hips. The worst we could come to expect is a honey trap and subsequently lighter wallet. The former is not an issue for me, as good boys always wrap up. And despite what you may have heard about me, I've always been good in that regard. I've been out of the game for a few years with help from TV personality and therapist, Dr. Angel, real name Alfie Adams. He's helped me overcome a lifetime of bad behavior inherited from my father. Anyone else part of the Shit Dad Club? We've had a lot to unpack. Of course, given his celebrity status and all-round panty-melting charm, you'd wonder how he got involved with the likes of me. But don't worry, we'll get to that.

For now, I really must focus on Olivia. She is attempting to chloroform me, after all. Dr. Alfie has heard of her. Hell, we've talked for hours about her to the point he's remarked on my unhealthy obsession. When I tell him about this, I'm sure he'll think I've had a complete breakdown of reality. Dr. Alfie thinks I put her on a pedestal, and perhaps he's right. I've never believed that my future held a conversation with her. She's too good, too pure. And yet, it seems even in my wildest dreams, I didn't imagine her being bad. How the tables have turned, sweet Olivia.

Despite the buzz of excitement I feel at being the focus of her attention, it does leave me in somewhat of a predicament. My first problem is a five-foot-six, blonde-haired pocket rocket who has successfully duped me into helping her to her car with the use of a fake sling and the promise of another smile that she's denied me for the last few years.

Of course, I had been thinking with the wrong head, so I followed her, lapping up her attention and light giggles.

Yes, angel, find me funny.

Laugh at my jokes.

I'll be the clown for you every day of the fucking week.

With the dribbled coffee on my shirt mostly dry, I held her books, helped her with the door, and held the luminous green matcha *fucking whatever* smoothie that she gets from this juice bar three times a week.

My heart thumped so hard that I felt it against my ribs. I was uncharacteristically quiet, waiting for her to make the next move. Not once has she spoken to me before. Most times we see each other, she purposely avoids any kind of interaction. On days I am graced with eye contact, it is accompanied by scowls, eye rolls, and a click of her tongue that I could find a much better use for.

I've tried to work it out for months, but finding nothing online to connect us, I accepted that all I would ever receive from her was a look of disgust, or worse, *indifference*.

But this morning, she looked nervous as she approached my table. Like she was deciding whether she could make a move or not. Like she is finally tired of waiting, and for the dumbest second of my life, I thought maybe that is why she's been so angry. Because she feels like I've snubbed her. Maybe I've read her wrong this whole time, and really, she is annoyed that I haven't asked her out that first day I saw her like I'd wanted to.

She struggled up from the wingback chair at the window where she always sits on Mondays, Wednesdays, and Fridays. Her Kindle hooked on her little finger as her thumb brushed over the screen at the rate of a professional speed reader.

She isn't her usual put-together self this morning. Her hair is thrown up into a loose bun, her usual styled braids or sleek ponytail nowhere to be seen. And I assumed it was the injury to her arm that's caused her dishevelment. A sling wrapping her left hand protectively.

And standing here now, it reminds me of a conversation with Dr. Alfie about lessons I've learned from my father. The most prominent being those who assume are those who are unprepared. And in our world, those who are unprepared best be ready to die.

Yeah, Alfie's signature eye roll had suggested he didn't like that lesson. Although it seems to fit this situation to a tee.

She stumbled and giggled as she attempted to carry her things. I instinctively reached to help her, fully expecting to be swatted away. But I was graced with pearly whites and a nervous chuckle. My raised eyebrows must have shown my surprise because her gaze softened as she looked down at me. Only a small bite of her lower lip gave any indication of nerves, and in my arrogance, I put that down to her wanting to ask me out.

I had never been so close to her. From a distance, she has seemed so ethereal. Whenever she leaned forward to pick up her juice from the low coffee table, never taking her eyes off the book she was reading, the light from the window created a soft glow around her. She looked angelic, otherworldly. But up close today, I could see a splattering of freckles. Her usual perfect makeup is rushed, and a small fleck of mascara sits on her cheek. If I had really thought about it, I would have known something was wrong. Especially since I've seen the video she posted yesterday where her arm was fine. Sure she could have filmed it weeks ago and spent time editing. But I know she's only just cut her hair like this since Wednesday.

Yes . . . I'm that guy. But I'm not a stalker. I'm . . . an admirer. Our time together in this juice bar, horrendously named Squeeze the Day, is the highlight of my week. A small respite to the otherwise debt-settling that I force myself to endure the remainder of my time. A punishment, if you will, for who I used to be. But in another way, this is a torture in itself. So close to someone so perfect who hates me so vehemently for reasons seemingly unrelated to my past. I've been so bad in my past life that even the new me needs to be punished.

So when she stumbled to my table this morning, I thought for a second my debt had been paid. I've repented enough, suffered enough, and deprived myself for long enough that, finally, something good might happen.

"Such a gentleman." She smiled warmly when I helped her pick up her things.

"Only when absolutely necessary," I quipped and that's when I saw it, her real smile. Not the poised ones from her fitness videos and not the polite ones she gives other patrons of Squeeze the Day. This one was real, and it was all for me.

"Well, helping a damsel in distress should count as necessary for a 'sometimes' gentleman." She practically purred.

I was putty, and her hands were wrapped around me, molding me the second she speaks. So, of course, I allowed her to lead me down the corridor toward the back of the café.

The fact that it is ill-lit with no cameras didn't seem dangerous. I'm Austin Black. Bad things don't happen to me. I do bad things to others—mostly those who deserve it. And if I'm honest, I just didn't see her as a threat at all. And if I give myself some credit, neither does anyone else. The café owners, Jenny and Anthony, waved cheerily as we made our way out the back.

I opened the door to her jeep, not questioning how she can drive with an injured arm. She asked me to place her things on the back seat, and I did. She stood so close to me that the hairs stood on the back of my neck. This was it. This is the moment I had been imagining for so long. I wasn't going to ask her out; I was going to tell her I'll pick her up. I'd promise her the best goddamn date she's ever had. We'd laugh about why it's taken so long for us to do this. I'll take her hand in mine, ending our night with a soft kiss that a gentleman would give. Never pushing her. Letting her set the pace. And if I were the luckiest son of a bitch in the entire solar system, she'd take me to bed, and I'd finally see what's underneath her workout gear she's only ever given hints of.

You're nearly brought up to speed. In just a few more seconds, I will have that resigned yet confused look on my face. Because I take a deep breath and turn just as a popping noise fills my ears. Olivia's mouth downturned, her smile and sling both missing, replaced with her usual scowl of indifference.

My eyes seek out the popping noise. A small black box in her hand crackles inches away from my crotch, the electric spark flashing in the dimly lit alley.

She is braced, ready to strike at any moment. But to

anyone more than a few meters away, we must look like a couple readying ourselves to return home.

And because I'm an idiot, the thought that we look like that to others makes me smile.

"I'm going to need you to hold this cloth to your mouth, please."

Her casual tone suggests she's asked me to move the books to another location or perhaps open the door for her. But the words replay in my head, and somehow, I am still confused, even after staring at the white rag in her perfectly manicured hand.

"Umm... what?" I chuckle, her politeness throwing my center of gravity off kilter. I'm not nervous about my physical safety, but her detached tone is unnerving.

"The cloth," she repeats. "Hold it to your mouth. Maybe sit in the car first. I won't be able to lift you." She's patient, like she's practiced this, fully expecting my confusion.

"Why would I make this easier for you?" I smirk, glancing toward the back door of the café, which is slightly ajar. Surely, someone will come out and witness this any second now.

The taser pops again as she grips the little black box tighter.

The Seattle sun, which earlier was so unwelcome, seems now like a warning. Like something is off about the day. Like seeing a cat on a leash or a rabbit in one of those rucksacks with the mesh cloth so they have a view of the world. *Unsettling.*

"I'll taser your dick and balls unless you do what I say. So lie back and hold it to your mouth..."

Jesus Christ.

I haven't exactly been using them lately, but still... There's no need to threaten Austin and the Chipmunks. They're an essential part of me. What would I do without my cock and balls? Well... pretty much everything I've been doing for the last year or two, but still. You don't just threaten a man's junk, for fuck's sake.

"We could maybe go for dinner first. You know, before we get into the kinky stuff." I waggle my eyebrows at her.

Her eyes lock with mine, and she waits. The back door swings open, its signature thump hitting the red brick wall as Jenny's laugh sings through the air. She's not looking over at us, instead concentrating on swinging a large black trash bag over her shoulder before stomping to the industrial trash bin. Any minute, she'll turn back around and see us here.

Olivia's eyebrows knit together, and her hand slips for a second. For a moment, I'm worried she's going to drop her arm and drive away, and our interaction will be over. I make a mental note to bring this up with Dr. Alfie because even I can recognize that wanting to chloroform yourself at the back of a juice bar isn't *normal*. Even if we don't use that word in therapy, Dr. Alfie is gonna have to do some real work to convince me this is something anyone else would do.

But then again, have they seen this girl? She's perfect. I know men who would have seriously done some reputational damage for a woman. Crawl on broken glass, cut their wrists, wear matching outfits on vacation. You know, real heinous stuff.

And I realize I'd wear his-and-her fucking everything. I'll get the embroidered robes and fluffy slippers. I'll wear the t-shirt that says "If lost, return to Olivia" as her t-shirt reads "I'm Olivia." We'll be that old couple in Europe roaming the streets, making everyone gag.

For now, I have a choice. Accept that the girl has put in top effort, chloroform myself, and see where this goes. Or, do the sensible option, twist her hand back, taser that beautiful tanned sliver of stomach she's taunting me with, and make a run for it.

Curiosity gets the better of me. Who the fuck is this girl I've been watching for two years? And how has she so successfully Ted Bundy'd me?

I might have been known as a cold, calculating bastard in my former life, but I have been looking for a punishment that goes beyond her usual scowls for a while now. In the ledger of life, I'm in massive fucking debt. If I ever want to balance the scales, I need to do something drastic. Or something drastic has to happen *to me*. And while I try to convince myself that this is just for punishment, being under the control of Olivia Daniels is too delicious to refuse.

Dr. Alfie is going to have a fucking field day once I tell him about this.

I take the cloth and hold it to my mouth, letting the blackness take me under, and the dank gray walls of the alleyway slip away.

CHAPTER TWO

Olivia

Well. There's no going back now. I have a brawling six-foot-something man in my back seat taking a self-imposed nap—kind of.

And not just any man. Austin Black. King of The Unseen, despicable human being, torturer, murderer, and my brother's boss. He's in over his head, my brother that is. He signed up to some organization offering advanced career progression and opportunities to earn fat checks. He's nineteen, and while I'm only twenty-four, he's been my responsibility since he was fourteen and our parents died in a car crash.

Money was tight and I know that's why he's taken this gig. He was tired of scraping by. There wasn't just an emotional hole left when our parents died; there was a financial one, too. I can't say for sure, but he's not exactly working nine-to-five while he purchases obscenely expensive things and comes home all hours of the day and night, if he comes home at all.

I was honored to raise him into adulthood. There was no way I was going to let him go into care when I was an adult and capable of looking after both of us. We were both grieving, and life was lived on a tight budget and not a lot of fun. He had this part-time job during his final year of high school, but I hadn't thought much of it. I'd been busy studying and working. It wasn't until just under two years ago that a seed of doubt started to build inside me.

Since then, his curly shoulder-length hair has been styled short on the sides with blond wavy hair on top. He's still as short as me, but he's built up muscle over the last few years, like he's working out. He regularly comes home with scraped knuckles and mud all over his clothes. I've asked him to explain what it is that he's doing, but he just laughs it off and says I worry too much.

I'd even gone as far as to follow him one day, and that's where I spotted Austin. I didn't know who he was at that point, of course. But he ruffled my brother's hair affectionately when no one was looking, and that was when I realized Danny had an entirely separate life I didn't know about.

After a little online sleuthing, I found a Reddit thread on The Unseen. The stories they told were horrific. Acts of violence littered the anecdotes, with commenters adding their own version of the legends they'd heard. Reading between the lines of the hopefully exaggerated stories, it seems that The Unseen is a subset of a larger enterprise named The Organization. This at least had some genuine articles from reputable newspapers. The leader? John Black, sixty-five years old, white hair, muscular build, with an imposing height. If he wasn't running it with his brains, the blurred photo of him on *The Seattle Times* news website would suggest he could certainly do it with his brawn. Even for a sixty-five-year-old, the guy was jacked.

According to the exposé article, his two sons, Augustus and Austin, worked with him to run The Organization, and for all intents and purposes, Austin cleaned up messes—or rather, made messes and then cleaned them up. There were no photos of Austin, but he didn't match the one the website showed of Augustus so I had assumed it was him up until Danny let his name slip in conversation one night.

When I followed Danny, he went back to the same warehouse repeatedly, and all sorts of trucks were coming in and out at all times of night, too. I was never brave enough to leave my car to check it out. The Reddit thread had given me nightmares, but I continued to watch from afar nonetheless.

Once Austin had started coming into Squeeze the Day just a few weeks later, I'd panicked. At first, I thought he knew I'd been watching him, and panic traveled up my throat that I was in danger. When I made eye contact, he observed me with a curiosity that made my skin crawl, but there was nothing familiar in the way he looked at me—more of an appreciation, as sick as it made me feel. I knew I couldn't risk spying on Danny anymore. It would be risking his life if Austin found out I was observing his operation, whatever it was. It was obvious The Unseen didn't want people to know what was going on behind the dull gray roller doors of their warehouse.

What I had managed to find out really was just rumors. The Unseen stupidly have matching tattoos, which Danny described to me as *an initiation* when I asked him about it. But he wouldn't tell me what the initiation was for. I only know it's a tattoo for The Unseen because a girl I went to high school with dated someone who works for Austin, and that guy also has the same tattoo: a blindfolded brunette staring up to the sky as a tear rolls down her cheek. Also, my brother is nineteen. He's about as subtle as lighting a bag of shit on someone's doorstep and ringing the bell. So when I said he came home with scrapes and bruises, it was true, and it was all the time. And unless he'd got a side gig digging graves at the cemetery, there was no reason for him to come back late at night covered in mud. The third concern came with the amount of cash he started to throw around. He handed me a bundle of one hundred dollar bills one night accompanied by a Post-it note with a smiley face on it. No explanation. Just money. Covered in dirt. All he'd said when I pressed him was that it was a bonus for a job well done.

So drastic times call for drastic measures. Danny won't listen to me. He's made up his mind. And besides, as he jokingly said one night when I caught him coming home at 4 a.m., "there's no way out now."

But it's not funny, and my parents didn't leave him in my care so that he would get killed by some gangster that has shitty taste in coffee. I mean, who goes to a juice bar to order coffee, anyway?

The plan is to: one, temporarily house him in my basement; two, keep things chill; three, flip the switch and make him believe I'm a psycho and that his life might possibly be in danger. And finally, when he agrees to let my brother go, I'll let him go, too. But not before Danny and I have enough time to get out of town. See? A four-part plan. Easy.

I pull into my driveway. It's our parents' house and is looking a little run down. My mom used to garden and keep everything full of flowers. Now, the path is overgrown, the weeds creeping in through the cracks, and the grass needs mowing—well, hacking might be a better word.

I pull out the trolley I'd prepared and place the blanket on top. Bending my knees and engaging my core, I drag him out by hooking my arms under his armpits. Linking my fingers across his chest, I drag him out of my old Land Rover Defender —another item left over from my parents' passing.

I let his legs flop out of the vehicle and angle him so his ass hits the trolley. I place him down gently, making sure his head isn't gonna hit any overgrown bushes on the way up to the house. It's the first time I'm grateful for no porch—I hop the trolley over the lip of the entryway and pull him through the hallway, just like I'd practiced last night.

I reach the door to the basement and brace myself for the next phase.

Call me a genie and marvel at my magic carpet. This bad boy helps me transport this hunk of muscle down a flight of stairs with no obvious injuries, and I only hit his head once—*obviously not on purpose*. But with no lasting damage, I pull his legs up onto the mattress I prepared and roll him over.

As unseemly as it is, you can't have an angry murderer wandering around your basement. When considering whether you should chain someone to your heating pipe, it's always better to err on the side of caution. One huge prison-style chain later, and his hands are connected loosely to his stomach with enough room that he could, well, alleviate himself without his pee flying round like a hose pipe, and he could, at a stretch, use his hands to eat. I've left some hand sanitizer so he can swap between both tasks with clean hands.

Unfortunately, wrapping the chain around his body has been a little tricky, and I did have to balance his head on my chest as I wrapped my arms around him. Despite being the most despicable man on the planet, he smells heavenly. And when he sighed deeply, face on tit, his warm breath cascaded down my crop top making my nipples ache.

I'm absolutely not attracted to him. I mean, I can see the appeal, of course; I'm not blind, or nose blind, or deaf—he has quite a lovely voice as well, in all honesty. But he is an awful person, dead set on being the villain in this situation. And *yes*, that is said without a trace of irony, as I do appreciate he's the one who's chained up in my basement.

I gently place him back onto the pillow and pull the blanket over him. I don't want him to think I'm an animal. I don't actually want to hurt him. Just maybe scare him enough that he will set my brother free the moment he wakes up. Speaking of which, he should be waking up in a few minutes.

Okay, deep breath, the hard part is done. Getting his big ass down the stairs and tied up. Now, it's just a negotiation, and I do those all the time.

I look around the basement. The light is shining through the small window on the north side of the house. It isn't large by any means, but there's a lamp I've placed close to his bed, which he could use if he needs more light.

The space is pretty empty, except for a big storage rack filled with equipment for my business. I'd made sure his chains were short enough that he couldn't reach anything else in the room, but honestly, what was he going to do? Throw a yoga mat at me?

And that brings me to my actual real-life can-you-believe-it day job. I work as a fitness instructor posting exercise routines online, creating videos to inspire others to get fit and take on new challenges. My channel is growing, but I have done well over the last few years to build a strong following online. I am starting to see the benefits of my hard work with sponsors, ads, and companies contacting me to review and promote their products.

The basement was meant to be a studio space to create videos, complete workout sessions, and store old equipment when it wasn't in use. Danny had been building me the space when he was in high school, but since he'd started working for Sleeping Beauty over there, he hasn't had the time.

Austin stirs, and a low grumble reverberates from his throat. He tries to pull his hands up to his face, but the clink of metal halts his movement.

My heart thumps against my ribs. The reality of the situation is starting to sink in. My body is acting like I've been trying to bench press one hundred kilos rather than thirty.

What the fuck have I done?

Visions of me being hauled out of my house in handcuffs, headlines like "Wannabe Fitness Influencer Kidnaps Beautiful Man" scan across the back of my eyes. I wish I could say I didn't mean to do this. But who can say they accidentally chloroformed and kidnapped somebody? *Sorry, your honor, he slipped on the cloth and then fell into my basement. Oh, the chains? Well, I didn't know who he was, so I thought I'd take a precautionary measure.*

His snuffles get a little louder, and I step away from him. Maybe I could gauge his reaction in the shadows first before revealing myself. My eyes fix on him as his strong, long fingers run over the length of chains. His strength is clearly returning. His body movements suggest he is assessing his situation, tugging on the chains, his head moving around to look for anything familiar. . . to look for me.

"Hello?" his gravelly voice calls out.

"Err, hi."

He strains his neck around, and I give him a small wave from my corner. Attempting to sit up, his head swirls, and he flops back down onto the pillow.

"Fuck," he groans.

"You're probably still a bit groggy from the . . . well, the . . . you know . . . stuff."

"Stuff?" he repeats, turning to look at me once again, this time with more success.

"Yes, the um, well, the cloth with the. . . you know . . ." I draw my empty hand up to my mouth and take a big inhale before rolling my eyes back and pretending to pass out.

He frowns, confused, obviously. I am acting like a lunatic.

"I'm still asleep," he mutters, moving his neck back to a normal position and closing his eyes. "I'll wake up in a minute, and I won't have helped the crazy girl at the fucking juice bar."

"Uh, rude. I'm not crazy," I snip, stepping out of my corner.

"Sure you're not, imaginary person in my head."

"Why would you be dreaming about me?" My heart rate picks up as I remember the few times I've caught his eye at Squeeze the Day. Hunger is the name I would give the looks he gave me. Like he's dying for a treat that doesn't contain seeds or some sort of vegetable in it, like what Jenny offers at the juice bar. Something that no food could satisfy.

"I always dream about . . ." he stops mid-way through a breathy sentence and lets out a rip-roaring snore.

"Brilliant," I mutter.

I drag over the wicker chair I'd been storing down here and place it by the shelves containing my gym equipment. He'll be able to see me when he wakes up, so I sit back in the chair and wait. Any presumptions of getting comfy are thwarted as I can't seem to sit still. Instead, I tiptoe cautiously over to him and tug on the chains one more time—they're solid. There's no way he's getting out of here. Despite this, in a last-minute panic, I trap his wrists together with a cable tie.

I'm still baffled that I've made it this far. He's the head of the formidable Unseen, but really, he's just some guy. Distracted by a pair of swinging hips and boobs squished into a crop top. It's kind of pitiful. Sure, my behavior today has probably been a little bit of a shock. I'd only ever scowled at him or ignored him, which I'm sure irritated him even more. He didn't know me or why I hated him.

Despite his pathetic performance earlier, I can't let empathy dictate how this goes. I could be soft, forgiving . . . none of which are bad traits. But this is life or death, and I need him to do what I tell him.

He's quiet for a while, and for a moment, I think he might be dead. Leaning into him, I get a whiff of his cologne. He smells woodsy, like pine and fire, like a man who knows how to take care of himself in the wilderness, which only irritates me further. His face is soft like this, almost angelic. I shake my head, reminding myself that this man is cold and calculated. Despite his warm brown eyes and dark hair, he is the devil wrapped up in the trappings of a hardworking man. Even now, passed out, mouth slightly parted, he's cruelly handsome.

He stirs a little, his breathing quickening as his chest rises and falls more rapidly. Maybe he's waking up for real this time. I'm not sure I want to be here when he finally realizes his situation. I'm worried he's going to be aggressive and violent, but mostly, I don't think I could handle him yelling. He's going to be furious when he realizes he wasn't dreaming.

I bite my thumbnail and glance around the room one more time. The space is soundproof to a point. We are out in the middle of nowhere, which will explain why I was more than happy to drag an unconscious man out of my vehicle in the middle of the day.

Despite the location being ideal, my nerves get the better of me when I think he may scream out for help. I know I'd give in quickly and let him go. And I can't do that without getting what I need first.

His fingers grip the chains once more and tug. The cable tie cuts into his skin as he tries to maneuver his way around the restraints.

My mouth is dry, but my palms are sweating uncontrollably. Just wake up, get this part over with, and then I can calm down. I'll make a nice smoothie to treat myself with some extra peanut butter. Just what I deserve for kidnapping. A nice little treat.

His eyes flutter open, and he rolls onto his back. He's still for a moment and then lifts his cable-tied wrists, inspecting them slowly.

"So I wasn't dreaming . . . huh," he mumbles.

"Nope . . . not dreaming," I reply cautiously.

He's silent as he turns his focus to me. I feel the heat of his gaze the second his eyes land on mine.

"How are you feeling?" I ask, like a nurse to their patient.

He pauses for a moment to consider the question. "Not as bad as I thought I would."

I nod, swallowing again. I need some water to fix this dry-mouth situation.

"And how are you? You look a little peaky," he adds, staring at me.

Oh god, I may just let him go now. Does kidnapping work like the five-second rule when you drop food on the floor? You can still eat it as long as you pick it up in five seconds. Ten seconds if it's really something delicious. Maybe if I back out within a minute of him waking up, we can just pretend that this never happened and go back to me scowling at him at Squeeze the Day.

Why isn't he scared? Why isn't he screaming out and asking who I am and what he's doing here?

"I'm fine, thank you," I clip.

"First kidnapping?" he asks, his eyes focused on me.

"I don't make a habit of it."

He rolls back onto his back and closes his eyes. "It's not

for everyone."

He looks goddamn relaxed. Like he hasn't just been kidnapped and this is all going to just work out. But he's not in charge here. I am.

"Do you want to know why you're here?"

"I'm sure you'll let me know when you're ready," he replies dismissively.

My heart goes from a mile a minute to feeling as if it has stopped altogether. He thinks I'm weak-willed and probably going to let him go any minute. Well, guess what? I have the stamina of a racehorse. I take on gym bros every damn day, and half the comment sections on my videos are full of steroid-guzzling gym junkies telling me how I should improve my form. I can handle an arrogant gangster who has nothing better to do than take a nap.

So I channel my inner bitch. I brought him here for a reason. He wants to be patient? Well, guess what? I can play that game, too.

"I'll tell you what, we'll talk about it when you're less tired." I push my fingers out in front of me to inspect my nail polish. I should really redo these before my next video. "There's enough food and water for a few days. Your bucket is over there." I point to the corner of the room.

He turns his head and eyes me. For a split second, concern flashes in his eyes. That is until the length of his gaze rolls down my chest and to the tight leggings clinging to my legs. I temper my body's reaction to his assessment. It's not like he hasn't seen me in tight clothing before. It's practically a uniform. His eyes linger on my thighs. Oh . . . he's a leg man for sure. Good to know. It has been feeling a little hot in here. It might be time to get out the shorts to make him a little more amenable.

I walk up the stairs calmly, swaying my hips confidently since the poor guy deserves a treat after being tied up in a basement.

When I reach the door, I wait for a moment, but I hear

nothing.

I close it, lock the door, apply the dead bolt, attach the padlock, and then I run to the bathroom, sink to my knees, and throw up.

CHAPTER THREE

Austin

This isn't too bad. I've been in worse situations. Sure, I'm tied up and chained to a hot water pipe, which thankfully has yet to turn on. But I've put others through worse, and I'm not sure this entirely counts as torture.

The comfy bed, the memory foam pillow, the handmade blanket. She's gone out of her way to ensure I'm comfortable, which has me slightly concerned I'm here for the long haul. But darling Olivia, *such a pretty name*, looked sick with guilt. I bet she's up there pacing as I lie here relaxed. The thought brings me a little joy.

The chains are good quality, not thin or wispy. She's obviously done her research. The cable ties are an added touch —quite simple to remove if you know how, but I'll leave them on for now.

I have a reasonable amount of room to move around despite the death-row-style chain around my waist binding my hands and feet. I'm almost surprised she left out the Hannibal Lecter mask.

I can bite, too, baby.

I scan the room. It looks like it's under renovation. The flooring is half complete, and spare wooden boards lean against the corner. Sports equipment fills the industrial shelving unit: yoga mats, blocks, weights, medicine balls, and even one of those shaking dumbbells that tone your arms is on there. Not sure I can imagine her using one of those very often. She seems more of a no-frills kind of girl.

My mattress is pressed up against the corner of the room, next to an array of pipes that connect to a water heater on the other side of the basement. The wooden stairs hug the far wall, and from my position, I have a full view of the entire space. Despite the concrete floor beneath my mattress, a worn rug had been placed at the side so I could stand without placing bare feet on the cold floor.

Paint is peeling on all four walls, a small yellow water ring stains the ceiling on the far corner, and the window rattles as soon as there is a light breeze. Basements generally aren't where people's interior design skills should be judged, and I bet that given her effort to make me comfortable here, the upstairs of the house is significantly homelier.

Standing up, my knees creak a little, and I try to stretch my muscles loose. I step off the rug and reach as far as possible. The chains impede much exploration. Like a dog tied to its kennel, I'm kept on a tight leash.

I can't see anything obvious that I've missed. The wicker chair she was perched on earlier has a little cushion. I attempt to reach it, but it's a few yards away. No luck there, but its presence forms a small ball of anticipation in my chest. Perhaps she'll be spending some time with me down here after all.

Now that I'm standing, I pat myself down, checking my pockets. My phone and wallet are gone. *Clever girl—always remembers the details*.

However, she's left my shoes on, which means she probably hasn't checked the small pocket inside my boot.

It's a little James Bond. But when you're the boss, you can indulge in a little excess. Besides, my past life isn't entirely in the past, and it's good to be prepared.

I lean back against the wall, balancing so I can awkwardly lift my foot and pull it over my knee. Lifting my jeans, I slip my fingers past the tough leather and into the side of the boot. I unhook the piece of string that's wound around a small button and pull out the tiny burner phone. Switching it on, I call Luca, my right-hand man, oldest friend, and a ruthless bastard.

He answers immediately.

“Boss, fuck, I thought you were missing. You never miss Friday lunch. You know I like to get your opinion on the new experiments.”

“I am . . . technically. Although I’m starting to think I should miss Friday lunch every now and then. I’m starting to get a reputation.”

“You know you love trying the new product just as much as I do, old man,” he jests, despite being only six months younger than me. “So, where are you? I’ll come pick you up.”

“No need. I’m with someone, and I want to see how this plays out. Can you cover things for a few days?” I keep my voice steady and words vague.

“Yes, boss. What’s your favorite animal?” Our code question for situations like this. Another habit from our pasts that we haven’t been able to shake. My answer determines the message I want to convey.

“Polar bears.”

Cold. Ruthless. Killers. And complete goofballs.

I’ve told him I’m fine, and he’ll believe it now.

“Wait, did you feel that?” He panics.

“What?” I lower my voice, glancing up toward the staircase.

“The world has stopped turning . . . hell has frozen over . . . Austin Black is taking a day off.” He snickers.

“Fuck off, or you’ll be getting a permanent vacation.”

“You’ll have to catch me first, boss.”

He’ll never let this go. Luca was the fastest in our school, ran like a fucking whippet on cocaine which got him out of many sticky situations. You know the phrase you don’t need to be faster than a crocodile; you just need to be faster than the guy next to you? Yeah, that was Luca, and unfortunately for me, I was the guy next to him. I'd been caught by a few crocodiles in our thirty years as friends, but luckily, I'd made it out alive.

"I'll call you if I need you, but otherwise, it's radio silence until then. I should be no more than a week."

"Yes, boss." He still sounds unsure. He's my right-hand man and as ruthless as they come, but we grew up together. We're basically brothers in every way except by blood.

"I'll call each day to check in—when I get the chance."

"Thanks, boss."

I hang up, taking a deep breath. Time for my second phone call and the one where I'm not the boss. An excited thrill rips through me as I dial Dr. Alfie's number. He's not going to believe this happened. I mean, sure, he'll be furious. But he'll realize my obsession has been reciprocated, and I just need to work out why.

I started talking to Dr. Alfie two years ago. I'd been working for my father since I was fourteen and raised to be a ruthless killer. Actually, no, that's not right. I was raised to be obedient. To follow orders. The killing was a byproduct of that arrangement.

Then, one day, I couldn't take it anymore. I'd lost all ability to function, let alone whip some fucking runty drug dealers into shape. I lost my edge. I hesitated. So, at Alfie's suggestion, I took a week off. And well . . . that week turned into two years. Of course, as far as everyone was concerned, I still worked for my father. God forbid anyone thinks there's trouble in the regime.

During my initial week off, I got blind drunk and tried to fuck anything with a pulse. As I was puking my guts up, clinging to the wrist of some poor woman who was trying to get back to her friends, I looked up, and that was when I saw it: a huge fucking billboard of Alfie Adams from high school.

Now you might think we'd rekindled some sort of friendship, but in reality, I was an asshole in school. Not more than I am now, just different. The kind of high school bully who doesn't stand up for others and makes himself look bigger by cutting everyone around him down.

Dr. Alfie had made it big on some network show where they called him Dr. Angel. What had been a scrawny specky nerd had turned into the ultimate glow-up. He filled out, his muscles hard and his suits tailored. Hell, he wore the fuck out of those suits. On occasion, he'd wear tortoise shell-rimmed glasses, giving an intellectual, academic vibe. The man had style.

And not only that, he had the women of the Pacific Northwest eating out of the palm of his hand. He was gruff, straight-talking, and commanding. Hell, he put me in my place a few times, and I'm not ashamed to admit it: the man would have made an excellent gangster. You know, if he hadn't taken the Hippocratic oath to be caring and considerate or whatever they fucking promise the community. Maybe he should be a Daddy instead.

Despite our difficult time together in high school. I'd stormed into Alfie's office with the intention of threatening to kill him unless he helped me. I mean, sure, a few threats were made, and once his current patient had left shaking and in tears, and thanks to me, a thousand bucks richer, he agreed to be my therapist.

There were conditions to our doctor/patient relationship, of course. He couldn't repeat a goddamn word I said, and I couldn't kill anyone anymore. Easy. I didn't want to fucking kill anyone anymore anyway. It's the whole reason I sought him out.

And the past two years, Dr. Alfie—or Dr. Angel when I try to irritate the fuck out of him—and I had been working toward my goal of cleaning my ledger and building a life that I could be proud of. One where I wasn't controlled by my father or his business and where I could take ownership of my own actions. Of course, there was a teeny tiny problem with the self-loathing and self-sabotaging side of me, but hey, therapy is a process, and I'm not afraid to say that he's basically saved my life.

No one knows about our sessions, and they never will.

If it ever got back to my father, he'd kill him. Of that, I'm certain. And I've grown rather fond of the handsome bastard.

And despite what he'd tell you, I'm sure the grump is quite fond of me, too. I was supposed to have a session today, and one of the rules of Dr. Alfie is that you never miss a session without good reason. I'd say that getting myself kidnapped on purpose by the woman I've been semi-stalking for the last two years might give me a free pass, but that remains to be seen.

"Mia, hi. It's Austin. Can you patch me through to Dr. Alfie, please?" I ask Alfie's receptionist.

"Are you sure? He's miserable today," she responds in a hushed tone.

"I'll deal with him, don't you worry," I reply softly.

I like Mia. She's never acted afraid of me and always seems to know the right thing to say. Even with Alfie, she's kind, considerate, but she doesn't take any shit from him. She practically runs his whole business. He better pay her well to put up with his mood swings.

"Austin. You know how I feel about missed sessions."

His annoyance permeates through the phone and scratches at the insides of my ears. *God, he's annoying.*

"Good reason coming your way. Do you remember Olivia?"

He sighs in that exasperated way that only he can muster. "The same Olivia you've talked about at every session for the last two years? That Olivia?"

"That's the one. Well, you're not going to believe this." I do love to tease him.

"What?"

I've piqued his curiosity now.

"She kidnapped me. Me! Can you believe it?"

"Austin . . . are you alright? You seem happy about this, and this doesn't sound like a good thing," he replies using his doctor voice, the one that's without judgment, but really is ready to press a secret button under his desk that tells Mia to call emergency services.

"Well, like you said, she's finally paying an interest after two years. Of course it's a good thing. Besides I'm fine, and this way, I can get to know her more. Once she comes back into the basement."

"Okay. So you don't want me to alert the authorities that you've been kidnapped?"

"Absolutely not. This is a perfect opportunity to lay some groundwork," I say quickly.

There's silence on the phone for a minute, and I finally hear him sigh. That's what you need to do in these situations. If your therapist can't make you better, you can one hundred percent make them worse.

"Can you promise me you're not in any immediate danger?" he finally asks.

"Safe as a baby at a fire station."

"And she doesn't appear to be unstable?"

"Nope," I quip.

"Did she explain why she kidnapped you?"

"Not yet, but as you taught me, I'm trying to get that delayed gratification."

"That's not a good time to use that, Austin," he huffs out, and I can practically see his eyes roll to the back of his head.

Silence permeates through the phone as I hold my breath.

Finally, his gruff voice sounds out. "Then I can't believe I'm going to say this, but it *might* be a good idea for you to see this through."

"Yes, doc! I knew it."

"But you will need to be back for your Friday session next week *in person*. Otherwise, I will immediately alert the authorities."

"Understood. That's more than enough time." I ponder how much I can learn about her in a whole week.

"Dare I ask, enough time for what?"

I grin. "To make her fall in love with me, of course."

"Of course." He clicks his tongue. "I trust that phone is a burner you've managed to keep hidden?"

"Yes. It was my backup one in my boot. I told you it was sensible to keep one. You told me it was me clinging to the insecurities of my past, and I should get rid of it."

"Yes, well, good thing you never listen to me, isn't it?"

I chuckle. "Certainly is. I'll call you if anything goes awry."

"Please do. Good luck, Austin."

I hang up the phone. Thank god Alfie isn't a conventional therapist. Imagine having to actually act normal for someone. Now, I just have to convince my dream girl that I am worth more than storing in her basement.

Olivia Daniels. Christ. I rub my face awkwardly with both palms. I'd been thinking with my dick when I placed that cloth on my mouth. As if, somehow, I could get her into bed after she kidnapped me. I glance over to the bucket she'd left me. That is a slight concern. Her clearing up my piss and shit bucket doesn't exactly scream, "Take me to bed." And I plan for her to do just that when the time is right.

The afternoon light from the one window soon fades away, and a golden luster fills the room, softening its sharp edges.

I click on the lamp and the warm glow douses the room into a soft light. Lying back on the bed with not much to do but wait. I've been hoping she would come back down by now, but a few hours is nothing. I'd kept prisoners chained and waiting for days, sometimes a full week, to weaken them. Keep them wanting for basic interaction so that they were so malleable that there'd be no need to break them. Of course, there was always the exception. Regardless, I didn't do those things anymore. My new business is somewhat of a PG-13 operation.

The slide of the dead bolt from the top of the stairs pulls me out of my thoughts and back to the present.

"Hello?" Olivia calls out, as if to make sure I was still alive.

I could play dead, but I'd rather start off on her good side.

"Hello."

She makes her way down the stairs, gingerly descending each step.

"How are you?"

"Quite well, how are you?" I reply, smirking. Such a strange tactic she's using.

She huffs a little as she hops off the final step. She is holding a plate of food in one hand and some clothes in the other.

"I brought some things for you," she mutters, her cheeks flushing pink.

"Thank you. Although I'm not sure how I'm going to change my clothes."

She holds my gaze for a moment before running her eyes down my body. Her piercing stare dips lower and lower until it lands directly on the chains around my waist. Pulled down by gravity, the main link is right in front of my dick. Realizing she must already know this, having put the chains on me, she would have been up close and personal while I was knocked out.

My mouth waters at the thought. *Is she thinking about it now?*

Letting out a sharp breath, she moves closer and then bends to put the plate of food in front of me. Her eyes never leave mine, and like a snake and a mongoose, we are at a standoff, waiting for the first one to strike.

She puts the plate down within my reach and quickly steps back. She continues to back away as I reach down to pick up the plate.

Her left shoelace hangs down the side of her sneaker, and her right foot presses down on the end.

"Careful, your lace!" I call out, probably a little more

booming than necessary.

Her eyes widen, and her instincts kick in. She attempts to lift her leg, her shoe remaining in place as her body recoils.

It almost happens in slow motion. I try to reach her, but my chains restrict me. Her hands are outstretched as she falls back into the shelving unit. Her ass hits the ground, and her face contorts. The medicine ball rolls slowly toward the edge. It teeters along the lip of the metal shelf before finally tipping over the edge, succumbing to gravity.

"Move!"

Olivia tilts her head just in time, but the medicine ball hits her shoulder with such force that the impact pushes her head toward the ground. Her skull cracks on the concrete floor before she can stretch out her hands to brace for the fall. Within seconds she lies unconscious, blood pouring out her head like the Trevi goddamn fountain.

"Fuck!" I cry out.

What the fuck have I gotten myself into?

I shift myself as close as possible. She is still breathing, thank god. The blood fountain coming from her head has quickly slowed into a pulsing trickle.

I had hoped I could keep the damn cable ties on a little longer to remain in her good graces, but needs must.

I put my hands together in a clenched fist prayer position. Pulling my hands sharply away, the cable tie snaps. I rub the red lines around my wrists, discarding the plastic over my shoulder. I am still chained to the wall, but at least I can now reach above my head and move my hands more freely.

I stretch for her calf and drag her limp body toward me as gently as possible. The blood stain smears over the rough concrete floor. It isn't much, but my stomach still rolls at the thought of her being hurt.

When I can reach her stomach, I pull her body around, rotating her so I can rest her head on my knee and take a better look at the gash on her forehead. The bleeding is lessening.

I pull off the first item of clothing she has brought down

for me and scrunch it in my fist. Hopefully, she won't mind me using it to stem the bleeding.

I press it to her forehead, dabbing up the blood that hasn't dried yet. Her eyebrows crinkle together as her nose scrunches up. Her hand reaches for the wound, and I pull it down to stop her. Her long, slender fingers squeeze mine, and a warmth courses through my body. Her hand feels so small.

Don't get a fucking boner right now, man. Not the time, and a bit fucking weird, given that the girl's unconscious with her head in my lap.

Her eyelids start to flutter open. *God, she is so pretty.* She moans, her body rolling as she tries to wake up. *Not helping the dick situation at all.*

"What happened?" she groans, her fingers linking with mine.

"Hey, you're okay. You just hit your head pretty hard, so take it easy," I whisper, not wanting to scare her.

"Am I in the hospital?"

"Umm . . . no."

She's going to panic, in . . . three . . . her eyelids open up, two . . . she realizes her head is in my lap . . . one . . . I give her hand the gentlest of squeezes and—

"WHAT ARE YOU DOING?"

She jumps off me, practically rolling away GI Jane style. Not gonna lie; I don't hate the image that conjures up, but she stumbles back, hand clutched to her head.

I raise my hands, palms facing her, surrendering immediately.

"How'd you get the cable ties off?"

Ah, shit.

"I couldn't reach you with them on, so I snapped them off."

She stares, her eyebrows knitting together like she is trying to calculate the trajectory to the moon, glancing between me, the bloody t-shirt, and the red stain on my pants where her head has been resting.

"You could have killed me," she says.

No use lying about it. "Yes."

"Why didn't you?"

I pause for a moment, mulling over my answer. I can't tell her the truth. That I've thought of her for years and only frequented that god-awful juice bar to catch a glimpse of her. Not yet, at least. It's too soon.

"And live without ever knowing why you brought me here?" I grin. "I couldn't possibly."

Her frown softens a little, and she perches on the wicker chair she sat on earlier today.

"So, you do want to know why you're here," she murmurs.

"Wouldn't you? If you were abducted."

"Well, why didn't you ask me earlier?"

"I thought it would annoy you most if I didn't ask you anything."

She nods.

Practically a written confession. I'm obsessed with you.

"And why are you telling me that now? I'm not letting you go, you know."

I smile. She sounds so sure of herself. "Hmm. I think you've had more than enough excitement for one day. Are you ready to tell me why I'm here?"

She sighs. "Give me a minute."

She heads back up the stairs cautiously, returning with an ice pack she holds against her forehead. She winces every now and then, and when she pulls it back, I notice a little red bruising starting to show now the swelling has subsided.

"Your shoulder got hit as well. The medicine ball hit there first."

She touches her shoulder and sighs. "I thought it was sore. Figured I'd overdone my workout yesterday."

She places the ice pack on her shoulder for a change and then crosses one leg over the other, leaning back into the chair, her eyes closing for a moment.

I'm slightly concerned she has a concussion, and I'd rather not be stuck down here if she gets into trouble while she's asleep.

"Why don't you tell me why I'm here?" I suggest, hoping this will keep her awake and lucid.

"Hmm. How about I tell you what I know about you and if I get something wrong, you let me know."

"This would be more fun with alcohol." I laugh.

She points to her head. "Head injury."

I point to my mouth. "Chloroformed."

She laughs. "Touché."

I tilt my head, assessing her, and realize I could use this to my advantage. "How about if you get one wrong, I get to ask you a question and you have to reply honestly."

She bites her plump, pink lip before turning back to me. "Deal."

"After you." I bow a little, which causes her cheeks to pinken.

She steadies herself before taking a deep breath. "Your name is Austin Black."

"Correct. I'm so glad you've abducted the correct person."

She ignores my sarcasm. "You're the head of The Unseen."

I pause, not confirming or denying. "Not many people have heard of The Unseen."

"Incorrect. Not many people have *seen* The Unseen. You shouldn't be surprised that plenty of people have heard of it."

I click my tongue, annoyed that she's right. My reputation precedes me whether I want it to reach civilians like Olivia or not. That's not within the bounds of my control.

She's dropped that bombshell pretty quickly, obviously wanting to get this show on the road. I suppose it's my turn to share some truths.

"Your name is Olivia Daniels."

"Y . . . yes," she replies, eyes widening.

"You're a fitness blogger with a following of 400,000 subscribers."

"Technically I'm a vlogger with a V, old man," she says. "But wait, how do you know my name?"

I shrug, brushing off the "old man" comment despite the sting it leaves. "It's my job to know things."

"Did you know I was going to kidnap you?"

An odd question, but somehow, I wouldn't be surprised if she'd googled the best ways to knock someone out without permanently injuring them.

"I hadn't expected you to smile at me that morning, let alone talk to me. So no, I didn't expect to be abducted either."

"Why didn't you expect me to smile at you?"

I arch an eyebrow and tilt my head. She knows why, but she wants me to admit I've noticed the way she scowls at me.

"Okay, okay." She rolls her eyes, but I can feel her softening as she smiles down at her lap.

"My turn," I say. "How do you know who I am?"

Her fingers sit in her lap, and I notice her squeezing them together. She rolls her bad shoulder, and a flicker of concern takes root in my chest.

"Do you know someone called Danny?"

Yes. More than one. My brain calculates who could be linked to Olivia.

"It's a common name."

"Danny Daniels."

Danny Daniels, Olivia Daniels. They're related. She's doing this for a family member. Brother perhaps? They have similar coloring.

I think about what I know about Danny. He's young and eager to please. A ruthless motherfucker when he wants to be. But he's not only a dumb worker with a penchant for fist fights, although he does have that. He's smart, keen, logical. He installed our new security software. He's quick on a computer. Orphaned, if I remember rightly, which fits with my knowledge of Olivia. I'd technically poached him from my father's company, offering him a better deal that had a much longer life expectancy. But I vet my staff, especially those who have worked with my father, and from memory, nothing came up about a sister. I'd certainly know, given that I've been all but stalking his for the last two years.

"I know him," I concede.

"You're his boss."

If she thinks The Unseen is a part of my father's business, then he obviously hasn't told her what he's really up to. Seems odd, given that what he's doing now is significantly safer than what my father had him running around doing.

"His boss's boss, if we're being technical."

Not technically a lie, as he does report to Luca, who, in turn, reports to me.

"You're no one's boss at the moment, if we're being technical," she quips, causing me to grin.

"Touché."

She grins back. Olivia Daniels, angel on earth, has a bad streak. Fuck me, she couldn't be any more perfect.

Come lie your head in my lap again, sweetheart.

"Okay, so I'm technically Danny's boss's boss. How does that get me into your basement?"

"I want him out."

"Out of what?"

"The Unseen."

"How exactly would you know he's in The Unseen? It's, without sounding obvious, *unseen*."

"Listen, your 'first rule of fight club is that no one talks about fight club' crap doesn't really work when my idiot brother is coming home at all hours of the day and night, covered in blood, bruises, and god knows what else. I found a burner phone, and I saw his tattoo. It didn't take a genius to work out what it meant."

Ah, yes, the tattoo that new recruits had started getting. It's rather dumb, but I can't say I hate the design. A beautiful brunette, blindfolded, chin tilted up toward the sky. What relevance the brunette has to my organization is anyone's guess. But it's subtle, and the work of the resident tattoo artist, Andre, is second to none.

The burner phone, blood, and bruises must have been from under my father's tutelage. I poached him when I first set up my business. Around two years ago.

"If my understanding is correct of these types of organizations, it's that, once you're in, you're in. There is no leaving."

"I thought you might say that," she replies quickly and coolly.

Too quick and too cool.

"And that answers why I brought you here. Because your rules may be solid now, but give it a few days, and I think you'll be willing to let one measly employee go."

She stands up and saunters toward me. Being locked up might not do it, but the curve of her ass might.

She leans down, close enough for me to touch her. Close enough for me to smell her. Salt and a hint of perfume that invades my senses. That's her first mistake, aside from getting knocked out.

"And you've played your hand, Austin."

The way she murmurs my name sounds so familiar and warm. No one speaks to me so softly anymore.

I want to smile. God, I never thought I'd be close enough to see the freckles across her nose, like constellations I want to map out. Today, it's been three times. I'm practically giddy.

"And what's that, Olivia Daniels?" I tilt up my chin, my eyes drawn down to her lips.

She grins widely. "You like me."

My eyes snap back to hers. She pauses for the perfect amount of time, and then, just as I open my mouth to retort, she retreats. She bestows a final smirk on me and saunters toward the stairs. Her hips sway, causing her ass to swing left to right like a pendulum I can't keep my eyes off. Oh, she's good.

"Goodnight, Austin," she calls out.

"Goodnight, Killer."

She pauses, turning to eye me up and down, considering the nickname I've christened her with. "Not yet."

And then she's up the stairs, the light is out, and I hear the click and slide of a dead bolt.

CHAPTER FOUR

Olivia

I roll into the middle of my queen-sized bed, stretching my arms high above my head and releasing a big yawn. The homemade blanket my mom made is bunched up; I must have kicked it off in the night.

One of my favorite parts of the day is waking up early before anyone else. Ticking off my to-do list before some people had even gotten out of bed gives me the feeling of accomplishment that no degree or corporate job ever could.

As my feet hit the floor, I lift my hands up as high as I can before bending down to touch my toes, stretching the sleepiness from my muscles.

First off is a to-do list for the day, ensuring I cover as much as possible now that I've got a houseguest to attend to.

- Breakfast for myself and houseguest
- Workout—using new equipment sent to me by Zen Yoga
- Plan out upcoming posts
- Lunch for myself and houseguest
- Check social stats and reply to comments
- Long-term planning
- Call with accountant at four
- Dinner and social time with houseguest
- Bed ~~(alone)~~

Alone seems an unnecessary addition to "bed." And yes,

I write "bed" on my to-do list. Those who don't understand the utterly gratifying feeling of ticking something off their list wouldn't get it. But those who are relentless list-makers like myself wouldn't bat an eye.

I chew the end of my pen, thinking if there's anything else I can squeeze into the day, but honestly, I think with the head injury, what I've already got to do might be too much. I should maybe try and take it easy today.

Images of Austin come to me suddenly and so vividly. Maybe he's an early riser like me, and he's waiting for me to come down to talk to him. Is he lonely? Hungry? Sleeping okay?

Sleep had evaded me last night. Thoughts of robbers and killers creeping their way into my house and up to my bedroom seeped through my subconscious until all I could do was listen for every creak and groan of this old house. Most likely because of the man locked up in my basement, but honestly, I kept feeling like there was someone walking about the house.

I've never been scared to live alone and never had an issue with creaky floorboards and drafts. I've been taking care of myself and Danny for so long that my childhood fears were long gone. But last night felt different. Maybe it really was just because Austin was here. Or maybe someone had come looking for him and decided to search my house in the middle of the night.

My plan is to subtly interrogate him today. To find out if I should expect any unwanted visitors. Then maybe I can search for that person online, just so I know what they look like.

I bite my thumbnail as I pace the living room. What in the hell am I doing? The bright light of day was shining through the window and showing me all the fucked-up things I'd done in the last twenty-four hours. What was I doing kidnapping a man who would *obviously* have people out looking for him? I bet they're on their way here now. I'd put myself and Danny in irrevocable danger.

But he does like me. His actions last night proved that. Maybe I could swing this in my favor just quick enough before anyone realizes where he is. I lift my fingers to the scab on my forehead and wince. I'm lucky; the injury could have been so much worse.

He did help me when I got knocked out, so I can hold faith that he is, at least, a tiny bit of a good person. But only because he wouldn't let me die on the floor. And if we're thinking clearly and objectively, which I absolutely am when it comes to this man, that bar is too low to be set as a standard for men.

I do have one other thing in my favor. And the thing is that I'm a woman. And the thing about being a woman is that, more often than not, our ideas and actions are overlooked by others. And who would suspect a fitness vlogger of kidnapping? In the words of Elle Woods, our lord and savior, exercise gives us endorphins, and endorphins make us happy. Happy people just don't kill their husbands.

And no, Austin Black is not my husband, not my boyfriend, or my lover.

But the last option has crossed my mind. Woah. No. No. No. Thanks very much. We'll call time out on that thought.

My head thumped from my thoughts ping-ponging back and forth, relentlessly swinging between one possible outcome and another. I need to calm down, stick to my routine, and follow my list.

After quickly checking that the lock and deadbolt to the basement are still in place, I head to the kitchen to make breakfast.

I unlock the door, take a deep breath, and head down the stairs carrying two plates. I always think meals are much better shared and even with a reluctant house guest, it's important to keep up good manners.

"Morning, Killer," Austin's throaty voice sounds out.

His eyes roam down my pink silky sleep shorts and

strappy top. The lace trim is black and makes me feel pretty, even barefaced, with my hair poking out at all angles. My first reaction is to scrunch my body and cower. His eyes on me feel like he's looking at his next meal, wondering which piece of me to bite first. Heat builds low in my core without permission, and I can't help but take him in as well.

His dark hair is mussed from sleep, his face perfectly at ease, as if he hadn't just slept with a chain around his waist that connects him to my hot water pipe. He's removed his shirt since last night, his strong chest exposed as the blanket covers just below his waist. His abs are visible. I can't help myself. He is fucking built to perfection. I have no doubt we could work out together. Those muscles aren't just for show; this guy is strong—all the more reason to keep him chained up.

He smirks, and my eyes are drawn to his as he arches an eyebrow. I ignore it.

"Good morning. Scrambled egg on toasted rye, spinach, and cherry tomatoes."

"If your method of torture is a good night's sleep and delicious food, you're doing a great job."

I hand him the plate cautiously, and he takes it just as gently, bowing his head a little with a smirk that could melt my panties clean off, if I were wearing any, that is.

I pull up my chair and tuck in. I'd forgone cutlery, thinking it was probably sensible not to hand a knife to the man I was holding in my basement. So I pick up the toast and take a big bite, watching as Austin does the same.

In less than three seconds, an audible groan escapes him.

"Fuck . . . what is that? It's delicious."

I try to contain the twitch in my cheek pulling at my lips. "I put turmeric in. It's good for your blood pressure, and it's said to help with muscle soreness after working out."

He nods, taking another bite. "There's something else . . ."

"Chili flakes. Just a sprinkle."

"It's the best breakfast I've had in a while," he says, taking another enormous mouthful.

I keep eating, chewing each bite, and sitting quietly. I know it's not sane to want the approval of my captive, but I just can't help myself. When I hear him mutter, "I need a new chef," I almost jump for joy. I'm damn good at my job, and although cooking isn't fundamentally what I do, it's an intrinsic part of my business, and offering recipes is something I've been looking to do more of.

Feeling the need to explain myself, I say, "I, uh, have things I need to do today. But I'll be back at lunchtime with some more food."

"What do you have planned?" he asks as I take his empty plate.

"The usual. I'm reviewing some new gym equipment for a supplier, and then I'll be doing some socials this afternoon. Pretty standard."

"Do you like what you do?"

Not a question I would have expected him to ask, and suspicion rises in my throat. I know he's only being nice so I let him leave. He's probably kidnapped enough people to know that if you can't initially fight your way out, you have to play the long game and win their trust. But that won't be happening with me.

"I do. I get to do what I'm good at and share it with the world."

He nods. "You help people."

Yes, exactly. "I try to."

He smiles, a small dimple forming beneath his day-old stubble. He looks good with a bit of scruff. His normal look is so clean-cut, with sharp lines. The rough ironically softens him.

"You might be the worst kidnapper in the world. I'm pretty sure you're meant to make me feel awful while I'm here. Not give me a comfortable bed and a nine-hour sleep."

"You're not here to be tortured. You're here to listen. And eventually, once I've won you over, give me my brother back."

He ponders my words, and I head toward the stairs, eager to get my day started.

"Olivia . . ."

I turn and see he's pulled one foot up onto the bed, his arm resting on his knee. The picture of relaxation, leaned back against the wall. If I took his photo and posted it now, my following would increase by ten percent within a day, I'm sure of it.

"Have you thought that your brother might not want to be set free?" He speaks softly, like the tone of a police officer who has come to tell you that your relative has been in an accident. There's a pity in it that I can't stomach.

Of course I've thought about it. But he's nineteen; he's too young to commit his whole life to this man. Our parents would never have allowed it.

Heading toward the stairs, I don't reply. I don't want to argue with him, and regardless, it doesn't seem the best way to get him on my side.

"I'll be back later, okay? Think things over."

"Wait . . . how's your head?"

"Oh." I pause and turn back around. Placing the plates on the shelving unit, I run my fingers through my hair and push it back, revealing the scab running along my forehead. "It's not too bad."

"Are you gonna go to the doctor today at least?" he asks.

I'm surprised, shocked even. Why would he care whether I go to the doctor? His face is concerned, his voice sincere. I can't read any manipulation from him. Either he's a master at it, or he's genuinely concerned.

"I'm okay, honestly. If I get any symptoms, I promise to go straight to the hospital."

His brows knit together but he eventually gives me a small nod.

"Talk to your brother, Olivia."

Ignoring his last suggestion, I pick up the plates and

return upstairs to work through the rest of my list.

◆ ◆ ◆

Austin's concern for my well-being threw me into somewhat of a tailspin. The warmth in my chest grew cold at the mention of my brother. He wasn't going to let him go. That much was clear.

At least not yet.

It seems that, in addition to this parting gift, the universe saw fit to grace me with more challenges today. My mom always used to say bad news comes in threes, but I disagree. It comes in threes, and then you just start counting from one again.

Of course, I've been distracted, imagining ways to convince Austin to let my brother go, my thoughts drifting to some dark places: I could deprive him of food and water. I could take away his mattress and blanket. This could escalate into something truly torturous. I have the imagination, but none of the follow-through.

I'm not a *bad* person. I'm just doing a bad thing.

And the worst part is I think he knows it.

I hope that's enough to ensure there won't be any long-lasting repercussions to locking a man in my basement. Because as soon as I stop imagining torture, the inevitable guilt kicks in.

I've tried reviewing a product sent by a local sports clothing store that's building its brand. They're small, local, and a product I genuinely enjoy wearing. They've given me a few things to try, and I've made sure to give honest reviews. But this morning, with the weight of a five-pound dumbbell on my chest, I know I'll have to redo the reviews tomorrow.

I jot down a few thoughts in my notepad for my next attempt. Perhaps a small clip to show that the fabric doesn't turn see-through when you bend over. Sure, I'd have to show my ass, but I could make it a funny clip. This is the kind of thing women would do in a changing room. It's one of the hardest things about ordering online. You can't tell how good the quality is unless you try it on.

After finishing up my notes regarding upcoming posts, I relax for the rest of the morning. My brain is too wired to do any genuine work, and my head is thumping from last night's injury downstairs.

I've made a simple sandwich for lunch and, of course, one for the houseguest, replacing his water bottles, too.

I don't say a word to him when I go down, the cowardly torture method I've gone with, and despite his somber expression, I can tell he wants to talk. I leave without a word and only hear a muffled *fuck* as I'm ascending the stairs.

My heart squeezes as my body naturally comes to a slow pause at the top of the stairs.

No.

He's not your friend.

Or your houseguest, no matter how many times you call him that.

He's holding your brother hostage.

Fuck him. Calm down—not literally.

When I return to the basement with dinner six hours later, my muscles ache from the poor workout and stretch I've done. My shoulder is burning, and my head is thumping. I throw back a few Advil to take the edge off and prepare myself for a silent dinner.

The afternoon has gone worse than the morning. I feel like crap, but I've received more bad news that has sent me into a tailspin. My rage is seeping out of me, and I know I won't be able to hold it in around him. So I'll give him his food, eat, and get out.

When I knew I was going to kidnap Austin, I had planned to eat with him. I knew it would be a good opportunity to lay some groundwork. And honestly? I enjoy eating with others. It seems so pitiful to eat alone watching some Netflix documentary or listening to a podcast. I miss having Danny around.

And after this afternoon's events, I need a distraction, and what better one than the chained-up man in my basement?

I can hear Austin adjusting his position on the mattress as I'm walking down. The chains clink together like a cat with a bell around its neck. At least he's still alive.

"Hey, how are you?" he asks softly as I hand him his dinner. Spaghetti bolognese, my mom's recipe. The reminder of her warms my chest until my body feels somewhat renewed.

I pause for a moment, truly thinking about my day and how it's gone from bad to worse.

"Fine."

Lies.

I twist spaghetti around my fork and take a big bite, saving myself from answering truthfully.

Now, for the most part, I'd say I'm a positive person. I live in the now, but plan for the future. I love the business I'm building, but parts are repetitive, and parts are negative.

My channel started a year ago when I was learning the ropes at community college to get a degree in business. I wanted so much to live my own life and be my own boss. Working for someone else comes with a level of security, but honestly, I have too much rebellion running through my veins to be told what to do all day long. Sure, you know when your next paycheck is coming, but the lack of flexibility and vacation days, not that I really took any of those, fills me with a sense of impending dread when I think about applying for *real* jobs.

When Danny and I were orphaned at such a young age, I knew I wanted to build something that was mine, that would take care of us.

So, I worked as a personal trainer on the side while I studied at college in the evenings. And when I realized how much I enjoyed doing it and wearing comfy workout clothes all day, I knew I had to incorporate it into my business plan.

After years of hard work, the videos really took off around six months ago. I started doing short reels to entice followers on my other social media platforms, but ultimately, the bulk of my money is earned through my channel. Currently, my subscriber list is around 400,000, but it's steadily climbing each month. Luckily, it's started bringing in some revenue for me, which supplements my product review and affiliated marketing.

As well as circuit workout videos, which is what I initially started with, I've now done courses to be trained in pilates, stretching, and meditation to create a more holistic approach to health. As well as a short cooking series which did okay—focusing on easy, healthy snacks for work.

Most of the reception I get is positive. Some of it is lewd or crass. A lot of it is people making suggestions that I should improve my form or *leave it to the experts, honey*. I chalk it up to people being a little jealous or maybe just bored. The trolls are inevitable.

But then there are some seriously malicious attacks. And today, there have been a few repeat offenders.

Millie Gilbert is another fitness vlogger and my virtual nemesis. She'd started her channel a few years before I had, but I hadn't heard of her until she began commenting on my videos, claiming that I'd stolen her routines and passed them off as my own. Despite my videos being posted before hers.

There was no truth in the matter, so I ignored her comments, allowing them to be drowned out by the more positive ones.

I'd ended up having to block her completely after her repeated attempts to brand me as a cheat and a thief.

It hurts because I've worked hard on my business, and I'm really proud of where I've got to today. But the video I was tagged in over one hundred times today was from her account, so I knew I'd be discussed at some point.

What I didn't expect was to see Travis, my ex, sitting

alongside Millie with a somber expression on his face.

Travis is a self-proclaimed finance bro. However, I would like to point out that he's not six-foot-five, nor does he have blue eyes or dark hair. He is, however, a total douche. We dated for six months, and once he saw the success of my channel and the potential earnings, he was convinced he could become an influencer discussing finance and how to invest in stocks and crypto. His videos lacked thought and intelligence, and he rambled about how men were just better than women at investing.

I tried to give him pointers to improve and reach his target audience, as in men like him. But he said if I could do it, it really wasn't that hard, and I should *stay in my lan*e.

So I did. I kicked him out, stayed in my lane, and since dumping his ass, gained an additional 100,000 followers. I generally don't like the energy that gloating puts out into the world, but revenge really is a dish best served cold.

His repeated attempts to get back into my life certainly helped my ego, but it got rather annoying with his incessant whining about how I was intimidating to him.

I'm not intimidating at all. *He* was intimidated, and that's not something I can control. So again, I just blocked him and moved on. But after watching the eight-minute-and-twenty-three-second video, my stomach's been rolling. Bile is bubbling away, threatening to roll up my throat at any moment. I am furious and stressed, and I can do nothing about it. I have no one to turn to. No one is here to support me. My parents are dead, and Danny is god knows where.

Millie had essentially recruited Travis to confirm her story. That I'd taken her ideas and profited off them. His bitterness at our break up and his subsequent lack of success is glaringly obvious to me, but to my followers? This could break my business.

So no, I'm not fine. But what am I supposed to say to the man sitting on my old mattress in my basement? I could hardly spill my guts to him and have a good old cry, which, if

I'm honest, is desperately needed. I need my mom. I want her to tell me it is all going to be alright.

So I'll lie, get what I need from him, and get him out of my life.

CHAPTER FIVE

Austin

I was hasty to say being in this basement would be a breeze. Yes, the bed is comfortable, yes, the food is so good my nonna would be proud, and yes, Olivia hasn't bothered replacing the cable ties on my wrists. But lying without so much as a book is annoying, to say the least. With nothing but my thoughts, the hours drag, and all I can do is wait for her to descend the stairs again.

I've checked in with Luca: everything is running smoothly, and my absence hasn't been questioned yet. It's only a matter of time. I can't speak for long, as although the burner has a freakishly long battery life comparable to a Nokia 3310, I don't know how long I will be down here.

So, aside from the very quick check-in, I'm left to my own devices.

And when I should be worrying about my business, the employees who work for me, and my own safety from a person who has decidedly acted very out of character, all I can think about is the hurt look on her face when I suggested that perhaps her brother was happy where he was. He didn't need his sister valiantly riding in to defend or save him. Danny is a man, a man who has made his own decisions and hasn't made any suggestions to me that he is unhappy with his choices.

And the trouble with my thoughtless comment is that it puts her in a difficult position. She abducted a man for a reason that may not be true. It's only logical that she would be thinking about her next steps. If I don't give her Danny, or Danny doesn't acquiesce, she either lets me go and assumes I'll come after her, or she kills me. Or tries to kill me. The girl is strong, clearly. But I have at least eighty pounds on her. There's no way she's taking me down. Unless, of course, she asks me nicely, like with the chloroform, and then apparently, I'll just fucking happily do it for her.

The sun has set, and all natural light has left the room, leaving sharp, elongated shadows across the half-renovated basement. I leave the light off, hoping the darkness will help me regain some much-needed sleep I've lost over the years. I expect she'll be down with some more food soon, but after lunch, I can't be sure.

When I finally hear the faint slide of the dead bolt, I hold my breath in anticipation. But she walks silently down the stairs holding two bowls of what smells like spaghetti bolognese with parmesan cheese on top. My mouth waters and maybe it's the fact I've been alone in this basement all day, but the sight of her fills me with such relief.

"Hey, how are you?"

"Fine."

Well, at least she's talking. Kind of. Not sure if monosyllables count in terms of a conversation.

When she comes closer, I can see how tired she is. The gash on her forehead is angry and molten. Gray shadows rim her eyes. Perhaps the lighting down here has exaggerated her tiredness but my gut says probably not.

She sits on the chair opposite my mattress and begins to eat.

I eat half my bowl before I can't take the silence any longer.

"I'm sorry I upset you." The words taste hollow. "It wasn't my intention to make you lose hope."

She looks up, her mouth slightly agape as she holds the fork up to take another bite.

"Oh . . . Oh no." She swishes her hand in front of her to bat away my apology, spaghetti sauce flicking across the floor. "I'm just in my own head. Nothing to worry about."

"Tell me."

I'm not sure what possessed me to say it. She seems to be wondering the same thing as she does an adorable head tilt.

"We've never spoken much before. Why start now?"

"We've never spoken before *ever*," I correct her.

She smiles. "I'm sure you said hi to me once. I was awful and ignored you."

"I can understand why now you've explained."

"I have a feeling we're going to go around on a loop here." She hitches her foot up onto the chair so she can almost rest her chin on her knee. I lean back against the wall and lift my leg as well, mirroring her.

"Hmm. okay. So let's talk about something neutral," I suggest.

"What's a neutral topic between captive and captor?"

I think for a moment, choosing from the list of questions I had banked up this afternoon.

"Why did you get into personal fitness?"

"I've been meaning to ask how you know that. You called me a blogger the other day. How did you know?"

How did I know that? Oh, right, she doesn't know that I've been watching her videos for the last two years only to masturbate to ones of her doing pilates or talking about healthy work snacks. No, I'm not ashamed. Her smile, her hair, her beautiful face and body are only enhanced by how fucking sexy she is when she's talking about her passion. And the whole time I've been semi-stalking her at Squeeze the Day. With each new video that was posted, it felt like a personal gift to me. *Merry Fucking Christmas—I can watch you on the other four days of the week from the comfort of my own home.*

"I didn't." I shrug. "But the constant leggings and crop tops, excessive amount of gym equipment, and the fact that you have time to sit in a café three times a week at 10 a.m.

just to read would suggest you don't have a typical nine-to-five. And everyone your age has an online presence. Am I wrong?"

Jesus, that's a ramble.

"Spend a lot of time monitoring the younger generation, do you?" she quips.

"I'm not that much older than you."

"That's exactly what an old person would say."

A laugh rumbles from my chest, and I throw my head back, clunking it against the wall.

"Fuck, that was your fault." I lift my hand awkwardly to rub the back of my head. The chain just about lets me reach.

"Mine? Typical Boomer, blaming us young'uns for everything."

"Fucking BOOMER? If I wasn't chained up, I'd—"

Her eyebrow raises, her lips parting ever so slightly. I can see her perfect, pink tongue peeking out.

"You'd what?" she whispers.

For a moment, I think she's scared. But I notice the subtlety of her movements; after all, I've watched her for years.

Her thighs clench, and she leans toward me, not away. Her voice lowers, and the slow movement down her throat suggests that the thought of me out of these chains makes her mouth water. Maybe it's inevitable that we'll get there. Maybe she's been fantasizing as much as I have. But it's too soon. I don't want to scare her. Only last night she panicked at waking up with her head in my lap.

And there goes my dick again. Perking up at the thought of her in my lap.

"Nothing . . . I was just playing," I lie.

She looks away, almost disappointed. The ape in my chest is spinning in circles and pounding with triumph. *Oh, she fucking likes me. I may well have played my hand, Olivia Daniels, but you've played yours, too.*

Now, I just need to play the game better than her.

"So." I clear my throat. "Your fitness journey. How did that come about?"

"I started while I was in community college. I ran sessions for extra cash. I really enjoyed it, so I thought I'd incorporate it into my master plan."

"Ah, then we'll do what we do every night, Pinky . . . try to take over the world," I quote in a high-pitched voice.

"Oh my god, you watched *Pinky and The Brain*?"

"Olivia." I lean forward. "I was obsessed with *Pinky and The Brain*."

She giggles, her eyes crinkling in the corners as she relaxes back into her chair.

"Well, yes. Sort of, I guess. I wanted to build something that was mine. I was taking care of Danny while he started high school, so I needed work to be flexible. I also wanted to get my degree in business, so I had to get creative."

I know the answer already, but it would seem odd if I didn't ask. "So . . . your parents?"

"Car accident." She summarizes—not explicitly telling me they're dead, but then I suppose she doesn't need to.

I nod. "Sorry to hear that."

She shrugs, moving on from the topic swiftly. "What about you? How did you get into whatever it is you're into?"

"I thought you knew what I was into?" I smirk, feeling the mood shift.

"Help me understand you and what my brother has gotten into." Her voice softens.

A difficult question to answer. Two years ago, I'd had somewhat of an epiphany. I don't much believe in fate, or destiny, but I'd been born into the life I'd been born into. My role as second son had another meaning besides being the younger brother. I was groomed to do the shit jobs, the dirty jobs, while August kept his nose clean to eventually be the face of our father's business.

As my world darkened, August was living in the light. The shadows comforted me, accepted me covered in blood, sweat, piss, and shit, none my own, not that that would be better. My reputation grew each year until everyone feared me. My father was so proud, proud of the monster I had become. My brother feared my ambition would grow beyond my station. Beyond the tasks our father had assigned me.

Of course, I indulged in the fantasy of living a normal life, having someone to come home to at night, take long walks with, and live somewhat of a simpler life. I'd dreamed that night of a life that was so ordinary, so unbelievably mundane. I could taste the percolator coffee first thing on a Saturday morning; I could smell the clean linen bed sheets wrapped around me and the most beautiful woman in the world—long blonde hair, golden-tanned skin, and a smile that filled her whole face. And she looked at me like that, like I made her that happy.

After experiencing the worst day of my life, something only Dr. Alfie knows about, I'd gotten black out drunk for a week or two before stepping aside from The Organization completely. It was the reminder of that day that led me to Dr. Alfie. And then, bumping into one of my father's associates, for the first time in my life, I panicked. I ran into a random juice bar, and that was when I saw Olivia. Sure, I hadn't imagined her exactly, but she was so strikingly similar. My fantasy girl had come to life, and she was more than what I had imagined. She was kind, hardworking, and ambitious. She was someone I could look up to, build a life for, and *change* my life for.

So I'd left my father's business. I'd struck out on my own and created The Unseen. And although the general opinion is that The Unseen is a branch of my father's business, it couldn't be further from the truth. My father allows the rumor mill to assume, but he knows nothing about my operation. If word got out about its true existence, that his son had left the business, his reputation would be destroyed.

I wasn't lying when I said that no one left this business alive. But I may just be the exception.

To add insult to injury, I had taken a few of the boys with me when I left. Luca, of course, a few others that we'd gone through the ranks with, and Danny—the tech genius that's setting us up to be legit.

The option wasn't there for them to quit. There were no resignation letters and fond farewells in this business. But I wanted to move away from senseless violence. I have a ledger to balance out. And right now, I'm still in massive fucking debt. Besides, their staying with me keeps them safe. I'm not forcing them to stay, and they know the risk if they leave: they're on their own. And that means they'd be fair game to my father. At least continuing to work for me means they're protected.

Olivia deserves someone better than a man with so much blood on his hands.

I shrug. "It's a family business. I didn't have much choice."

"You have a choice now, though."

I smile. "Yeah, Killer, but I don't make the rules."

"What's the point in being the boss if you can't make the rules?" She wiggles her eyebrows, attempting a tactic of playful teasing despite the undertone of desperation seeping into her voice.

"I'm not the boss. My father is."

"Yeah, that's what everyone thinks." She leans back, relaxed. It's an act. She's about to pull the pin. What has Danny been telling her?

"I have a theory," she continues.

"A theory about me? You've been thinking about me an awful lot, Killer. You know you could have just asked me on a date. You didn't need to go through all this trouble." I lift the chains and let them fall back down over my thighs.

She rolls her eyes. "As if you would have said yes."

"In a heartbeat. Have you seen yourself?"

She stutters, her lips slightly parted. For a split second, she seems surprised by my admission, but then the flush crawls up her skin, and my chest thumps wildly. She's not embarrassed; she's pleased.

I implore her to understand with my eyes, pushing every honest thought I've had at her so she knows how serious

I am. Once she's composed, she deflects, just as I knew she would. And that's okay. We're taking baby steps.

"How about, if my theory is correct, you do me one favor of my choosing?" she says.

"Nice try." I laugh.

"Scared?"

I raise an eyebrow and let out a deep sigh.

"Terrified. You're a loose cannon. Unpredictable. Acting out of character and desperation. If we both make it out alive, the two of us will be looking over our shoulders until one, or both of us, decides to do something about it."

"And what would you do?"

"I haven't decided yet. That depends on how well you keep feeding me." I tap my stomach.

Her eyes roll again, but I can tell she's softening. "I'll bear that in mind."

"So what's this theory then?"

Taking a deep breath, she pulls up her other leg so she's sitting cross-legged on the chair.

"I think you're the boss. Like the real boss. I don't think your dad has anything to do with The Unseen." She pauses for a moment, waiting for a response. I say nothing, so she continues. "My brother is nineteen. There's no way in hell he's idolizing a man in his mid-sixties. But a thirty-something-year-old? Sure, I can believe that."

She's so close. I almost want her big, beautiful brain to work it out.

"You're charming, accomplished, and have a reputation for taking no shit. You're handsome . . ." She flushes, tilting her chin down. "Of course he'd look up to you."

It astounds me that for someone who isn't in our world, she's astute and nearly on the fucking money. Without knowing our internal politics, she could never guess the full truth, of course, but still. She's fucking smart. And that's without mentioning that she thinks I'm handsome. *Fuck, I'm a goner.*

She looks up through her lashes, waiting to hear my thoughts. But what can I say?

She doesn't realize the game she's playing, or maybe she does, and she really is just that desperate. I have to put her straight. I have to make her hate me just enough that she forgets this endeavor and moves on. I can't outright tell her I'm not part of The Unseen. The name allows my team a level of protection in addition to my own. If people found out what I was actually doing, that protection would disappear immediately. My father is included in that. As soon as he changes his mind, I could be dead, and so could her brother.

"How old are you, Olivia?"

"Twenty-four . . . why?"

"You have a lot of life ahead of you. I'd suggest you keep out of shit you don't understand. There are a lot of people who wouldn't hesitate to hurt you for what you just said."

"But not you," she says, lifting her chin in defiance.

Fuck, she's so brazen. Pushing her away is going to be harder than I thought.

"No, not me. I'm not exactly in a position to hurt anyone right now."

She glances down at the chains. I'll let her believe that's all there is. Not that I am cleaning my ledger, for her and for me. To prove that I could be more than what I was born into.

"Are you going to let my brother go?" she asks again.

"No."

"Then you're hurting me," she whispers.

She uncrosses her legs and steps in front of me with her hands out so I can pass her my plate.

I hold it out to her but run my fingertip over her knuckle. Her quick intake of breath tells me she's shocked. Her feet staying put tells me she liked it.

"I'm making you feel something, Killer, but I don't think it's hurt."

Her pink lips press together in a flat line. Seems I've struck a nerve.

"Good night, Austin."
"Good night, Olivia."

CHAPTER SIX

Austin

I wake the next day, the smell of bacon filling my nostrils.

"Morning," a soft voice whispers very close to my face.

Did I get laid last night? My morning erection is ready to go if so.

I roll to my side, ready to reach out to the hopefully soft, naked body lying next to me, but the clink of metal wakes me faster than any alarm clock.

"Have you been sleeping okay? Comfortable enough? I can get you another pillow or different bedding. You're probably used to something a little fancier than what I've given you."

I rub my hand over my face and blink my heavy eyelids open.

Bright eyes and freckles fill my vision, her warm breath tickling my chin as she inspects my face. *Fuck, why is she standing so close?* My eyes dip down as if following a homing beacon. A sheen of sweat coats her chest as her tits threaten to spill out of her crop top. Does she realize how dangerous this is? You don't get within grabbing distance of your hostage.

"Are you feeling okay? You look a little peaky. I can get you medicine. Maybe you're not getting enough vitamin D . . . Actually, you're definitely not. Your skin is sallow and lifeless."

Fucking rude. There goes my morning wood.

"Maybe I should get you a supplement."

"Or you could let me go."

Please don't.

"Are you ready to let my brother go?"

"Not happening, Killer."

"I can wait you out," she snips.

"Well, at the moment, we can call this a wild weekend together. Any longer, and people are going to start looking for me."

She frowns, retreating out of reach, and as I sit up, I try to stretch out the muscles in my back. The chains have been digging under my ribs. Not unbearable, but uncomfortable all the same.

She looks at my bare chest and the indents in my skin. Her brows knit together as she presses her lips into a flat line. Despite knowing better, she appears so innocent like this, but it looks like the guilt is kicking in.

Handing me the plate, she says, "You don't seem too bothered about me letting you go."

I start eating the bacon and egg wholemeal sandwich she's brought me. It's got chili flakes in again, and spinach. It's fucking delicious.

"It'll happen, or it won't. You're going to do what you're going to do," I say before taking another bite.

"But . . . but I took away your freedom. Aren't you upset?"

I shrug. "It's no more than I deserve."

A flicker of concern reaches her eyes. But she doesn't seem scared for others. She seems scared for me.

"And your people will be looking for you, won't they?"

"Yes."

"This soon?"

"The same day, Killer."

We're on day three. She must know that this is inevitable. I'm not going to lie. Not that she would believe it, anyway. Of course my people will be looking for me; she just doesn't need to know that they know exactly where I am already.

"I could torture you," she blurts out.

"You don't have it in you to hurt someone, Olivia. We both know that."

"You don't know me."

I shrug again. Finishing off my sandwich, I place the plate on the side of the bed and lean back, trying to stretch my aching muscles. I work out every day, so my body is starting to feel the effects of this little vacation. I'm not getting any younger, and the body forgets itself quicker after thirty.

Regardless, she's shamelessly checking me out, and fuck, it feels good. I'm in good shape; I know this. But given her profession and how fucking out of my league she is, the monkey jumping around my rib cage is pounding its chest, screaming, "Mine. Mine. Mine." She's feeding my ego as well as my stomach.

"I'll bring you some vitamin D supplements."

"Don't go out of your way, Killer. You'll let me go soon, and I'll get my sunshine then."

"I've kidnapped you . . ."

I let you.

"I've held you hostage for three days . . ."

I could have gotten out of these chains and out the window in less than twenty minutes, but sure.

"And you still don't take me seriously. Maybe I really will torture you. Then you'll know how serious I am."

"Sounds like foreplay to me," I wink, and pink singes her cheeks.

She moves to pick up my empty plate, and I reach out to grab her wrist. My grip is light, non-threatening, but she gasps all the same.

"I will smash these plates on your head if you don't let go of me."

Pressing my two fingers against her pulse point, I can

feel her heartbeat racing. I rub my thumb against the smooth skin of her wrist. She could pull away easily but she doesn't. She's waiting to see what I do next. At least she has her weapon of choice ready.

Ignoring her comment, I say, "I'll make you a deal."

"You're not in a position to make a deal."

"Consider it something interesting to keep my mind occupied. You've given me far too much time to think."

"Perhaps that's the real torture."

"The comfortable bed, eight-hour sleep, and delicious food kind of outweigh the negatives of being locked in your basement."

"Ah, so the fact that you don't deserve those things doesn't weigh on you. Interesting."

"Those things are pretty basic. Surely everyone deserves those, regardless of who they are," I argue.

"If you thought you deserved them, you wouldn't keep bringing it up."

I pause for a moment, I should really mention this to Dr. Alfie. "Perhaps you're right."

My self-inflicted four-hour-a-night sleep routine is a form of punishment in itself, but I don't want to admit that to her. "Is this where I discover the true meaning of Christmas and change my life by moving to a small town and falling in love?"

"Would that be so awful?" she murmurs.

I lean forward, my eyes dropping to my thumb circling her wrist. Her eyes follow mine, and she inches closer, too.

"I couldn't think of anything fucking worse. And I think you're the same."

"You don't know anything about me."

"You've said that already."

"And yet again, you're not listening."

I smirk, drop her wrist, and notice the tiniest of furrows in her eyebrows. She steps back like I've stung her.

She likes me. She fucking hates that she likes me, but she does.

"Perhaps I haven't met the right woman," I say, attempting to break the tension and failing miserably.

"Oh, so you are into women then?"

I smirk, how clever she is at gathering information. "I'm open to all things Killer, but yes, I'm interested in women."

"I thought by the way you're holding my brother hostage, you were interested in him."

I grin. "No, you didn't."

She turns, hiding the tug of her lips I spot for a brief second.

"No . . . I didn't. I knew you liked women."

"And how did you know that?"

"At Squeeze the Day, you were practically drooling one day over a lady who walked in. She really was quite beautiful."

"That can't have been me." I shake my head.

"It was, I remember," she says, practically pouting. Sweet Olivia is not a good poker player, I see.

"Impossible."

She rolls her eyes. "And why is that?"

"Because I've only ever looked at you at Squeeze the Day."

Her mouth opens, but nothing comes out. She steps back further before turning on her heel to head toward the stairs.

I smile, stretching out my legs in front as much as I can in these chains.

"Our deal, Olivia?"

"I'll think about it," she replies without turning around.

"All I ask is that you bring me a book. It is quiet when you're not here with me."

She stops to turn. Her eyes drop for a split second on my bare chest, and I squash the urge to smirk.

"That's all you want from the deal?"

"Please?"

Not a word I often say. My commands are followed

regardless of social etiquette. But Olivia Daniels is not from my world. She's kind and thoughtful, and I have a strong suspicion that deep down, she thinks everyone else is too. And for the life of me, I can't bear to be the person to break it to her. There are bad men out there who would relish taking advantage of her kindness. Fuck, I'm sure some already have.

"I have a few old books I'll bring down to you."

She returns with some old paperbacks, and she places them on the floor by the bed.

"Thank you, Olivia." I bow my head.

I watch her throat bob up and down, the swell of her breasts overflowing the tight sports bra she has on. Does she realize her presence alone is torture enough? Being so close, I can smell the faint scent of her perfume; receiving kindness from her when she hates me, it's too much. I know I can't do anything about her brother. Danny would be in an unbelievable amount of danger if I did. Or he'd be back working for my father, and that might be just as bad. I'm sure he'd be punished for moving to my side. I can't take that risk. I like the kid. Sure, he's all bravado like most nineteen-year-olds. But he's a good kid and works hard. And even if he wasn't all those things. He's her brother. Nothing can happen to him. No. There's one way to leave, and that's in a body bag.

And as I hear the click and slide of the lock, I'm alone.

I hear shuffling and muffled footsteps at the furthest point of the basement ceiling, which I assume is either the kitchen or the living area. Given that the muffled footsteps quickly quieten, my guess is that it's the living area.

I pull out the phone from my boot. The charge was about fifty percent, so I have a few more days available. I hesitate for a second, but decide it's more important to speak to Dr. Alfie today.

The phone rings, and Mia answers in her normal, cheerful, professional voice.

"Mia, it's Austin. Austin Black."

"Yes, Austin." She laughs. "I know who you are. Do you

need Dr. Adams?"

"Right away if he's available."

"It's your lucky day, a patient canceled. I'll put you through," she chirps.

"You're the real angel, Mia. Don't let him forget."

"I'll expect that to be reflected in my Christmas tip." She laughs before clicking silence.

I make a mental note to give her the biggest tip she's ever seen. Alfie is going to be furious.

He's quick to answer, and as soon as I take a breath, his deep voice rumbles through the phone. "Austin, how is everything going?"

How is everything going? I really should have thought more about what I wanted to talk about. He'll only have a limited time before his next patient or my battery runs out.

I get as comfortable as possible, given the chains, and keep my voice low.

"It's . . . going well. Given the circumstances."

"How does Olivia seem?"

"Surprisingly unfazed. She's more than I thought she could ever be. I mean, I know I've thought about her a lot. Thought about us together and what that would look like. But I'd never imagined her to be anything other than . . . good."

"And do you think that changes your fantasy?" the doctor asks.

"Yes and no."

"Explain that for me."

God damn, he's so professional. If I were listening to someone telling this story, I'd get them to stop so I could make some popcorn first.

"She's exactly what I thought she was: driven, kind, caring. She's actually taking care of me. It was a bit disconcerting at first. I mean I have the comfiest mattress, soft bedding, one of those pillows that molds to your head. And the food, it's been good, like really good. She's cooking homemade dinners and then eating them with me. We're talking and, I think, flirting."

"Sounds like you're enjoying yourself," he says coolly.

"I mean, I am. I don't want it to end. Is that crazy?"

He pauses for a moment before asking, "Why don't you want it to end?"

"If it ends, the fantasy is over."

"Hmm." He pauses. "Is this really your fantasy, though?"

"I mean, for being kidnapped, it's damn near perfect." I laugh, attempting to rub my hand along the back of my neck, but the chains have tangled, preventing me from getting further than my collarbone.

"Okay, but every time we've spoken about Olivia in the past, you've always talked about the man you wanted to be. The type of man that someone like Olivia would deserve."

"Yes, that's true. I want to be someone who is capable of being good."

"And what do you think Olivia sees when she looks at you right now?"

I falter for a moment. Fuck. I look around the room. It's dark, dingy, and unkempt. I look down at my body. It's chained and aching. My beard is growing. My hair is a mess. I know for sure I've got death breath. My next deal with her is going to be a toothbrush. I'm actually surprised she's forgotten it.

"Austin?"

"I'm here. I'm just thinking."

"Okay. I have another patient coming in. But I want you to think about that and then call me tomorrow. Do you have access to the time there?"

"On my phone."

"Good. I'll call you, and we can have a longer session. But one more thing before you go." He pauses, waiting for my acknowledgment.

"Yes?"

"You sounded surprised when you said she was taking care of you."

"Yes, I said it to Olivia as well, and she said it sounded

like I thought I didn't deserve basic comforts."

"Do you think that?" His voice raises slightly.

"The ledger isn't clean, doc."

"Austin, you're making tangible steps to becoming a better person. To become a better man. I think a good night's sleep and some comforting food is exactly what you deserve."

I take a deep breath, and the dust down here causes my eyes to prickle.

"Tomorrow, Austin."

"Thanks, doc."

Olivia

Can I physically torture someone? No, probably not. Can I let someone think I could torture them? Absolutely.

I'm not above mind games, and this is how I'm going to win this particular battle with Austin Black. That and the shortest shorts on the planet.

I'm at the hardware store picking up some heavier-duty cable ties—for emergencies only, of course. The scent of sawdust and oil fills the air, and I inhale deeply. There's something so comforting about the smell of a workshop. Maybe it's the possibilities of what can be created with just a few materials and tools. Taking something raw and sculpting it into something purposeful.

I panicked when Austin grabbed my wrist this morning. He was so calm, not rough at all. His fingertips had caressed my skin to the point where I couldn't move. I was frozen, waiting to see what he would dare to do next. *Not sensible*. And the only way I'm going to get me and Danny out of this mess is if I keep my head on straight.

No messing around with the guy I've tied up in my basement. No more talking, no more flirting, and absolutely no more checking him out.

Because despite the effort I'm putting in to be a

reasonable captor—and fine, maybe make him like me a little so he'll give me what I want—it's not working. He's well-practiced at the game that I'm still only learning to play.

Frankly it's a miracle he's still tied up down there. It's a miracle I managed to get him in the car at all.

I can be smart about this. Everything he does is a ploy to get me to release him. Sitting with his shirt off, licking the crumbs off his thumb when he finishes eating, the flirting, the softly spoken man who I know is a killer, the gratitude, the pleasantries. The list goes on and on. And every single tactic is there to throw me off guard and let him go.

And I know what will happen when he gets free. I'll die. Because you can't abduct the head of The Unseen and not face repercussions. Even if he likes how I look in a crop top and bike shorts.

And that comment about the café . . . *I've only ever looked at you in that café.*

My heart raced a mile a minute when he'd said that. Of course I'd noticed. It would have been hard not to. His presence in the café almost made me find somewhere new to get my matcha green goddess smoothie. But Jenny makes the best smoothies, and I wasn't going to let some man, especially the worst kind of man, stop me from doing what I wanted to do.

His eyes would follow me around the juice bar. I could practically feel them staring at my ass as I placed my order. They followed me as I took my usual seat by the window. I swore one time I heard him growl at someone who tried to sit in my seat first. They quickly moved to the back corner, and his eyes were on me again. But the second I looked back, his eyes would dip low, and he'd take a sip of coffee. As soon as I stopped looking, his eyes would crawl back to me, watching me intently while I tried to focus on whatever book I was reading.

It wasn't creepy; it was more curious. And I had to wonder why he hadn't ever spoken to me, given that he seemed interested at the very least. I'd quickly determined he didn't know who I was, despite me following Danny to his warehouse on a number of occasions. He seems very chatty now though.

After I finish up at the hardware store, I head to Squeeze the Day and take my seat in my usual spot by the window.

I can't help but glance over at the chair that's usually occupied by Austin.

"He must be running late," Jenny says as she brings me my juice.

"Who?" I ask, but I feel the blush flow down my neck and spread on my cheeks.

"Girl, the hottie that you're always having a stare-off with."

"I don't stare off with anyone."

Oh god, she knows. I'm going to prison.

"Uh-huh, sure, and the beetroot smoothie doesn't turn your poop purple," she replies sarcastically, and I cough on my drink.

"Purple?"

"Fluorescent purple. Your pee, too. You know, if you're ever trying to mix it up a bit." She points down to my green kale smoothie, which fortunately does not turn my poop green.

"I'm good, thanks."

"Between you and me," she whispers, leaning down to me, "I think he only comes in here for you."

"For me?" I laugh nervously. "He's never even spoken to me." As far as she knows anyway.

"Well, he doesn't seem like a man of many words. He's one of those strong, silent types. You know, the broody ones."

He's actually been rather chatty stuck in my basement.

"I think you've been on the mushrooms again. Seeing things that don't exist," I joke, my heart fluttering so fast my skin was practically humming.

"Well, he only happens to come on the exact days and times that you do. I think that's an unlikely coincidence."

"Obviously, he has a routine." I shrug.

"He practically stares at you."

True.

"I haven't noticed."

"You have." She laughs, picking up my straw wrapper.

"I haven't."

"You're blushing."

Deflect, deflect, deflect.

"Is this how you treat all your customers?"

"If you mean whether I've been daydreaming about two of my most loyal customers falling madly in love in my café so that I'm mentioned at the wedding, then yes. Things get a little repetitive here, and my imagination helps pass the time." She cocks her hip to the side and arches an eyebrow at me.

I grin up at her despite the smoothie feeling lumpy in my stomach.

If Jenny has noticed our animosity, then maybe others have too. Maybe someone knows about the girl in the café, and they'll come looking for me.

She heads back to the counter and then returns with a coffee cup in hand. I frown, and not because I don't like coffee or order it. But I just wouldn't order it from here. I had it once on a particularly tired day, and let's just say it isn't their best drink on offer. It does make me wonder if he's ever actually had anything good.

"What's this for?"

"If you bump into him, you should give it to him. He orders the same thing every time, so it's the right order."

"I can't just give a random man a coffee," I splutter.

"Not random, and who knows what might happen? He might end up being the love of your life." She slides the coffee toward me using the tips of her fingers. Risky move, given how clumsy I know she is. She once spilled an entire drink on me.

"Doubtful," I mutter.

"Well, maybe the universe will throw you a bone. And besides, he's got to be better than Travis. I saw the video he and Millie posted, by the way. How are you feeling?"

"It's stressful for sure. I'm not sure whether to take any legal action or not, but overall the support online seems to be okay. The odd few comments are negative."

She nods before getting distracted by another customer.

Before she has the chance to return and pepper me with more questions, I pick up the black coffee and head home.

◆ ◆ ◆

"Hey, I brought you a coffee from Squeeze the Day," I call out, stepping down into the basement.

"Rule number two, Killer: don't give your hostage anything hot that they could throw at you."

His voice is husky and sends an unwelcome shiver down my spine. Each syllable reminds me he's real and he's here.

"Well, it's a bit cold now, to be honest. But it would ruin my outfit if you threw it at me, so I'd appreciate it if you drank it instead." I wink.

"Just a thought." He takes a sip.

"What's rule number one?"

"Don't come within touching distance."

I laugh. "Well, I've done that a few times. But I think I'll be fine. We've accepted the fact that you don't mind being chained up for some reason, and besides"—I shrug—"you like me."

"Rule number three."

I roll my eyes before taking a seat in my usual spot opposite his bed.

"Go on."

"Never trust your hostage. They will do anything and everything to get out of your grasp. That includes gaining your trust and appealing to your better nature."

"Sure. If I end up making a habit out of holding people hostage in my basement, I'll be sure to follow those rules."

"You know who I am, yet you're not scared of me. Why is that?" he asks, sipping the coffee, and for a moment, I think

I see him wince, but his usual smirk pulls in and hits me like a truck. I might not think he'd physically harm me, but this man has a whole arsenal of weapons at his disposal.

"Oh, I'm terrified of you. It's why I want Danny out. He deserves a good life. He's smart, he's incredible with computers and could be doing something with that."

"You don't seem scared though." I see he deflects my comments on Danny.

"No? Maybe I'm good at acting."

He takes another sip and leans back. His shirt is still off despite it not being that warm down here. He isn't wrong about hostages doing whatever they can to gain favor. He's noticed me checking out his broad chest with splattering chest hair. His shoulders and biceps aren't just from lifting weights. This is a man who has worked out for years. The scars on his chest and one down his forearm only make his body more intriguing.

My mouth waters at the thought of touching him freely. If I'd thought about this differently, I might not have needed to abduct him at all. I could have seduced him, learning each contour of his body while I did it. But I can't—even the thought is preposterous. This situation is hard enough now, but at least I've been upfront. He knows what I'm doing and why I'm doing it.

I don't have the strength to emotionally manipulate someone. Especially not him, who I've learned can be kind when he wants to be. He's gracious and easy to talk to. And his body runs circles in my brain night after night. You know when you take one look at someone, and you can just tell they would know exactly what to do? Too long, I've worked to get myself off in bed with a partner. Focusing so much to keep in the moment. Nothing stills my brain. Whether it's a lack of skill or something wrong with me, finishing during sex has always been a difficulty.

"Nah, I think you're curious." That damn smirk is back.

"Curious?"

"Yeah, curious. I have a theory."

Of course he does. I lean back into my chair, attempting to appear relaxed.

"I'm not what you expected," he begins.

True.

He doesn't wait for me to respond. "I'm not a mindless killing machine."

Maybe not mindless.

"I'm not angry or demanding."

I keep my eyes fixed on his despite the overwhelming urge to look away.

"I understand why you've done this. Hell, I would do the same thing if it was my brother. Well, a hypothetical brother that I actually like. Not my idiot older brother."

I ignore that comment even though hearing a small tidbit about his life seems to warm my chest. "Then you know why I have to keep you here."

"I do."

"So you'll let Danny go?"

He shakes his head but has the decency to look sad about it. "I said I understand. I'm empathetic to your cause. But this is not going to turn out the way you want it to, Olivia. It's just not."

He leans forward with his bare feet flat on the ground. His elbows are resting on his thighs as he leans forward. Like a doctor breaking the news to a patient's relative, he's bringing himself down to my level, speaking softly as if not to frighten me. But I am frightened, despite what he says. I know he's working on me. Seeping into my thoughts and my body, too. It hums for him. Every time I'm close to him, I feel like I'm charging up; my battery always feels overflowing when I'm near him. The excess energy needs a release, and I don't know how to get rid of it.

"Okay. So abducting you isn't going to work. What will? There must be something you want. I can take his place. I can —"

"No." His deep voice is sharp and raised.

"But—"

"No."

"I kidnapped YOU. I'm in this already whether you like it or not."

"Do you think I . . . your brother would want you in this life? You're not a bad person, Olivia. This is not the life for you," he says like he knows me.

"There are things about me you don't know. Things I've done," I lie. Honestly, I've had a relatively drama-free existence up until a week ago when I got this crazy idea. Now, I'm having threats to my business, and my favorite juice bar employee is trying to set me up with the guy I have chained in my basement.

"Can't be worse than holding someone hostage."

Why does it feel like he's holding all the cards when he's the one in chains?

"Let's change the subject," I say, done with this conversation.

"Okay. Tell me what was wrong yesterday."

"I don't want to talk about that."

He says nothing, sipping slowly on the coffee. Staring at me. Damn it, I hate awkward silences.

Eventually, I sigh, and his dimple surfaces under the scruff of three days with no shaving. It only encourages me to talk.

"It's probably silly to you, my business."

"Why would it be silly?"

"It's online."

"Explain," he demands softly.

"I have a channel, which is like a video—"

"I understand what a channel is."

"Okay, sometimes people don't know." I hold my hands up in surrender.

"Older people, you mean."

I blush. I mean he is older, but not old, as in he can't

understand what an online presence is. I remember trying to explain it to Gran before she passed, and she just thought I was scamming people.

"I didn't mean that you're old. You're just older than me, and I can't imagine your line of work would require you to watch many fitness videos."

"You'd be surprised, but go on."

Okay, that's ambiguous.

"I create exercise routines, film them, and post them online. I have a subscriber list of around 400,000 people. The videos are popular, fun, and meant to be for everyone. I try to do inclusive exercises so that if you're not fully mobile, there's an option for you, too."

"That doesn't sound silly at all, Olivia." His eyes are fixed on mine.

I smile awkwardly.

I don't need his approval. I don't need his approval.

"Well, there are some other people that are also in this line of work. One in particular is not very nice or kind. Her videos are all about aesthetics, appealing to a male audience, which isn't in itself a problem, but, well . . . she fat-shames people."

"And no doubt her videos aren't as popular as yours."

"No, although she is growing. It's not like she's not doing well. She's built up a good following of around 100,000 but she's been doing it longer than me so I think it annoys her that I have more subscribers."

"So what's the problem?"

"Well, she started dating my ex, and since then, they've been leaving comments about me on my videos, saying that I'm a thief and a fraud. That I had stolen all my workouts and passed them off as my own."

He nods again.

"It's not true. I work really hard to create content that will work well for people. I build my videos from the ground up . . . Actually, Danny had helped me set everything up at the beginning. He was amazing, really. So I haven't done it all myself, but I've worked hard nonetheless."

Another nod.

Maybe Jenny wasn't wrong about the strong, silent type with this one.

"But yesterday . . ." I turn away as my eyes start to prick. I take a deep breath, fiddling with my fingers in my lap. "Yesterday, they posted a video, calling me out. And Travis, my ex, said that I showed him how I would copy videos. It's a lie, but I don't know where to go from here. I don't know if I need a lawyer or if I should message them or block them. I just don't know what to do. And now I'm rambling to the man I've held hostage in my basement for the last three days. What the hell is wrong with me?"

"Well, aside from abducting someone rather than just asking them on a date, I'd say you're just a victim of jealousy." He winks.

"I . . . I don't want to date you," I splutter.

"We'll circle back to that." He smirks, and a flutter hits me in my core. "I'm going to take a wild guess and say that you broke up with him."

"Correct."

"Another guess would be that he didn't have your drive or work ethic."

"Correct."

"Final assumption for him, apart from being an entitled, work-shy scrounger, was that he wasn't exactly . . . fulfilling in the bedroom."

He stares me down, forcing me to look him in the eye.

How does he know that? I feel the flush of my cheeks, my neck, my chest; everything must be crimson.

Was Travis good in bed? No. He was a racehorse. Slapping his pelvis against my butt cheeks at a ferocious rate with no skill or finesse. He thought the harder the better, which left me unsatisfied and, honestly . . . reluctant to do it a lot. At least it was always over quickly.

My lack of response has apparently already answered for me.

"Okay, so correct on three counts. Well done for dumping him. At least he's this other person's problem now."

"Mmhmm." That's all I can muster up for a response.

"You could get a lawyer if you want a long, drawn-out case which will cost a whole lot of money, or you could post your own video in response . . . but that only makes people assume there's some truth in it for you to respond to. Or you can do nothing and hope that it goes away."

"Like I said, it seems like a lose-lose situation. And I don't like losing."

He smiles, and I shrug.

"What?"

"People don't often surprise me. And you seem to at every turn."

Warmth spreads in my chest, and I forcibly stop myself from overthinking this. He's saying what I want to hear to get out of here. Obviously, he's going to play to my weaknesses. He knows he can manipulate me. I crave more praise from him. Hearing it from someone so established, regardless of what he does, makes me feel so validated.

Silence fills the room. I'm not sure how to respond to that. I think it's complimentary. But it only makes me wonder what he thought of me before.

"I should get some work done. Did you read the books?" I divert the conversation to safer territory.

"Yes, they were very enlightening. I especially liked the highlighted sections." He laughs.

"The what?" I frown, trying to remember which books I had given him.

"The highlighted sections in *Black Silk*. Very educational."

Oh, shit. *Black Silk* is an erotic romance I bought after breaking up with Travis. I'll tell you, he's not wrong . . . it *was* enlightening.

"I . . . uh . . . that one wasn't meant to get in there."

"No doubt. I'll take more of those if you have them. The non-fiction nearly sent me to sleep."

He liked it?

"Umm, sure. I'll bring some down later."

He grins up at me, and I head up the stairs, my legs feeling heavier with each step.

CHAPTER SEVEN

Austin

As she heads up the creaky, wooden stairs, I can't help but smile. Her energy was lighter once she'd unloaded some of her concerns about Millie Gilbert and Travis Burns. Yeah, I fucking know their names.

Travis Burns, twenty-eight, currently unemployed. Has a Finance Bro channel that consists of him mostly talking about being an alpha, not realizing that an actual alpha doesn't need to talk about how much of an alpha he is. Pathetic.

And Millie Gilbert, twenty-two, Fitness Influencer—started her channel six months before Olivia did and has had relative success in the last few months. She's done well, but Olivia was light on the specifics of Miss Gilbert's content. She's fucking rude, shames people on her videos, and does those awful before-and-after shots that only suggest someone's value lies in their weight, not their happiness, not their confidence, not their personality. Is attraction a thing? Sure. Can I acknowledge that Olivia is beautiful? Absolutely. But if she were as vapid as Miss Gilbert, she'd be fucking ugly.

As the door clicks shut, I wait for the slide of the lock. Once it's in place, I take out the burner. The battery is getting dangerously low.

"Luca, I'm running out of battery. Give me an update."

One of the blessings of knowing Luca for so long is that he gets straight to the point.

"I have someone working on a profile for both Millie Gilbert and Travis Burns. You'll know the last time they sneezed by the time we're done."

"Good. And no word of this will get back to Danny, correct?" I remind him.

"Yep. He's working the warehouse this week, so he's out of the loop, and I let the boys know it's a need-to-know only."

"Good, I'm going to need another burner. Do you have the address I gave you yesterday?"

"Yes, boss."

"Good. Woman living alone, not to be disturbed. This is an in-and-out job. I'll have the basement window open for you to pass the phone and give me an update on tonight."

"I'll be with you before 1 a.m."

"Get going. Remember, this is a need-to-know only."

"Boss, quick question?"

Here we go.

"Why the fuck are you choosing to stay in this woman's basement?"

I inhale slowly, closing my eyes to count to five. Dr. Alfie says ten, but if I did that, I'd spend my whole damn day counting. "I hope no one can fucking hear you right now."

"Give me some credit, Austin."

Luca and I grew up together. He calls me boss for show, but I know he's alone when he calls me Austin.

"Okay, okay. I don't know, man. I'm following a hunch here."

"A hunch about what?"

Yeah. A hunch about what? Do I even fucking know?

"As soon as I know, you'll know."

"Your old man was sniffing around again."

Fuck.

"I bet he was. What did he want?"

"He said he wants an answer. Said you'd know what he meant."

And I do. My father, after two years of me not working

for him, has decided it's time for me to return to the fold. He didn't tell me why, only that fun time was over, and it was time to get back to work. Our meeting last week has been playing on my mind while I've had time to think. I wasn't lying to Olivia when I said that the quiet had been torturous.

I'm not up-to-date on the ins and outs of what's been happening in The Organization. I only know what I need to know. Luca keeps an ear to the ground, but he's somewhat aware that I needed a break from it all. Ironically, despite not coming from a family like mine, Luca is way more suited to it. Don't get me wrong, I was good at what I did. Too good. But Luca doesn't have the same emotional range that I do. It keeps him detached. He compartmentalizes, whereas I jumble the different parts of my life together. At least, that's what Dr. Alfie believes. I'm not good at separating things. Hence why I dove into being an enforcer for my father—I did that and nothing else. No girlfriend, no friends outside of work, no me time. Everything was for the job. Until that one awful day. And then again when I saw Olivia. And going back to that reality just isn't possible anymore. Now, I've had to build a new version of myself that fits the world that she lives in.

My father forcing me to come back is certainly going to be a problem. But how much of one remains to be seen.

"Yeah, I know what he means. I'm mulling it over. Hence why the basement is an attractive option right now," I concede.

"He's gonna keep coming back. Are you sure you can't sneak out in the night and be back by morning? It would help for people to see your face."

"It's been three days. You can manage this." Teaching my staff to be self-sufficient has been the hardest part. Normal companies, or at least good ones, empower their staff to take ownership of their work. These guys have lived and breathed hierarchy their whole adult lives. But things are different, and with the culture I'm trying to grow—*yes, I said culture*—it's going to take a long time for them to trust me.

"What's your timeline?"

"I'll be back by the end of the week."

He hesitates for a second.

"Okay. See you tonight."

◆ ◆ ◆

"When they died, my whole world turned upside down. I had a fourteen-year-old to look after and I barely knew how to look after myself. It was the hardest thing I've ever done, taking charge like that. But I wouldn't change it." She nods like she's reassuring herself. "I kept a roof over Danny's head and he graduated from high school. I couldn't do much but if he needed something I made damn sure he was going to get it."

The love she has for her brother is undeniable. I'm almost jealous of the bond they have. Augustus, my older brother by a few years, and I have nothing in common. We were taught to hate each other and everyone else whilst we were growing up. It's a miracle I even had Luca as a friend. Augustus wasn't an option but he saw my value as soon as our father made him accept it.

The emotion in her voice, the way it cracks when she talks about Danny almost makes me cave. I knew things would have been tough, orphaned at the age she was. But I hadn't realized she'd taken on the role as mother for Danny when she should have been learning about herself, finding out what she wanted to do with her life.

I'd always known what I was going to be. Always known what my life would become. But she had the promise of a happy future where she could make her own way, build her own life. And it was snatched away from her in the blink of an eye.

If I wasn't already obsessed with her, I'd be falling hard now. The sheer grit and determination she must have to turn to the world that had fucked her over and not let it ruin her kind and happy nature, baffled me. I can't say this to her. So I say something weak instead.

"Danny's a good kid. You did a good job, Olivia."

It's midnight, and Olivia has talked my ear off for hours now. I am starting to think she's much better at this kidnapping business than I originally thought. If she isn't going to torture me into compliance, she might very well charm me. If I weren't so concerned that Luca would be imminently tapping on the window, I would be having the time of my life.

She is snuggled into her wicker chair, feet tucked under her legs, sipping on cold water that matches my own. Wearing a pair of black, silky sleep shorts and a t-shirt that has a goose with a knife in its mouth with the words "Peace Was Never An Option" on the front.

She is funny, beautiful, and relaxing more and more around me. Just her sharing the story of her family dying feels monumental. Is this what Dr. Alfie talks about? Feeling responsible for others when you care about them? I have a warm feeling in my chest that makes me want to do better. Be better. To deserve the time she's giving me when she could be treating me like a piece of shit. Hell, I've done worse when I've chained people up. I've tortured them, I've hurt them, their families. The feeling that I don't deserve this kind of trust sits uncomfortably on my chest. And despite that, I want more. I want all her secrets. I want her to feel comfortable to share anything with me. Watching her from afar was sustaining me, but now that she's given me real attention, it's like I'm starving for it. I'll do anything for another five minutes. I'm almost praying that Luca doesn't come with the phone. I don't want it if it means she leaves me here alone.

I've used the blanket to cover up the chains. The more she forgets about me being tied up, the more she can see this as something more than this particular situation. I'm beginning to accept that my attraction for her is more than skin-deep. More than just an infatuation with a fantasy girl. She is my fantasy girl, but amplified. Before, everything was black and white, but with every conversation, more and more color is seeping in, bringing life to everything. Even in this half-renovated basement.

When I really think about going to that juice bar for two years just to watch her read three times a week, her kidnapping and putting me in her basement really isn't that crazy.

And despite her adorable anecdotes and the difficulties she faced building her business whilst looking after her brother, she's bright and caring and genuinely believes it will all work out. I've never met someone so refreshingly positive. I'm sure she believes that I will just hand her brother over. And given that I so willingly put a chloroformed cloth to my mouth, it's no wonder she would feel that way.

A tap at the window stops her mid-sentence.

"What was that?" she asks, getting to her feet immediately.

I stand, too, wanting to grab her, but I forget about the chains and stumble.

Instinctively, she's at my side, grinning. "Steady there, big boy."

It's honestly like she's forgotten I'm here—technically—against my will. Her hands are on my arm, stabilizing me. I could wrap my hands around her throat and squeeze until the light leaves her eyes.

"Rule number one, Killer."

"Right . . ." Her hands are still on me, her eyes are fluttering, pushing the limit. See? An eternal optimist.

But she has to learn. Luca will tap again any minute. She needs to learn as much as Luca needs to see that I'm not completely thinking with my dick. I don't need anyone in my ranks, even if it is my oldest friend, thinking I'm not fully in control.

I snap my hand out and grab her by the throat, the clink of chains ringing against the sharp exhale of her breath. I'm careful to squeeze only the side of her neck and not her windpipe. Her right hand instantly pulls at my wrist, and a slight panic reaches her eyes, but it quickly morphs into something else entirely. To drive home my point, I squeeze the tips of my fingers and thumb, leaning into her closer so my lips brush against the shell of her ear.

"I warned you, Olivia."

She quivers beneath me—in fear or something else? I can't tell.

"And I warned you," she says. Her right hand stops pulling me away, instead moving her own hand over mine, guiding my fingers to increase their pressure. It's my turn to exhale sharply now; our noses are almost touching as our breath mingles together.

I could tilt my head down to meet her defiantly raised chin. I could press my lips against hers and run my tongue along the seam of her lips. But before I can make my next move, her left hand snakes up the inside of my leg, cupping the hardening bulge in my pants.

"You don't know me," she whispers.

She squeezes firmly, not enough to hurt, but the warning is there, and fuck does it turn me on.

I push her head back so my lips tease against hers. My eyes drop down. I pull back the smallest amount. "Not yet. I want to, though, Killer."

"I don't think you could handle me."

"Want to renegotiate that deal we were going to make last night? I could prove you wrong."

Tap. Tap.

Fuck.

Her hand is off my erection and my wrist. I release her neck, and she storms to the window.

"It's just the wind," I say lamely.

"How would you know it's just the wind?"

She unhooks the window and lifts it up. She attempts to look out, but thankfully, it's too dark, and hopefully, we've been loud enough that Luca will keep out of sight.

"Get away from the window. You don't know what's out there."

"What are you worried about?" She frowns, looking over her shoulder at my corner.

Think, think, think.

"It could be a rabid raccoon."

"A rabid . . . raccoon?" She laughs, letting go of the window and allowing it to swing shut. "Are you worried about me?"

"Just worried about who will let me out of here when you go crazy with rabies."

"I think it was eradicated a while ago."

"I'm not willing to take any chances, Killer." I wink.

She heads back toward me, forgetting the tapping for now. I breathe a sigh of relief as she pads over to me barefoot. She must be getting chilly now; the concrete floor is cold on my feet.

She checks the time on her smartwatch and says, "Shit, I'd better get to bed. I didn't realize how late it was."

She picks up my plate from dinner and starts to head upstairs.

"Sleep well, Olivia."

"You too, Austin." Her sweet voice rings out as I adjust my hard-on.

Luca wastes no time before comically poking his head through the window. Like a sketch from an eighties movie where the kid is sneaking into his girlfriend's bedroom, and he wants to check if the coast is clear. But thank god, I don't have to worry about Luca trying to get in my pants.

"And now it makes sense," he whispers.

"Shh. The door isn't even fucking locked yet," I hiss.

"*You too, Austin,*" he mimics her voice with scary accuracy.

"Fuck off, Luca."

He laughs. "Alright, alright. I'll take the phone and the pick with me. Or would you rather I hang out for a bit? I've been waiting for ages; I thought she'd never shut up."

"Hey, don't fucking talk about her like that," I warn.

He slides into the basement, his small frame easily fitting through the tiny window. It's always been to his advantage. Some would be a little self-conscious if they were his height, but Luca takes it in his stride. His tiny, tiny stride.

He jumps down to a squat position and hops back up, holding his hands out in surrender.

"Okay, so now I know why you're here, what's your plan?"

"Fuck, I don't know, man. I realize this is a little out of character."

He shrugs, looking through all the old gym equipment she has stored on the shelves.

"If I were to tell you that I thought it was more strange that you stalked her at a café for two years and didn't make a move, would you believe me?"

He fucking knows about that? Dammit. I thought I'd been more careful.

I press my lips in a line and breathe slowly through my nose.

"That's my private time, Ireland."

"Oooh, you called me by my last name. You are pissed." He laughs.

"Give me the fucking pick."

"I thought you would have done it yourself by now. You're losing your touch."

I work quickly on the lock, and within thirty seconds, the chain is off me. My shoulders roll back in relief. I'll be able to sleep without a crick in my back tonight, and then I'll slip them back on when she comes down in the morning.

"Let's get out of here then."

"No, man, I'm not done here. I told you. I'll be back at the end of the week."

He rolls his head back, looking to god knows who for assistance. "What's your endgame?"

If he'd asked me this yesterday, I wouldn't have had an answer. Hell, if he'd asked me this morning, I still wouldn't have known. But after tonight, the way she practically purred when I grabbed her throat, the sweet way she curled her legs underneath her when she told me all about her childhood, the way she snuck glances down my body and grabbed my dick the first chance she got. Yeah, I have no doubt. Olivia Daniels is fucking mine.

"My endgame is becoming the biggest producer in the Pacific Northwest. I want our products everywhere. I want to be so big, so legit, so loved that my father doesn't stand a fucking chance at taking us down. The rest is none of your goddamn business."

He smirks, looking up toward the staircase. "Sure thing, boss."

Luca meanders back over to the window, hauling himself up as I roll my shoulders a few more times. I could do a little workout now to stretch off my limbs.

"Oh, Austin." Luca's head pokes back through the impossibly small window. "You might want to know that she didn't lock the door."

He grins manically before disappearing into the night.

I don't think; I just move. Creeping up the wooden stairs, hugging the walls so I avoid any loose floorboards.

I reach for the handle, and my mouth waters in anticipation. Although it's not locked, she might have an alarm triggered. Or she may have security cameras set up around the house. Given that she is committing the bigger crime here, I'd assume she wouldn't want the evidence. I risk it and twist the handle, the door creaking open.

My heart thunders in my chest at such a rate that I'm surprised I haven't woken her yet.

I'd done this a hundred times, snuck into houses in the middle of the night. But my aim was to get caught those times; I wanted my victims to know I was there. But Olivia isn't one of my victims, and I'm not ready for her to catch me just yet.

I move around the house, noting where to find the basement door in case I need to quickly make my way back. The house isn't new by any standards; it looks to have original floorboards and wallpaper that is starting to peel at the corners, although, in the dark, it is hard to tell.

The left of the basement door leads toward the kitchen and backdoor. To the right, the hallway weaves into the living room. I move stealthily, the moonlight guiding my way and helping me envisage Olivia's day-to-day.

Her yoga mat and a ring light are tucked in the corner against a plain white wall that I recognize from her videos. The couch against the other wall is worn in. It looks soft and homely. It's clear to see Olivia hasn't decorated this room. Presumably, she hasn't changed much around the house since her parents died.

I look at the coffee table and see a notebook and a laptop. Firing it up, there's no password so I start to snoop. I log into her email, reading through bills and a spreadsheet of a monthly budget for the home.

She has lists upon lists that I can go through, but it's the notepad that draws my attention. I pick it up, the pages hiss between my thumb and finger as I flick through, picking a page at random to read. I quickly realize it's a journal.

Danny got home at four a.m. last night, covered in mud again. I don't know what to do. I keep trying to ask mom and dad for a sign that I'm doing a good job with him but the silence is overwhelming. I used to still feel their presence but it's fading now. I don't know what I can do to bring him back home where I can keep an eye on him. I feel like I'm reaching a crossroads where I either do something drastic, or I let him go. And I'm not ready to give up on him.

Fuck me.

I flick to the most recent entry, my pulse quickening.

I wonder sometimes if all the goodness in me left when mom and dad died. Would they be proud of me? I don't feel very proud of myself right now, but I can't go back, I have to push forward.

What's done is done. And the man in my basement is dangerous, unpredictable and a master manipulator. I feel him softening my resolve. And the worst part is that I'm willfully allowing it. I need to hold myself accountable for what I've done here, and I do. I just wish there were someone here to take care of me. To help me out of the situation I've put myself in. I wish I had someone who could understand this pain I feel.

I throw the journal down like it's burned me. Despite all the work I've done with Alfie, I'm still so selfish. I can't see further than my own experience. Kidnapping is so disgustingly normal for someone like me, I've failed to see how emotionally traumatic this is for someone like Olivia. She was desperate when she abducted me. Desperate enough to face prison for her brother, and I've treated her like nothing but a joke. When really, I could be doing something to bring some fun into her life. Make it easier so she's not so burdened.

I turn to the stairs. There is no light on to mark my way, but my feet guide me there, anyway. With each step, I'm shown a new glimpse into Olivia's childhood as photos adorn the walls. Smiling faces, happy memories. There is even one of Danny's graduation, which could only have been a year ago. A tug in my chest aches for something I've never had, but I'm pleased that she could add to the wall of happiness despite everything she's been through.

The upstairs is smaller than the downstairs; only four doors come off the hallway. The open door leads to a bathroom with a small tub and a built-in shower. My dick twitches at the thought of Olivia soaped up and naked, beckoning me with a come-hither look of want and desire. I'd trip over my own pants getting to her, I have no doubt.

Two doors are shut, one of which has a "Keep Out" sign taped to the front. I presume that's Danny's childhood bedroom. The one to the right, and by my calculation, looking to the front of the house, would be the master bedroom. Something tells me Olivia wouldn't have taken her parents' bedroom, so I ignore that and head to the end of the corridor to a door that is almost closed. The crack of moonlight slips through as the curtains aren't fully closed.

Slipping into the room, I beg my racing heart to calm the fuck and down and let me enjoy this. If I'm going to do better tomorrow, I'm going to remain selfish tonight.

Holding my breath, I step toward the bed. She sleeps on her back, one leg straight and the other bent to the side. Her arms are sprawled up above her head, the thick blankets covering one breast and not much else. The warmth of the evening has stretched into the night but no doubt, the cold night air would seep in eventually.

It would be reckless of me to step forward to lay the blanket over her. But I've been careful for the last few years. I've controlled every urge I've had. And now, Olivia is almost daring me to do something out of character, just like her.

I crouch beside her and push a lock of hair out of her face. Her face twitches, and she brings a hand down to flap in front of her as she scrunches her face up. I freeze, suddenly terrified that I might frighten her, but she quickly relaxes, her mouth opening as she lets out a snore loud enough to wake the dead.

I slap a hand to my mouth and pinch my nose for good measure, holding in a laugh that would be sure to rival the noise she is making.

I pull the blanket up and over her, once I'm sure she is settled.

I could kiss her forehead; I'm close enough. But there would be enough time for that. I have to be patient.

Fuck, I'm good.

Dr. Alfie would be so proud.

◆ ◆ ◆

"What the hell were you thinking?" I have to hold the phone away from my ear. Dr. Alfie is screaming so loudly. He's fucking reprimanded me before, but goddamn, the man has a set of lungs on him.

"I tucked her in. What's wrong with that?"

I mean, yes, okay. I know what's wrong with it. But honestly, the whole situation is fucked-up. I'm not sure tucking her in and watching her sleep for twenty minutes really calls for this kind of response from one's therapist. The therapist they are paying.

"You know damn well what's wrong with it. Austin, you've worked really hard to get where you're at. Now, you're using your previous skill set to invade someone's privacy. Someone you have been arguably stalking for two years."

"Arguably, yes, but it wouldn't be prosecutable. I looked it up."

"Austin . . ."

I can practically see him pinching his nose in that resigned way that lets me know I've disappointed him. Even from a fucking basement, Dr. Alfie can make me feel a new level of low.

"I know, I know. It won't happen again." "I promise" is on the tip of my tongue, but I can't bring myself to say it. I know I want to go up tonight, but it depends if she forgets to lock the door again.

"Good. Now, did you think about what we discussed yesterday?"

That's what I like about Alfie. He takes you at your word, despite mine being worth about as much as a used tea bag. If you say you'll work on something, he believes you. Right up until you fuck up, and then he goes over what went wrong. A little gnaw of guilt starts to build as I fully intend to go back on my word, but I squash it down. Despite his exasperation, he doesn't hold grudges. He moves the fuck on. It is actually really fucking healthy.

"Did you think about what you want to get out of your time in the basement?"

"Yes, I want her to see me as someone she could be

with."

"Okay. And how do you plan to do that?"

"Flirt like crazy, make her see how perfect our chemistry is, how much fun we can have together. She works so hard all the time. She could use some fun in her life. I was thinking I would build the tension a little. She's already shown me she's attracted to me and she knows I'm attracted to her. We just need a little more anticipation and the promise of some fun so she can loosen up a bit. But just as I'm about to make a move, take a step back and tell her I wouldn't want her to feel like she was taking advantage of me. I think the self-sacrifice will show her that I'm serious and that I want her, which will in turn make her want me even more. She'll see me as someone who wants something long term."

"So, to be clear, you want to manipulate her into sleeping with you?"

"What? No . . . I just need to build the tension."

"Why?"

"Why what?"

"Why do you need to build the tension? You're both already in a heightened state. Why do you feel the need to add to it?"

"I . . . I don't know."

"Think about it. But until then, I have a suggestion."

My chest feels tight. Have I been playing this all wrong? After I read her journal last night, I thought she would want someone to bring some fun into her life. But Alfie is right. I have been trying to manipulate her feelings, even if it's not for the reasons she thinks—letting me go. I've been doing it to get closer to her, to stay closer to her. But is that so wrong?

"What's the suggestion?"

"When we first started our sessions, you told me that you want to be a person that is easy to love."

"I remember," I reply cautiously.

"If Olivia was to be loved by anyone else and be happy with them, is this the way you would want them to behave with her?"

She shouldn't be played or manipulated. Despite my intentions and my long-term plans to be with her, she doesn't know that.

"Fuck. No, of course not."

"Good. Otherwise, we'd be having a different conversation."

"Okay so what do you suggest? I can't help but flirt with her."

"Keep flirting, but she needs to see the real you. The one that you've grown to be in the last two years. But you have to look at this from her point of view. At the moment, she just knows the enforcer. She thinks you're dangerous and dangerous is not long-term. You want her to see you as a long-term prospect, is that correct?"

"Fuck yes."

"Okay. So let's work on that."

"What do I need to do?"

"I think this is going to be hard for you, but you should be yourself. You're funny, you're charismatic, lean into that. She'll be able to let her guard down with someone who's approachable and she enjoys spending time with."

"Okay, I can do that. But you know that what you're suggesting is insane, right?"

"It's unorthodox, I'll admit," he says in his unrelenting professional tone.

I'll take doc's advice, but I'll be adding my own flair for sure.

"And Austin, remember that you've worked incredibly hard to become the man you are today. You deserve good things to happen to you, too."

"Thanks, doc. I gotta go. I'll call you in a few days."

"Bye, Austin."

We hang up, and a renewed sense of purpose fills every corner of my chest. All I have to do is wait for her to come down those stairs.

CHAPTER EIGHT

Olivia

Another video was posted last night. This time with clips of my own videos compared to Millie's. It doesn't seem to matter to her or the ninety-five percent of commenters that my videos were posted before hers. All that matters is she's creating enticing videos that cause drama.

The video was removed by the site after I flagged it. I'm not sure how it worked so quickly, but both videos that called me out have now been removed, thank goodness.

Now, I just need to focus on my work. I have a fitness expo coming up to prepare for and videos to create.

After braiding my hair, I slip into a bright pink crop top and shorts, ready to take on the day. As I descend the stairs, my heart flutters at the thought of seeing Austin. We talked for hours last night. I feel like we're really connecting.

Despite my brain screaming at me to cool off, my heart is thumping wildly for this man.

He is kind, funny, and attentive. And I think I might have been wrong about him. In fact, I know I have. Despite everything that has happened, I think this could turn out okay. But I'm not going to let one evening fool me.

I reach the basement door, my feet halting immediately. It's closed, but the locks aren't in place.

I quickly check over my shoulder and peek my head into the hallway. I have a clear view of the living room and the kitchen from my position. I listen for a moment, but I can't hear anyone else in the house.

I twist the handle and pull the door toward me.

Silence.

I take a step down, and I hear chains clinking together.

"Olivia?" Austin calls out.

Act normal. He cannot know you were so googly-eyed last night that you forgot to lock him in. Despite him being chained up. It's not a good look, and no doubt, it would be against one of his rules.

"Hey," I call out cheerfully, "good morning."

Stepping down the stairs barefoot, I get to the final step, leave my hand on the banister, and take him in.

Mussed hair, his stubble filling out along his jawline. His eyes are a little puffy from sleep, but he's stretching over the mattress in a way that makes my mouth water. His abs are on display, begging me to run my fingers over them.

I reach for my throat, remembering the way his hand squeezed me last night. I've read about it, of course. Romance novels often discuss *hand necklaces*, but I've never felt comfortable enough to ask for it with people I've slept with. Hell, I didn't even know I liked it until last night. Austin seemed to know what I needed. He'd been so tender despite being in control, and as soon as I gave him the green light, he'd squeezed the tiniest gasp out of me. What would it feel like to have him do that as he pulses inside me? Whispering filth into my ear as he toys with me.

"You feeling okay, Killer?"

I give myself a little shake. "Oh yeah, all good. Did you sleep okay?"

"Yep." He frowns, and it seems like a stupid question now, given how uncomfortable he must be.

He's looking at me like I'm missing something. Why am I down here again? Damn, I forgot to make breakfast first. As if my body needed to see him more than it needed food. I need to rein this in.

"Oh, I haven't made breakfast yet. Sorry, I'm a little out of sorts today. Umm. Any requests?"

He grins. "How about the first breakfast you made me? The one with the spice in it. I can't remember the name."

"The turmeric?"

"Yes! That's the one. That was the best thing I've had in years."

I smile, and it occurs to me that I'm fully allowing him to get to me. I'm not even trying to stop him anymore.

"Sure, I'll make it now."

"Thank you." His eyes remain fixed on mine as he rewards me with a genuine smile. My insides are gooey, and I have a sudden desperation to please him. This can't be good right? I need to regain some semblance of control.

◆ ◆ ◆

"What are your plans for the day?" he asks, tapping his bare stomach in appreciation, and I grin again. His breakfast lasted all of two minutes once I handed it to him.

"I have a few fires to put out, nothing major. Just normal work stuff," I say, popping the last crumb into my mouth.

"The same fire as the other day?"

Yes. The ones that are trying to ruin my life and my business.

"Umm, possibly."

He nods.

"I'm sure you have a different way of dealing with things at work." I laugh awkwardly.

His smile drops before his head shakes a little. Guilt drips into my stomach, but he quickly recovers as if remembering something.

"Nah, it's all lawyers and admin for me nowadays."

Lawyers and admin?

"Right . . . lawyers and admin," I say, making air quotes

with my fingers.

He sighs and shakes his head again. The mood is so different from last night. I thought coming down here this morning would feel the same: exciting, vulnerable, and like I was on the brink of something. But now I'm just confused.

"Wanna play a game?" he asks.

"Wow, that sounded just like the horror movie quote."

His lips twitch before he lowers his voice a few more octaves, repeating himself, "Wanna play a game, Olivia?" His voice is scratchy, and honestly, it's kind of doing it for me. Like, yeah, I'll play a few games.

"How about twenty questions?"

"That seems very tame," I tease.

"Okay, let's make the questions good. And if you refuse, you have to do a dare."

"What kind of dare can you do in a basement?"

"I can certainly think of a few things," he says, his voice dangerously low, "but feel free to use your imagination, Killer."

I swallow hard. "Twenty is too many."

He shrugs, waiting me out. I suppose it's not like he has much to do around here.

"Let's make it five."

"Fine, but I have one condition."

"Okay?" I say hesitantly.

"No work-related questions."

I open my mouth to protest, and he raises an eyebrow in defiance.

"Fine," I concede, concerned at how quickly I give in to him.

"I'll go first, as I'm the guest."

I laugh, but he ignores me.

"What's your favorite color?"

"What's my favorite color? You're going to waste one of your questions on that?"

His eyes light up, and I get a flash of his teeth. "It's not a waste. I've been dying to know."

I think for a moment. “Yellow. But not the bright, garish yellow. More like a soft lemon.”

“Soft lemon. Got it.”

“Same question for you.”

He rolls his eyes but smiles again. “It depends on my mood.”

“Okay, and what is your mood today?”

His eyes dip down to my bright pink crop top and shorts, and my heart starts thumping wildly. I know what he’s going to say before it even leaves his lips.

“Pink.”

I turn away, trying to cover my manic smile with my hand. I think my skin has turned beetroot.

“There it is.” He sighs like a whimpering puppy.

“Could you stop?” I laugh, launching my chair pillow at him.

He catches it with ease and shifts it behind his back so he can get comfy.

He raises his hands in surrender, although I’m sure it’s another ruse to lead me into a false sense of security.

“Tell me your most embarrassing moment,” I say.

“Hmm . . . not really a question, but I’ll allow it.”

I fight the urge to roll my eyes. I don’t want to give him any reason to change his mind.

“The day I came into Squeeze the Day for the first time . . . the first day I met you, I was running away from a business associate of my father’s.”

“Okay . . .”

“I’d had a meeting with him the week before; his wife had attended, and she’d been running her foot up and down my leg all evening. No matter how many times I shifted, she found my leg and kept winking at me over her wine glass. I thought she was a thrill seeker, desperate to do something, or someone, right under her husband's nose. That was until I felt his foot on my other leg. It turns out they were both interested. I kindly declined their offer and then when I saw him in the street a few months later, I was too embarrassed to speak to him. He'd shouted my name a few times, and I ran into the juice bar and tucked myself behind that man who was as big as an SUV. I'd ordered a coffee, which, by the way, was disgusting. And then I saw you. I just had to pray that the guy wouldn't follow me in and try to talk about the proposal in your vicinity."

"You're not into sharing a woman?"

He laughs. "That's what you took from that?"

I shrug. "It's not that uncommon."

His chin dips, and his nostrils flare for a split second. Is that possessiveness I see?

"What they get up to in their own time is on them. I wasn't interested because I wasn't attracted to either of them. My turn."

I grip the bottom of the chair, leaning forward, braced and ready to spill my most embarrassing story, too.

"Have you ever been shared?"

Oh, shit. Not what I thought he was going to ask.

It's nine in the morning, dammit. This is a nighttime conversation surely? When a blanket of darkness can hide the flush of my skin that the morning light just can't.

"I . . ." I feel the heat spread, and his eyes calculate the probability of whether it's my inexperience that's causing me to blush or the memory of being shared by two men. "No, I've never been shared."

I swallow hard, watching his reaction.

He breathes slowly through his nose, nodding, his shoulders relaxing. "Good. Not many people want to make it pleasurable for everyone involved. It's good you haven't done that."

Good? Is he one of those people? Why did I limit us to five questions?

"Haven't done that *yet*, you mean," I say, eager to provoke him.

"Yet?" he parrots, his mouth gaping slightly.

"I can't speak for the future." I shrug.

Oh god, what am I doing? Shut up, Olivia.

Austin rolls his shoulders back and pulls his head down toward his shoulder to the left and then to the right, stretching out the neck muscles he's been clenching. His eyes are closed, and he takes a deep breath.

"What was the name of your stuffed toy when you were a kid?" he swerves to the point of whiplash.

I can't keep up.

"I . . . I have a crocodile," I say, and he seems to nod knowingly as if he's met the stuffed toy already. "He's called Chops."

"Chops. Great name." He grins, all tension seemingly dissipated.

"What was the name of your stuffed toy?"

"Are you just going to ask the same questions as me?"

"Depends. Yours have been quite insightful so far."

"I had a polar bear. But I couldn't say polar, so I called him Pillow Bear."

Imaging a small dark-haired boy with his thumb in his mouth and his polar bear tucked under his arm, my mouth tilts up. I can imagine another little one running around our feet, joyfully clutching his own stuffed polar bear. Austin picks him up and swings him around as he reaches for me.

Good god. Lock this down, you maniac.

"Are you missing Pillow Bear? I'm sure I can find something to keep you company at night."

He raises an eyebrow, and I inhale. That one was a hundred percent not on purpose.

"I didn't mean it like that."

He holds his hands up in surrender. "Hey, you said it, not me. I have certainly been missing something to hold at night."

Oh god, does he have a girlfriend? How had I not even considered this? Of course he does. He's gorgeous, filthy rich, and dangerous. He's irresistible.

"Do you have a girlfriend?"

"Is that one of your questions, Killer?"

I hesitate, but decide to commit. "Yes."

"No, I don't have a girlfriend, or fiancée, or wife. No significant other."

"Good." I nod, mostly for myself. I knew I hadn't made this up . . . whatever *this* is between us.

"Yet," he adds with a wink.

"By my calculation, we have one question left each. Let's save this for later. I want to think about mine for a while, and I really need to get some work done."

I pull my phone out of my pocket and see another new video I've been tagged in. I can feel my brows knit together. What am I going to do about this? The posts are coming in thick and fast. Not only is it Millie and Travis, but comments are spreading across multiple platforms, while I'm wasting my time flirting with a man I'm trying to convince to release my brother. I haven't even mentioned Danny during the last twenty-four hours. What am I really doing here?

"Hey, is everything okay?" Austin's soft voice brings me back to the basement.

I shake myself off. "Yeah, just work stuff. I have to go do some things. I'll be back later, okay?"

"Sure, I'm here if you need to talk, Olivia. I might be able to help."

I nod, grab his empty plate along with mine, and head back upstairs.

By the following afternoon, I've worked myself into such a state that I find it hard enough just to drop food downstairs. I barely say more than a few words to Austin. His worried look guts me every time I drop something down to him. I've included a few more books as well to keep him occupied, but otherwise, leave him alone.

By mid-afternoon on Tuesday, my despair has all but taken over. The comments are relentless and the private messages are coming in thick and fast until the inboxes across all my platforms are unmanageable.

My phone is blowing up, and eventually, I can't take any more. I pick up my phone, flip it over, and head to my channel.

I've been tagged again in another video. I suck in a deep breath and brace myself for another onslaught of insults and accusations.

I hit the play button and watch.

Austin

I'm sitting up on the bed, reading another romance novel, when Olivia skips down the steps. Like a puppy bounding along, she hums a tune low in her throat.

"Hi," she says, smiling shyly.

"Hi." I grin. "You look happier this evening." And thank fuck for that. I would have picked the lock and consoled her myself if she had stayed so despondent.

"Oh, yeah. Some good news, kind of."

And she's come bounding down to tell me.

"Kind of?"

"Well, I'm not sure it can count as good news if it means something bad happened to somebody else."

"Depends if they deserved it or not." I shrug.

She thinks for a moment. "I mean, yeah, they did deserve it, but I still don't want someone to be hurt."

I had a small doubt in my mind, but now it's been eradicated. She really is just a good person through and through.

"Care to share your news?"

She bites her lip. "You might think I'm a terrible person."

"Doubtful, Killer."

"The video of Millie Gilbert and Travis, you know, my ex."

"Ah yes, the disappointment in bed."

Her eyes pop out a little, and she tries to hide her grin.

"Yes, that's the one . . . well, they'd been posting videos about me that aren't true. You know the ones I told you about?"

"Yes, I remember."

"Well, they released another video. Apologizing directly to me and their *fans*." She says the words fans while making air quotes with her fingers. "They wanted to reflect on recent events that they felt were cosmic karma for what they had done to me."

"Is that so?"

"Yeah. Do you want to see the video?"

"Rules one and four, Killer."

"What's rule four?"

"Don't hand your hostage a phone."

She laughs. "I'll hold far enough away. Are you gonna give me a grade at the end of all this?"

"If you like roleplay, sure. I'll play your teacher, Olivia."

She flushes beautifully, and I smirk, rubbing my stubble with my hand. I like the rough feel against my palm. I've missed seeing her like this. So relaxed and happy. We've been getting on so well. I thought I might have pushed too far with the flirting, sending her into a tailspin. When really it's external factors that have caused her discontentment. A hum of energy buzzes through my chest. I'm on the right course; I know I am. She's going to see me as more than a monster.

"Show me this video."

She pulls out the phone, the app ready. She holds the phone in front of me, but her loose grip suggests she's not worried about me taking it. She's so close I can smell her shampoo. A hint of cotton, fresh linen, and citrus fills my nostrils, and I inhale deeply. Our thighs graze as she watches over my shoulder, chewing her thumbnail.

A short, slim girl with long blonde hair fills the screen. She's in a black legging and crop top set, similar to what Olivia wears. This girl is polished, her hair styled, and her makeup perfect. However, I still notice her bloodshot eyes and puffy face. The man next to her looks to be in his mid to late twenties. With sandy blond hair pulled back with a hair band—it isn't long, but it falls past his ears. His vest top is loose and baggy, his chest on show. They hold hands as they look somberly at the camera.

"We've had a little time to think over the last twenty-four hours, and we need to be honest with our followers. Our previous video, which called out 'Train with Olivia's,' Olivia Daniels, was inaccurate . . ."

A small cough can be heard in the background as Millie's eyes flit to someone behind the scenes.

"Actually, no, it wasn't just inaccurate. It was an outright lie. I used to look up to Olivia, and I wanted to achieve everything she had. But in trying to build my own brand, I chose to tarnish hers instead of focusing on myself. When I met Travis, who used to date Olivia, it felt like I would always be in her shadow. So to Olivia, I'm sorry. You're an inspiration to us all. If you haven't seen her videos, her work is amazing, and she'll get you fit in no time at all. Go and subscribe. I'll be taking a hiatus while I reevaluate how I conduct myself with my channel."

She gives a small hiccup before looking at Travis. While Millie could almost be considered sincere, her crocodile tears are for no one but herself. Her great epiphany is the result of Luca and the boys stopping by and making it very clear how this will go if they don't remove the videos. Essentially, her livelihood will be destroyed. All for the sake of making a shitpost for this treasure sitting to my right.

"I, too, would like to apologize to Olivia," Travis grits out, less convincingly than Millie. "I was hurt when you broke up with me. I wanted to punish you for your success when my channel was so lacking. Millie and I brought out the worst qualities in each other: jealousy, pettiness, and cruelty." He clicks his tongue and pushes it into his cheek before continuing.

"I, too, will be deleting my channel to focus on how to conduct myself in the future. I just hope that I can learn how to be a man who accepts his wrongdoings and tries to be a man worthy of someone like Olivia."

A small sob slips out of Millie, and the uncut video is posted for all to see.

It has over fifty thousand views already and hundreds of comments. Ironically, this video might actually make them go viral. Shame Luca insisted they delete all their other videos and backup files. If they did want to start another channel, it would be from scratch.

Most of the comments support Olivia, but I'll be ensuring Luca discovers the identities of those who are particularly bad.

"So, what do you think?" she asks me, pulling the phone away and slipping it into her pocket.

She hasn't moved away from me. Instead, she pulls her feet up onto the bed and crosses her legs.

I lean back, scratching my jaw.

Play it cool, man. Let her relax. Let her find this position and proximity the most normal fucking thing. Let her feel natural.

Shrugging, I say, "Maybe they found Jesus overnight?"

She laughs. "Travis isn't the type, and something tells me Millie isn't either. Although I've only met her once at a fitness event. And look at this: all their other videos have been taken down . . . It's odd. I could never imagine either of them doing something so drastic."

"So what do you think happened?"

"Well. I think Danny may have had something to do with it. Maybe he contacted them online or something like that?"

"Maybe."

And why the fuck didn't Danny do something about it? This is his sister, dammit. If I hadn't intervened, this would still be a big fucking problem for her.

"If I wasn't thinking clearly, I would think it was something in your ballpark."

"Interesting thought, Killer. Shame it couldn't be me,

isn't it?" I lift the chains and wiggle them playfully before dropping them back down and leaning back. I'm begging my heart to calm down. She's so goddamn smart; she can fucking read me like a book.

"So, am I a terrible person for being happy?"

She leans on her left hand, her pinky finger no more than an inch from mine. She cares about my opinion. The video's only just been posted, and her first instinct was to tell me. This is more than her trying to get her own way when it comes to Danny. My gut instinct tells me she's feeling this as much as I am.

I mirror her position, leaning back on my hand.

"You're a good person, Killer. You take care of your brother, you take care of your business, you're even taking care of me. Despite what I am to you."

"And what's that?"

I hesitate for a moment. I don't want to remind her of what I am to her. But the selfless part of me wants her to know he's still in there. I want her to protect herself. Even if it's from me.

"A bad man, a captive . . . a threat."

Something shifts, the air becomes thick, and my breath catches in my chest.

In low, hushed tones, she replies, "You're more than just those things, Austin."

"Yeah?" I swallow, my gaze dipping down to catch her tongue running along her bottom lip. "What else am I to you, Olivia?"

We're practically whispering to each other now. Sharing secrets at the back corner of a classroom, desperately trying to ensure no one else hears. The image of her squeezing my hand around her throat two nights ago floods my vision. Her lips part, letting out a low whimper. She has a dark streak in her that even she hasn't explored yet. When would she have had the chance? I could be the one to unravel her. Teach her things she's never dreamed of doing.

I lift my hand slowly so as not to startle her. She's led this shift in our dynamic, but she could just as easily flip back. Her eyes track my hand until I cup her cheek, using the pad of my thumb to brush her lower lip.

"Answer me."

"Wh . . . what was the question?" Her heavy whisper circles us both, until we're wrapped in a gauzy cloud, everything else blurred and fuzzy.

"What else am I to you?" I lean in again. Her chest moves more rapidly, her perfect breasts squeezing out of the pink crop top she's chosen for the day. How desperate I am to rip it clean off. For two long years, I've been waiting for her to give me unfiltered access to her perfect, soft breasts with puckered nipples. I salivate at the thought.

"I . . . I don't know."

I drop my hand so my fingers trail along her throat. I want it to haunt her thoughts the way it has mine. How good it felt to have my hand wrapped around her neck. How close she was to me. The risk she put herself in must have been exhilarating, I have no doubt. But if it was with another man, I'd have to punish her. I'd never hurt her, but she doesn't know that. Olivia is taking more and more risks. It's up to me to manage that. Let her explore her thrill-seeking in a safe way.

Trailing my fingers down, stroking along her collarbone, but heading down to the valley between her breasts. I trace the perfect handful along the bulge from the constricted sports bra, feeling her skin tingle beneath mine. Everywhere I touch lights up, aching for more. My own body is fully invested. My skin hums, my mouth waters. I lean and press the gentlest of kisses to the corner of her jaw, right below her ear. It's all I would allow myself, for now. The tiniest gasp escapes Olivia's mouth. And another thread of my carefully tied restraint snaps.

Fuck it.

I squeeze her breast, rubbing my thumb where I can feel her hardened nipple beneath the fabric. Fuck, I'd give my left arm to be able to run my teeth over it now. Kissing down her neck, I feel her swallow. A small moan escapes her parted lips, and I can't help but smile against her neck. Her body sings for me, and I can play it like I was born to do it. Maybe after all these years of watching her, I've memorized all her micro-pleasures. The way she trails her fingers over her neck when she reads, tracing her collarbone. She likes it rough, biting her own lip hard, so only to imagine it done by someone else.

With all the willpower in the world, I press one final kiss to her neck, drawing my fingertips back up to her cheek.

"When you figure out what you want me to be, I'll be waiting, Olivia. I can be patient."

Lies. I'm not fucking patient. Every limb is protesting. My chest aches, my lungs are scorched like I've been trying to keep up with Usain fucking Bolt. My dick throbs against my leg, pressing against my sweatpants like it's trying to take them off.

Despite my body's silent screams, I draw away, leaving the ball in her court.

CHAPTER NINE

Olivia

What. The. Actual. Fuck.

CHAPTER TEN

Olivia

"Listen, if you focused a little more on listening to your body, you'd understand that it's not all about lifting. You've got to be more in tune with yourself. Yoga or pilates is a great way to do that. It's the focused breathing."

I watch his eyes roll under his eyelids, and despite my attempt to stifle a laugh, a small giggle escapes me when he mutters, "Focused fucking breathing," under his breath.

After last night, I've decided a little bit of exercise would be a good idea to defuse some of the growing tension between us. I anticipated this situation would be difficult, but I hadn't predicted how my body would respond to his presence. I can tell he is starting to feel cooped up and uncomfortable, regardless of what he says about the eight-hour sleep and good food.

We haven't spoken about last night, but it has been playing on a loop in my brain since then. I can't believe that in a few short days, I've gone from grabbing his dick to encouraging him to squeeze my throat and letting him trail kisses down my neck. I allow my eyes to close as I remember the way he felt in my palm, hard and ready. Knowing I have such an effect on him makes my lower belly throb—another pair of panties soaked. I just know he could make my body submit to him if he chooses to. But after last night and the neck kisses, which were honestly heavenly, he said the ball was in my court. So far, he's stayed true to his word. Despite lingering looks, deep sighs, and the occasional arm flex, which I'm sure he is doing on purpose, everything has been very PG-13 this morning.

"Close your eyes," I encourage.

"This would help if I didn't have chains under my back."

"Oh . . . sorry, I forgot about that. There's not really much I can do apart from what I've already done."

He now has just one long chain around his waist which pretty much gives him more range. He still can't reach anything to use as a weapon, though. He can't reach the window or the stairs. But there is more give, and it means we can do these classes together.

"It's fine, Killer. Show me your moves."

We finish up our class, and I give him space to wash himself and change into fresh clothes.

After lunch we sit in amiable silence, both of us reading our respective novels.

I know in my heart that he isn't the man I thought he was at Squeeze the Day. And even though he won't release Danny from his contract or whatever it is that keeps him there, I can't keep him here forever.

I worry about what might happen if I let him go, but ultimately, I don't think he will hurt me. Maybe that's dumb and naive, but I think . . . I think he actually likes me. No one could fake this well. He's calm, assuring, caring . . . flirtatious, but not too much. It's clear there's a dark side to him, but he hasn't given me reason to fear it.

"Austin . . . "

"Mhm?" he replies, engrossed in his book.

I swallow hard. "We should talk about what we're doing here."

"Well, Helena is about to get ravaged by a wolf that's been stalking her . . . I can only imagine he's going to shift back into human form and turn into Lance, the guy she's been crushing on. There will be some form of trivial argument about deception, invasion of privacy, blah blah blah, and then we'll get to the good stuff."

Not quite where I thought this was going to go. But he'd been rushing through our yoga today so he could get back to reading.

"That being . . ."

"Oh, I forgot you've never had good sex, Killer." He winks. "But pay attention to these books. I've even learned a thing or two."

"Like how to shift into a wolf?"

"The big, bad wolf, baby." He winks again, and my heart somersaults.

Yep, he's definitely flirting. And his admission of learning something from the books he's been reading is surprising. I've never met a man who admits to having something to learn, especially not from what they find to be a *silly* romance novel. That's what Travis used to call them. Unrealistic standards for men, set by women. But I can't understand how someone being devoted to their partner and making their body sing from orgasms is unrealistic—or unreasonable. The wolf shifter bit, I can understand.

I bite my lip, my heart thudding like the *Jaws* theme tune, steady at first and then altogether speeding into ominous territory where I'm likely to get eaten. It's a wonder he can't hear it.

Maybe he can because he suddenly looks up.

"What's going on, Olivia?" he asks, turning his book over onto the mattress and giving me his full attention.

God, I love it when he uses my name. It's always soft and understanding; it tells me he's ready to listen. He calls me Killer when he's flirting or playful, which makes my lower belly surge with heat. But *Olivia* is something special. He enunciates all four syllables like he's tasting them.

"I . . . I think we need to discuss the future. You can't stay here indefinitely and . . ."

"What day is it? I've lost track," he interrupts.

"Umm . . . it's Wednesday now."

"I've been here since Friday. Five days total." He lifts his head and counts using his fingers. It's oddly endearing.

"Yes."

"I'm free for two more days."

What the fuck is he talking about?

"Austin. I don't think you understand. I'm talking about letting you go . . . now." I let a big breath out. I'm actually going to let him go. I think I'm going to miss him. Christ, what is wrong with me? I thought Stockholm syndrome was the other way around.

"And I have until Friday. So think about it. I'm in no rush."

He's gone mad. I might need to drop him off at the hospital.

"Austin . . . I think maybe you've got this thing. I read up on it. It's called Stockholm syndrome. You kind of end up liking your captor. It's actually super unhealthy, and you should really go and talk to someone about that when you get out."

His face transforms, his smile stretching like it's being pulled by his ears. His grin turns to laughter; his laughter turns to silent gasps of him clutching his stomach.

This is it. He's a goner.

I can't be responsible for him.

I can deal with my brother's psycho boss. I can't deal with a genuinely unwell person. Especially when I've chained him up in my basement for nearly a week, and now he's lost it.

He rights himself, swiping at a glisten of tears in the corner of his eyes.

Oh god, I've made him lose his mind. Is this worse than killing someone? Will a jury give me the death penalty? No . . . I think they got rid of it in Washington a few years ago. Okay, I have to google that later. Can the police see what you search for in incognito mode?

"I should go and leave you to calm down."

The *Jaws* theme tune is gone, replaced with some high-pitched violins screeching like I'm running away from the murderer in a slasher movie. My breathing is getting erratic. What the hell am I doing? I've abducted someone, held them hostage, acted like they're not really a hostage, and then offered to let them go. I've gone so back and forth I'm like one of those awful shake rides at the fair. No wonder he's losing it. He doesn't know what's up or down anymore.

I head to the stairs, running two at a time. I need a contingency plan. I have to think.

"Olivia, wait . . . Let me explain," he calls out, panic replacing his humor in 2.2 seconds. More evidence that he really has lost all sense of reality.

Ignoring him, I run out the door and swing it shut. The gravity of what I've done is finally hitting me square in the chest. There is no one I can turn to. Not a friend who would back me up, no parents, and I certainly can't go to Danny. Austin will think he was involved. No. Best to keep him out of this.

Nausea runs through me, and before I can think, I run to the bathroom quickly and vomit up my breakfast. My hands shake, my skin has a cool sweat clinging to it, and I feel awful. I know what I need to do. I have to face the consequences and just hope and pray for a miracle that the man in my basement really isn't the awful bastard I thought he was.

Because if he is, I'm as good as dead.

I give myself twenty minutes to panic. Then I eat some crackers and down some water. After brushing my teeth and washing my face, I feel a little better. All I need to do is go down there, unchain him, and then hope that I don't get murdered. Should I drive him into town? Call a cab? I suppose if I do get murdered, I won't have to worry about the logistics of him getting back home.

I stare at my face in the small bathroom mirror. I look surprisingly fresh. My skin is plump, and my hair is smooth and silky. Having him here has done wonders for me. Selfishly,

I wonder what it would be like to keep him around. I know . . . I know I can't. Obviously.

But he's not the horrible beast I thought he was; at least, I'm ninety-nine percent sure. He could be someone I could actually fall for. If he weren't holding my brother hostage, that is.

I tie my hair back and run my hands down my black-on-black leggings and crop top. It's practically a uniform, but far from the usual bright colors I wear. Today is all business. Or a funeral. We'll see.

I step out of the bathroom and somberly walk down the stairs. Rounding the corner, I reach for the basement door, but see it's open. The door is a hair-width ajar, and I can hear a voice that doesn't belong to Austin.

I hold my breath, desperately trying not to make a sound as I strain to hear the hushed voices.

"I told you, I'm handling it. I'll be back by Friday." That's Austin.

"Boss, I can handle this right now. What are you doing? Playing with your food?"

In a low growl I hear Austin spit back, "Say that again, Luca."

Luca. Danny had mentioned him. He's someone from work. But how the fuck did he get in my house? I quickly turn my back against the door so I can still hear, but dart my eyes around the rest of my house so I can check for any other "employees" that may be lurking.

"Boss . . . I'm sorry. We've known each other for a long time. You're like my brother."

"Then why are you questioning me now?" Austin hisses, using a tone I don't recognize. This is the man I've been afraid to meet.

"Because you've got to admit, this is out of character for you."

"Well, I'm shaking things up. Things need to change, Luca."

What things?

"You've stalked this girl for two years."

Stalked me?

"I didn't stalk her."

What the hell?

I draw my hand to my chest, like one of those cartoons that's trying to push their heart back in their chest when it's pulsating out. Except this isn't love I'm feeling. I feel . . . scared? No. That's not it. I can't put my finger on it, only that my body is taking charge; my brain needs a second to catch up.

"Fine, you turned up where you knew she would be for two years. Never said a word. Never made a move. And now what? Now you're playing house."

"We're hardly playing house, Luca." I hear the chains clink together, and I can picture him holding them up to him.

"No, you're letting her think she has an out. And she doesn't. If this gets out, you're done. I won't be able to protect you."

"This isn't going to get out, because it's going to be resolved by Friday," he hisses.

"You'll take care of it?"

"Yes, Luca. I'll take care of it. Now can you please fuck off? It's the middle of the day, and she's upstairs."

"I'll help clean up the mess. Give me a call when you're ready."

I hear a grunt and sharp smack of wood hitting wood, which I have a strong suspicion is the basement window. Could someone really fit through there?

My heart sinks into my stomach, and I have a strong sense that I may just vomit again. I'm such an idiot. Of course he's going to kill me. The mess will be my body. Danny's never going to know what happened to me because his psycho boss will dispose of my body, so he'll never find it.

I chew my nail, feeling so fucking pissed off. To think I liked him. Have I got such awful taste in men? Travis is one thing; I didn't know who he was when we first met. But surely

I'm not stupid enough to be duped by someone I knew was bad when I met him.

I'm not one to sit on things. In fact, I'd rather get this over with. I shoot a quick text to Danny, letting him know I love him. I try to keep it casual, but really, what can I say?

I move down the stairs quickly, and I hear him scramble for the chains. When I reach the bottom step, I see him holding them in front of him with a small metal stick in one hand. He's not trying to get loose . . . He's trying to lock himself back up.

"Olivia . . ."

His eyes dart between me, the window, and then down to the chains in his hands. He looks at them like he's holding a pile of snakes that might bite him at any moment.

I thought I'd still have some semblance of control here. But no. He's free to pounce as soon as he's ready. He swallows hard, and I watch his throat roll. Panic laces his eyes as his mouth grimaces. Maybe he feels bad about what he has to do next.

"I heard you talking to your friend," I mutter, glancing down at the chains in his hands.

"Loose word for what I think of him right now."

"You're going to kill me," I whisper.

"No." He shakes his head, his eyes imploring.

If I'd been a weaker woman, I would have believed him. I don't let him finish. "Let go of the chains, Austin."

"Olivia, let me expl—"

"Let. Go. Of the chains."

He drops them to his feet. His eyes pierce mine, boring into me, penetrating my mind and body. His body is perfectly still; he somehow seems even bigger now. Like the chains have constricted him these last five days. Finally, he can stretch, righting himself to his full height. He keeps his hands folded in front of his stomach, as if he's about to kneel and pray. But I know the man that's inside. I heard it only a few minutes ago. He can flip at any moment and I can't be here when that happens. Despite his stillness, I can feel my heart pressing so hard against my chest I might just break a bone. My chest is heaving, my shoulders moving to allow more room for the oxygen I can't seem to get in. And for the first time in my life, after fighting for everything I have for so long, for everything Danny has, I run.

I spin on my heel, grab the wooden banister, and take the stairs two at a time.

"OLIVIA!" Austin bellows.

He's quick to chase, but he doesn't know my house.

I reach the top of the landing and slam the door shut. I don't try to turn and lock it because I can feel him a breath away from me. I keep going. Running through the hallway, I reach the living room. I find the drawer I'm looking for, pull it open, and grab the taser.

He's quick on my tail. Seemingly knowing the layout of my house—maybe his friend has let him know.

"Olivia, just listen to me for one second!"

I turn, and he's only a couple of yards in front of me. He holds his hands up, his bare chest finally showing some signs of exertion from the chase. He breathes in deeply, holds one palm up, and says, "Give me the taser, and then I can explain everything."

"I'm not fucking stupid, despite what you and your friend think. I know . . . I know you're going to kill me. And it's no more than I deserve for what I've done. But I . . . I just thought . . ."

"Thought what, baby?" His voice is soft. This is the Austin I've grown to know. The lie I'm so eager to believe.

Playing with your food.

I flip the switch on the taser, and it crackles menacingly.

A flicker of uncertainty meets his eyes as he glances down at the taser. He must have some sense about him, as he raises his other hand in surrender as well.

"I just want to explain what's going on."

"What's going on . . . *Austin*," I spit, "is *I* kidnapped *you*. I chained *you* up. I have a taser, which I'm going to use on *you*."

He has the audacity to grin. "Oh, I don't doubt you could, baby. I know you like it a little rough."

The air is sucked out of the room as my body betrays me. My breath deepens, and the heat between my legs spreads to my belly. I'm on fucking fire right now, and I need a cool douse of water to calm down.

"This isn't funny. This is my life."

"And I'm telling you, your life is not in danger. Not from me." A part of me wants to believe him. But that's crazy, right? This whole situation is fucked-up.

"You're a liar."

"I've never lied to you. Not once." He steps closer.

"I don't trust you."

"I've only ever been honest with you."

"You stalked me." I'm whispering now; the hurt laces my words, and he has the decency to look chagrined as he stares at my worn floorboards.

He hesitates, running a hand over the beard he hasn't been able to shave in my basement.

"Technically, I only went where I knew you would end up. I never actively followed you anywhere," he explains.

"That's just semantics, you fucking psycho." My words aim to hurt, but they lack the impact I'd imagined in my head.

His face softens more still.

"I only ever went to Squeeze the Day. I never followed you anywhere else."

"I don't believe you," I whisper, my hand falling just slightly. "You let me take you, didn't you?"

He takes another step forward until he's so close he can reach out and touch me. I could jab the taser into his stomach right now if I wanted to. But I don't. I don't want to hurt him. The realization hits me all too hard, and I try to shake the thought. Have I lost all sense of self-preservation? I grip the lifeline in my hand tighter, steeling myself to go against my very nature.

"Olivia," his voice steady, he says my name like an oath,

like a promise.

I peek up at him through my lashes. He's crowding me now, and half of me is screaming to run. He's caging me in. It's a trick. It's a lie. But I don't care. I deserve what he's going to do.

"I promise you. If you could put down the taser, I'll explain everything."

My hand lowers again. I want to believe him. I want to be able to trust him.

He lunges quickly, grabbing my wrist. He shoves me hard against the wall, and my breath leaves my lungs, the back of the taser squishing into my stomach. With every bit of strength I have, I push the back of the taser with my hip and thrust into him. The crackling hits his bare stomach, and he convulses in front of me.

His body revolts, jumping away from me. I watch his head nod up and down rapidly, his jaw jutting out as the electricity vaults through him. I cover my mouth with my hand, trying not to laugh. I can't move; I'm part scared of him killing me, part scared he's going to taser me right back for laughing.

"Are you fucking laughing at me?" he groans once he regains control of his body. He's keeled over still, hands on his thighs as he tries to compose himself.

"Yes, you look ridiculous."

If I'm going to die, I'm going to die. At least I can make him feel like an idiot before I do.

A manic smile pulls up his lips, his eyes deranged. "You're gonna regret that, Killer."

He grabs the taser from me, presses the button, and jabs me as swiftly as it pulls away.

"FUCK!" My hand grabs my thigh where he stung me. "THAT REALLY HURT!" I scream at him.

He throws the taser across the room, and it skids across the wooden floorboards, crashing against my bookcase.

He leans one hand against the wall, one hand clutching his side where a pink cluster of angry veins are collecting. He leans down, his height becoming all too smothering against mine.

"Now that we've got that out of our system, let's talk."

I swallow, my eyes darting around the room, looking for anything I could use to defend myself against him. He leans in further, and I know it's futile. I know that he could snap my neck right now if he wanted to. But he doesn't. He waits. He's still panting, still unbalanced from my brief assault. A warmth glows, and I fight the urge my lips have to tilt upward. Am I enjoying this? I didn't enjoy being tasered at all, but the chase, the height difference, the feeling of helplessness. Do all bodies react like this when they're about to die? Probably not. I'm really starting to think there might be something wrong with me.

"Fine. But I'm getting the taser back," I say, shifting toward the bookcase.

"No more tasers." His hands palm the wall as he leans down, his nose an inch from mine. His corded forearms cage me in, my back against the wall, and I know resistance is unavailing. Part of me likes that it is. At least I can pretend he's forcing me to stay this close to him.

"This is my hostage situation. I'll hold my taser if I want to."

"No."

"What do you mean *no*?"

He grabs my wrist and drags me toward the couch. Despite my protest, he pulls me down onto him. He spins me around and pulls me onto his lap so my back is on his chest. I poke the spot where the taser hit him in the hopes he might release me, but all it does is make his abs clench.

He twists and swings his legs up so he's lying down on the couch, his head on the armrest. His thighs squeeze me tightly so I can't shift, and all I can do is twist so at least I can look up at him from my stomach. From this angle I can feel every contour, every muscle, every hard thing about him. My cheek rests on his chest, my breasts on his stomach. His heart beats so calmly it's unnerving.

I feel his dick between his sweatpants throbbing into my stomach.

Holy hell.

I blush furiously and try to stay as still as possible.

"Now that we're comfortable."

His legs bend so his feet cross under my ass, and he pulls me in further so I'm basically thrust against him. *Fucking pervert.*

"Let's talk."

"Who said I was comfortable?" I spit back, digging my nails between his ribs.

His hands move from my back to grab each wrist.

He hoists me up so quickly that our lips are almost touching. "I will restrain you, Olivia. But I know you like to be the one tying someone up, so you'll get that one for free. But I will gag you if you don't behave, understand?"

My mouth waters, and my eyes can't stop themselves. I dare to look down at his lips; the filth that comes out of them has my body singing. It's like we're drawn to each other in a way that I just can't explain. It's more than physical. It's chemical . . . emotional.

I nod.

"Good. Now slide back down and get comfortable."

He releases my wrists, and I do what he says. He is silent for a moment as I wriggle into position. Once I've settled, my cheek is back against his chest, and my left arm is hanging loose by the side of the couch. I sigh and close my eyes. Might as well lean into whatever this is.

While he runs the fingers of one hand down my back, he sweeps my hair out of the way and uses his other hand to stroke my head. If I hadn't already closed my eyes I would do so now. The way his deft fingers delicately run through the strands of my hair is heavenly. Had I not just been tasered by this man, I would strongly suspect that this is what a real relationship could be like. Afternoons on the couch, cuddling, kissing, rough fingers teasing each other until eventually neither of us can take any more, and we tumble into bed.

Maybe I'm just touch-starved. That's a thing right? I haven't had a relationship in so long, but I haven't been held like this either. Not even a hug. This job is so isolating sometimes. It's weird to think how little I'm physically around people. And now that it's just me and Danny, it's hard not to feel a certain level of relief at being held by this man who, despite his obvious flaws, could protect me if he chose to.

"That embarrassing story I told you. About the man and the wife who were propositioning me. My father had given them the okay to pursue me. He'd told me what they wanted, and he didn't outright say it, but I knew the expectation was that I would agree without question. In addition to that, something had transpired a few days after. Something had happened while I was on a job that put into question a lot of my own behavior, which ultimately led me to make some changes in my life."

I try to shift but he holds me tighter, continuing to stroke my hair. I'm desperate to look at his face, but I let him keep me pinned down.

"That's awful. Your father should never have put you in that position."

"It was no worse than I deserved." He sighs.

"That's not true. No one deserves to be treated like that."

He ignores my comment and continues, "When I saw you for the first time, you were unbelievably kind to someone who spilled your drink all over you."

I remember that. It was Jenny's first day.

"You told them not to worry and said something about dog poo and a client or an ex who I instantly wanted to dismember."

I smiled but stayed quiet, my fingers beginning to stroke along his ribs.

"You were kind and funny, with a gentleness that I'd never seen before from anyone. Kindness is not common in my line of work, and you . . . intrigued me."

He pauses for a moment, but when I don't respond, he continues.

"So I started going to Squeeze the Day, drinking their god-awful coffee, to prove to myself that you couldn't have been as kind as you were that day. There had to be a fault or a flaw that would prove me right."

"Why would you want to be proved right?" I murmur. The weight of his hand on my back and the other running through the strands of my hair felt glorious. Like stepping into a warm bath or curling up under a blanket on the couch.

"Because then I wouldn't have to obsess over you anymore. I could move on. Stop drinking that piss water they call coffee and just get on with my life."

"I'm not perfect. I have flaws."

"Olivia." He laughs. "I know you have flaws. You just fucking tasered me after chaining me up in your basement."

I chuckle as tears prick at my eyes, threatening to spill. I don't understand where this emotion has come from. Austin continues rubbing my back, petting me like a cat curled up on his lap. The thump of his heart beneath me creates a rhythm my breath falls in sync with. My whole body aches to align with his.

"I thought you were sunshine incarnate. But you have a dark side, which is equally enticing. I watched you for two years, Killer, and I didn't learn half of what I learned from living in your basement."

His legs loosen from caging me in, and I shift so I can look at him.

"So you're not going to hurt me?" I already know the answer. At least, I hope I do. But I feel the need to ask it all the same.

"No, Killer. I'm not going to hurt you, not now or ever."

"I still don't believe you. I'm just . . . me. I don't think I merit this kind of fascination."

"Well, we'll work on that then, won't we?" He smiles

before booping my nose with his fingertip.

He shifts, and all of a sudden, I feel cold without him.

I'm sitting upright, facing him on the couch, and my heart begins to race. I think he's going to kiss me. I lean in as he holds my hand, running his thumb over my knuckles.

"I've got to go and sort some things out. We'll talk soon, okay? Think about what I've said."

"I . . . wait, what? Where are you going?"

"I have a business to run, employees to manage. As you may have heard from Luca, they're needy fuckers."

I roll my eyes, and he smirks. Drawing my hand to his mouth, he presses a brief kiss to my knuckles. "I'll see you later, Killer. Ice that leg for me."

And with that, he strolls right out the front door, no shirt and all, and I'm left dumbstruck.

CHAPTER ELEVEN

Austin

That went better than expected. A light tasering, a cuddle starting with some light wrestling, and a heart-to-heart. Who knew getting a girlfriend could be so fucking easy? You just have to wait for someone to chloroform you. And yeah, I said girlfriend. I could do a TedTalk about finding your soul mate because if they exist, then Olivia fucking Daniels is mine.

Her public persona may be so sweet it could rot your teeth, but the girl is dark. She's not afraid to break the law, and by that, I mean federal law. She's racking up a hefty number of years behind bars for the shit she's pulled just this week. But hell will freeze over before I let that happen.

If I know her well, she's about to freak out in about two minutes. So I'm going to leave her for a few hours to come to terms with what she's done, what I've said, what is going to happen, and then I'll head back.

I swing open the door to Dr. Alfie's with such force the handle whacks against the wall.

"Austin Black. You are a fully grown man capable of opening a door properly without whacking it and scaring the shit out of me and the other patients. Close it properly." Mia stands, hands on hips and looking fucking good in a tight pencil skirt and loose blouse with one button below decent.

How the fuck Alfie hasn't put a ring on her yet is beyond

me, not that I'm interested. There's just one girl for me, and that's exactly what I need help with. I'm almost certain that the loose blouse is for Alfie's benefit.

"Morning, Mia." I grin, heading straight to his office.

"He has a patient, Austin. You can't just barge in there." Mia hisses as she moves around her desk toward me, her heels clipping against the floor.

The other patients are watching intently, obviously enjoying the show.

"I said no. Sit down and wait your turn. Which, by the way, is Friday. You're two days early."

"Yeah, no can do. This is an emergency, Mia."

I push through the door, holding my hands up in surrender the moment I see Dr. Alfie's face of thunder.

"Austin. So glad to see you're alive. I'm a little busy right now." He points at his patient, who is holding a soggy tissue to her nose. "So, if you could kindly speak to Mia about making an appointment."

I turn to his patient. "Miss, I realize you're in the middle of something here. But I will pay for your next ten sessions if you leave right now."

I pull out a wad of cash that I'd picked up from the office and start counting bills. Her bug eyes flit between me, Mia, and Dr. Alfie.

"Austin, no. We've talked about this. You can't just barge in here on a whim when it suits you."

"Did I say ten appointments? I meant to say ten appointments plus three months' rent."

"Deal," the mousy woman states with such certainty.

"Verity, you do not have to do this, and of course, your session today will be comped," Alfie interrupts.

"Verity, pleasure to meet you. I'll pay Mia upfront for your sessions. If you could leave your details with her, I'll send over the money for the rent. Let her know how much it is as well please."

"Thank you. Austin, is it?"

"Yes, ma'am."

Alfie rolls his eyes, folding his arms over his chest. I know he's unimpressed, but you can tell he's keen as a bean to find out what's been going on.

As Mia guides her out of the door, she looks past me to Alfie. "Sorry, Dr. Adams. I tried to stop Mr. Black here."

"Not your fault, Mia. Thank you for taking care of Verity." He's so polite, but I see the way his pupils dilate.

I take a seat on the couch, making myself comfortable.

"Austin, I don't need to tell you how fucking inappropriate that was," he hisses. "My other clients are just as important as you and deserve to be treated with respect and dignity when they come here."

The vein in his forehead is protruding quite comically, which is a big indicator to me that I need to look contrite and keep my mouth shut.

I nod. "I'm sorry. But I just got out of the basement, and I need your help. It won't happen again."

"You said that the first time we had a session."

"Well, that was two years ago, so I've done well for a while, and this is sort of an emergency."

"Not an emergency, Austin, although I am glad to see you're alive and well. I take it that things went well with Olivia if she let you out?"

I look around the beige office. It's supposed to be calming, neutral tones with a few non-descript decorations dotted around. The couch is a darker shade, bordering on brown, comfortable, and has a few throw pillows that I may or may not have held to my stomach when we were talking about some particularly dark shit. The back wall has Alfie's desk and a wall of books, mostly psychology ones, but I've noticed the Dr. Seuss ones, too. When he went to talk to Mia one time, I pulled them out and read the inscription; both of them were from his lovely receptionist. If I'm not mistaken, there's something going on there, but today is not the day to further piss Alfie off, so I keep it to myself.

He leans back and puts on his professional face. His jacket is off, and his sleeves are rolled up to the elbow. He does this to disarm people. It makes him look softer, less of a doctor and more of a barman you're about to spill your life story to. I know this because it fucking works. The second he leans back all relaxed, I want to relax, too. I just need him to throw a towel over his shoulder and pour me a drink. Then I'll spill all my secrets.

"Tell me what happened."

I give him the rundown of the last few days, including the escape—sort of—from the basement and the conversation we had just before I left. He doesn't ask questions, but lets me talk and run through the events as they happened. Now he's up-to-date, he taps his forefinger to his lips.

"So you've left her there."

"Yes, I wanted to give her some space so she could process her feelings."

"That's . . ." He raises his eyebrows. "Very mature of you, Austin. I'm proud of you."

Warmth fills my chest, and I want to smash down the feeling. I hate that I'm seeking validation from a man my own age, no less someone I went to high school with.

"What are you going to do next?"

"Well, I'm going to ask her out on a date. It seems like the next logical step."

He nods. "And how did she feel about your admission about your father and the expectations he had of you?"

"She was upset for me, I think. She told me it wasn't right what he did."

"How did that make you feel?"

"Good and bad. I don't want to be pitied. I want her to see me as a strong person. Not as a weak person who was used and treated badly."

He nods. "That's understandable. But perhaps she sees you as strong because you walked away from that situation. She understands a little of your world, so she must realize that it would have been extremely difficult for you to say no to your father."

"Yeah, I didn't get a bad vibe from her. I just hope that it stays that way."

"Good. I think you should continue to be honest. You've worked very hard to get where you are now. She deserves to know how hard you've been working. Whether you give her the reason why or not is up to you."

"And what is the reason why?"

"Well, you tell me."

"I didn't want to do bad things anymore. Or at least I didn't want people to be frightened of me anymore. When I saw those kids watching me beat the shit out of their dad, I wanted to die. I'd never felt worse than when I had at that moment."

He nods. "Any other reason?"

"Can I have more than one?"

"I'd be surprised if you didn't."

"I wanted to be someone that was worthy of someone like her. I don't think I'll ever get there, but I wanted to try."

"Ultimately, that's for Olivia to decide. But I think you have more in common than you originally thought. Olivia in your fantasy is just that. A fantasy. You put her on a pedestal no person could ever reach—"

"But that's where you're wrong, doc. Her dark side is just as intriguing to me. It actually makes me like her more. That she has this side of her that only I know about."

"I'm glad she's exceeded your expectations, but you will need to be patient in this situation. She is going to have a lot of catching up to do. Not only have you had years of cultivating feelings for her, but she's had less than a week of you being in the basement convincing her that you're not a terrible person. She seems to like you, but she'll find that conflicting with her original feelings. You'll need to be calm, consistent, and very, very patient with her. There will be a lot of up-and-down emotions."

"Emotional rollercoaster. Got it. I've got this, doc. I want this so bad; I'll do anything to make it work. I'll ask her out on a date and be very patient."

"Good idea. From what you've said, the physical aspect of your relationship is not the problem, but her mind and her heart need to catch up. You don't want to jump the gun and lose her before it starts."

"Thanks, doc. I'll . . . settle up with Mia now."

He rolls his eyes. "I'm glad you're back. Let's keep our normal session on Friday."

And because his mood seems to have improved, I decide, rightly or wrongly, to push his buttons further. "Oh, one thing, doc. One of your patients was flirting outrageously with Mia. If I were you, I'd put a ring on her soon. Let everyone know she's off-limits."

He shifts in his chair, and I can practically see him trying to work out what patient it is.

"I don't know what you're talking about. Mia is a professional. She would never jeopardize her position here."

"Whatever you say, doc. But she sure did look good today."

I swing the door shut behind me as I see the vein pulse in his forehead one more time.

"Are you causing trouble?" Mia asks, arching her perfectly shaped eyebrow.

"Giving him a gentle nudge, that's all."

"Here's your bill. I've added a tip for me." She grins. "For the trouble."

I sign the form and swipe my Amex, shoot her a wink, and head back to the office to do some hand-holding.

◆ ◆ ◆

After a long day, where I have to explain myself to my employees more times than I would fucking like, I slip out of the car and head up the pathway. It's late, and it's too dark now, past 11 p.m. I wonder if Olivia might be in bed.

I twist the door handle, and the door swings open. She should really be locking her door. Anyone could walk in.

She gasps and is clutching her arms around her chest.

She's been waiting for me it seems.

"Hey, Killer. I'm beat. Do you mind if I go straight to bed?" I ask, sliding my shoes off by the door.

"Listen." I can see on her face how scared she is. "I . . . I don't think it's a good idea that you're here. We need a clean break. Pretend this never happened, okay?"

"You've got a bruise." I rub my thumb along her thigh.

"Yeah, you fucking tasered me."

My mouth pulls before I can stop it. *There's my girl.*

"I have to work again tomorrow, but we're going out in the evening. Is seven good for you?"

"Wha—" She frowns. "No seven is not *good* for me."

"Okay." I shrug. "Eight is fine."

I head toward the basement and turn, "Goodnight, Olivia."

Her mouth agape, her stance has changed, so she's standing, leg cocked, fists clenched on her hips. God, she's a sight. With all the strength I have, I descend to the basement and leave her to go to bed alone, praying that Dr. Alfie's advice to take it slow works.

◆ ◆ ◆

After hours of meetings, welcome-backs, and a birthday cake for Hannah (yeah, a fucking *birthday cake*), the team is settled. Luca and I are sitting in my office, sipping on a warm amber whiskey from Kentucky.

I lean back in the leather-bound armchair. Yeah, it's old-school. But if my father did one thing right, it was decking his office out so it looked like an old British smoking room. He even had a smoking jacket made for himself, monogram and all. Despite being a little eccentric, I haven't gone that far. Dark greens and mahogany perfectly blend with the wainscot walls. I've taken inspiration from my father's style, but I like to think that mine is more comforting, whereas his is dark and not a place you want to linger. I've collected a few books, of which I'll be adding my most recent reads to the shelf. My whiskey collection is world-class, too, something that seems to impress Luca more than me. My vice is purposely putting myself in dangerous situations with unpredictable women. Well . . . one woman.

"Explain it to me," Luca snips.

I sigh. If anyone else talked to me like this, their tongue would be nailed to the desk, but Luca is my oldest friend. The shit we pulled when we were younger, it's a miracle we're both still alive and kicking.

"She's the one."

"The one?" he asks dumbly.

"Yep," I pop the "p" the way Olivia does and take another sip of my whiskey.

He says nothing and just stares, one eyebrow arching mockingly.

"I know this is hard for you to understand. This isn't our usual style, but did you really not see this coming?"

"No . . . I'm just surprised you finally worked it out. I thought you never would." He downs the remainder of his drink and gets up to pour another.

"Bastard." I hold out my glass for him to top me up.

"Hey, you were the one watching her from afar for two years. And I'm guessing you found out she's Danny's brother by now?"

"You knew?"

"Yeah, because I'm not a fucking simp like you. I do my research."

"Fuck off."

"With pleasure. I have a date as it happens. I might take a leaf out of your book and become a one-woman man." He winks.

That's as likely to happen as it is for Olivia to be ready to go on our date without a fight tonight.

I look at my watch; it's six thirty. I should start heading over to Olivia's to finish the argument we're bound to have before she finally agrees and make our reservation for eight.

"Meeting booked for tomorrow?" I ask.

"Yeah. Danny's ready."

"Good. You gave him the research points?"

"It's all sorted, boss," he snips. Luca's been doing this for as long as I have, so I'm not sure why I still nag him on the details. But he lets it go quickly.

"Good. Enjoy your date. I'm heading out too."

"Well, if you don't make it in by tomorrow, I'll know where to look first."

I grin back at my oldest friend. "If I don't come in by tomorrow, don't come looking for a few days."

We clink glasses and down the remainder of our drinks. The burn of the amber liquid sears down my throat, and I grab my jacket.

It has been a busy day. After nearly a week off, there is a lot to catch up on, but also plans to make.

My time in the basement has been thought-provoking. But most of all, my conversations with Olivia have made me reassess a few things. I've been coasting on my father's coattails for too long. I want to step away from his shadow and build on something fresh and new. Something completely unrelated to his shady business dealings.

We've worked hard over the last few years to build The Unseen to where it is now. We've used technology that my father's business had harnessed over the years to grow marijuana plants underground and repurposed it for something legal. Which I understand, is not usually how scientific breakthroughs go. Usually, people start with good intentions, but my father ran out of those in the 1970s, so it's my turn to make up for it.

Luca moved over from my father's business with me

and has remained under my protection, a novelty my father has permitted up until now. We haven't had any trouble. Danny also came over, as we needed his tech skills to get up and running. He's a practical kid. Knows his way around a computer, and he's started to automate our growing system, too. We started out in a basement, and now we're working on three underground levels of growing capacity, hence the name "The Unseen."

Since then, Hannah has started as our social media and marketing campaign manager, and Jack is a sales rep. Hannah is quiet, unassuming, but strategizes like a fucking tiger stalking its prey. She's sharp, witty when she wants to be, and has Jack completely wrapped around her finger. Jack is suave and smooth, a typical car salesman type with slicked-back hair, a sharp jawline, and a shark-like smile. We tolerate his cheesy one-liners and too-white teeth because he's doubled our customers in six months since he started, so he's worth his weight in gold.

Despite being separate from my father's company in every legal sense, the general rumor mill assumes I am still under The Organization's umbrella. It is time for that to change. The business has to move on, or we'll be going the same way as my father's business will in five years—six feet under. At least I have the foresight to see it coming and make changes. Dad is still operating under smash-and-grab warfare.

Jimmy, my driver, pulls up to Olivia's house. The red brick pathway is bordered by flower beds full of bright, tall flowers. Blooms of oranges, pinks, and yellows guide me to her fire-engine red front door. The place could do with a little maintenance. The grass is overgrown, and the flowers are descending onto the pathway in a bid to take over. Let's face it. I'm not sure when Olivia could fit in household maintenance on top of her extra-curricular activities.

I smile, shoulders relaxing for the first time since I left this morning and let myself straight in. Yeah, I'm not fucking knocking.

"Olivia?" I call out.

I walk into the living room and see her pacing. She's holding her chest again, eyes wide, biting her thumbnail.

She looks up at me and steps back.

"What happened?"

I reach out to her, and she flinches.

"Olivia. I need you to tell me what happened. Now."

The closer I get, the angrier I feel. Her eyes are red from crying; her cheeks are sunken and sallow. Her usual fight has left her eyes.

"Is this about us?"

Please say yes, because I can deal with that. I know how to deal with that.

She nods. "Please don't hurt me."

"Hurt you? Olivia, I've been thinking about taking you out all day."

Her eyes pop open, and her lip quivers.

"Oh god, I meant to take you out on a date . . . not, you know, take you out, take you out." I chuckle nervously.

I cautiously place my hands on her arms and rub them up and down. *God, she's freezing.*

"Come here, Killer." I pull her into my chest, and she lets out a small sob.

"I thought you'd come to your senses once you left. That you'd come back to take care of the problem. But then you just went down to the basement, and I . . . I mean, who does that? And then you're back again, and I just can't stop thinking about that guy saying you were playing with your food. And that's what it feels like. It feels like you're playing this game, and I don't understand the rules. I'm just waiting for it to be over. Because I can't live like this. I'd rather you just get on with it and kill me because I can't stand the waiting."

Jesus. This girl.

"One, no one is dying. Except maybe Luca for referring to you as food. Two, you've been so scared all day. Why did you stay? Why didn't you run?"

"I figured you'd be able to find me."

That's fucking true.

"You're not wrong, baby. There's nowhere you could go that I wouldn't be able to find you. But, Olivia. I need you to know that I'm not going to hurt you." I stroke her hair, and her breathing begins to even out. "I meant what I said yesterday. And this is not what I meant when I told you to think about what I've said. Don't doubt me, Olivia. I need you to trust that I'm telling you the truth."

She pushes me away, "Well then, you're crazy, Austin. I kidnapped you . . . I tased you."

"I tased you back. So I think we're even on that front."

"It's not a joke! I keep thinking there's either something unbelievably wrong with me . . . or you . . . or both of us. I keep going round and round, and I can't make sense of it."

"Not everything has to make sense, Olivia."

"This should, Austin. I mean, you get free from the basement, where you've not really been chained up, and then you ask to take me on a date . . . It's ridiculous."

"Okay, this is going to take time. I'm a patient man."

"Doubt it."

"I was chained in your basement for five days."

"Technically, not chained."

"Well, Luca, the guy you met, he gave me the pick a few days ago. I've just been unchaining them while you've been asleep so I could get comfy. And that really was the best mattress I've ever slept on. I wanted to get the full experience." I take her hand and run my thumb over her knuckles.

Changing tack, I ask, "Are you ready for our date?"

She looks down at herself and laughs.

"I'm wearing workout gear."

As if I fucking care what she's wearing. "You could wear a trash bag, Olivia. I'll take you anywhere."

I push a loose strand behind her ear and drag my fingertips down her neck before gripping firmly. It's a risk, but I think she needs me to take control right now.

"Go get ready, baby. Wear whatever you want."

"Okay."

"Okay?" I smirk.

Her eyes roll, and she nods.

Our drive into the city is so smooth, it feels like we're elevating. Not a single bump or swerve the entire time. It is as if everything uncertain and chaotic is bubbling inside the vehicle. Thankfully, Jimmy is driving, so I can keep my focus on Olivia.

Her nose is almost touching the blacked-out window, her body turned completely away from me. Not a great start. She isn't talking either, but I wouldn't know what to say if she did.

Part of my role with my father was playing a part. Generally speaking, people are more terrified of long silences than they are of verbal threats. The silence leaves room for guessing, for imaginations to run wild at what torture you have in store for them.

Perhaps Olivia is better at this than she thinks. She did successfully kidnap me with a little help, and now she has me sweating and pulling the collar away from my neck.

The balance of power has shifted astronomically in the last twenty-four hours, and I've mentally prepared that this might not be a smooth transition for her.

Sure, she's agreed to a date, but she's taken a lot of cajoling.

At least I've finally had a real shower. I've trimmed my beard, tidying up the scruff. Running my hand over the bristles, the sound was soothing. From the way her eyes dipped, I bet she liked it too.

I still remember how she descended the stairs, the light from the upstairs window lighting her up from behind like some ethereal creature. Her red sundress embroidered with daisies that seemed to float along the fabric. The hem fell just above the knee, showing off her toned legs. The bodice squeezing in at her waist and tight enough that her tits pressed against the fabric into a sweetheart neckline.

Her loose waves cascade over her shoulder, preventing me from reading her face. At least she's not crying anymore. I'm sure her anxiety today has been an accumulation of overthinking and guilt over what she's done. I just have to reassure her that this is the best thing that could have happened for us. It's led us to tonight.

I cough lightly. She's like a deer in headlights, and I don't want to startle her.

"There's a restaurant called Harvest. We're going there."

She turns, eyes wide and beaming.

"Harvest? Oh my god. I've wanted to go there for ages."

I smile. "Good." I reach out for her hand and draw it to my lips, kissing her knuckles.

Thank god I've done something right. I dare not look at her face, so I take my turn to stare out the window. She doesn't let go of my hand the rest of the way.

◆◆◆

"This isn't chicken." I stare down at my plate before looking over at Olivia's across from me.

The restaurant is the perfect setting for a first date. We're on the patio, a miracle in itself given that we're in Washington State, but they have heaters on now that there's a chill in the air.

The string lights twinkle above us, creating a night sky usually unseen in the cloudy Seattle night. She has my jacket around her shoulders and is eating a chicken burger with wholegrain mustard mayo, lettuce that came from my indoor farm, and a wholemeal bun where the wheat was grown in the field down the road from Olivia's house.

This is why I chose Harvest for tonight. I knew Olivia would love that they knew exactly where all their ingredients came from, and it meant I got to try out some of my products in actual meals. It also helped that when I was sneaking around her house the other night, the menu was open on her laptop. But hey, why spoil the magic by telling her where I get my intel?

However, my chicken with brown rice and sesame broccolini is coming up short on a few key ingredients.

I push my fork around the plate as Olivia peers over the top of her burger.

The lines around her eyes deepen, and she turns away to focus on something else, pressing her lips together.

"Are you laughing at me, Miss Daniels?"

"Absolutely not," she snorts. "I just never thought I'd see the day when you'd be eating a grilled eggplant salad."

"Is that what this is? It's very . . . squidgy." A bit of eggplant flops back onto the plate with a squelch, and my stomach heaves a little.

Pull it together, man.

I shovel some in my mouth. *What the living fuck?* My tongue pulls to the back of my mouth, trying to escape the slimy invasion that's now resting on my tastebuds.

Olivia is watching me intently as she takes another humungous bite of her burger, looking very fucking pleased with herself.

"Definitely not chicken." I retch. "Where's my meat?"

She laughs, and bits of burger spray out of her mouth. Good. We can both be disgusting.

"Oh my god." Tears pool in the corners of her eyes. "If you don't know where your meat is by now, I'd suggest you go see a doctor."

I grab the underside of her chair and drag it closer to me. The wooden legs screech across the stone floor, and neighboring tables turn to us.

I lean my arm on the back of her chair, and as my lips brush the shell of her ear, I place my right hand on her knee, lifting the fabric of her dress a few inches so I can squeeze her smooth skin.

"I can assure you, no doctor visits are necessary, Olivia."

"Austin!" she hisses, pulling the fabric down and over my hand so no one can see.

I lean down to take a bite of her burger before she has a chance to stop me. "Yeah, that's fucking chicken," I say, licking my lips.

The old lady at the table nearby tuts before focusing back on her dinner. Her sour expression suggests she, too, was mistakenly given the eggplant salad.

"You've got no manners," she whispers as I lean back in my chair.

"I don't think you want a man with manners, Olivia."

"Oh, is this where you tell me what I do want instead, and it just happens to be all of your qualities?"

"You want a man who takes what he wants. Because that's what you do. You're a woman of action, and you want to see that reflected in your partner . . . whoever you choose," I add with a wink.

"I'm still not convinced by this." She circles her finger in the air from my head to my chest and back again.

Oh, a challenge. What a chore that must be for some people. "I told you I'm patient, Killer. Are you nearly done? We have a quick stop on the way home."

Yeah, I said home. That little basement is my new registered address.

"How was your chicken, sir?" the waiter emerges from the shadows like a fucking jack-in-the-box. Olivia loses it, and starts laughing embarrassingly loud.

"Apologies, George. Miss Daniels here had an edible before we arrived, so she's a little out of sorts right now."

This only causes Olivia to laugh harder. She clutches her stomach, and I worry she might choke on her burger.

"Oh, don't worry. I took an edible the other day and stared at a lamppost for three hours. Best afternoon I've had in weeks. I'm just glad she's enjoying herself," the young waiter whispers after glancing around to check no one could overhear.

I take the opportunity to swipe another bite of her chicken burger and without having to lie, I tell George the food was delicious and settle the bill.

"Sir, this is coming from my manager. He's asked me that if you're to return, you'll need to be a little more conscious of the other guests. Otherwise, we can reserve a private room for you."

"Of course, not a problem." *We won't be returning.*

Olivia is breathless and trying to regain her composure but ends up yelling, "How was the chicken?" at the top of her lungs before falling into fits of giggles again.

"However, if you have the name of the person who sold the edibles, I'd love to get their details," he whispers.

"Next time, George." I slap a one hundred dollar bill into his hand. "I'd better get her home."

My arms are snaked around her slim waist, and I end up hauling her out of the restaurant and to the car.

"That was the best meal I've ever had." She grins as I open her door.

"Me too." And it really was.

We stop for ice cream. Olivia orders strawberry, and I take chocolate fudge. We swap halfway through until the last bite, and we swap back so she can have strawberries as the final taste in her mouth.

It feels strange to indulge her with this. I haven't had such a fun dinner in years. I felt young again, as if life is meant to be more than what I've been doing. Olivia doesn't have an easy life; she works hard, unbelievably hard. But she enjoys the little things and doesn't take herself too seriously.

When we reach the house, I walk her down the path after sending Jimmy home with the car. She doesn't tell me I can't stay, so I assume she's fine with it.

She unlocks the door, and as we step into the house, the glow of the living room light warms the room. The date has gone better than I could have imagined. She leaned into me, held my hand, and let me touch her. She's been as playful as she was when I was under her control in the basement. It gives me hope that she's believing me when I say I'm not going to hurt her. But I temper my feelings. I can't overwhelm her with this. It's new to us both, but this change in dynamic is much more difficult for her. This has been inevitable to me since last week, probably since before then. But she tased me yesterday. So I'm going to have to live up to my word and be patient.

She stands, looking at the floor awkwardly. I run my fingers through her hair, with my other hand cupping her jaw. She licks her bottom lip before biting it lightly.

Fuck.

Any other date, any other woman, I'd take. Take her mouth, take her tongue, take her to bed. I'd take and take until there was nothing left for her to give.

I use my thumb to pull her lip down, all while she's looking up at me with a mixture of lust and apprehension. It's too soon, I know this.

"Tonight was better than I could have imagined. You're perfect, Olivia."

"You were mostly a gentleman, something that surprised me."

I grin wickedly, desperate to spar a little longer with her.

Sighing, I run my fingers down her arm. When I reach her hand, I draw it up to my lips and kiss her knuckles.

"Good night, Killer."

She frowns a little, and with a sag in her shoulders, she whispers, "Good night, Austin."

For the second night in a row, I willingly descended the stairs to the basement alone.

◆ ◆ ◆

Rolling over for the fifth time in as many minutes, I'm torn between striding up the stairs to pin Olivia to her bed or going for a run to shake off my discomfort. I never used to consider options. I would take what I wanted, when I wanted it. And it was clear Olivia wanted me as much as I did her. At least her body did. But as discussed with Dr. Alfie, I'm in this for the long haul. My dick is protesting, but my chest is puffed out with pride. My control around her is hanging by a thread, but I cling to it like a life preserver. I won't let my past dictate how I behave now.

That being said, there's nothing wrong with watching her for a few moments as she sleeps. That wouldn't technically be breaking the rules. And given that I've already watched her sleeping once before, it doesn't really count.

With that justification, I slip out from under the blanket and pad up the stairs. Despite not being locked in the basement, my heart rate increases as I sneak through the moonlit hallway and into the living area. Reaching the stairs, I keep my feet close to the edges of the steps so as not to creak any loose floorboards.

My mouth waters in anticipation as I take the final step on the stairs. A red glow hums from her room and the door is open an inch. Perhaps she's not asleep yet.

I stalk toward her bedroom door and position myself so I can peer through the crack. A small moan rings through my ear, and my first concern is that she's having some kind of nightmare. I could push my way through, smooth back the hair from her face, and soothe her out of her bad dream. But I pause for just a moment as another moan escapes her lips.

The blanket ruffles around her as I watch her bent knees part.

"Yes, Austin, just like that."

Holy shit.

The gods are testing my resolve today, testing the strength of every fiber of my being.

I watch through the crack, undoing the button of my pants and slipping my hand down beneath my boxers. I'm as hard as stone, no surprise there. I grip the base of my cock, pulling upward; my release is imminent. Like a goddamn teen who's seen a girl naked for the first time, I'm ready to blow my load at her soft whimpers.

I can't hear any noise except her own, so I know she's only using her fingers. How I wish she'd kick off the blanket and expose her bare pussy for me.

"Yes, please . . . I need it. *I need you.*"

Fuck. Me.

My girl likes to beg, and I store that tidbit away for later.

Her breathing quickens, and I watch as her head pushes back against the pillow, her back arching, legs falling further and further apart. She's close. Her left arm reaches up and grips the bar of her bed frame. Her knuckles turn white from the strength of her hold. She lifts her hips, and I practically thrust mine into the vise hold I have around my cock. She cries out my name one more time, and I lose all semblance of control. I pump myself faster and faster, and as her hips pulse up and down into her fingers, I allow myself to come. My orgasm powers through me, pulsing up to my head, causing my eyes to roll back into my skull. My toes tingle as my blood soars around my body. I have never fucking come so hard. Euphoria settles through me like an anchor falling through deep water.

I pump myself a few more times, relishing the power she has over me, the sticky residue of my orgasm coating the inside of my briefs and my hand as I watch her come down from her own climax. She brings both hands on top of the blanket now but stares at the ceiling, smiling, a small giggle reaching her lips.

She pulls her knees back together and swings her legs off the bed so her feet touch the floor. Her panties are around her ankles, and she pulls them up before I have the chance to see any more of her.

As she heads toward me, I step back quickly. She's not ready for the real me to invade her fantasy. I'm halfway down the unlit hallway as she opens the door. As I creep carefully down the first step, I watch her swing into the bathroom, switching on the light so I can see the burgundy panties and matching silky sleep top in all its glory. Olivia washes her hands and then leans against the vanity. She glares intently at herself, until a small curve breaks on her lips, and she caresses her collarbone with her fingertips. The flush of her orgasm still stains her neck, and I fight back the urge to creep up behind her to run my tongue along the flush.

She sighs, smiling to herself again before flicking off the light and heading back down toward the red glow of her bedroom.

CHAPTER TWELVE

Olivia

I've read the same paragraph six times before he finally arrives. He orders his coffee, or piss water, as he calls it. His usual spot is open, and I stare at it while he undoes his jacket in the wingback chair opposite mine by the window. My expectations were off; I wasn't sure if he would acknowledge me or give me space. But sitting right at my table uninvited, like this is no big deal, is not what I expected.

I hear mutters around from other regulars, and Jenny is bug-eyed at the counter, practically clawing at Anthony to look over at our table. I give her a wide-eyed, confused shrug and turn to Austin.

He picks up his coffee mug and pulls out one of my paperbacks that I've given him down in the basement. *The Howl of Desire* is the title, and the front cover models a six-packed man with furry claws and wolf ears. It isn't my favorite novel, yet the shifter element has turned out to be surprisingly enjoyable.

Austin takes a sip of his coffee and proudly flips a page.

Jenny brings over my juice with raised eyebrows. She's uncharacteristically quiet, but her face speaks volumes.

"Good morning, Jenny. How are you?" Austin perks up, grinning.

I'm not sure I've ever heard him talk to her before. Usually, his stony silence vibrates from ten feet away.

"Oh, yes, um . . . good, very good. You . . . wanted a new seat, I see?" she stammers out.

I blush furiously and pretend to start reading again.

"Yes, Olivia finally made a move. She practically dragged me into her car the other day," he teases, although Jenny doesn't realize quite how accurate that statement is.

"I was just telling her to ask you out the other day. Did you get the coffee?"

"I did! I didn't realize you'd given her a nudge. We'll have to mention her in the wedding speech, won't we, Killer?"

"Killer!" she squeals, turning to Anthony on the register. "They even have pet names for each other."

The. Entire. café. Is. Watching.

Despite how uninterested Anthony is, heads turn, old ladies mutter, and I even get a wink from one gentleman in the corner. *Lord, help me.*

"I don't have a pet name yet, but I'm sure she'll come up with something soon, won't you, Olivia?"

"I can think of a few names right now," I say through clenched teeth.

"It's still new." He winks, turning back to Jenny, while crossing his leg over his thigh. The perfect image of a man relaxed and in control. I want to strangle him.

I can't believe I wanted this oaf to kiss me last night. And despite the annoyingly rapid rate he's taken over my life, I feel a sense of relief that he sits with me today. He could have sat in his usual spot, watching from afar as I scowled. We could have continued the same old game, but this means something.

Even if he didn't kiss me last night.

Why didn't he kiss me last night?

Jenny talks to Austin for a few more minutes before Anthony calls her over to help a customer.

Once the usual hum of the café has resumed, he leans forward, downs the remainder of his coffee, and stands, buttoning up his suit. I stand too . . . I'm not sure why, but it makes him smile.

"Plans for the weekend?" he asks.

"I'm having an *Ideas Afternoon* on Saturday. And I have to film a few videos. Other than that, no plans."

He nods and runs his palm over his scruff. I can practically feel the roughness. Just the sheer sound of it sends heat south of my navel.

"I'll be back tonight, and I'll help. With the videos," he clarifies. "And you can tell me all about what an *Ideas Afternoon* entails."

"You'll help?"

"Sure. Sounds fun. Then we'll go out." He doesn't ask. He's not giving me any options, I suppose.

"Okay."

"Good." He cradles the back of my head and kisses my hair. "I'll see you tonight."

He waves goodbye to Jenny and Anthony and sweeps out the door. The only proof he's been here is his empty mug and the ring of the bell as the door jumps back into place.

I slump back into my armchair, more confused than ever.

◆ ◆ ◆

The wind whips my hair into a frenzy, and the crunch of gravel beneath my shoes accompanies my pug-like breathing. Despite the incline, I feel like I'm practically bounding along the trail. The dark greens, browns, and grays of the mountains blur past me as I push my legs harder, feeling like my thighs could start smoking at any point.

Deep breaths accompany mine as we laboriously climb the hill. As we reach the precipice and the trail flattens, I feel my breaths sounding less winded.

"You're fucking fast, Olivia. I could barely keep up." Austin huffs as he bends, resting his hands on his thighs.

"I've gotten quicker lately. I've been doing a series of

marathon training videos to help keep me motivated."

He hums and stares out at the view. Parts of Obstruction Point can look quite barren; the earth looks scorched in places with pockets of trees littered around. That is until you reach the dense forest, then the trees cover the floor in darkness. Roots and moss take over every surface available, even the trees.

"You're doing a marathon?"

"That's the plan. I want to hit every fitness milestone at least once in my life," I say just before I take off running again.

"Already, woman?" I hear Austin behind me.

"I bet I can beat you down to the lake!" I call out over my shoulder.

It's only a few more miles until we reach the freezing body of water, so I pick up the pace. It's mostly downhill now, so I know I can push myself. The ominous sound of Austin's footsteps behind me, building speed, gaining on me, has the hairs on my neck standing to attention. Given the kind of man I know he is, at least the kind of man I thought he was, being chased is somewhat thrilling. Who am I kidding? I've never felt so much adrenaline coursing through my body. My legs threaten to turn to noodles at the thought of him catching me, as if they *want* me to be caught.

I was sure he would have made a move to be more physical the last few days. Our date had gone so well on Thursday, but we'd stayed in and watched movies last night, and then today, we both worked before heading out for this run. He stayed down in the basement both nights—*unchained, of course*.

Once he left Squeeze the Day yesterday, Jenny had rushed over wide-eyed ready for me to fill her in. But really, what could I say? I definitely couldn't tell her the whole truth, so I just said what I could: we went on a date, nothing had happened, and I was waiting to see what would transpire next. Frustrating, but accurate.

Despite the inner turmoil regarding Austin that is

quickly taking over my life, I've received more comments on my videos about possible copyright issues. I've lost around 2,000 subscribers since Millie's last video blasting me personally, which hasn't put a huge dent in my numbers, but it's still a devastating blow.

Although Millie seems to be keeping her word and not posting videos directly, there are way more trolls than usual, and I can't help but be suspicious that she's behind it.

I sent an email to a lawyer this morning asking for advice before doing some bookkeeping and general admin for the business. It was rather dull and not what I wanted to focus on, but keeping on top of it kept my anxiety away. Processing my thoughts, I feel Austin closing the gap between us. We're close to the lake now.

"I'm coming for you, Olivia. You can't outrun me."

What a delicious threat.

I laugh. "Sure, old man."

"Oof, you wound me. I'm not old."

"You're a lot older than I am."

"Not. Old," he huffs out.

Before I can reach the edge of the lake, I hear a loud growl, and his forearm snakes around my stomach. He tackles me into the long grass, breaking my fall by rolling me on top of his chest. I laugh into the crook of his neck and try to wriggle free, but he cages me in.

"Cheater!"

"I never said I followed the rules, Killer."

I roll my eyes at his use of my nickname. "Hmm, that doesn't surprise me much."

"No?"

"I think you're used to just taking what you want."

"Is that what you did?" Goosebumps spread across my skin, chasing the path his fingertips made.

"What I did?"

"Yeah . . ." His eyes sparkle. "When you took me?"

I laugh, slapping my hand against his chest. "That was

cheesy, even for you."

He grins, a dimple appearing on his cheek.

"What can I say? I like to throw you off, be a mess of contradictions."

And that really is a perfect way to describe him. He's chaotic but meticulous, funny but authoritative, frightening but comforting. I'm exhausted by my attraction to him. He draws me in, and I wonder if I'll ever truly see all of him. I don't think I can fully relax until I know what I'm up against.

Avoiding his penetrating eyes, I rest my head on his chest and bask in the warm sun.

"I have an idea for your *Ideas Afternoon*," he finally says.

"Oh yeah?" I mumble, feeling myself dozing off to the rhythm of his chest contracting and expanding with each breath.

"You could do a self-defense series."

"Self-defense? That's . . . interesting. How would it work, though? I'd have to do it with someone."

"Would you?"

"Well . . . yeah. I couldn't defend against myself," I say, propping myself up on my elbow and tapping a finger against my lips. "I could hire someone. Some big beefcake to make it look legit."

"Umm, no. That won't work," he says all too quickly.

"Why not? It was your idea." I laugh.

"Well, they'd have their hands on you, and I'd have to cut them off if they did that," he says softly, brushing hair out of my face. He speaks so softly, in fact, that my breathing hitches and my lungs twinge. He doesn't often remind me of who he is; he doesn't need to, I suppose. But I have no doubt he's deadly serious.

"What's the alternative?" I ask, eager to find some level footing when it comes to this man.

"You could use a woman?"

"Who says I don't like women?"

"You don't like men or women, Olivia. You like me," he

says casually, like it isn't an acknowledgment of everything unspoken between us.

My lips curl at the edges, threatening to break out into an all-out grin. *Oh, he's jealous.*

"Well, maybe I'll keep it fair and hire a man and a woman. They can tag-team me," I murmur, lifting my head to gauge his reaction.

"Olivia, I'm warning you."

"We could do different scenes, you know. What if they snuck into my bedroom, and I had to defend myself there?"

"Olivia . . ."

"Or maybe the shower. You know, really catch me off gua— AH!"

I'm flipped on my back, my wrists trapped beneath his right hand as he presses me into the grass. He's straddling my waist and he bends so his nose is touching mine.

He strokes my lip with his thumb before trailing his fingers down my neck and my shoulder, making his way across my collarbone and down the center of my chest.

My sports bra is pressing my breasts up, squeezing them in tight so they look much bigger than usual, and I thank god the padding doesn't reveal my hard nipples. *Fuck.* What is happening to me?

He exhales slowly through his nose, his chin dipped close to his chest so he can watch where his hand roams. He's mapping me out, learning every ridge, every crevice. When he circles the swell of my breasts, I let out a small whimper. His eyes draw back up, and his wicked grin boasts like that of a winner.

"I'll do it."

God, yes, let's do it right now. I lick my lips, my eyes dipping to his soft lips. *Finally.*

He seems to realize what I've inferred and smirks. "I meant, I'll do the videos, dirty girl."

With a press of my wrists, his weight is off me, and my hands are released. He sits back, still straddling me, but now his hungry gaze is back on my chest. I feel him harden, and the bulge in his shorts tells me all I need to know.

"I don't think that's just what you meant."

He looks away, a grin breaking out across his face. He's smiled more in a week than the whole time I've known him. That must mean something, right?

"Not yet, Olivia. Come on. Let's head back and get a solid plan."

"I'm not sure how we're going to get the leader of The Unseen in my very popular, if I do say so myself, videos without being *seen*."

◆ ◆ ◆

"This could work . . ." Austin murmurs before spinning around with a Chewbacca mask on—movie quality, of course.

I tug on the hairy mask. "I'm not sure your skin will thank you for doing a workout in this."

I pull it off his face and throw it onto the couch.

Maybe this is how The Unseen have managed all these years. With multiple different masks from movies. I mean, how did he get these all ready in time if it wasn't for that?

"Okay, what about this one?" He pulls on a thin plastic mask with thick Xs across the eyes, which glow in flickering neon red. The lips appear to be sewn shut. It looks terrifying. My core tightens despite.

"It's a little scary. I'm not sure the viewers will go for it."

"Well, we can try, see how it is, and then review?"

He pulls the mask up so it's resting on his head, his hard jawline and thick stubble replacing the horror of the mask with another unsettling feeling. Which is really the mask? He's different from what I have imagined. He's calm, soft, and caring. He acts like he longs for something he can't have, and deep down, I feel like it could be me. But he's still the monster

I've heard so much about. He murders, steals, and hurts with a level of cruelty I can't possibly imagine.

"Why are you doing this, Austin?" I whisper.

He stares at me for a moment, uncertainty flashing across his eyes. "Surely you know . . ." He drops his chin, his thumb brushing over my cheek. His eyes are burning into mine, imploring me. With just a touch and a look, he commands my entire body, my entire being. I lean in, as if I could even stop myself.

"Say my name again for me," he murmurs, his lips a breath away from mine.

I swallow, my eyes closed, entranced by the smell of him, the taste of his breath, the heat overcoming my body. My other senses have taken over, leaning into the assault his very presence has on them. Like an addict, I crave more, knowing that indulging it may ultimately kill me. I can't seem to care now. Maybe not ever. Not as long as he continues to cradle my face and look at me like he might drag me down to the depths of hell with him.

"Austin . . . I . . ."

"OLIVIAAAA FROM BOLIVIIAAAAA! Where are you?"

My eyes snap open, and I seize Austin's wrist and tug him to the back of the house.

"Where are you?" My brother's voice hollers out of the hallway. I hear him shuffling out of his jacket and slipping his shoes off, no doubt leaving them in the middle of the entryway.

"Olivia from Bolivia?" Austin chuckles as I snap open the basement door and push him toward it. Once again, I feel the warm muscles of his chest pounding as my palm pushes against him, urging him into the basement. Why am I always trying to lock this guy up?

"Shhh . . . get in there, please."

He steps back but his hand stops me from closing the door. In a low growl he whispers, "Keep it open, Killer."

I nod, but push the door so it's open by an inch. His

silhouette haunts the exposed line, and I retreat toward the living room with a finger pressed to my lips. The head of the silhouette moves slightly in confirmation.

"Danny, you could knock, you know."

"Livvy llama, what are you doing?"

"Nothing," I hesitate, hating to lie to my brother. "I've just been working."

"Yeah, you work too much."

"Says you! I've not seen you in weeks."

He shrugs, unperturbed. "You got anything to eat?"

I huff. I'd really rather not do this right now, although it is nice to see him in one piece.

"Come on . . . I know I've been a bad brother. But I've come to make it up to you. I have a good meeting with the boss next week. He wants to run through some of my ideas to make us more modern and really lean into the social media side, like you."

"Really?" I can't help but glance at the basement.

"Yeah, looks like he's coming around to pushing us toward the twenty-first century. The old man even knows how to edit a video now, thanks to me."

He's bragging, but how could he put his business on social media? My mouth parts slightly, my brow furrowing as my brain kicks into overdrive.

"Now I can really use some of my other skills. Maybe I'll even be an influencer like you, Livvy." He winks at me before grabbing an apple and taking a big bite. Juice sprays, and he mumbles through the crunch. "I forgot you never have any fun food here."

"Why the change of pace?" I ask, ignoring his jab.

"No idea. Bossman went away for a week and came back with some fresh ideas, I guess."

He flops down on the couch, stretching out his limbs so they cover three pieces of furniture as opposed to the usual one. I suck in a deep breath and steal another glance at the basement door. I can't see him but I can feel his eyes on me still.

I consider moving out of his field of view, but something holds me in place. I like knowing he's watching me.

"Sounds like things are changing. Maybe that means you'll get a promotion. And a pay rise?" I say a little louder.

"I'm fairly compensated, don't you worry." He laughs while pulling out his phone.

"Maybe some more vacation days then."

"What is wrong with you today? You're being real fucking weird. We've talked about this: I'm not moving jobs; I'm happy where I am."

"Happy or unable to leave?"

"I don't want to leave, so that's a redundant question."

How I wish Austin would make him redundant.

"I just think there are better companies you could be working for," I hiss quietly.

"I didn't come here to get fucking lectured by you, Olivia," he snaps back, rising to his feet.

I hear the basement door creak enough to reveal the fury of Austin's features. He's Mount Vesuvius and my living room is Pompeii. I'm preparing to get covered in hot spitting ash as Danny shucks his head in annoyance. The blood drains from my face, and I feel like everything I've been worried about is going to come true. He's going to hurt me, or Danny, or both of us.

But as soon as his furious gaze moves from the back of Danny's head to mine, his composure changes instantly. His mouth softens, his teeth no longer bared and ready to snap; his brow smooths; he leans back, pulling himself back into the shadows until I can't decipher his features.

"Fuck, that was out of line, Livvy. I'm so sorry." Danny pulls me into a hug, and I start to breathe again.

How can he flip so easily? And I don't mean my brother. He's always quick to anger and quick to apologize. But with Austin, I don't know his moods. I assume he'd be quick to murder, quick to bury the bodies. Not quick to lose all sense of fury with one look from me. It's unsettling to be unaware of how to manage him.

"It's okay. I just worry about you."

"Well. I'm more worried about you right now. I've seen those Millie—*I'm a twat*—Gilbert videos. What the hell is she doing? And with Travis, that fucking weasel."

"I know, I know. I've emailed a lawyer to see if there is anything I can do. Until then, I just need to wait. They're professing their opinions at the moment, so there's not really a lot that can be done, unless I sue them for slander."

"Done. Let's fucking do it."

"With what money, Danny? I make enough to cover the house and put a little aside, but you know Millie has her family money to fall back on."

"Together we can sort something out."

"No . . . I'm going to see what the lawyer says, and then I'll get a plan together."

He pauses for a moment and shuffles back and forth from his heels to his toes. "There is an alternative option."

"And what's that? Use your new muscles to go all gangsta?" I laugh.

Silence envelops the room like an oil spill. It seeps slowly until everything is sticky with it.

"Danny, no. I don't want you getting messed up in that. Not at all. I don't want to hear anything of the sort, okay? Besides, it would only make things worse. I'm sure she'd somehow find out I had something to do with it."

He scoffs and shakes his head, leaning back into the couch.

"What?"

"Livvy," he says, his voice barely above a whisper, "there's a reason why it's called The Unseen."

"Okay . . ."

"Those who see us aren't around long enough to tell the tale." He laughs, throwing his head back. "Just kidding."

I swallow hard and try to avoid glancing over at the basement doorway.

We relax for a while. Danny catches me up with what he's been up to. It's a watered-down version. I give my own PG-13 version of what I've been doing, too. I omit to mention that his boss is in my basement, not locked up this time. Danny doesn't know that I know him. Or at least, I don't think he does.

I never mentioned his visits to Squeeze the Day or the way he watched me. I never considered why before, and I suppose the answer is still unclear.

Eventually, Danny leaves with the promise that he'll be back soon to visit. This means I could see him tomorrow or in a few weeks.

With the click of the front door, the basement door creaks open ominously. Austin heard the way Danny spoke to me earlier. And although my brother was quick to apologize, I still can't seem to recover from the sick feeling Austin's expression left in my gut.

His mask slipped, and for a second, I caught a glimpse of the monster that lies beneath. Like boiling water on a stove on the cusp of bubbling over. The hiss and spit of the steam puffs into the air, a constant reminder that at any moment, the peaceful tranquility could be annihilated in one swift eruption.

He stalks toward me, his face soft and comforting. Is this the face of a man who comforts the loved ones of a man he's just killed? Or is about to kill?

"I've got to take care of a few things. I'll be back, okay?" He drops a kiss on my forehead.

"Wait. How much did you hear when Danny was here?"

"Everything's going to be okay, I promise." He cups my face, his eyes swimming with an explanation I can't decipher. Before I can protest, he lets me go and picks up a set of keys, the door swinging shut behind him.

CHAPTER THIRTEEN

Austin

The wrought iron fence lines the property between red brick pillars. Guarding the top of these pillars are stone lions, their pose hunched as if peering over at those who dare enter. Teeth bared, stance ready to pounce. I press the button on the silver box, which seems out of place with the old-fashioned entrance.

The buzzer clicks off, and an unknown voice answers. I state my name and purpose, and after a brief hesitation, the gates slowly open. The gravel drive is going to destroy my wheel arches, but I need to do this. The obnoxiously long drive is littered with armed guards, all eyeing my car suspiciously. And why wouldn't they? I've only been here a handful of times in the last ten years. It's not like we socialize.

I pull up to the manor house. Corinthian-style columns adorn the front of the house, with two large doors ushering you into the foyer. If you're not born with class, you can just buy it.

I don't expect him to be standing outside the front of the house, but he is. I would have thought he'd have me brought to his office so he could finish some work while I watched and waited. Perhaps if I'd given him fair warning of my arrival he would have thought to do that. Power plays are his strength, but only when he's prepared.

"You're wearing jeans," he remarks with a slight hint of

disgust.

"Hello, brother. What a spectacular observation." I look down at my jeans and mahogany leather boots.

"I haven't seen you in anything but a suit since we were teenagers. It looks . . . odd."

Not sure if that's a compliment or not.

"And you're wearing the Tom Ford. Your best one, in my opinion, Augustus."

He sniffs, tugging at the bottom of the suit, flattening the crease where he's been sitting in it. He eyes me suspiciously, despite my compliment being genuine. We're not often nice to each other, but if we are, it comes at a cost.

"Why are you here?"

"We need to talk."

"Obviously," he sneers.

"Can I come in?" I ask.

He eyes me up and down once more before turning back into the house. He leaves the door open for me, so I presume that's an invitation.

I follow him to the west wing, yes, the *west wing*.

Leading to his office, he heads straight for his liquor cabinet. A crystal decanter houses the warm amber liquid, and he uncharacteristically pours me a glass before taking a seat in his large wingback chair, which reminds me of an overcompensating villain chair. The top almost reaches above his head, and I have a sudden vision of him spinning on it for a big reveal, stroking a cat while he's at it.

The rest of the room is lined with old books and artifacts, some of which I know to be stolen. A particular painting hangs from an old-fashioned frame. I'm sure I read about it in the papers a few weeks ago. Didn't that get stolen from a museum?

"I don't have all day. Let's get down to it."

His face is stony. A surge of annoyance grates at my skin. Danny and Olivia were so happy to see each other. And despite a few choice words that Danny needed to have removed from his vocabulary, they've always seemed to get along. They support each other. They love each other.

"I wanted to let you know Dad has been harassing me to compete with you for the business. I've told him I'm not interested."

He sits for a while, his face white and pale. The guy is lacking vitamin D, that's for sure.

"Why are you telling me this?"

I sigh. "I'm tired of fighting with you. It should have been me and you *against* Dad this whole time, not each other."

He smirks, the curl of lip mocking. "It was hardly a competition. I'm the oldest and it's my right."

I don't want to argue the point. "Agreed. And I want no part of the business. I have my own endeavors that keep me busy. I came to warn you that Dad might try and make it seem otherwise."

He nods, sipping on his whiskey. I do the same, feeling the burn of the amber liquid warm my tongue and throat. We sit in silence for a while. I used to be comfortable with this. Eager to let the other person speak first like it was a competition to see who could hold out the longest. But today I don't have the patience, not when I have Olivia waiting for me.

"Listen, August. I'm sorry for the part I played in our rivalry. Dad set up this competition between us and it was like there was this constant need to earn his affection. He was only happy when we were clawing at each other's throats. Like somehow it would make us tougher. I'm realizing that's not true. We could have worked together, been loyal to each other, not to him."

"A little late for that, don't you think?" he snips.

"Perhaps . . . Perhaps not. That's up to you and me isn't it?"

He grunts, not agreeing but not refusing—a small victory. Olivia may well have turned me into an optimist.

"Do you even want to run the business?" I ask.

"It's not about what I want," he states so matter-offactly, it's as if it's written in stone.

"Why not?"

He stares me down like if he gives me just enough time then the answer will dawn on me. I arch my eyebrow in retaliation, which seems to be enough.

"Who are you, and what have you done with my brother?"

"What do you mean?"

"The jeans, the repentance, the . . ." He swishes his hand in front of him, swirling it around so his signet ring glimmers. "The hippie nonsense you seem to be sprouting."

"I don't think discussing our childhood trauma counts as hippie nonsense, Augustus. But yes, I have relaxed a little in the last year or so. Taking a step away from Dad's business has cleared some things up for me about how I want to live my life."

"How new-age of you. I'll stick to what I know."

"Of course." I drain the rest of my whiskey and slap my hands on my *jean-covered* thighs. "I've said what I wanted to. I'll let you enjoy the rest of your Saturday night."

"Who is she?" he asks, taking another casual sip.

"What?"

"The woman." His grin spreads wide enough that his teeth are bare.

"What woman?"

"Don't play dumb, Austin. Despite Father's insistence on making you into an enforcer, you do have a brain. So tell me, who is she?"

My heartbeat picks up, which I note is rather telling. I don't want Augustus to know anything about Olivia. I don't want him anywhere near her at all. And yet, if I want to rebuild this relationship, I need to learn to trust.

"You don't know her. But she's not like us." Technically, not up until a week ago, anyway.

He nods, and the lines around his eyes lose their sharpness.

"Then you should let her go. This isn't the life for her, Austin."

It might be the kindest advice my brother has ever given me. The only advice, actually. And he's right. This isn't the life for Olivia. But I knew long before I met her that it wasn't the life for me either. I have to prove that I'm out of it. I have to prove that I'm worthy of her. Because she's it for me. And as much as I'm trying to be a good person, that doesn't extend to letting her go.

◆ ◆ ◆

I let myself in. And while it usually brings me great joy to see the shock on someone's face, catching my father with his pants down, dick-deep in some poor, unfortunate soul, has me reevaluating my scare tactics.

His forehead has a vein popping out like a hernia. His head is thrown back as he repeatedly thrusts into the poor girl, who's biting her lip hard enough to bleed. He is slamming into her like a jackhammer.

"Glad to see you can still keep it up at your age, Dad."

"Austin, I'm busy," he puffs out, continuing to thrust.

"Off you go, sweetheart. I'll see you get your tip, pun not intended." I sigh, closing my eyes, but unfortunately, that image is seared into my retinas.

My father eventually relinquishes his grip on her hips and slaps her ass like he's trying to get a horse to start moving. The poor woman scurries out the door, clasping her clothes at her chest.

Unfortunately for me, my father is butt naked as he wipes his brow with the back of his arm and heads straight for the liquor cabinet. How remarkably similar he is to my brother. Or my brother is to him. Unlike Augustus, he doesn't hand me a drink, so I take the initiative to pour myself a glass as my father locates his slacks and pulls them up, covering what little modesty he has.

His office is old money. Deep mahogany wood carvings house first editions, and he has a rifle on the wall that apparently belonged to Teddy Roosevelt. The dark green walls and paneling mirror mine to a point. But if I do say so myself, mine elevate the room; his dark-on-dark furnishing seems to make his office seem cave-like. A dragon hoarding precious possessions and discarding anything he deems invaluable. Like that woman who's just escaped his greasy clutches.

"Here to finally take a seat at the table? I'll make sure it's wiped down before you do." He smirks, his eyes flitting down to where the young woman was pressed down, ass up over his desk.

"I can assure you, the desk would be burned if ever I was to take the helm, Father. But luckily for you *and your desk*, I've come to officially hand in my resignation."

I pause to let him digest that first tidbit.

"No."

Okay, well, let's ignore that.

"I'll be stopping all official duties as your enforcer and cease completing any contracts or otherwise henceforth."

"Hence-fucking-forth? What the fuck have you been reading?" he hisses; a blob of spit hits the desk, inches away from my hand. I have the good sense to pull my drink away from his firing range. I can't help but think of all the fluids he hasn't wiped up.

And if he must know, werewolf smut, where the heroine really does save the day and allows the hero to feel safe enough to be vulnerable. Only with her, though. Only ever with her. Erotic, exciting, and honestly, quite therapeutic. Smut really has it all. Speaking of, I need to get the next book in the series from Olivia when I get home.

"Nothing you'd like, Daddy dearest."

His mustache starts to wiggle on his top lip as he rolls his thin lips together. The bristles rub against the end of his nose. How is he not sneezing all the time?

“The week I gave you before your little vacation to god knows where wasn’t a time for self-reflection. It was a deadline.”

“And here I am, before the weekend is up, letting you know that I’ve made my decision. And my little vacation did me wonders, thanks for asking.”

“Clearly not if you’re throwing everything away.”

“You’re under the impression that this is a negotiation. It’s not. I’m not interested in being your enforcer, your successor, or anything else you may think to offer me. This isn’t about money or titles or what you want me to do. It has to do with what the business does and what you do. I’m not doing it anymore, Dad. I’m done.”

“You’re done when I say you’re fucking done.” He spits again.

Say it, don’t spray it, old man.

I sigh, wishing I could rub my eyes a few times.

“I’ve not really worked for you for a long time, Dad. This isn’t going to be any different from the last two years.”

“Austin, your brother is not up to this and you know it.” His voice tinges with desperation.

“I’ve already spoken to Augustus to let him know I’m out.”

“Oh, and how did he take that?”

“He was rather indifferent, actually.” Not quite a lie. “He was busy with work and didn’t have long to chat, so we kept it short.”

“How wonderful to hear you’re getting along.” His tongue clicks.

“Quite remarkable despite all the effort you put in to make us hate one another.”

He nods, smirking. Man, I wish I could bitch-slap that right off him.

“I tell you what, if you don’t come back, neither of you can work for me.”

What?

He laughs manically. "Oh yes, this is perfect. If you're not there to keep your brother in line, then he's of no use to me. I'll rid myself of him, and he'll only blame you. What a novel idea."

He tips his drink to his lips, his eyes fixed on mine, goading me to make a scene. He's always thought me weak, and in a way, he's right. I worked for him for years, doing unspeakable things, but in the end, my body, my brain, my fucking heart just couldn't do it anymore.

I remain silent, stewing on my next move. Mine and August's relationship has taken one tiny step forward today, and in one conversation with our father, I might as well have not bothered. There is no recovery from this. Because Augustus will see this as my fault.

I move to stand. The conversation is over, and he knows he's won this round.

I reach for the fake diamond door knob and roll my eyes. *Fucking pretentious twat.*

"Oh, Austin?"

I twist back, and he's made his way to the side of the desk once again, pulling down his zipper.

"Send the girl back in."

CHAPTER FOURTEEN

Olivia

The rest of the day, I try to avoid thinking about Austin. It's terrifying how quickly he's taken over my life.

I work on a few things for my channel, re-doing the product review from the week before and editing a few other videos from the "almost done" column on my planning spreadsheet.

However, the evening feels mainly like a distraction. I am tempering my emotions, reminding myself that Austin wouldn't hurt Danny, because hurting Danny would hurt me.

Still, he left without so much as an explanation. Is he going to talk to him? Or is he going somewhere else? He's left me alone on a Saturday night, so presumably, he has plans. Plans he can't tell me about. Although my thoughts run rampant, they don't quite make sense in my mind. It's like I am trying to convince myself that he must be doing something bad. If only so I expect the worst from him. If I do that, then at least I won't be disappointed when this inevitably hits me like a pie to the face. Luca's voice rings in my ears: *What are you doing? Playing with your food?* I need to protect myself at all costs.

I curl up in bed, tucking the blanket right up to my chin. The soft light from the lamp fills the room in a pink hew as I attempt to read. I scan over the same sentence five times until I finally admit defeat.

For the past few days, Austin has been letting himself into my house at night and heading straight to the basement. I've been trying to tempt him to change paths, but it hasn't worked so far. The red light that bathes my bedroom filtered down the stairs, tempting him from the downstairs hallway. I know he's seen it. I checked one evening, and the glow practically lit up the wall against the stairs. But even my suggestive lighting hasn't been enough to encourage him. Am I hoping the books I've lent him will encourage him to make a move? Sure. But the man has the patience of a priest.

Well . . . a good priest.

Finally I hear his car pull up and the jingle of keys at the door. Closing it shut with a gentle click, I can practically feel him pause. There is no shuffling, not a sigh or even a sneeze. Silence descends on the house for a few moments.

I hold my breath, waiting for his next move. The clomping thwack of rubber soles against wooden floorboards thuds up to my room, footsteps as heavy as the frustration building in my stomach. As his steps grow fainter, I realize he's headed toward the back of the house.

I roll into my pillow, exasperation and annoyance hitting me all at once as my veins start to heat. *Fuck him.* He could see my light was on, and he left me when he said we were going to spend the day together. Presumably, that means the night, too.

I pull the covers off me, ready to fly down there and tell him what I really think. As my feet hit the floor, I spin and see him leaning against the doorframe. I inhale sharply and take a step back into my bedside cabinet.

"Fuck, you scared me."

"Hey, Killer." His eyes slip down to my bare thighs.

"How'd you get up here so quietly?"

"I took my shoes off." He shrugs.

"You've done it before?"

"Take my shoes off?" He smirks, tilting his head slightly as he takes in my silky pink pajamas.

"No . . . come up here."

He looks away. "You've seen me sleep, I thought it was only fair I should see you sleeping too."

"Is that your *thing*?"

His smile turns from a small smirk to an all-out grin in half a second. "No Killer. I like my companions awake. Why? Is it yours?"

"You have a lot of companions, do you?" I can't hide the jealousy that laces my words as I avoid his other question. The thought of waking up with his head between my legs has crossed my mind once or twice.

"Not many lately. I've been a little preoccupied, if you haven't noticed."

"So tonight . . ."

"That's what you think?" All playfulness vanishes as hurt takes over.

"I don't know what to think anymore."

He sighs, entering my room for what I assume is the first time but who really knows? He takes a seat on the bed, tugs my hand, and draws me in between his legs. His thumb skates over my knuckles, and I can feel his breath on my chest. His eyes level with my collarbone, and I watch them dip down to the silky fabric covering my breasts.

"Fuck," I hear him whisper before his chin lifts and his deep brown eyes meet mine.

"Are you jealous, Olivia?" he asks softly.

"I was worried." I lift my chin, my jaw jutting out in a hard line. I'm practically pouting. *Of course I'm fucking jealous.*

"What are you worried about?" His thumb brushes over the thin strip of skin exposed between my sleep shorts and my top. His touch burns my skin, and I fight every instinct to step back. My breathing quickens, and my gaze fixes on his lips. God, I want him so bad. My body knows it, my mind knows it. My heart is teetering on the edge, desperately pleading with the rest of me to stand firm.

"A few things," I mutter.

"Yeah?" He drops a kiss on the swell of my breast. "Let me alleviate some of your concerns."

His tongue peeks out as he drops open-mouth kisses through the fabric of my top. My hardened peaks swell as he masterfully sucks, scraping just the right amount of teeth over them. A surge of heat travels fast to my lower belly, like being dragged out to sea by an unforeseen current; I'm swept away almost instantly. My mind quiets for the first time in hours, focusing solely on the feeling he draws out of me. If he dared slip his hands to the inside of my shorts, he'd find me wet and wanting for him.

Another throb hits me as he finally snakes his hand between my legs, pulling me closer to him as his hand spreads over my ass cheeks. I could ride the bulging veins on his forearm if I wanted to. And fuck, do I want to.

He releases my nipple, twisting me slightly so he can tend to the other one. The damp fabric from his spit rubs itself against my overly sensitive buds, causing a delicious roughness.

At last, he talks. "There's no one else, Olivia. There hasn't been for a long time. What's your next concern?"

I whimper as he follows the same tortuous routine with his tongue and teeth on my left nipple, which has always been more sensitive than the right. My head lolls back, and I rest my forearms on his shoulders, my fingers playing with his hair.

"Olivia . . ."

"Hmm?"

Can't think.

Can't breathe.

"What other concerns do you have?"

"I thought you might hurt Danny for what he said to me."

His lips pop from the fabric, his mouth parted and his brows knitted together.

"Don't stop, please," I beg.

He withdraws his hand back between my legs and

gently moves me to the side. Standing and heading toward the door, his head bent low and shaking. He mutters something to himself. My heart hammers in my chest, sinking like an anchor, hitting the seabed with such force that everything living swims as far away as possible.

"Wait, where are you going?" I whine desperately.

"Downstairs. You're not ready. You don't trust me."

"You stormed out after you heard my conversation with Danny. What was I supposed to assume?"

"Did it ever cross your mind that if I wanted to confront Danny, I would have just come out of the basement?"

Well, fuck.

"I . . ."

"So all afternoon, you just thought I was either fucking someone else or hurting your brother?"

"Austin . . ."

"Answer me."

"Y . . . Yes, that's what I thought. At least a small part of me did. But you have to take some responsibility for me jumping to those conclusions."

"You kidnapped me, remember? You brought yourself into this world, and now you act like I'm the one that's tried to harm you. I've never, not once, caused you harm, and yet you fear me so much."

"Because I know what you're capable of," I practically shout.

The remark lands just how it means to. His lips part in disbelief, and he shakes his head again, disappointment rolling off him in waves. His explanation makes sense, but I need to be right more than I need him to point out the flaw in my argument. And now I've hurt him—the big bad wolf, wounded by the puny human.

He tilts his head to the ceiling. Praying to someone, maybe. How to deal with a paranoid girlfr— *companion* who, after having her nippled sucked to the brink of an orgasm, has decided to kill the moment by freaking out.

He steps toward me, and the squeeze in my chest loosens a fraction. Clasping my hands, he brings them to his lips and presses hard against the skin. He's been so angry, so upset, and now he is comforting me. My heart is a yo-yo; the constant rise and fall is making my head spin.

"I like your brother, but I like you more," he says, his voice even and calm.

"Okay?" I say as a small sob slips out.

He brushes the tear that has rolled down my cheek. "Well . . . you love your brother. If I hurt him, I'd hurt you."

"And you don't want to do that?"

He laughs. "Why would I want to hurt you? I've been trying very hard to date you."

I nod slowly, looking down at my toes.

"I . . . I've heard things."

"Hmm." His thumb rubs over my lip. "What have you heard, Killer?"

"You're a bad man."

"Rarely."

"Then how have I heard about it?"

"I make an impact when it counts."

I nod, my shoulders slumping down from exhaustion.

"I'll let you sleep, sweetheart. And I'll give you some space to work through these feelings, okay?" He sounds resigned. Guilt overtakes me. I have done that to him. I've brought up things I have no real knowledge of. Going off rumors and hearsay. I've ruined what could have been us finally spending the night together.

"Wait . . . I don't need space. I'm sorry."

"You do, Olivia. But I'll be watching. And when you're ready, I'll be back."

"Please stay."

"Why would you want that if you think I'm a monster?"

I feel alive with you. I feel safer with you. I feel happier when you're here.

My mouth parts, but I'm not ready to tell him yet. To

accept how quickly these feelings have developed.

"I'll be back when you have an answer for me."

He leaves, this time through the front door. I hear the crunch of tires on the gravel road as I throw myself into the bed and weep as silently as the house I'm left alone in.

◆ ◆ ◆

Austin hasn't lied when he said he would give me space —something I desperately want to avoid. I've looked for him everywhere. He doesn't turn up to Squeeze the Day on Monday or Wednesday. Now, it's Friday, and I'm heading to a fitness expo for the next three days.

He's left his number on a scrap of paper with a note saying "for emergencies." Is telling him I'm sorry an emergency? Or that he's left me so unsatisfied that I've punished myself by not relieving the ache he's built in me the entire week?

As soon as the words came out of my mouth the last time we spoke, the regret hit me as hard as that medicine ball hit my shoulder. I roll it back, reminding myself of the pain.

Despite my willpower, I've left a note for him where he's left his. Informing him I'll be back on Monday and that if he needs me, I assume he'll know where to find me. It's a tease, a challenge of sorts. I have no doubt he knows exactly where I'm going and when. I think he'll expect me to come running back. Part of me wants to. The other part is wanting to give him what he's asked for. He said he could be patient . . . well, so can I.

The time apart has made me realize that I want to see where this goes. I want him here with me.

Scanning my phone for the airport staff, I walk through when the scanner dings.

"Oh, miss." The impeccably dressed air steward turns to me. "I have a new seat for you if you don't mind."

"Oh, okay. Sure." At least she isn't saying there isn't

space on the flight.

"You're in row one." She smiles, her perfect white teeth glistening.

As soon as my butt hits the chair, I know it's going to be a good day. No, *good* doesn't cover it. The day is going to be spectacular.

I have the row to myself, not a soul to either side of me or behind me. Which means no one is behind me to kick my chair. When an opportunist decides to sit in the second row, he is met with a stern-faced air stewardess who informs him that if he does not return to his assigned seat, he will be arrested the moment the tires hit the ground.

I am offered champagne, chocolate-dipped strawberries, and a full meal.

At one point, the co-pilot comes out of the cockpit, takes one look at me and the empty seats, and with a flirty wink, asks, "What did you do?" in a British accent.

The air stewardess with sharp features leans in even closer until he cowers, gives me one final wink, and hops back into the cockpit.

My luggage is first off the carousel, and then I'm greeted by a driver from the convention.

I could get used to this kind of living.

And now, as I walk around the convention center, the bustling fitness community is swarming in. Dance-offs are happening between the chairs. Salsa classes are taking place in one of the connecting rooms. Music is playing, but it seems to alternate between genres with every stall I pass.

I am smiled at as fliers are thrust into my hand. This isn't my first convention, but it is certainly the biggest and the first I've been invited to personally.

I check my calendar. My first stop is a new brand that has reached out to meet.

I head over toward the stall and am greeted by a short brunette with a huge smile. She is so bubbly she is almost jumping.

"Oh. My. Gosh. JOSH, she's here!" she squeals, reaching out to shake my hand as she straightens her spine and pushes her shoulders back, her high ponytail swinging.

A head, which I presume is Josh's, pops around the back of the stall. "Oh lord, brace your ears," he warns.

"Nice to meet you. You must be Nicole?"

"Oh god, you know my name. YOU. KNOW. MY. NAME." She hops as Josh's head disappears around the back of the stall, eyes rolling as he goes.

I decide not to tell her it is on her name tag. "Of course. I'm excited to see what products you have. Truthfully, your brand is the one I'm most excited about seeing this weekend."

It's the truth. They run an eco-friendly clothing company out of Texas that has great reviews so far. It just needs a little more exposure to get their name out there, which is where I come in. It helps that the clothes are gorgeous. As well as your simple basics, they have cowboy-inspired workout gear that works well for anyone with extra flair. The fringe tassels look amazing when you spin around in a dance class.

I play with the tassels on a light yellow top, which I think would go well with my lavender shorts. A small cowboy hat is embroidered over the top left-hand corner.

"Oh, that would be perfect for you. Although, if you don't mind, I have a few options put aside for you that I thought would suit you."

"Absolutely, you're the expert—although I'm definitely going to buy the yellow one."

"Take it! As a token of our appreciation for meeting with us so soon on the weekend."

"She's giving the stock away again," Josh mutters to himself.

Nicole leans in. "Josh doesn't technically work for the brand. He's, err, helping this weekend. He lost a bet with my brother."

"A bet?"

"Yes, my brother was supposed to come with me, but in

poor form after too many beers, he made a bet Josh couldn't refuse."

"Okay, now I'm intrigued."

"Nicole, you're supposed to be introducing her to the brand to develop your business. Not gossiping about your brother and his friend."

"You're my friend too, Joshy," she teases.

His jaw clenches ever so slightly, and I swear I hear him mutter, "Yes, I know we're just friends," before diving into another merch box.

Interesting.

"Well, if you're free tonight, I don't have any plans. The three of us could go for drinks and dinner?" The invitation slips from my lips before I realize what I'm saying.

I haven't been out with friends, albeit new ones, in a long time. My business has been my sole focus—before Austin, at least. But the thought of letting loose with a few new people seems like a great idea as long as I don't do anything to mess up the business prospect.

No tequila. That's for certain.

"I love that idea! But can we do it tomorrow night? We're going to be quite busy tonight with setup, and I think this one"—she throws her thumb back over her shoulder toward Josh—"needs an early night."

I stifle a giggle, and before I move to the next stall, she reaches out to grab my forearm. "Quick, before he sees." She hands me the light yellow tassel top in my size, blocking Josh's view with her body.

She gives me a small wink, and as I turn, Millie Gilbert rounds the corner, arm in arm with my ex. I haven't seen him in months. He stopped coming around once I'd threatened to call the police on him. My first instinct is to run and hide, perhaps behind the stall with Josh—he wouldn't mind, would he?

But I've done nothing wrong; I've only ever worked hard to get where I am. I'm not going to cower like a scared child in the face of two bullies. Besides, they apologized on their video, and despite my suspicion about the increase in trolls, they haven't posted anything since, so maybe this would all be okay.

I only wish this weren't happening right in front of Nicole and the brand that I want to work with.

CHAPTER FIFTEEN

Austin

Chasing Olivia Daniels around the West Coast is the first time I think I might have a problem. Have I been invited to a fitness expo before? No. Have I paid an obscene amount of money to get a last-minute ticket? Yes. I almost tell the event manager that I am here for a woman, but from their shrewd look and rolling eyes, I don't think it would land quite like I want it to. Does it kind of sound like stalking? Yes. But as we know, I'm not completely averse to some light stalking. Besides, watching Olivia sleep is only scratching the surface of my obsession with her.

Thank god Luca is busy, or he'd be up my ass about this. Squeeze the Day is one thing; actually following her around is another. And I've avoided the subject completely with Dr. Alfie. Deciding what he doesn't know can't hurt my impending admittance to the hospital.

I know her schedule, so I head straight to Cowgirl Clothing. An image of Olivia in Daisy Dukes and a shirt undone, teasing me with the curve of her perfect breasts, fills my vision. I rub my eyes. Christ, I'm fucking doomed. For the love of all things holy, don't let her be in those short shorts because I will pick her up like a sack of potatoes, throw her over my shoulder, and growl at anyone who dares try to stop me. But I pause for a moment. I spot her laughing with a small brunette who has leaned in to tell her a secret. Her eyes dart around, she looks happy, in her element. The woman passes her a lemon-colored top with tassels, and she quickly slips it into her bag as the brunette winks. She gives a small wave and turns right into . . . *Oh, shit.*

As I stride over to Olivia, I watch as Millie Gilbert's face softens, looking up at me. She's a tiny, no-more-than-five-foot powerhouse. She's defined, her toned and tanned stomach on display with a pierced belly button. Her neon orange athletic wear is blinding and I can't help but think of a traffic cone.

"Hey, Killer." I drop a kiss on top of Olivia's head as I snake my arm around her waist, pulling her into me.

Her pretty mouth pulls apart as she glances up at me. She fits so perfectly tucked into the crook of my arm.

"You're here," she whispers.

"Thought you could leave without saying goodbye, did you? You're going to pay for that," I whisper so only she can hear. Her breathing hitches, but she pulls herself together to slide her hand over my stomach. I can't help but tense; the thought of her hands slipping lower takes over as my cock wakes up. He's been asleep all week—too sad that I've denied him a night thrusting into Olivia. I can't even get myself off. The poor guy just isn't up for it. Sulking at what could have been, suddenly fucking miserable at the thought of my fist.

Fuck, I've missed her.

I turn back to Millie and the ex in time to see Millie's face sour and Travis turn absolutely feral.

"Friends of yours?" I ask dryly.

"This is Millie Gilbert. She has her own channel, and this is Travis . . ."

"I think you mean I *had* my own fitness channel, Olivia. I was forced to delete it, remember?" Millie interrupts.

I ignore her, turning my attention to Travis. "So you're the guy who thinks he's due royalties from Olivia's channel? The guy that has about eleven subscribers."

Travis's face begins to blow up. His lips twitch open and closed, open and closed like a goldfish swimming in circles. I have nearly a foot of height on him, so if he does anything stupid, I know it'll be easy to flick him away like the annoying gnat he is.

"And you"—I flick my gaze lazily to Millie—"I thought you'd have an epiphany of some sort? Something about reflecting on your past actions. At least that's what your apology video to Olivia suggested."

Millie's shocked face moves between me and Olivia. I can feel her tensing beneath my arm as she grips the back of my shirt. My girl is brave, though. Face forward, she's cool, calm, and collected. Millie watches her movements, and a triumphant sneer flashes across her face.

"Oh, I see . . ." Millie draws out. "You've hired a bodyguard to make yourself look important. Oh, bravo, Olivia. You really know how to work the room."

"Not a bodyguard . . . but we do love a bit of roleplay, so thanks for the tip," I snap back, pulling Olivia a little tighter against me.

Travis has almost turned purple, the poor sausage.

"You okay over there, big man?" I say jovially, insincerity woven between my words. I've been working on being a better person, but I'll make an exception for these two idiots.

"Who exactly are you?" he spits out.

"I'm Austin, Olivia's boyfriend."

"*Boyfriend*?" he splutters. "What happened to you focusing on your career and not having time for a relationship?"

I hesitate a second, allowing Olivia to answer if she wants to. She remains stony-faced, so I jump back in.

"I guess people find the time for the right person. But as I've already said, we really must get going. Lots of people to talk to."

I quickly spin back to the stall, where the brunette is gaping at our interaction. The tall, dark-haired man standing protectively at her side gives me a small nod. I return the gesture, tuck Olivia in closer, and shield her from standing close to them as we walk away. Once we're out of the hearing zone of those two goblins, I pull her between two stalls. "Are you okay?"

Now that Travis and Millie can't see us, I allow myself to take note of her. She's rattled, practically shaking. It's incredible what people have the power to make us feel. My poor Olivia is terrified of them, and no doubt it's not just physically confronting; they threaten her whole business, too.

A small whimper escapes her.

I pull her into my chest. "Not here, Killer. Let's go up to the room, and you can tell me what happened with Tweedle Dumb and Tweedle Dickface. But don't let them see you cry. They don't get to have that."

She pulls back and nods, taking a deep breath.

"Hey man, can I buy one of those?" I ask the stall next to us for one of their bottles of water.

"They're free." The guy says, handing me the bottle.

"You're a champ." I wink at him before handing it to Olivia. "Drink this. I have it on good authority that you can't drink and cry at the same time. Physically impossible."

"What?" she turns, perplexed.

"I stayed with my younger cousins in the summers growing up. The best way to get them to stop crying was to give them a glass of water. Worked every time. Although, it did end up meaning they would all run around with cups of water anytime one of them started crying. Honestly, I slipped on my ass so much that summer."

I peer up to the ceiling, remembering that it was truly one of the best summers of my life.

"We went to stay with my aunt in Austin, Texas. Her kids thought it was the funniest shit ever that my name was Austin."

"Austin in Austin, huh?"

"I know, right? That joke went on for weeks."

She smiles softly. "You're really not what I thought you

would be, you know?"

"You aren't either, Killer." I tuck a stray strand of hair behind her ear. "Now, do you want to go to the room for a moment, or do you want to walk around?"

"I actually have my talk in . . ." She glances at her watch. "One hour. I've got to get ready. Is my makeup okay?"

"You look perfect, Olivia."

She rolls her eyes but smiles. All traces of tears have vanished.

"Umm, quick question: why did you say the bit about roleplay to Millie?"

We jostle through the crowds, heading to the main stage where they're finishing up another talk.

"It's not totally off the mark."

"What do you mean?"

"Abductor and the abducted . . . I mean, usually, it's the other way round in traditional tropes, but I'm glad we gave it a fresh face."

She spins her face to mine like I've gone absolutely bat-shit crazy. Well, that's true, too. *Crazy for you, baby.*

"That was not roleplay . . . I actually kidnapped you."

"Olivia, you might not be ready to hear this, but I could have whipped that little taser off you in point five of a second if I wanted to. I liked you. Thought you were a fucking angel sent down here to punish me for two years. And then when you waltzed up to me all sweetness and light, you had me hooked. When I realized what you were doing, I wanted to know why. So I did what anyone would do."

"You're telling me you actually chloroformed yourself willingly? I thought you were joking when you told me that last week." She arches an eyebrow.

"You were doing so well. And you looked so serious; I didn't want to ruin your flow."

She laughs, slapping my chest playfully. "You're a real asshole, you know that, right? Like an idiot as well. What if I had killed you?"

"An angel of death, huh?" I tap my finger against my lip a couple of times. "Sounds hot. Let's add it to the roleplay bucket list."

"You're incorrigible."

"Ooh yes, Miss Librarian, use those big words for me." I wink, faux fanning myself like a high-society lady in the height of summer.

Crimson flushes over her neck as she shakes her head, fighting a smile that's pulling at her lips.

"Go get ready, Killer. I'll start working on that list. Smash it, okay?"

She heads over to the podium as the other talk finishes up. As the audience gets to their feet, I take the opportunity to get a front-row seat.

◆ ◆ ◆

Olivia shines like nothing I've ever seen during the talk. She's being interviewed by the editor of a well-known fitness magazine, and the questions largely revolve around social media and the use of influencers to promote products.

She is prepared for each question, reflecting on her experience of promoting and reviewing products honestly and authentically. Unfortunately, Millie Gilbert makes an appearance during the question section of the talk, but even then, she is graceful and fair with her answers.

When she asks what Olivia has to say about integrity in her branding and being honest with subscribers, the host holds up her hand, and I kid you not, says, "I think we've heard enough from you. Shall we try someone else?" *Priceless.*

Millie splutters into the microphone. Not only has she been shot down by Olivia, but she's effectively been dismissed by one of the legends of fitness journalism.

The crowd chuckles and Olivia gives me an awkward face. I just wink and love seeing her blush up there, knowing I'm the one affecting her.

"Are you single, Olivia?" someone yells out from the crowd as laughter breaks out from the audience. I jump to my feet, turn, and find the guy in question. His face falls instantly as I point my fingers to my eyes and then point them straight at him. He flinches like he took a bullet, sitting down immediately.

Motherfucker.

"I guess the gentleman in the front row has answered that question." The host laughs.

Olivia hides her face for a moment, smiling, "Don't mind him, that's just my bodyguard."

The crowd rumbles with more laughter.

"You'll pay for that, Killer," I mouth to her. She winks and turns back to the host.

After the talk, she is swarmed. For a moment, I think I might actually have to play bodyguard. But she handles the crowd like a pro, even if she is inching herself closer to me as she does so.

She takes a few selfies with some gym bunnies who claim they've never had such toned legs before doing her workouts. She says it's a real *Legally Blonde* moment, which I pretend not to understand, but *bend and fucking snap* all you like, my love.

I hold the cards and merch she's received as part of her introductions with brands. She has meetings booked in for later in the expo, and some online meetings next week, too. She's even been offered to fly out to Aspen to do a winter clothing line shoot. She almost squeals when we leave the booth.

"You've got to control your face a bit more," she says, taking a swig of water.

"What do you mean?"

"You've got this look on your face that says you're going to pummel anyone that gets too close to me."

"Excellent. That was just the look I was going for." I wink.

"If you're bored, I can give you my room key. I'll be done in an hour."

"I'm not leaving you. Besides, this is fun, seeing you in action."

She looks unsure, but nods anyway.

By the time we finish up, I'm dead on my feet. How she stays so fucking happy all the time, I have no idea. It must be exhausting putting your customer-service face on for ten hours straight. In my job at least, my face could show how I feel —which is mostly indifferent. She has to look happy regardless of what's going on.

Toward the end of the day, she slips her hand into mine. Her shoulders have slipped from their perfect posture and she lets out a large yawn.

"Tired?"

"Exhausted. We have dinner plans tomorrow night with Nicole and Josh from Cowgirl Clothing, the Texas brand, but can we just stay in tonight? I wanna get in bed, put on a movie, and just chill."

"Whatever you want, Killer. Let's get room service."

"Ooh, I've never had room service before! I'm going to go full Kevin McCalister." She laughs, rubbing her hand across her palm like she's throwing money around.

"Anything you want." She could have asked me to take her to dinner in Paris, and I would have said yes.

"We should get you a key to the room from the front desk," she says, pushing me through the hotel lobby.

"I have a room. I asked them to move your things."

"And they did it? Without asking me?" She frowns.

"I can be very persuasive when I want to be." I shuffle from foot to foot. I keep thinking back to Dr. Alfie's advice. Take things slow. Let her adjust. Don't rush her. Could this be too much? I should have asked for permission before moving her things.

We head to the elevator, and I press "PH."

"PH? We're going to the penthouse?" she squeals.

Relief surges through me. She doesn't seem upset; she seems eager and excited. She's practically hopping. I waggle my eyebrows, and as the doors open with a ding, I put my hand on the small of her back, guiding her through the corridor and to the room.

She steps inside, slipping off her shoes. Her toes wiggle slightly before she starts laughing.

"Austin, this is bigger than my house."

Her hand runs along the back of the couch before stepping around the front and flopping onto it.

"Food?"

"God, yes. I'm starving."

"Such a drama queen." I roll my eyes, but I love seeing her like this. So carefree. She seems so much younger like this; she's acting like a twenty-four-year-old, not burdened with the responsibilities of caring for her young brother.

"Says the guy who literally pretended to get kidnapped so he could spend time with me."

Her head pops up over the sofa, cautiously gauging my reaction, but as soon as I grin, she laughs.

"Shall we talk about this week?" I say, lifting her legs so I can sit on the couch with her legs draped over mine.

"I . . . I missed you. I know it's an odd thing to say."

"I've been right downstairs, baby."

She nods. "I know. I saw you've been sleeping in the bed in the basement. I just thought you've changed your mind or something. I thought I'd ruined it."

She looks so innocent like this, tucked into the sofa, holding a throw pillow against her chest like a shield.

"No, I wanted you to have space, to accept the new reality of me being around of my own volition. I wanted you to know that I wasn't going anywhere, that you can trust me to keep to my word."

"I do trust you."

"Olivia . . ."

"I do, I promise. I'm just scared. I've been on my own

for so long. I've been Danny's guardian and doing everything by myself. Even looking out for him. I mean, I kidnapped you. What was I thinking? But I wonder if I'd had someone to confide in, maybe I could have just talked it through rather than doing something so drastic."

"I'm glad it worked out the way it did. It led us right here."

And it's the truth. She's amazing, but she needs time to get used to this dynamic. Distance really does make the heart grow fonder. If I push her, she'll freak out and reactivate the taser. My balls shrivel at the thought.

I rub her foot, and she moans softly.

"So . . . can we go on another date?" she asks.

"Are you asking me out, Killer?" I tease.

"Yeah, I am." Her lips curl up, and laughter lines crinkle around her eyes. She's breathtakingly beautiful, even all squished up on the couch.

"Date two coming up. We'll go out when we get back home."

Home.

"Sure. Do you mind if I shower and you order food?"

"Of course. The room is over there." I point over her head and let go of her foot.

"Oh my god. THIS ROOM!" she squeals at the top of her lungs. They may just be able to hear her down in the lobby.

CHAPTER SIXTEEN

Olivia

The suite is insane. The modern decor is unexpected, given how old the hotel is. But it's light, breezy, almost a beachy vibe with a hint of old-fashioned features like the paneling and the embroidered chaise lounge in the corner of the room.

The whiter-than-white bedding has an outrageous amount of pillows and looks straight out of a magazine. Every surface of the ensuite is covered in marble, with a clawfoot tub on the left by a floor-to-ceiling window overlooking the city. A walk-in shower is surely big enough for two, if not three. The thrum of warmth in my lower belly hits me unexpectedly at the thought of what could happen this weekend.

Tonight has to be the night surely? We've been waiting and waiting, and now that I know we're on the same page, I'm ready for this to go to the next level.

After dinner, I reach my arms over my head in a faux sleepy stretch. There's no way I'm sleeping now. Not when I've been eyeing Austin up and down like he's what I've been ordering for dessert all night.

"Bedtime, Killer."

He walks with me to the room, looking so calm. He hasn't spoken much over dinner; he is probably as tired as I am after a full day of walking and talking.

Although I didn't know he was coming, I've brought my

silky sleep set I know he loves. It makes me feel close to him, and I'm suddenly so grateful I did. I can feel his eyes roaming over my skin as if it were his fingertips.

"Goodnight, Killer," he says in the doorway.

"Wait." I frown. "Where are you sleeping?"

He points down to a closed door.

"On the same floor this time, at least," I mutter, unable to quell the disappointment in my tone.

He steps into the room towards me, and hope blooms like a flower at the first sign of warm weather. Cupping my cheek, he says, "Still not close enough, Olivia." His chin dips until he drops the lightest of kisses on the corner of my mouth. He draws back, and the thought of him leaving me here alone leaves me full of desperation. I'm more desperate than the day I asked him to help me to my car, more desperate than when he chased me through the house when I realized he wasn't chained anymore. I pull him into me, his chest thudding against mine.

"Olivia . . ."

"Austin . . ." I push up on my tiptoes and press my lips to his. They're soft, smooth; he seems to freeze for a split second. The longest split second of my life, and I brace for disappointment. Brace for him to reject me again. But he moves. His fingers intertwine with my loose hair, kneading the back of my neck. In one swoop, his body presses against mine, and he spins me against the wall. He uses his foot to spread my legs, sliding his knee between them. The corded muscle of his thigh pushes against the ache of my center. My silky shorts smoothing his rough touch, I can feel them growing damp between my thighs.

It's like a switch has flipped. He finally has not only my permission, but my participation. I'm not waiting for him any longer. If I thought about it too much, this crazy situation we're in, I might back out. I might talk myself out of it. But there's no time to think. His lips are demanding, his tongue daring to taste the entrance of my mouth. I'm clinging to his shoulders, desperate to ground myself in the moment. Each time I feel like I've got my footing, he shifts again, tasting and touching from a new angle. The constant uncertainty leaves me breathless, unable to keep my balance.

His large palm hooks under my thigh, and he wraps my leg around him. And that's when I feel it. The tight fabric of his jeans can't keep him contained. He thrusts against me, and the length of him grinds between my legs. Pleasure thrills through me until I feel it zip around my shoulders and down my arms, goosebumps raising the hairs along my skin. The earthy scent of him fills my nostrils, engulfing my senses. There's nothing else to think about. Nothing but pure need binding us together. Was this inevitable? It's been two years since he came into Squeeze the Day, two years of scowling and hatred. Now within two weeks, he's turned my world upside down. What would Danny think of us? What would my parents think if they were alive? Do I even care at this moment? I haven't taken a risk since my parents died. I've been the dutiful daughter and sister, taking care of Danny. When others were partying, I was studying, building my business. I've done nothing selfish in a long time, and I need this. I need him. His dizzying obsession fuels a longing in me to be wanted, *to be loved.*

I'm drunk on his kisses, drunk on the feeling of his fingers digging into my flesh as he grinds against me. His whimpering moans roll from his throat in soft, needy growls. My body follows suit, gasping as he gyrates his hips against me again and again. Suddenly, I'm all too aware of the surge of wetness leaking between my thighs. His lips leave mine for a second, and he opens his eyes, his forehead resting against mine. A thumb grazes against my nipple; he remembers how sensitive they are as I arch and moan. He smiles wickedly before pressing his lips back against mine, his tongue licking and nipping at my mouth. He moves deftly, smoothing his other palm around my back and down to my ass, and in one thrust, he has my feet off the ground and wrapped around his waist.

"Austin," I breathe, "I've wanted this for so long."

"What did you want, Killer?" he whispers.

"You . . . this . . . from that first day. I . . . can't explain it. You've done something to me. It wasn't supposed to be like this." Was I really doing this? With a man that I know is dangerous?

"What was it supposed to be?"

"I was supposed to be in control."

"Is that really what you want? To be in control? Doesn't being out of control feel good?" He bites down my neck, and my skin lights up in uncontrolled goosebumps.

I want to lie. I want to tell him that I love being in control. I love the power it gives me to have everything in order, to be in charge. But the toll it takes has been catching up with me. The stress of managing my life, Danny's life, his supposed criminal boss. It's like I've snapped and now I'm running into dangerous territory. Territory that led me to chase a high I've only ever felt one time, when I stole him and chained him in my basement. Maybe it's recklessness? The utter stupidity of being in my early twenties with nothing to lose. Except my life, my heart, my willpower.

"I want to be out of control," I whisper.

He hums, his lips trailing down the column of my throat.

"You can let go with me, Olivia. I'm going to take care of you. Of everything… you just have to let me in."

He pauses; his head tilts back so he can look at me. I'm starting to understand. His intensity. His fascination. It's been longer for him, maybe since before the abduction. I can't believe it took me so long to realize. I have so many questions. Why hasn't he spoken to me before? Why has he left it up to me to do something so drastic before even talking to me?

He owes me answers, but the feel of his lips against my neck washes away all thoughts of the mystery he presents. As the heat in my belly reaches a precipice, he gently drops me back down on the floor with the utmost care. He steps back, running a hand over his mouth and stubble. He stares so intently. He's wavering; he might leave and I don't think I could bear it.

"I shou—"

He stops mid-sentence as I pull my tank top up over my head in one fell swoop. There's no tease, no timid display of embarrassment. I'm done fighting this. Hell, I'm fighting *for* it from now on. I want this. I want him. Regardless of how we got here. Regardless of the fact that I think he might be the head of a criminal organization, my gut tells me he won't hurt me. He'll protect Danny. He'll take care of us.

He hisses, turning his head away but snapping his eyes back, like his body knows he shouldn't, but he just can't stop himself.

I pull my shorts down next. I'm not wearing any panties, so when the silk fabric hits the floor, I'm bare.

I step toward him. "Take control, Austin. I want you to take control."

"Fuck, you're more than I ever imagined." His head shakes as his eyes dart around, jumping back and forth between different parts of me. I'm not sure he even meant to say that out loud. Just the thought of him out of control sets my lungs on fire.

"You imagined this?"

His head tilts, and his eyes sharpen as if to ask how I could be so dumb.

"No, Olivia. I've *fantasized* over this. I've *obsessed* over this. I've had this exact moment running through my head for so long, my dick is practically weeping with joy that it's finally going to feel that tight pussy and not just my fist."

I huff out a slow breath, running my fingers down his chest, exploring each muscle as I dip to his waist.

"Let's live out the fantasy." My voice is steady. I leave all doubt and nerves out of my voice. I give him nothing to use to back out. I know he wants this, but he has to make the move. And if he decides he can't, for whatever reason, I'll know. I'll end this infatuation now.

But he doesn't. He takes me in, and his eyes darken like a switch has flipped. This is the man I've known him to be all along. So in control. So dominating.

"Get on the bed, Olivia."

I do as he says, but take my time. I crawl up the middle of the king-size mattress, my knees sinking into the soft bedding.

He hisses again, and I can feel the burn of his gaze over my body.

I peek over my shoulder to watch him bite his fist. I want him to take control of me, but in doing so, he looks on edge. Hungry. Ready to pounce. I turn around, leaning back against the plump, soft pillows. My nipples are hard, my sex aching. I wait for his instructions as a flutter of nerves swoop through my stomach.

"Spread," he demands.

My legs fall apart almost instantly. His tone, his voice, he even looks different. He's still Austin, my Austin, but it's like he's been holding back. Allowing me to think I've been in control this whole time when really he's been the one pulling the strings.

His eyes drop down to my pussy, and he licks his lips. Like a hunter stalking his prey, he circles the bed, eyes roaming my body like he doesn't know where to start.

I'm throbbing, my pussy weeping with desire but he's taking too long. I pinch my nipples, then let one hand inch down my stomach until I reach my center. There's no resistance as I push two fingers inside myself. Pulling them back out, I circle my clit a few times and then draw my fingers up to my mouth. All color has left his eyes, his pupils as wide and dark as humanly possible. His chin dips, and he swallows hard like his mouth has been watering just at the sight of me. He's stopped moving now, his focus solely on my fingers.

I slip them between my lips and let my tongue roll between them, catching every last drop of my arousal. I moan; the tangy taste is unexpectedly sweet.

Austin pounces, *finally*. His head is in between my thighs, his tongue swiping instantly in one swoop from ass to clit. I cry out, my back arching, thighs spasming. I instinctively dig my heels in, pushing back from the overwhelming pleasure he's giving me, but his arms loop under my legs, and he pulls me back to his mouth by my hips.

"You're fucking delicious, baby. No wonder you couldn't resist tasting yourself," he says before lapping his tongue against me. With one hand, he pushes two thick fingers between my lips and curls them, hitting the rough-textured spot inside me perfectly.

He's relentless, unforgiving, and the second he hums against my clit, sucking it in with the slightest hint of teeth, I'm done for. I rock my hips against his face, my fingers at the back of his head, smothering him with my pussy. If he can't breathe, he doesn't let it show. He picks up the pace, rocking in tandem with the ebb and flow of my hips.

"Fuck, fuck, fuck!" I cry out, reaching for the headboard, trying to ground myself. The head of The Unseen is between my legs. *The man I kidnapped and chained to my basement is in between my legs.* He's lapping me up like I'm his last meal. Like it's his life's purpose to be here right now in this moment with me. And he's not even undressed. It's unseemly. My nakedness spread bare for him as he gives me so little of himself.

The waves of pleasure roll through me like waves against a shore. Crashing over and over until my legs are shaking, and each flick of his tongue shoots spams through my muscles. His lips lift from me as he carefully draws his fingers out, a rakish grin transforming his face as he slips his fingers between his lips and sucks them clean.

"You're the sexiest woman I've ever met."

"I'm hot, sweaty, fucking shaking, Austin. That was . . ."

"Amazing? Incredible? The hottest thing I've ever done? Yeah, all of the above." He grins, sneaking one more lick against my clit.

"Did I hurt you?"

"When you were fucking my face?"

"Oh god." I cover my eyes with my forearm. I feel the bed shift under his weight on top of me.

"Don't hide from me. That was the hottest thing that's ever happened to me. You used my mouth like your personal grinding pad. Fuck, it was sexy."

"Oh my god, you have the filthiest mouth!" I squeal as he kisses under my breast.

"I've been taking notes from all those dirty books you read," he murmurs, swiping his tongue along the fullness of my breast until he takes my nipple into his mouth, sucking hard.

"I can't fucking wait to feel you riding me, using those hips like that. Are you gonna show me how, Killer?"

"I need a second. My legs haven't recovered."

"In that case, let me help you."

He slips off his pants and then his boxers, the hard length of him springing free. I watch the head bob, his hand gripping the base of his thick, veiny cock. He crawls over the mattress, pushing my knees up into my chest and inspecting me. I feel my blood pumping furiously, spreading up my neck. He lines the head of his cock against my pussy, teasing my clit as he rubs it up and down.

"These fucking tits, Olivia. You've been teasing me with those crop tops for two fucking years. I'm gonna fuck these tits, baby. Not right now. Right now I need your tight pussy clenching me, but one day soon, I'm gonna fuck these tits, rub my come all over them so you know who you fucking belong to."

I tilt my hips up and he almost slips inside me. The grip he has on his cock tells me he's holding back. Maybe he's taking his time or maybe he's punishing me. I can't tell, I can barely think right now.

"Please . . ." A breathy moan escapes me.

"Fuck, I need to be inside you."

Stroking his cock, once, twice, three times. My mouth

waters watching him.

"Austin," I whine, hating myself for begging.

Is this what I've become? I used to have all the control; I had him tied up and wanting. Now he has me pinned beneath him, begging like a sex-starved maniac. He seems to like that, though, and he rewards my begging like he's been waiting for it. Pushing the tip of his cock through my folds, pushing deeper until my walls squeeze tightly, engulfing his length.

"Fuck baby, you're so fucking tight. Your pussy, it's sucking me in. You've been dreaming of this, haven't you? Tell me you have, Olivia."

"Yes, yes, I've been dreaming of this."

"Thoughts of my cock pushing into you keep you up all night, baby. You've been such a patient fucking girl for me, haven't you? Waiting for two long years until you couldn't wait any longer, isn't that right?"

"Mmhmm."

He pushes himself all the way in, his head rubbing against my G-spot as he pulls back out.

"So you took what you wanted, didn't you, Killer?"

He pushes in again agonizingly slow. He huffs a breath from his nose, mediating his breathing, but the grip of his fingers against my thighs tells me he's very much a man who is on the edge of losing himself.

"You took *me*."

Thrust.

"You wanted *me*."

Thrust.

"You wanted *this*."

Thrust.

"Begging me for it."

Thrust.

He pushes his palm flat on my lower stomach, somehow building the pressure tenfold as his pace quickens. His words speak directly to my pussy as it drenches him with its own praise.

"You're mine, Olivia. *Fucking mine*. You took me, and now I belong to you. You have me whenever you want me."

"Austin, please . . . I'm so close. I'm begging you."

"Beg, baby, beg me to let you come."

And I know he won't let me until I do. The pressure building brings me so close. His filthy words act as their own extension of his cock, rubbing every pleasure spot I have until I'm at the point of no return. The slap of our skin mixes with my moans. He grunts as his cock swells, pushing against my walls, demanding more room. I clench around him and he hisses, slowing himself.

Now I know what he likes.

"How are those legs, baby? Ready for a ride?"

"Yes, please let me."

He leans down, snakes one arm around my back, then flips me so he's underneath, all without pulling out. I slam down hard, and I swear the tip of his cock hits my cervix, causing me to cry out. His hands are straight back on my hips, and I'm learning that it's his favorite part of me. He controls the rhythm until I grip his fingers off me.

"I set the pace, cowboy," I whisper in his ear as I roll my hips over his cock.

I place his hands on my breasts, and he takes no time before pinching my already hard nipples before lifting himself up and rolling his warm, wet tongue around my hardened bud.

Bracing myself on the headboard as I roll myself over and over his thick length, bringing myself to the edge of insanity.

"Use me, Olivia. Use my cock. Take what's yours."

"I'm gonna come, Austin. I need to come *now*."

"Beg me, baby."

"Please, Austin, I'll do anything. Just let me come."

The pressure is at its peak—a few more rolls, and I'll be done for.

He pinches my left nipple hard as his teeth graze over the right. "That's it, Killer. Milk my cock and take what's yours.

Claim me. Come for me now."

I dig my nails into his chest, leaning my head back as far as I can, desperate to spread the pleasure throughout my body. Then it hits: the stark warnings have been there all along, but there's no way I could prepare for the realities of the pleasure hitting me.

"Yes, Austin. Austin, please don't stop, please . . ."

"Fuck, Olivia." He thrusts into me as I cry out, the waves of my orgasm flooding through my body. My pussy squeezes him, eagerly gripping his hungry cock.

I lift and slam back down, over and over and over. I'm leaning right over him, my weight on his chest. I lift my hips, letting my pussy slide up his length, before pushing back down.

"Yes. Yes, that's it. Keep lifting like that. Quicker baby, quicker for me." He's begging too.

I lift, slide, and slam repeatedly. His hands have moved back to my hips, assisting with the continuous flow of movement. He's practically using me like a toy to thrust into, and the thought makes me giddy. The head of The Unseen is using *me* to pleasure himself.

The slide of the head of his cock is hitting against my textured spot inside, and it's building yet another ball of warmth inside me.

"I'm close, baby, I'm so fucking close. Keep fucking going, just like that." He's practically whimpering.

"Austin, I'm gonna . . . I think I'm gonna . . ."

"Yes. Come. Come right now, baby, come for me."

My second orgasm thunders through me, my hips thrust desperately, eager to please him. Suddenly, he's roaring in my ear, his head thrown back into the silky pillow as his hips continue to twitch up into me. I'm damp and sticky and feeling so goddamn full. I slow the roll of my hips, a wonderful ache warming me. I don't want to climb off him yet, so I fold down onto his chest. Squeezing him one final time.

We lie there, allowing our lungs to catch up with

what's just happened. I've never, I mean never, had sex like that before. The dirty talk, the control he has over me, is all-encompassing.

"Olivia."

"Yes?"

"What the fuck was that?"

I giggle, lifting my head from his chest. "What do you mean?" I ask innocently.

"You're a witch. It's the only explanation," he mutters. "That's why I let you kidnap me. I'm powerless against you."

He presses between my ribs, and I squirm, my muscles tightening.

We both still.

"Killer?"

"Yes?"

"Did you just—"

"Please don't say it!" I squeal, burying my head into his chest. The tickling makes me squeeze my muscles, including my Kegels. I feel the aftermath of his arousal squeezing out of me and down his dick.

"God, you're fucking sexy." He kisses me hard, cradling my face with one hand before squeezing my ribs again.

I jump as fast as a deer running across the road, and I think I sound like one, too. I pull myself off him and roll to the side. He groans as I squeeze, the mess slipping down my thighs.

"Bad girl. I was enjoying that." He kisses the end of my nose. "Let me get you cleaned up. Two seconds."

"It's okay. I should pee anyway."

"Come on then," he says, holding out his hand.

I slip out of the bed, feeling shy all of a sudden. The man's just given me multiple orgasms, like *multiple.* I begged him to let me come. And now I'm feeling shy? His come is literally making its way down my leg.

I go about my business, and he uses the sink to wash his face. I smirk, knowing full well why it needs washing. He tuts at me, shaking his head, murmuring under his breath something that closely resembles "bad girl."

"Bath?" he asks.

"Maybe tomorrow. I'm pretty exhausted."

I wash my hands, and once dried, he picks me up bridal-style and carries me back to the bed.

"Will you stay with me?" I ask as he pulls the cover over my still-naked body.

He moves confidently to his side of the bed and slips under the covers.

"Olivia. I've been waiting for you to catch up. If you want me here, I'm here. If you need me to give you space, I will . . . reluctantly." He's teasing, I know. If I asked him to leave I know he would, but I can't think of anything I want less right now.

"I want you to stay."

"Good."

He pulls me into his side, and I place my hand on his chest and leg over his thigh. He sighs slowly, and when I sneak a peek, his eyes are closed, but he's smiling. He looks so peaceful. Suddenly, I'm no longer tired.

"Will you tell me something?" I ask.

"What do you want to know?"

"Tell me about your family."

CHAPTER SEVENTEEN

Austin

"Tell me about your family."

Such an innocent request. How could she know it's so loaded?

Her sweet eyes peering up from my chest, the warmth of her body is transferring to mine, like our bodies are molding together. If we stay here long enough, we'll become one big fused blob, and nothing would make me happier. I feel . . . cozy, calm, fucking *peaceful.* Sure, it might be because I've just had the best sex of my life with the girl I've been fantasizing about for two years, but in my heart, I know it's more than that. She's more than that. It's how I knew, when she told me to chloroform myself, that this was going to work out okay. It's how I knew that if I just gave her a little space and continued showing up, she'd see it, too. I trail my fingertips up and down her shoulder, leaving a trail of goosebumps in their wake. She's quiet, waiting for me to answer, and I fight the urge to fidget uncomfortably.

"I'm not sure you want to hear about my fucked-up family, Killer." I feel her cheek pull against my chest, and she nuzzles in, inhaling deeply.

"I really do, actually."

Fuck.

I can't say no, but god, I don't want to scare her off. She knows a little, but there's no way she knows everything.

"I have a brother," I eventually admit.

"I knew that. He's older, right?"

"Yep." I let the "p" pop.

"Do you get along well?"

"You know the answer to that already, Killer."

I feel her cheek pull again, her fingers dance across my chest, and I feel the tightness loosen. *Here goes nothing.*

"We were pitted against each other. Our dad thought it would make us tougher. Really, it just made us suspicious of each other. I didn't realize how abnormal that was until I saw you and Danny together."

"Not all siblings get along, Austin. It's okay. I know people who hate their brothers."

I nod, continuing to stroke her, and my shoulders melt into the mattress a little more. Maybe this bed can mold to us too. Not that long ago, I thought the basement mattress was comfortable, but it'll never top this. Having Olivia in my arms after fucking each other senseless. You can't buy that level of comfort.

I want to tell her more. But I'm not sure she can handle it.

"What about your father? He's the boss, right?"

Usually, when a woman asks about my father, my spidey senses are on high alert. There's nothing more suspicious than someone sleeping with me and then asking questions about The Organization. But with Olivia, I know she's just trying to understand me.

"He's a bad man, baby." I kiss the top of her head, inhaling the scent of her shampoo. "Let's not talk about him here."

"You can talk to me, though. Outside of this little cocoon." She lifts her chin, her face neutral.

I feel my dick twitch. *Fuck, I'm ready to go again.* The curve of her hip is accentuated by her leg draping over my thigh. Her waist dips low, and I trail my eyes along the ridge of her side before taking in her luscious round tits. If there is a god, they should have just stopped with her. She's perfect.

Her eyebrow arches. I smirk, taking in all her glory. Her lips part as she goes to speak, but I flip her over, pushing her shoulder into the mattress. A half-moan, half-yelp releases from her lips.

"Are you trying to find out all my secrets, Killer?" I let my voice drop an octave.

She bites her lip for me. "You know all of mine. It seems only fair," she whispers.

I push my hard cock against her as she widens her legs for me. "Not yet, but I will.

◆ ◆ ◆

Olivia gets out of bed at the ass crack of dawn. She is already showered, buffed, and polished, all before I roll out of bed. My lazy days in the basement seem to have gotten me out of my rigid routines.

Her lilac gym gear is her outfit choice for the day as she does a little morning yoga, treating me to a view of her perfect ass.

"You could join me, you know," she huffs, lifting her arm straight as she twists, face tilted toward the ceiling's panel moldings.

"I'm good here, baby . . . so good."

She glances over to see me leaning on my elbow, watching her like my own personalized show. I give her a small wink, and she laughs, losing her balance.

"So tonight, we're meeting with Nicole, right?" I ask, knowing full well that's the case. I've had Luca run a background check on her, the guy working at her stall, and her company. They are all legit, seemingly charming people. My instincts were right the first time I saw how protectively the guy, Josh, stood by the pint-sized Nicole.

"Yeah, she owns the brand I'm most looking forward to

working with. Her outfits are kind of country chic. There are tassels and sparkles, which makes it fun to work out in. I'm excited to get to know her a little better. Although I'm not sure Josh is coming. I'll text her to ask."

My guess is Josh isn't going to let Nicole out of his sight, but that's just one man's opinion.

The evening rolls around quicker than I expect. Olivia has another long day of meeting brands and giving talks as well as attending a few lectures on social media trends and business planning.

She returns to the hotel around four-thirty. Our dinner reservation is for eight, so we have a little time. But as much as I want to pounce her the second she's back, I have plans.

The massage tables are set up in the living room—two, one for each of us. I have no doubt that Olivia's version of self-care is actually after-care. She's been busy taking care of Danny for so long now. With her parents gone, who's been looking after her? She is so strong and independent—someone who works fucking hard to get shit done. But she's mine to take care of now. What's the point in having money if you can't spend it where it counts?

A snick of the door follows the buzz of the keycard. The soft spa music is playing over the low lights, ready for her to relax as soon as she steps in.

"Austin?"

"Hey, Killer."

I step up, taking her bag and phone, placing them on the side table before taking her by the hand. I lead her into the living area, where Janie and Chris are waiting patiently.

"What's this?"

"You've been working so hard. I thought we could have a little downtime before heading out tonight. What do you think?"

She turns to face Janie and Chris before leaning into me. "Do I get the big burly man?"

I practically growl into her ear. "The only burly man

touching you is me. Unless you want Janie's hands all over me?"

She frowns, assessing Janie for a second before shaking her head.

"I didn't think so. Now, head into the bedroom and get your robe on, woman. For god's sake, don't let me see you undressing or the two best massage therapists in L.A. will have been hired for no goddamn reason."

She giggles, skipping into the bedroom. She sticks her tongue out at me over her shoulder before clicking the door shut. A part of me is disappointed, but the other half is fucking grateful. We're on a tight schedule as it is, and I want this to be perfect for her.

◆ ◆ ◆

Fuck. Me.

Chris is kneading my muscles like I'm a lump of dough. My muscles are no match for his weapons of choice. His forearms slide over my skin. His thumbs find every lump and bump in my knotted muscles. I don't realize how tense I am until this man puts his hands on me.

I glance over at Olivia a few times, and Janie is giving her something much more in line with what I thought I'd get: therapeutic, relaxing, fucking calm. But no, Chris is taking the "let's beat the soreness out of him" approach. It doesn't help that Olivia's soft moans are all I can hear until I cry out, and she starts to giggle.

"Too much, sir?"

"No, no, perfect Chris. Just what I need."

Don't want to anger him more.

Olivia opens up one eye. She's obviously noticed my pained expression as she tries to hold in more giggles.

God, she's cute. I'd let Chris blend me into a smoothie every day if it kept her laughing.

After they leave, I pop open a bottle of champagne. Olivia starts getting ready as I hand her a glass.

"You know I could get used to this," she murmurs softly, expertly lining her eyes kohl black. Her lips part every time: the eye shadow, the eyeliner, the mascara. And I'm not talking *softly* parted; her mouth is gaping open.

"What the fuck is going on with your face right now?"

"Don't make me laugh, you brute. You'll ruin my makeup." She chuckles, trying to keep her mouth closed at the end.

"Okay, okay, I'll leave you be. But we need to leave soon."

"No worries. I'm basically done."

"Okay, I'll call the car now. I'm guessing I need to be on my best behavior tonight?" I smirk.

She gives me a pointed look. "Yes, no mention of how we met."

"We met in a juice bar," I say, deadpan.

"Okay, no mention of the whole kidnapping thing."

"Why would I want anyone to know you Ted Bundy'd me?"

"Ted Bundy'd you?"

"Yeah, you lured me to your car under false pretenses. I'm just glad you so politely asked me to chloroform myself and didn't hit me around the head with a baseball bat. I've never seen you swing, but you're strong as fuck; I wouldn't rate my chances."

She smiles, gazing up at the ceiling for a split second. And this. This is why I like her so fucking much. Because I'm telling her I have no doubt she could beat the shit out of me, and she looks so fucking pleased about it.

"No mention of Ted Bundy, please," she eventually says, throwing her phone and lipstick into an obscenely tiny handbag.

I salute. "Scout's honor."

"You weren't a Boy Scout." She eyes me suspiciously.

I smile. Of course I wasn't a Boy Scout. Had there been

a henchman boys club, my father would have sent me there. Unfortunately, that sounds a little too Hitler Youth, even for my dad's monstrous tastes.

"No, I wasn't. But I think I got my rope-tying badge if you're interested later," I murmur, stepping closer so my chest is at her back. I look up in the mirror, placing my hands on her hips. We look fucking good.

"Hmm." She turns to face me, smoothing her hands down my chest. "Here I thought I was the one who liked tying people up."

"I think you'd love to be on the receiving end. Give up some more of that control, Killer."

"But you know I like it." She pouts, and my lips pull to the side.

"I know a lot about what you like, Olivia. But I'm sure we can find out a few new things together." She inhales deeply, her eyes darkening beneath her hooded gaze.

"If I were a betting man, I'd say your panties are getting damp, Killer." I lift her chin with my finger as she swallows hard before parting her lips. "No time for that, baby. We've got plans."

"You would be wrong," she replies breathily.

"Really?" I arch an eyebrow. *Surely she feels this, too?*

"Yeah, but that's only because I'm not wearing any panties."

Fuck. She's living up to her nickname a little too well. My dick is gonna fucking burst. She's right about control; I've got zero of it. She's got me by the balls.

Olivia winks before slipping on her stilettos and flicking her blonde waves over her shoulder.

I adjust my pants, take a deep breath, and hope these are the most boring people on the planet so we duck out early and I can fuck her into the headboard for the rest of the night.

◆ ◆ ◆

The girls are downing margaritas like there's been a shortage and they suddenly have access to an open bar. Which I guess they do, since I've left my Amex with the bar staff under the strict instruction that no one else in my party picks up a check.

Olivia and Nicole are getting along like a house on fire, and despite Josh's initial apprehension, he seems like an okay guy, albeit a little obsessed with Nicole. But hey, can't blame a guy for that. I'm certainly not in a position to.

"So, you don't work together normally?" Olivia asks.

"Nope. Poor Josh here lost a bet with my brother and ended up taking his place helping this weekend."

Olivia laughs. "Sounds like something my brother would do. What was the bet?"

"It was a shuffleboard game. Don't ask. They're obsessed."

Josh rolls his eyes. "We are not *obsessed*, Nicolette."

He takes a sip from his bottle, and she looks at him all doe-eyed. He shifts uncomfortably and starts peeling the label of the bottle.

"Isn't that game for old people?" I ask, teasing.

His head snaps up, and I instantly hold my hands up in surrender. "Just kidding, man."

Everyone laughs, and Olivia places her hand on my thigh, giving me a light squeeze.

"It is weird, though, because Josh is the best shuffleboard player in Austin. He's won a load of competitions," she boasts.

"They're just bar games," he dismisses her with a swish of his hand.

"Not that one up in East Creek. You won like one thousand dollars that night."

"You remember that?" he turns to her, smiling.

"Who wouldn't remember winning one thousand dollars? It was so much fun. That night, I lost a bet and had to run around the pool table in only my bra and panties."

Olivia laughs. "We need to stay in touch. If I'm ever in Austin, I'm gonna hit you up for a good time."

"The whole bar saw her in her underwear," Josh says, throwing his hands up.

"I got so many drinks bought for me. It was the best night." Nicole smiles.

Taylor Swift starts to play, and Nicole squeals. "Come on, let's dance." She grabs Olivia's hand and drags her from the booth.

The locals make room for them on the dancefloor, stepping out of their way as they bend and snap or whatever else they're doing. All I know is Olivia looks like she's having the time of her life. She's relaxed, happy, and carefree as they take turns twirling each other around. I hope I've played a small part in making that happen.

I turn to Josh, who is staring just as intently at Nicole.

"So, how long has this been going on?" I ask him, pointing my finger between him and Nicole's chair.

"We're not—"

"Hey man, we're probably never going to see each other again. Lay it on me," I say, taking another swig of beer. Dr. Alfie would be proud. Making friends and offering to be a listening ear. Call me a regular human being.

"She's my best friend's little sister."

I nod. As if that fucking explains anything.

"She doesn't look so little to me," I say finally as he raises an eyebrow. "Okay, yeah, she is short, but you know what I mean. She's a grown woman."

"She's off-limits. Besides, I'm not interested in her."

"Sure, man, that's why you can't take your eyes off her and saw red the second she mentioned running around a pool table in her bra and panties."

He laughs, shaking his head before sighing. "Fuck, she's a fucking wild child. Just does whatever pops into her head. She lives in the moment, and that's not something I can do."

We turn back toward the girls—and *fuck*. Nicole is dragging Olivia to the pool table.

They shake hands with two guys and begin a game of doubles. My heart skips a beat for a second as I wonder what the bet is.

"Fuck me, she's gonna have her tits out in ten minutes, and her brother's going to kill me."

I look over to Olivia and realize she must have made the bet, too. And I suddenly remember she's not wearing any panties.

◆ ◆ ◆

"Austin, it's Saturday night. You know that's my off-limits time." The harsh drawl hisses into the phone.

"I know, Alfie, but it's an emergency." I look back through the window, and I can make out Olivia laughing with Nicole as she covers her ass when she bends to take her shot at the pool table. Thankfully, they seem to be taking care of each other despite the taller of the guys leering at them like they're his next meal.

"Are you in danger?" Alfie's voice has returned to his professional self, and I almost feel bad.

"Well . . . no. I'm at a bar with Olivia. And she's gone to play pool with some other guys."

"For the love of—"

He sighs heavily into the phone, and I roll my eyes. For a medical professional, Dr. Alfie Adams is kind of theatrical.

"Is she not allowed to play pool with other people?"

"She is . . . I just don't want to do anything I'll regret if one of them gets handsy," I admit.

"Then don't."

He doesn't elaborate, and the line is silent for a few seconds.

"What do you mean?"

I shuffle along the sidewalk out of the way of patrons entering the front door. I can still see them through the window, but I know Josh is making sure they're safe while I'm out here. Had he not been there, I never would have left the room. I know bad men. I used to be a bad man. Now that I have her, I have an awful feeling that I have something monumental to lose. I've never felt more vulnerable in my life. It'll either be someone taking her away from me or something I do that will make me lose her. That's why I needed to call Alfie.

"If you don't want to act a certain way, then don't. We've talked about her seeing you as a partner. What kind of partner do you want to be? What kind of partner does she want? You don't need to answer me now. But think about it and act accordingly."

"Right . . . and if something goes wrong?"

"You can't prepare for every eventuality, Austin, but you can be true to the person you're trying to become. Let your long-term needs guide you."

"Thanks, Alfie. I'm not going to do anything stupid," I say, and I mean it. I'm not going to fuck this up.

"Good. You've never been the jealous type, so I don't know why you're worried now."

"I've never had anyone to be jealous over before."

He laughs a little. "Yeah, I know what you mean. Listen, I've got to go. I'll see you at our session next week."

The phone clicks off and curiosity grows in me at his words. Alfie has never been one to share. Given his profession, I'm sure he has friends that he confides in, but I can't exactly be one of them while I'm his patient.

It's an odd sort of relationship. He knows everything about me, and despite going to high school with him, I know very little about his life. Although, I would bet my business I know exactly who he's talking about when he says he knows what it's like to be jealous.

I slip my phone back into my pocket and pull open the door to the bar. The crowd has grown, and the drinks are flowing. Holding my hand up to my mouth to mimic taking a drink, I catch Josh's eye, and he gives me a nod before turning back to watch the girls.

Suddenly, I realize I don't need to worry. If anyone is going to do something they shouldn't do tonight, it's Josh.

CHAPTER EIGHTEEN

Olivia

In hindsight, making a bet with two random guys when I'm on a double date with someone happy to admit she'd lost her last bet hasn't been my brightest idea. And because we're really doubling down, the fact that the head of The Unseen is sitting less than fifteen yards away might also be a slight issue.

I swallow down my nerves. How is Austin going to react? Is he going to do something drastic and make me lose my deal with Nicole? What would she think of me?

I bite my lip, frowning, but when I glance over to Austin, he gives me a small wink. The tension in my chest eases a little, and I realize he's not going to risk anything with me. But it feels good knowing he's there if I need him.

Josh, on the other hand, looks like a badger's just pissed in his cheerios. The vein in his forehead is alarmingly large. I almost want to tell him to get it checked out. I can see it on the other side of a crowded bar, acting like a beacon to other patrons.

We're at the back of the bar. It's darker back here with the light hanging over the pool table, illuminating the bright green cloth.

"Do you girlies know how to play?" The smaller of the guys smirks.

"Oh, we've played a few times. Usually, I get someone to

help me, though." Nicole laughs, leaning against her pool cue.

She slips a little and falls into the taller guy with dark brown hair. He's handsome in a conventional kind of way. Broad, tall, with a strong square jawline and straight nose. His hair is styled and swept back, but a few strands fall loosely over his forehead. He's eyeing Nicole like he wants to carry her out of here over his shoulder.

The smaller one, Jake, I think his name is, sets his attention to me, his friend clearly calling dibs on Nicole.

"Well, no help this time. You made a bet." He winks at her.

"Oh, I've practiced. I think we'll be fine."

Fine? I fucking hope so. Otherwise, I'll be running around this pool table in nothing but my bra.

Another glance at Austin, and he's rubbing his jaw curiously. Josh has turned purple.

We flip a coin, and I get to break.

I bend to line up the cue with the white ball, and it's then I realize how short my dress is. Short of flashing my butt at the entire bar, I can't do this in the correct position.

Nicole laughs, realizing my situation, and moves to stand behind me.

Not realizing what she's doing, Jake calls her out for assisting.

"She's err . . . not assisting. She's covering my ass." I swish the skirt of my dress, which falls indecently high.

"I thought you looked hot. Maybe bend over with her next time." Aaron laughs.

I laugh, too, but it feels forced. I glance back over to the table. Austin has lined up another drink for Josh.

We run a few turns, and they've potted four to our one. Aaron is looking practically giddy as he lines up to take his next shot.

"The air con in here is running a little cool, eh, sweetheart?" His eyes dip down to my nipples which I realize are poking through the thin lace of my bra and silky dress.

He misses, and I huff a breath of relief, covering my chest with my arms.

"You know what I've never understood about men?" Nicole murmurs, lining up to pot a striped ball into the top left corner.

She hits the white ball perfectly, and it clunks against the ball so hard I barely see it fall into the pocket.

"They don't understand that if they learned to shut up for a second, they'd still have access to view your beautiful breasts, Olivia."

She lines up again, thwacking hard as another ball goes in. I bite down a smile as Aaron's jaw slacks.

"But now . . . now you're covering yourself up because he couldn't keep his stupid mouth shut."

She lines up her shot, hitting the white ball at an angle. It bounces off one ball, *it goes in*, it rebounds into another, and god damn, *that goes in as well*.

"Men," she continues, "think the bar is their domain." She looks Aaron dead in the eyes as she takes the final shot, the black rolling slowly toward the top right corner. "When really, they just got hustled by a couple of *girlies*." The ball smoothly rolls into the pocket and clunks against the other balls.

A cheer erupts from the crowd. Apparently, our bet has drawn attention.

"Now . . . let's hope that air conditioning isn't too cold for *you*." She smirks, glancing down at his crotch.

I'm in awe. I squeal, wrapping my arms around her and squeezing tightly.

"You might be my new best friend," I say, laughing loudly.

Aaron's face is stony, like he's been deceived by some great trick when really he's just underestimated us. Well . . . Nicole. I didn't really do much.

"Fuck you, you cheated," he spits out, throwing his pool cue across the floor like a toddler chucking his toys out of his stroller.

Jake has the good sense to put his hand on his chest, murmuring something in his ear. Aaron doesn't see sense and makes his way around the table, pointing his fat finger in her face. Nicole must only be five-foot-three, maybe four at most. But the girl isn't just in the fitness industry; she lives it. She's strong as fuck and stares him down, not bending an inch.

He, however, bends right down into her face. That is before Josh strides across the room, and before I can blink, he punches Aaron right in the nose. Blood pisses out of his face as he screams. Chaos descends. Aaron takes a swing, which Josh easily ducks out of the way. He moves swiftly, raising his hand and then bitch-slapping him to add more insult to injury. Is there anything worse than getting bitch-slapped? Okay, maybe getting bitch-slapped by the guy who literally just broke your nose.

"Apologize to her," he growls, grabbing Aaron's collar and tugging him down so he has to crouch.

"FUCK YOU, YOU PRICK!"

Josh grabs his nose and squeezes.

Oh my god. I glance at Nicole, but she doesn't seem fazed at all.

"NOW!" Josh bellows.

The whole bar is silent, the air still as every patron waits to see what happens next. It's like watching a car crash in slow motion. You can't look away. You want to see what happens next; you just don't want to get sprayed with blood.

I feel Austin step behind me, his warm hand squeezing my hip. I regulate my breathing. He feels so calm behind me. But this is normal for him, isn't it? He sees things like this all the time. He *does* things like this all the time.

"I'm sorry," Aaron whispers, spitting out some blood onto the floor.

"Louder," Josh says, calmer now.

"I'm. *Sorry.*"

"Better. Clean yourself up. You're a fucking mess," he says, pushing him away.

Nicole steps back and picks up her bag.

"Time for ice cream?" she chirps as if we haven't just watched Josh punch a guy in the face on her behalf.

"I could use some ice," Josh mutters.

Austin, leaning over the bar, grabs a glass of ice chips and a paper towel.

"Five stars. Would highly recommend it." He winks at the bar staff before dropping a hefty wad of cash in the tip jar.

"Come back anytime." The brunette laughs, grabbing the tip jar and putting it out of reach of customers. Something tells me bar fights aren't uncommon here.

I give Austin's hand a squeeze before darting off in front to chat with Nicole.

"Okay, what the hell?"

"What?"

"Don't *what* me, young lady!" I giggle.

She laughs, looping her arm with mine, and we fall in step together. The boys are quiet behind, so I keep my voice low.

"You don't have boys defend your honor where y'all are from?" Her Texan drawl is really standing out now. It's thick and smooth; I like the way her words blend into each other.

"Well, some do, I suppose. I've never really seen a bar fight before. Actually . . . truthfully, I've only ever been in a bar once."

"Girl, you've gotta get out more. Your man must take you out, no?"

"We're kind of new."

She nods, grinning. "Yeah, you can tell. He's got that look about him. Like he'd take a swing at anyone that would dare look at you."

"Umm, I think you're talking about Josh with you right now."

She swishes her hand in front of me, dispelling my words. "That's never gonna happen. He's made it *very* clear."

"But you want it, right? I mean, hell, I feel like I'm

emotionally invested after watching that."

She laughs again, dropping a quick glance over her shoulder. "Like I said, not gonna happen."

I drop the subject, even though I'm dying to know who made that decision. If I had money to bet, I'd guess Nicole wasn't involved in the decision-making process.

After ice cream, we say our goodbyes with the promise of an actual business meeting next week. Austin draws my hand in his, kissing my knuckles.

"You looked like you enjoyed yourself until the pool table, at least."

I bite my lip, wondering how to explain without upsetting him. "I was worried you would be annoyed we were playing pool with those guys."

He nods, his face filled with caution, too. "Olivia, you can't control how other people react to things. And it's not your responsibility to do so. Did you want to play pool tonight?"

"Yes."

"And did you care who you played with?"

"I wish it had been with you, but no, I didn't really mind. I was having fun with Nicole."

"Good. That's all I want. For you to have a good time."

"You're not gonna go all alpha on me like Josh did with Nicole?" I tease.

He pauses for a moment, as if to carefully practice the words he wants to say. "That's not the dynamic I want our relationship to have. It might work for them, but it doesn't work for me. I've lived a lifetime's worth of violence, and in the last few years, I've worked very hard to build something different. Something away from my father and his organization."

The air around us is charged; it hums against my skin. *Does he not work with his dad anymore?*

"You have?"

He nods. "You're mine, Killer. But let's get one thing clear: I don't own you. No one owns you."

He stops me right in the middle of the sidewalk, tilting my chin up. Bending down so his lips brush the shell of my ear, he whispers, "There is one exception to the rule, of course."

"What would that be?" My mouth waters as his fingers dance across the hem of my dress, and I'm reminded of his promise to me earlier.

His finger slips between my legs, and he reaches the apex of my thighs. I let out a small gasp as he tickles his fingers delicately over my sensitive flesh.

"This pussy, Olivia. I own it." He pushes a little further in, and I glance around the empty street. To anyone, it would look like we're embracing. In reality, I'm dripping down his fingers.

"Mmhmm, anything. You can have anything."

"Just this will do. And maybe your ass." He winks. Withdrawing his fingers, he slips them between his lips. "Delicious."

"You're crazy." I laugh, taking his hand and dragging him back to the hotel.

◆ ◆ ◆

Our lips press together hard as he hikes my leg up around his waist. All sense of propriety gone as I grind my bare pussy against his crotch. His fingertips dig into my flesh as we vie for control. The elevator door dings open, and we fall through. He swipes the key card, fumbling with it until the little light turns green.

I jump up, wrapping my legs around him. He carries me into the room, his tongue licking mine, his teeth biting at my lower lip.

I pull the strands of his hair between my fingers and tug hard. He groans, throwing me onto the couch. I scramble, attempting to use my strength to pull him down on top of me. But this is where he has me beat. You can't beat those solid, broad muscles he has. Pulling me down by my hips, my butt sits close to the edge of the couch as my head is pushed up against the cushions. It's not a flattering angle, but Austin doesn't seem to care, and at least like this, I have a perfect view of him diving face-first into my pussy. But I can't arch my back; the position restricts the stretch I like to feel throughout my body.

He takes one final languid lick with the flat of his tongue before flipping me over. My knees hit the carpet as he pushes me down onto the sofa, my face squishing into the couch cushion. The weight of his chest is flush against my back as I feel his hard cock nestle between my ass cheeks. We're not even undressed. My dress is still on. Hiked up over my hips so I'm bare for him to see, but he's not even taken his shirt off. His slacks are on, even his fucking shoes. I'm aching to feel the heat of his skin against mine, but this feels dirty in the most delicious way.

The slap of his belt rings through the air as he wraps it around my middle. Holding on to both ends, he pulls it tight, and my ass slams into his crotch.

"I'm gonna fuck you hard, Olivia. If you want to stop, you just say stop, okay?" His voice is so deep I barely recognize it.

"Please, Austin."

"So good at begging, baby," he teases.

The sound of his zipper accompanies my heavy breathing. I hear him pull himself out, tugging at his erection as he lines up with the entrance of my soaked pussy. He slides in gently, nothing stopping him as he glides like a skater on fresh ice.

He pulls out slowly. "You ready, baby?"

"Yes. Please, Austin, I want it rough."

"Fuck, Olivia." He pushes again.

I expect him to start slamming into me, but he doesn't. He grinds deep, using the belt to pull me against him tighter.

His pace quickens, but the rolls continue. My ex used to fuck me like a jackhammer, just slamming repeatedly. But this is different. Austin isn't gentle. He's fucking me hard, but his cock is rolling in and out, reaching the deep spot near my cervix. His relentless penetration has moans rolling free from my lips.

"Don't stop. Please, don't stop," I beg him.

He drops the belt, pinching a nipple as his palm spreads against my chest, lifting me flush against his chest. His lips meet my neck; he bites, licks, nips. The heat in my belly is coiling tight, ready to spring open.

His zipper and slacks rub against the back of my thighs, and I'm reminded of how this must look: two people who couldn't even make it to the bedroom, they had to start fucking half on the floor.

He pinches my nipple hard, and then his hand snakes up to my throat.

"Do you trust me, Killer?"

His hand is ready to squeeze, but he's waiting for my okay.

My head moves up and down before I've really considered my options. But do I need them? I trust him to make me feel good. I trust him to stop if it doesn't. His thumb and forefingers squeeze the side of my neck. The blood flow is restricted, and he starts to pound into me. My pussy drenches his cock as he releases my neck, squeezing harder next time.

Thrusting, squeezing, releasing. Thrusting, squeezing, releasing. The pattern of his fucking sends me into a frenzy.

My hips ache from being stretched, the pressure lifting me higher and higher. I groan out, and my pussy starts to strangle his cock the way his hand is my throat.

"I'm coming," I cry out.

He releases my throat instantly, grabbing both my hips and pounding into me harder and harder.

"Please don't stop, Austin, baby. Please, please, please."

Each wave of my orgasm crashes through my stomach, my chest, and my legs; I can feel it in my toes. I'm crying, tears streaming down my face, the intensity of this flowing out of me.

His grip on my hips tightens, and some sick part of me hopes it bruises. I want his mark on me; I want to feel this for days after.

I tilt my ass up a little more for him and engage my muscles, squeezing him until I feel him swell even more.

"Fuck, baby. I'm coming now. Give me a little more."

I squeeze again. Reaching my hand between my legs, I roll his balls in my hand. His movements become more jagged, his cock pulsing in me as he unloads his warm seed, coating my walls. *Fuck, I love this.*

We're covered in a thin layer of sweat as he leans his weight over me, my chest pushing back into the couch. He pulls out of me, and I twist to look at him.

"Fuck, did I hurt you?" He takes my face in his hands, wiping my tears with his thumbs. The anguish on his face shows me just how much this man cares for me.

I'm shaking. "No, of course not, that was perfect. Just a lot. I think I can still feel you inside me."

"You're sure?" His voice wavers.

"I'd tell you if I didn't like something. That was the biggest orgasm of my life. I think my body didn't know what to do." I laugh.

"As long as you're sure," he murmurs, brow furrowed.

His rough hands trail lightly over my thighs, before he pushes his hands beneath me and carries me across the room.

"Austin!" I cling to his neck, realizing that my ass is exposed. I feel the evidence of his release seeping from my sex. He strides to the bathroom, carrying me as if I weigh nothing, carefully placing me on the tiled floor.

Turning the golden hands on the clawfoot tub, he sprinkles in some Epsom salts and some oils the hotel has left us. As the bubbles grow, he tests the water with his hand. Letting the water run, he begins unbuttoning his shirt. The man just fucked me over a couch, and yet, the slow seduction of undoing his buttons has my heart thumping like a racehorse on derby day.

He smirks. "Strip." He nods to my dress.

Mirroring his slow dance of movements, I slip one strap off my shoulder, caressing my collarbone as I move to the other side. The satin dress slips down my body, bunching at the curve of my hip. I wriggle it loose until it hits the floor. The hiss of zipper rings in my ear, and his slacks hit the floor along with my dress.

He climbs into the tub, sinking beneath the bubbles. He takes my hand and supports me as I sink down into the tub, my back leaning against his chest. I'm nestled between his thighs, and I feel him adjust himself as he hardens behind me.

"Ready to go again, old man?"

"Is that the nickname you've chosen for me, Killer?" He nips at my ear, tugging my earlobe between his teeth.

"If the shoe fits." I laugh, leaning my head back against his shoulder.

He holds me against him, his arm resting over my lower ribcage, pulling me tight against him. I'm so small compared to him; I love how he cages me in.

I sigh, closing my eyes, the warmth of the water engulfing me as the heat from Austin presses into my back. My fingertips skate over his thighs and up to his knees. I repeat the process, back and forth encouraged by the soft groans I hear humming by my ear.

After a few minutes of silence, I finally find the courage to ask him, "What did you mean when you said you'd worked very hard the last few years to build a different life?"

He stiffens behind me; the water sloshes as he shifts. I press my back into him, using my foot at the end of the tub to anchor me against his chest.

"Are you trapping me in the bath, Olivia?"

I twist my neck so I can assess his face. He's grinning.

"Maybe. You know how I like control."

"Ah, yes, but I also know how out of control you love to be as well."

His hand slithers down my stomach. His fingertips trail across the tops of my thighs, but I snap my hand over his to stop him. I bend my knee so I'm no longer pushed against him, and I turn.

"If you don't want to talk about it, that's fine. But tell me. Don't try to distract me with sex."

His lips part for a moment before pressing together in a flat line.

I lean my head back to let him digest that request. I'm sure he's not used to someone talking to him like that. I'm sure he's had everything done for him his whole life with the money he's grown up with. There are a lot of yes-people around men like that. I'm trying to be patient, trying to be understanding. He's different from what I initially thought he was; I know that. But despite our chemistry, despite our attraction, I still don't know him very well. And I desperately want to. I need to know that the man I'm falling for is worth the time and effort and won't leave me heartbroken.

"I told you about the day we met . . . at Squeeze the Day," he whispers, pulling me back against his chest, his forearm strapped around my chest.

"Yes."

"And I told you about the man I was running from—the man my father had asked me to sleep with. Him and his wife, I mean."

"I remember."

He nods, shifting uncomfortably behind me, before moving his hand up to rub his face.

"Fuck, I don't know if I can tell you this. I don't want to scare you away."

I turn to him, the water sloshing over the side of the tub as I reach out to cup his face.

"I can't promise you I won't be scared or unsure. But I really like you, and I want to know you better so that I can understand you and we can stop having these misunderstandings about who we both are. If you don't want to tell me right now, that's okay. But I'm going to keep asking questions because I want to know the real you, Austin. All of you."

I snuggle into him, kissing his neck before settling my cheek on his damp chest. He begins running his fingers through my hair; my eyelids close almost instantly.

He takes a deep breath. "I had been doing a job for my father and had taken the week off before I bumped into that guy. I'd been contemplating my next steps, and I'd even spoken to someone—a therapist. I knew I didn't want to have this life anymore, but I didn't know what to do about it."

"What changed to make you speak to a therapist?"

"My father had given me a job. I had to go and get some cash from one of our dealers. The guy only sells weed, but he had been skimming off the top. Despite weed being legal, we have the variety and the distribution the legal guys don't. It's technically legal to be selling, but you need a license—something our guys don't have. But we have the best product so our sales are still through the roof. At least they were two years ago. I have no idea what they're like now."

He continues to stroke my hair, and I drop kisses of encouragement on his chest.

"So I went round his house, and I told him to give me the missing money, and we'd be square. He told me he didn't have it. And I . . . I did my job. I beat the fucking shit out of him. He was crying, begging for me to stop, and I just kept pounding and pounding, screaming at him to give me the money."

I squeeze my eyes shut, trying to correlate the story to the man clinging to me like I'm his life raft. Scared that if he lets go, I'll flee.

"His kids walked into the living room, and they started screaming. The oldest one tried to hit me. Fuck, he was a fucking brave kid. He was whacking me with these crutches, and I realized he'd been skimming the money to pay the hospital bills for his kid who had broken his leg."

He takes another deep breath, and I pepper his chest

with more kisses, willing him to go on. I need to know this. I need to know how bad it is.

"I stumbled out. The kid gave me a good fucking whack, but I left, fucking drove off, went straight to a bar, and got blackout drunk. I'd never been more ashamed. Never been more afraid of myself. I thought I was going to kill that man. Right in front of his kids because he skimmed maybe a thousand bucks. It was nothing to me. I could have just paid for it myself. But my job was always my excuse. *I was just doing my job*.

"After a week of getting blackout drunk, I saw this billboard for a therapist. I recognized him from school—I'd been a dick to him back when we were kids, but I knew he was the only one who could understand me, the only one who could help me. So I went to his office the next day, and he's been helping me ever since."

"You haven't been working for your father in two years?"

"Nope."

"So, what have you been doing? What has Danny been doing?"

"It's different from The Organization. It's legal."

If that's the case, then why are there so many secrets? Why has Danny been so hush-hush about the whole thing?

I frown. "Do you still hurt people?"

"No. Not since that last job."

I shiver. The water has long run cold, and my fingers have wrinkled.

"I thought there was no redemption. I didn't even know good people. I mean, I have Luca. But other than him, everyone around me would either be terrified of me or use me to get to my father. I didn't trust anyone, and I still don't, really. But I wanted out of that life, and I've worked really hard to get to a place where I can actually enjoy life and not be suspicious of everyone I meet."

"And then I go ahead and kidnap you," I whisper. "I'm so

sorry, Austin."

"No, baby. Please don't say sorry for that. It was the best thing that ever happened to me. It got me away from everyone; it got me closer to you. It was exactly where I wanted to be. Please believe me on that, okay?"

I pull myself out of the tub, and he follows me, taking the hand that I hold out for him. I wrap the fluffy white towels around us, drying off before slipping into the bedroom. It's late, and exhaustion takes over.

"Come here," I whisper as I pull him into me. His head nestles into my neck as I cradle him. I wonder when someone last did this for him. He's held me like this a few times, and it's brought me close to tears. Being touch-starved will do that to you, and I have a feeling Austin has been touch-starved for a very long time.

"Thank you for telling me," I whisper, dropping a kiss onto his damp hair.

He clings to me again and falls into a deep, unburdened sleep.

CHAPTER NINETEEN

Olivia

Stepping over the threshold of Austin's apartment, I take in the blank walls and gray features. The sharp edges cut down to the uncomfortable-looking sofa that looks like it could have been delivered yesterday for all the wear it has.

There are no photos, no artwork, no throw cushions, and not even a fuzzy blanket for the harsh Seattle winter months.

I take another tentative step as Austin watches. His towering frame looming over me. He stands between me and the door, as if he's preemptively preventing me from escaping. *How the tables have turned.*

"I don't spend much time here. So I don't have much stuff," he says, looking around the room as if he's seeing it from my perspective. He's frowning, and maybe he realizes how odd it is that he doesn't have anything personal here.

I walk through to the living area, and a sleek TV screen is attached to the center of the dividing wall between the living room and the bedroom. Glass windows stand floor-to-ceiling, and I press my fingertips against them as I peer down at the bustling streets below.

"It's not really you, is it?" I say.

He pulls his hand up and rubs the back of his neck awkwardly. "No, I guess not. Like I said, I don't really spend a lot of time here."

"Where do you spend most of your time?" I ask innocently, even though a small part of me tugs at the separation of our work and home lives.

"At the office mostly. My office. Not my father's. I've had my own business for the last . . . wow, it's nearly two years. I started it once I left the family business."

I nod. I haven't asked him much about his business. If I could guess, I'd say he wanted to share more. Austin has been bringing it into conversation more frequently, dropping small hints. But I've never asked about it. I'm not entirely sure why, but the gnawing in my gut has prevented me from acting on my curiosity.

"You're unnervingly quiet, Killer. What are you thinking?"

What am I even thinking? That this is the weirdest apartment I've ever seen, or that I'm sad for him. Has he always lived like this? Alone, with no personal effects, nowhere to make him feel safe and cozy. No wonder he kept coming back to the basement. I'd left him things so he was cared for and warm, despite being chained up. I look around the bleak room and feel a sudden prick in my eyes. My back is turned to him so he can't see my face, but he must sense my unease.

He wraps his warm hand around mine. "Come on. Let me show you what I really do."

I nod, expecting him to guide me to another room, but instead, he picks up his keys, and we walk straight out the door.

Austin

I park the car in front of my warehouse and step out to open Olivia's door for her. Aside from the staff and the odd city health inspector, no one's been here. The warehouse is technically owned by a shell company, nothing that could be traced back to me. There are cameras around the whole building, partly out of habit, but partly out of concern that once my father realizes I'm building a solid foundation elsewhere, he'll bulldoze it. And my dream of a new life in the process.

I type the code into the security system and push the heavy door through. Stepping over the bund wall that sits half a foot above the ground, I hold out my hand to assist Olivia. She hops down into the warehouse, and her eyes bug out.

I grin, knowing that this must be the last thing she's been expecting, despite my attempts to engage her in conversation about my operation.

She lets go of my hand, her feet carrying her through the rows and rows of shelving units above.

"This is your business?"

"Yeah." I shift between my feet, waiting to see a proper reaction.

She wanders down the rows of plants. She leans up on tiptoes to study the different species.

"What's this one?" she asks, admiring the deep purple leaves.

"The technical name is oxalis triangularis. Here"—I snap off a deep purple leaf and hold it out to her—"try it."

She takes the leaf from me, frowning. I pull off another leaf and pop it into my mouth, chewing.

I've never thought I could be jealous of a leaf until I see Olivia slowly place the purple triangle onto her tongue. She chews, frowning until her eyes pop open in surprise.

"The flavor . . . It's so sharp. What is it?"

My lips pull upward. "It tastes like a granny smith apple, right?"

"Oh my god. Yes, it really does. Can I?" She points to the plant again.

"Yeah, go ahead . . . but just wait because I have more to show you." I tear off one more and hand it to her before taking her hand toward another section of the warehouse.

We wander hand in hand down each aisle. The viridescent greens contrast against the purple LED lights. The smell of earth fills my nostrils, and a sense of calm descends.

Each question Olivia asks leads to another and another. She's talking about superfood recipes, incorporating the protein- and nutrient-filled microgreens into her channel and showing her followers how they could build a small hydroponic system like mine.

"Are you trying to put me out of business?" I tease.

"Oh gosh, I'm sorry. I got carried away. But Austin, this is amazing. What you've built is unbelievable. It's huge here. And there are so many varieties of plants, things I've never even heard of. And the flavors . . . I just can't believe it."

"And they're more nutritious. For example, the pea shoots here have forty times more nutrients than an actual pea." I pick off a shoot and pop it in my mouth. She follows suit and chews, humming her approval.

"So, you sell these to restaurants?"

"Yes. It's done better than I could have imagined. It's good to build something beneficial for everyone involved."

She nods, running her fingers along the industrial shelving units we use to hold the plants.

"How did you learn all this?"

And here is the part of the tour that I don't want to give. I knew she would ask. That's why I brought her here, so I could explain where I came from and how I'm working to change. I want her to know her brother is safe working for me because we don't do anything illegal. Even if the only reason I know how to do it is because my father has run a cannabis empire for the past twenty years. Underground, just like my farm is.

Could she accept this part of me? We've all but avoided talking about it for the last few weeks. Wanting to build our relationship on something other than the fact that I'm her brother's boss and that I used to be a very bad man. Maybe I still am. If I weren't, I would have had this conversation earlier, or better yet, I would have let her go. But as usual, my selfishness has prevailed.

"My father's business, I can't go into too much detail about it. But I learned about growing plants underground there," I eventually say, wandering down each aisle and inspecting the plants so I can avoid looking her in the eye.

"I had guessed that, but why move to edible plants? You're basically a farmer, which is . . . surprising."

"Why?"

She laughs, and it's nice to hear something so sweet in a place that's been built off the back of something so terrible.

"I just picture a farmer in dungarees and a straw hat, not a black suit, black shirt, and a master at giving orgasms with his tongue," she whispers.

"Olivia Daniels. You forgot about my cock," I tease, grabbing her hip and squeezing until she hums her approval.

"Hmm." She taps her finger against her lip. "Maybe I need a reminder."

I huff out a small laugh, adjusting my pants. "Going back to your question." I take a step back to ease the growing tension between us. "I'm a farmer. The practice is called vertical farming. It's basically eradicated the need for huge amounts of space, soil, and pesticides. It's organic, really healthy, and tastes incredible."

"So, I know why you left your father's business"—she places her hand in mine and gives me a reassuring squeeze —"but why did you get into farming?"

Good question.

I think back to two years ago when I left The Organization. My father was furious, of course, and wouldn't get off my back about getting back to work, throwing easy jobs my way. I'd been talking to Dr. Alfie, but after meeting Olivia for the first time and then subsequently learning her schedule, she'd been a regular reminder of how much I wanted my life to change.

Sitting with Alfie in his office, discussing what I was going to do, we'd talked about the sense of urgency I constantly felt. To complete a job for my father, to get answers out of someone, to get money out of someone, it was all urgent, urgent, urgent—all the time.

And when he asked how I felt each time I sat in Squeeze the Day, I told him I felt calm and peaceful. I'd sit and drink the awful coffee, and I'd subtly watch Olivia read her book for an hour. She rarely did anything else; she never spent time on her phone. It was almost like decompression time for her, a time to escape reality into whatever she was reading. She'd always looked so at ease.

It's odd that now that I know her better, I realize she has been struggling so much. Looking after her brother, building her business. Yet, she has better coping mechanisms than me, a fully grown man.

"I wanted to watch something grow," I finally say.

Her smile stretches ear to ear, but she dips her head to hide it. I can't work out why, and then she whispers something equally confusing.

"You're a good man, Austin Black." Her palm cradles my cheek, and she drops the lightest of kisses against my lips.

My eyes prick, and is it hot in here? Something must be off with the temperature control.

"I . . ." My brow furrows. My shirt suddenly clings tightly around my neck, and I swallow down words of dismissal or self-deprecation. "Thank you."

She smiles again, but this time, she doesn't hide it. Taking my hand, we walk along a new aisle.

"So, you can grow everything year round?"

"Yes, everything is temperature controlled, so there's no seasons to worry about. We even started experimenting with fruit."

"Really? Like what?"

"We've been growing strawberries for the last six months. They've done surprisingly well, although they take significantly longer to grow than the leafy greens. I'm not sure they'll be profitable until we grow them on a larger scale. But that means more space, and we can't get that until they start selling, so it's a catch-22."

She nods, but before we can discuss further, Luca's

ringtone interrupts us.

"Luca," I say, picking off a strawberry that's ready to eat and feeding it to Olivia. Her lips wrap around the sweet red berry as the juice squeezes out. My dick throbs watching her pointed tongue lick a stray drop from her lip.

"Boss, we're headed back now. We're around thirty minutes away."

"Hey, boss," I hear Danny's voice in the background.

"Tell Danny I say hi," I say, my thumb rubbing his sister's lip until she draws it between her teeth and bites playfully. I roll my eyes, but the only rolling my dick can think about is rolling her into bed.

"I'll be gone by the time you're back."

"No problem. We'll talk later," he responds, and I hang up.

"Time to go, Killer. Unless you want to explain why you're here to your brother?"

She pouts playfully. "But I was hoping to see your office."

I pause, and take her in, her eyebrow arching, her chest puffed out as she pulls my hand toward her stomach. My fingers skate across her exposed skin almost instantly. It astounds me how fast I've fallen into a habitual role with Olivia. Our movements flow together, so synchronized, that she knows what I'm about to do before I even do it. And visions of taking her to my office, locking the door, and bending her over my desk fill me with a sense of unhinged desire.

"Do you know how unfair this is?" I whisper accusingly, retreating from her with my hands on my hips. There's no need to be quiet, as only the plants can hear us now. I've made sure there is no one around for our little tour today.

"What's that?" She steps forward into my space, running a finger down my chest, inching dangerously close to my belt buckle.

"Do you know how long I stayed away from you? I was worried that I would corrupt you, but it's *you* corrupting me,

Killer. I just brought you here to show you my plants," I say with faux disgust.

She grins, her steps eating up the distance between us. I play the game, stepping back again, letting her take the control I know she craves. She keeps pushing, right until my back hits the wall. She moves between my legs, my erection pushing against her belly, and she rises on her tiptoes.

"Well, you've shown me your *plants*. Now I want to see something else that grows,'" she flirts, running her hand up my inner thigh so close to my throbbing erection.

Her hooded eyes dip down to my lips. Lust spills from her tongue as her words have me quite literally by the balls. My cock is painfully tight against my briefs as if it's reaching down to her palm itself. She's leaning into me further, and she uses her hips to push her hand against me, cupping me now until I look up to the heavens. It's there I'm reminded of the security cameras I had Danny install.

"Olivia," I breathe out, "we're being watched here. And as much as I know you're an exhibitionist, I don't want my staff, your brother included, seeing you squeeze the life out of my dick."

She hops back, blushing. "I, err, didn't realize there were cameras. You can erase that, right?"

I nod, grinning. "I can, from my office."

Her eyes dart up, and she licks her lips. "Lead the way."

I pull her along the back wall that she's cornered me into and up the stairs. The dark corridor leads to my office and I unlock the door, ushering her inside.

She steps in, and instantly, her fingers are pulling up her crop top, her bare breasts greeting me before I can even get the door closed.

"So needy, aren't you? So desperate for my cock, you can't even wait until we get home."

I unbutton my shirt slowly, and before I'm halfway down my shirt, her leggings and panties are off, too. She backs away from me, lips pouting, eyes full of lust. As her ass hits the desk, she leans back, spreading her legs a few inches, enough for me to want to bite down on my knuckles until they bleed.

She crooks her finger and beckons me, but I know this woman: she wants to be watched, wants to be teased. She loves the anticipation of it. So once my buttons are undone, I remove my shirt, folding it over the back of a chair.

"Sit back on the desk properly, Olivia." She scoots back, lifting her ass up as her eyes never leave mine.

"Lift your feet on the desk."

She follows my instructions without hesitation, leaning back slightly as she does. Her knees are up, and I can no longer see her breasts.

"Spread your legs."

She smiles, slowly parting her knees until I get a clear view of her glistening pussy.

"Is that all for me, baby?" I croon, taking in the sight of her.

She nods as her eyes dip low to the bulge in my pants.

"Yeah, I've got something that's all for you, too. But first, I need to taste you, Olivia."

She whimpers as I drop to my knees, spreading her legs even further. I run my tongue along the inside of her thigh, halting as I reach her lips. I pause for a moment, inhaling through my nose. Fuck, my girl is wet; her arousal taunts me, but I want to draw this out for her. I dip to her other leg, licking until I reach her mound.

She hooks her legs over my shoulders, leaning back on her elbows; she watches me like I'm about to bless her. Anointing my tongue along her pussy is the only blessing I can give, but it still makes her eyes roll back and scream to god.

I reach the crest of her seam, flicking my tongue over the tight bundle of nerves as she tugs at my hair. She's sweeter than the strawberry I've just fed her. More essential than the nutrients the plants growing below us provide. If I could tap her, I would. I'd drink her nectar every fucking day, and I know it would sustain me. Fill up every need I have.

"Don't stop, please, Austin. I've wanted this all day."

"You had me this morning, twice, if I remember rightly," I say, popping my head up before she tugs me back down.

I lap my tongue over her slick arousal; it coats my beard and my lips. Hell, I might get some on my forehead when she tugs me down so hard. Her hips roll onto my tongue as she contorts her back, stretching her stomach muscles.

She quickens her pace, and just as her shallow breathing halts, I pull back, standing up and stepping between her legs.

"I was about to come," she whines, her hands slipping between her legs.

"Uh-uh," I snap, grabbing her hand before she can finish herself off. I unzip my pants, the snick of the zipper filling the silence as Olivia lets out a breathy whimper. She sits up, eager to take my dick into her hand, but I step back.

Footsteps sound out in the corridor.

Fuck.

I can hear Danny and Luca chatting, and I know Luca has a key. Did I even lock the door as we came in? I've been so distracted by Olivia removing her crop top. Dammit.

I pull her off the desk, grab her leggings, and burrow her into the closet, clicking the door shut behind us. I hold my finger up to my lips, and she gives me a small nod.

"What the hell is this?" I hear. "A little small for the boss, isn't it?"

"Put it back, Danny. You don't know what's been done to it."

"Gross."

I hear the light plunk of something hitting the ground, and I realize it must be Olivia's pink crop top. I only have her leggings in my hands. I turn to her standing so boldly naked. She comes up behind me, and her hand snakes down my stomach and into my pants.

Fuuuuck.

My eyes roll back, and I brace myself against the door

frame, biting down hard on my knuckle so as not to make a sound.

"He must have left like he said," Luca says, a little louder than necessary, and I wonder if it's for my benefit.

"Okay, I'll leave him a note on his desk," Danny replies. "It's kind of messy in here. Do you think someone's been in here?"

I hear Luca snicker as Olivia pumps my dick, rolling her palm up and down my hard length.

"I think the boss is fine if that crop top has anything to go with it."

"Yeah . . . crop top. Maybe he's got himself a lady friend. Maybe that's why he's been in such a good mood lately," Danny laughs.

The little shit. If only he knew his sister is tucked up behind me, stroking my cock like it's her personal fuck toy. Well, I guess it is.

Before I let her take me over the edge, I snap her around until her back is flush against my chest. She yelps, not too loud but loud enough that they might hear.

I hold my hand against her mouth, and I feel her hot, labored breath from her nostrils warm my fingers. I slip my other hand down. Using three flat fingers, I take the arousal seeping out of her pussy and smear it over her clit. It's wet and slippery, and her swollen bud almost vibrates against my fingertips. I rub in tight circles, my other hand fixed against her mouth. Her pussy is puffy, begging to be filled, letting me know she's ready. I know how she likes it, rough and wild. I build her up, my fingers spreading her lips as the heel of my palm leans in against her clit.

She tilts her head back against my shoulder, her eyes wide and begging.

"Do you want to come, Killer?"

She nods against my hand.

"I don't think you know how to be quiet."

She nods more vigorously this time, whimpering like a

baby kitten.

"If you can come quietly now, I'll reward you with my cock later. Do you understand?" I whisper against the shell of her ear.

She nods, and I remove my hand from her mouth, dropping it against her neck, finding the perfect position to squeeze the column of her throat just the way that makes her pussy contract. As if like an on-button, I slip my fingers further between her lips and find a new wave of slickness coating me. It would be so easy to slip my cock into her now, but Olivia's inability to be quiet is an obstacle, to say the least.

I can still hear Luca and Danny rustling around my office, and as much as I want them to get the fuck out, the fear of being caught certainly has its perks.

I pull my fingers out and focus on her clit again, over and over, circling her sweet bud until she hikes her leg up against the doorframe and braces herself against my chest, forcing my back into the shelving unit. A few papers fall down with the force of her bucking. I can hear Luca say it's time to lock up, and then finally, the click of the lock lets me know we're alone.

"Come for me now, Killer. Show me how fucking turned on you are," I whisper into her ear.

She pushes back against me again, one hand pinching her nipple and the other behind her back, palming my erection.

I'll never be able to set foot in this closet again without thinking of her sweet moans and the slap of her pussy juice against my fingers. I can see her muscles tensing now, her breathing becoming more shallow. She's bucking against my hand, so I barely have to move. She's such an active participant during sex. I've never met anyone so voracious, someone who so incessantly takes what they need. She's not scared of me. Not scared to take her pleasure, and I fucking love it. I squeeze her throat a little harder now, and she breathes in a quick gasp.

A moan cries out, and she reaches the apex of her

orgasm. She rolls out each wave, whimpers rolling out in tandem with her hips.

"Don't stop yet. I'm still going," she whispers, using her hand to press down on my fingers now.

After another thirty seconds of writhing, she slows her hips, lowers her leg from the doorframe, and slumps back against me. My dick is almost crying out.

"Have they gone?" she asks.

"Yeah, baby, they've gone. You didn't think I'd let you come before, did you? I knew you couldn't be quiet." I smirk.

"I always used to be quiet."

"What do you mean?" I ask, opening up the cupboard door to check that Luca and Danny have actually left. It's empty, but I spy Olivia's crop top on my desk.

"With other guys," she says simply.

I turn to face her, dark possessiveness seeping through my bloodstream so fast that I'm surprised I don't transform into one of those fucking werewolves Olivia has me reading about.

"Did you just mention your previous lovers in my office after I made you come all over my fingers, Olivia?"

"I . . . yes," she replies, a hint of nervousness lacing her voice.

"Go to the desk and bend over."

"Austin?"

"Now!" I snap.

She hops over, covering her breasts as she does.

I walk slowly to the door, ensuring it's locked this time. It is, but I consider slipping a chair under the handle for extra security. But then again, I know my girl loves the risk of being caught. I know I'd hear someone if they tried to unlock it. We'd have time to hide again.

Her face turns toward me in confusion, but she waits patiently, lying her top half over my desk like I requested. When I step behind her, I push her down by her shoulder so her breasts squeeze against the wood harshly, her tits bulging out the side of her chest. She whimpers a little, biting her lip as her fingers grip the long edge of the wooden desk.

I unzip myself again, lining myself up against her swollen sex, the evidence of her orgasm messy against her inner thighs. I use the head of my cock to smear her juice up and down her seam.

"Do you enjoy provoking me, Olivia? Is this what you want? For me to punish you?"

She pauses for a second. "Yes."

"Yes, to which question?"

"All three," she whispers, lifting her ass a little higher by standing on her tiptoes.

"Fuck. I can't see straight when I'm around you. I've been trying to be so good for you. I've been trying to be a good man, and it's like you're begging me to be bad," I admit. We're in a scene, playing our roles, but the honesty is seeping through. How can I correlate the man I want to be for her and the animal she draws out?

I slide into her wet heat, feeling her muscles contract, strangling my cock as I push myself further in. She huffs out a breath, her knuckles white from gripping the desk. I'm so deep now I've bottomed out. Her ass lifts even higher, and she snakes her hand down between her thighs.

She rolls my balls in her hand for a few moments, and I pull back, losing her touch but slapping straight back in. She cries out, whimpering, moaning, begging me for more. Her hand is still between her legs as I push into her punishingly hard.

"Are you touching that needy little clit of yours, Killer? Gonna rub that little nub until you come all over my cock?"

Her moans are her only response. I love her like this, so wet and needy, she can barely form words. I'm only rewarded with grunts and moans until I spill into her, taking her over the edge with me. But we're not there yet. I push on, gripping her hips so hard I'm going to leave bruises. My chest puffs out at the thought of marking her, keeping her as my own forever.

"Are you going to mention former lovers to me again after I've made you come, Olivia?" I ask.

She moans again, and I pause, waiting for her to respond.

"Please don't stop, Austin, please. I'm so close."

"Answer my question."

"No, never. I only meant that you're the only man that's ever made me scream like that. You always make me come so hard. Please, Austin, I'm begging you, please let me come on your cock. I need you. I need you so badly."

"Fuck, baby, you're so perfect, you know that?" I slam into her, and she cries out a string of yeses. "You're so fucking perfect. The way your cunt squeezes my cock, I'm close to coming in seconds with you. Did you know that? The way I always have to hold myself back because I'd blow my load like a fucking teenager otherwise."

I thrust into her, the desk moving forward a few inches from the force of it. The desk rattles, my chair wheels away from the desk, and the computer screen shakes, dangerously close to falling on Olivia's head or the floor. I pull her back into me so that only her elbows are propping her against the desk.

"Rub that clit for me, baby. Rub it just the way you like. I want to feel you strangle my cock with that perfect pussy, okay? Can you do that for me?"

Fuck, I sound so desperate. So fucking on edge all the time. This woman is changing me, building me up to be a desperate sap, and I fucking love it.

"Yes, Austin, I can do it. Please, I'm so close. Don't slow down."

"Come for me now, Killer. Take what you need."

Her pussy contracts as her usual loud cries fall by the wayside for a guttural groan that lasts anywhere from ten seconds to ten minutes. The tightening muscles around my cock pull me over the edge with her, and my thrusts become jagged and uneven. She milks me for everything I can give, and as I finish, I step closer to the desk so it can take our weight.

Leaning over her, I pepper kisses down her back, whispering promises I shouldn't be thinking about making.

"You're mine, Killer. I'm not letting you go."

With a sheen of sweat on her back and her ruffled hair, she's perfect. Looking thoroughly fucked, her hooded eyes sink into a deep tiredness.

I pull out of her, my come links us together, and as the remainder seeps out of her, I use my fingers to force it back in. Her pussy flinches as I push in and out of her swollen lips.

She sighs contentedly, and I pause to give her a break. Picking up a pack of tissues, I wipe her clean and myself.

"Did you like the way I spoke to you during that, Olivia?" I ask, doing my best to keep my face neutral. As Alfie says, I need to keep up good communication, and punishment isn't something we've discussed before.

She grins, nodding, looking up at me through her thick lashes. She's biting her lip, and I know she means it. But still, we should discuss it, right?

"You know I was just playing with you, right?" I say, helping her into her leggings as she steadies herself by resting her hands on my shoulders.

I'm looking up at her from my knees, and like a queen I've come to worship, she's looking down at me adoringly.

After she's pulled up her leggings, I pull her crop top over her head. She adjusts the tight fabric so her breasts are comfortable and fucking bulging out the top. She must notice my face because she giggles as she leans her forehead against my chest. It tugs at my lips, too. I don't think I've smiled so much since I was a kid. She really is a light that shines on everyone around her. You can't help but feel warm.

"What do you mean, playing with me?" she asks, squeezing her arms around me.

"I mean, you can talk to me at any time about any former partner or anything else you want to talk about. When I was punishing you, it was just for fun, but if you don't find it fun, I won't play that way again."

She frowns. "You know I loved that, right? That was one of the best orgasms of my life."

"I know, I fucking felt it, Olivia. I thought you were gonna bruise my dick; you were squeezing it so hard. I'm gonna start calling your pussy anaconda for the way it squeezes me to death."

She laughs, and she reaches up on her tiptoes, nuzzling into my neck and lacing her arms around my chest.

"But I just want you to know, if you don't like something, you can tell me, and I'll stop straight away," I add.

"I know that Austin. I trust you."

"You do?" The back of my neck tingles, and it feels like Olivia has dropped a barbell in my stomach. I'm not sure why; it's clear she must have some trust in me to be doing what she's doing, but to hear her say it so blasé like it's nothing is surprising.

I thought I would have to earn it more.

"Of course. I meant what I said earlier: you're a good man."

And for a second, as she rests her cheek against my chest and snuggles, I really believe her.

CHAPTER TWENTY

Austin

The temperature of Alfie's office is a cool sixty-eight degrees. We sit in our usual spots: him with his notepad resting on his knee and me sitting on his comfortable, but not too comfortable, couch. His office is neutral, inviting, and warm. Despite his direct approach to therapy, I've learned that he wants our environment to be a comfort.

I think of my own apartment and how clinical it is with its sharp lines and right-angled edges. Even Alfie's office looks more homely than there.

And I haven't been back in weeks, at least not to sleep. Olivia and I have fallen into somewhat of a routine together, working, playing, fucking. And then she curls up against my chest, and I fall asleep holding her, breathing in the scent of her shampoo as she tucks herself under my chin.

It took me all my strength to pull myself away this morning. She has a slow start on Fridays, her day truly starting when she enters Squeeze the Day for her fluorescent green smoothie. This morning, we'd sat in amicable silence, reading our respective books. She'd inched the toe of her sneaker up my calf when she thought no one was looking; I welcomed the distraction. It seems I'm incapable of not touching her when she's in my vicinity.

I relax back on the couch, pulling my right foot over

my left knee and smiling. Alfie usually lets me start the conversation so I can steer the ship, as it were. But today, I'm content. I'm not sure I really need this session.

He smiles at me, which would be unnerving if it weren't so genuine.

"You seem well, Austin."

"I am. I feel good," I reply.

"Business going well?" he asks, although I know what he really wants to ask. He's getting all the boring bits out in the open first.

"We're still growing. The experiments are going well. The staff are happy. Pizza Friday is a hit."

His lips tilt up again and he jots something down in his notepad. I lift my head slightly, but the fucker always angles it so I can't see anything.

"We'll have to get you back in time for that, then," he says, nodding toward the clock.

Truthfully, I don't give a shit about going back to the office right now. Sure, I love my work, and who doesn't love pizza? But all I can think about now is getting home to Olivia and slipping into her as she practices her downward dog.

I curb my thoughts; no need for me to get an erection during therapy. Alfie won't be too happy about that.

"And how is Olivia?" His voice is smooth and relaxed. But this is what has caused the most change, and he knows it.

Without hesitation, I say, "I'm in love with her."

He pauses for a moment and jots down another note. It used to irritate me the way he would let my words linger in the air like that, but over time, I've grown used to it. Alfie never responds without thought.

"You've had a very intense few weeks, and that would definitely bring some heightened emotions out of you," he replies cautiously. He places the notepad down on the coffee table between us. Lifting his ankle over his thigh, he mirrors my position—another Dr. Angel tactic. When something gets interesting, he's all ears.

"It's not that." I shrug. "She's the one."

"Austin, you don't have to analyze these emotions so quickly. Give it time to marinate."

"I'm not trying to convince you that I love her, doc. I'm just letting you know that's where I'm at," I reply, moving my ankle back down to the floor. I watch him copy, and I almost want to laugh.

He observes me for a moment before nodding, picking up his notepad, and resuming his usual position.

"Have you told her?"

"Not yet. I've listened to your advice, and I'm taking it slow." As much as I know my emotions, I know I run hot. Olivia still has some catching up to do to meet me where I'm at. I'd love to go all in, let her know I'm in this with her, forever, if she'll have me, but my girl is skittish, and I have a long way to go to prove to her I'm worthy.

We sit quietly for a moment until I say, "I showed her the business."

"Really?" his eyebrows raise, and I get a little kick in surprising him.

"Yeah, she loved it."

"So, she knows you're not working with your father anymore?"

"Yeah. She knows a little bit about what happened. Not everything; I don't want to scare her. But I told her why I left. And then I told her what made me stay gone. I showed her around the warehouse and then . . ." I cough. "I showed her my office as well. Just, you know, giving her the tour."

I try not to smirk nearly as much as I try not to let my pants tent. Images of Olivia splayed before me as I fucked her over my desk mean I haven't been able to work in my office for a week. Every time I sit in there, it takes me two seconds, at best, to have my dick in my hand or, at worst, turn right back around to Olivia's house, where I take her all over again.

"You need to be careful, Austin."

I wave him away. "It's fine. I took care of the cameras,

and her brother was out on a job with Luca. I made sure we wouldn't be caught."

He shakes his head. "I'm not worried about her brother finding out, Austin. I'm worried about your father."

My father. Fuck. With all my fucking feelings, the old gremlin has fallen out of my thoughts completely.

I know my security is tight. Luca and Danny are aware of the situation. Aware of what it could cost if my father dug his way in. Danny isn't aware of Olivia of course, but still, they both know for their own safety, and mine, they need to be vigilant.

"I have procedures in place." Procedures might be a slight understatement. Despite my legal business, I still have some of the boys on the books to inform me of any strange behavior when it comes to my father. I don't trust him or my brother, as far as I can throw them.

A small chime indicates that our session is up. I slap my hands down on my thighs and go to move.

"Be careful, Austin. You've come a long way, which is fantastic. I'm very happy for you. But you still don't know the lengths your father will go to. He's always thought you'd come back into the fold. You being with Olivia will change that reality for him."

I ruminate over the doctor's words as I wave goodbye to Mia. My father would have made a move by now if he knew about Olivia. He's not a patient man. We don't go out much, certainly not in the city. If anything, I've been overly cautious with her. Hell, even her brother doesn't know. The only person who does is Luca, and I trust him with my life.

Pulling out of the parking lot, I cruise back to the office so I can participate in the team bonding that is Pizza Friday.

Once the boxes are empty and the biodegradable plates are placed into our compost, I call Luca into my office. My conversation with Alfie is niggling at me and I want to take some steps to ease some of that anxiety.

"Any news on my father?"

"No, boss. Nothing to report."

His speedy response calms me slightly but does nothing to quell the ache Dr. Alfie has left with me. *The fucking bastard.*

I know I've been lax recently, but isn't this the whole point? To not have to look over my shoulder all the time? I wanted my life to be free from that kind of bullshit, and it's been working. But now his words sit with me, and honestly, it's unsettling.

Luca grabs a couple of glasses and pours us both a generous serving of scotch. Then he takes a seat and leans back, just like Alfie fucking Adams did not two hours ago.

"Spit it out, Luca."

"Did you at least return her crop top? Or was it a souvenir?" He smirks, taking a sip and hissing slightly.

"I'm not going to talk about Olivia. But thank you for covering for us."

"I'll do a follow-up report; send out a few more feelers regarding your father." He stands in preparation to leave the room.

I thank him again. Luca has always known what I need without me having to ask. I'm sure the doubt in my mind is only worrying over having something—*someone*—so precious in my life. But Alfie was right to caution me.

I lean back in my chair and look around at all I've built. I open up the blinds and look down at the warehouse floor through the window behind my desk. Rows and rows of growth, each plant meant to be consumed. I've done the right thing. I've made steps to become a better man. I know this, and I desperately want the latter to be true.

◆ ◆ ◆

Spending Friday afternoon seeking out my brother is not at the top of my list of things to do, but I have to. And being a better person includes being a better brother.

He doesn't greet me at the door this time, and I'm not

entirely surprised. August is, despite what my father thinks, a quick learner. His doorman greets me pleasantly, his wrinkled face giving me a polite smile as he takes my jacket. He guides me down the same corridor as before, enunciating that my brother is in his office *in the west wing*.

I thank him, slapping him on the shoulder and squeezing gently. The poor man scuttles away before I can open the door. And because I'm polite and a good boy, I give the door a knock before I enter. And that's a lesson I've learned after visiting dear old daddy the last time. I'm a quick learner, too.

"Come in," my brother calls out.

I step into the office. Everything is very much the same as last time, except my brother.

Holy shit. He's wearing jeans.

I try to contain my smile, failing desperately. Have I become an influencer? Our father would have a conniption if he could see the two of us now. Maybe I could convince August to become a farmer like me. I'm sure he'd like the harsh lighting and lack of weather in my operation.

"Brother, how are you? Good week?"

"I've had better. How about yours?"

Still painfully polite, I see.

"Drink?" I ask, inviting myself for one while I'm at it.

He checks his Rolex and tuts. "Might as well."

I pour out the same amber liquid as last time. Either my brother fills his decanter up regularly, or he doesn't drink at all. I'd guess the latter. He really hates being out of control.

"My week has been good," I say, handing him his glass. He takes it and sips it delicately. "So, come on, tell me what was so terrible about your week."

"Should I expect regular heart-to-hearts now that you're in love?" He snickers.

I roll my eyes, even though a twinge of satisfaction runs through my body. Even August has noted a change in me.

I lean back, taking in the artwork I saw last time,

the waves crashing into some famous ship of some famous explorer. It surprises me that August seems interested in this kind of work. But then, I don't know my brother very well.

He finally responds to my question. "Father called me and told me I was fired. I've ignored him, of course, carried on as usual, but it does make things rather difficult when the head of The Organization has been sending rage-fueled emails for the past week."

"Hmm . . . can't imagine what would have caused that." I wink.

"Austin."

"August."

He throws a look my way that only an older brother can. It hits me with guilt. What would Alfie suggest?

"I should have called sooner and warned you. I apologize. It's not in my instinct to give you a heads-up, but I should have."

He nods, adjusting his t-shirt. He's only thirty-four but the way he carries himself, you'd think he was significantly older. The man just can't relax. Even in jeans and a t-shirt, he looks painfully uncomfortable.

"What are you going to do?" I ask.

"Hope that it blows over, and he'll need me for something soon, forgetting this whole debacle." He flourishes his hand in my direction.

"Well, I appreciate you not blaming me for this."

I hear him mutter, "Fuck," under his breath, and he sighs heavily. I want to laugh; surely he's not that annoyed? This is classic Dad.

"Dad fed information to those trolls of Olivia's. He forced them to close down their accounts. Threatened them. I believe he destroyed their equipment."

No. That's not right. *I* instructed Luca to take care of Millie and Travis. Why would my father be taking credit for that? And how the fuck does he know about Olivia? My heart rate spikes, and I can feel the slosh of whiskey in my stomach, begging to come back up.

"Why would he do that? That only helped Olivia."

My brother shrugs. "Maybe he thought it would encourage her to dump you, and your inevitable heartache would lead you back to The Organization."

I keep my mouth shut. That means my father and brother don't know about the basement. They must think we've just spent the week inside her house.

"Well, he did her a favor. I'll have to thank him," I mutter.

Why the fuck would he do that? Surely he can't think that would work? My father might actually be losing it. Even this is out of his realm.

"He won't stop. If he thinks that didn't work, he'll go bigger. You know this. You did this."

I understand his insinuation, and it grates like nails on a chalkboard.

"Yes, alright, August. I don't need a fucking reminder. I know what I've done."

He holds his hands up in surrender before picking up and draining the remainder of his drink. That's my cue to leave.

"I'll keep my ear to the ground," he snides because he just can't help himself. "Which might be fucking difficult now that I'm fired because you won't fall into line. You better hope this doesn't have any bounce back on me."

Always the big fucking brother, trying to act like he's doing his bit for the family all the time, when really, he's just looking out for himself. My jaw aches from my clenched teeth. I fucking hate that I've come here to make amends, and now I'm only just hearing about shit to do with my girl. Luca clearly isn't hearing shit from my father's team now.

With clenched fists, I rest my knuckles on his desk, tilting into his space, forcing him to lift his chin and look up at me.

"Stay the fuck away from Olivia. If anything happens to

her, I'll burn the whole organization to the ground." I point my finger right in his face. "You can take that straight to Dad."

I storm out, grab my jacket from the doorman, and wheelspin out of his embarrassingly ostentatious driveway. It occurs to me that out of the two of them, only my brother has mentioned Olivia. My father wouldn't be able to resist shoving that in my face. How can I be sure it was Dad and not August who trashed Millie and Travis's equipment? And what the fuck is going on with Luca? He knows fuck all about anything, and now apparently, my Dad's the one that got to Tweedle Dumb and Tweedle Dipshit.

CHAPTER TWENTY-ONE

Olivia

My heart pumps furiously. My lungs burn in a way that I haven't felt in a long time. Hurtling my thighs forward, I press on, desperate to make him work for it. The hunt. I can feel him closing in. In the end, his stride is almost double mine, and my capture is inevitable. The thrill of being hunted by him is delicious. I run my tongue along my lips, pressing forward, the thud of his footsteps behind me. I turn to glance around and see his masked face, and giggle. His head tilts just like in a horror movie.

I dart to the left and start to zig-zag toward the camera. His cape flaps in the wind, and as I faux scream, hands flat on my cheeks in a mock surprise, he reaches out one gloved hand, gripping my shoulder.

I dip, duck, bend my knees, and crouch down. My right hand reaches over my shoulder and grips his upper arm as my left arm reaches across my chest to flip him over my shoulder. His body surges over my shoulder as I use his weight against him. Flipping him over onto his back, I press my foot onto his chest as I gaze into the camera with a thumbs-up.

A few seconds pass, and as I try to catch my breath, he grabs my ankle, pulling me on top of him.

"You weren't supposed to make it so hard to catch you, Killer," he murmurs, the plastic mask scraping along my jawline.

I tilt the mask slightly, revealing the scruff along his jaw and his soft lips reaching up to mine. My lips graze against his, our labored breath mingling together. I pull back just as he reaches up to close the space.

"Olivia . . ." he growls as I smirk.

Before I can respond, he rolls me on my back, one knee between my legs, and he pulls the mask all the way off, flinging it somewhere into the field. He presses his lips into mine with a harshness I can't quite put my finger on. It's not desperate, but it's in need of reassurance.

I reach to cup his face and smile at him. And with that gesture, he softens, dropping smaller pecks across my lips, my chin, my cheeks, my eyes . . . my whole face, really. Until I'm laughing, and his kisses are all teeth with how far his smile has stretched his lips. He rolls onto his side and pulls my leg over his, keeping our connection.

"What's next?" he asks as I nuzzle into him.

"Well . . . that should be a good intro. We'll need to actually show some self-defense moves. Which means you'll need to put your mask back on. Unless you want to become influencer famous and really lose all chance of working for your father?"

After Austin's confession last week, we've talked about the changes he's made and the work he's been doing to build a life that is his own. He's also told me about a conversation he had with his father about taking over the business. The answer was a resounding no, of course. But as I watch him talk about it, he looks almost fearful.

"Tempting. Not wearing a mask would certainly help my case against taking over. I can't say my father or his associates would want someone being thrown around by a woman taking over the helm."

"Hey!"

"Killer, I think you're a fucking powerhouse, and the fact that you can take me down does nothing to shatter my ego —clearly." He adjusts himself through his sweats, and I can't help but roll my eyes.

"Nothing could shatter your ego," I tease, cupping his dick through the soft fabric. "But you were saying?"

"Fuck, Olivia." His eyes roll back as his chin tips upward.

"You were saying?" I repeat.

"I was saying that although the patriarchy is alive and well for those gremlins, the fact that you can tackle me to the ground bears no problem for me, given that you make me rock hard while doing it."

My lips tip upward as I take him in. He's been insatiable, but then again, so have I. I can't keep my hands off him. Which might explain why this intro scene has taken half a day instead of half an hour.

"So, is that a yes or a no to the mask?"

"I'll keep it. I don't want to put you in danger, my love."

My love. Be still my beating heart.

"Besides"—he hesitates for a second—"I have a feeling my father is well aware of what I'm up to. If he knows about the mask, he'll really think I'm not suitable for the role."

"Oh, I don't know. You're giving me some boogeyman vibes. He might go for it," I tease.

He lightly pinches my nose, making a honk noise while he's at it.

Rolling over so he's on his back and staring at the sky, he takes a few breaths, and I run my hand over his chest until he clasps it in his hand, bringing my knuckles up to his lips.

We're still for a few minutes until Austin stands, pulling me up by my wrist so easily that I brace myself against his chest.

"Where did that mask fly off to?" he mutters as if he didn't launch it away himself. I shield my eyes from the sun, as Austin heads over a small grassy mound. Once he's located it, he pulls it back over his face and gives me a thumbs-up. How this man was ever an enforcer I have no idea; he's such a goof.

The next few weeks pass in the same way. Austin is disarmingly charming on camera. His contribution to my work is sincere and never mocking. He favors the Ghostface mask, but others make appearances too: Leatherface, Bane, Darth Vader . . . always the villain. I wonder if these masks are truly how he sees himself.

The videos I've edited and posted are received well, incredibly well. The comments are craving more and more of the "Masked Man" as he's been dubbed. Comments are curious; some speculate as to whether he's my boyfriend or just a camera-shy self-defense instructor I've hired. The buzz surrounding our videos has filled me with a sense of pride, and Austin is asking me daily for updates on views and comments. We go through them together. He jots down notes when he thinks I'm not looking. He seems . . . invested. Like this is as much his as it is mine.

I offer to give him a share of the money our videos bring in, but he laughs and says no. He is just a participant; I am *the brains* behind the operation.

On days we aren't creating videos, he works. He discusses upcoming experiments and the plants that are growing well. Before the basement, I thought he was a two-brain-celled thug, no better than a monkey with a handgun. But in reality, he's so smart. He tells me all about pH levels and soil acidity. That using certain soil for one plant won't work for another. It's fascinating work, and you can tell he's this encyclopedia of knowledge. The fact that it's legal and Danny won't be in danger has removed any uncertainty I once had about him. He'll look after Danny. It's a promise he's made and one I trust him to keep.

The days vary, but the nights are routine. We cook together, play games, stream something, and when we've teased each other enough with gentle caresses, one of us drags the other to bed. He hasn't been down to the basement in weeks; it's almost like a crazy, long-forgotten dream. Like an old movie in black and white, the memories of it are soft and dreamlike.

We're lounging on the couch in my living room. I'm

watching him unapologetically as his brows scrunch and relax, scrunch and relax.

"Austin?"

"Yeah, baby," he mumbles, eyes scanning the pages of the latest novel he's reading. I haven't read this one; he's bought it himself. His brow furrows as he turns a page.

"We've been, umm, spending time together for a few weeks now."

"More like a month, Killer. I count the basement." He winks, turning his book over and focusing on me.

I smile, looking down at my lap. He makes this so easy, but a small part of me doubts he'd want to be official. In our public life, he hides his face, and when we do go out, it's mostly to smaller, local restaurants, not anywhere he would be recognized.

"So . . . I guess what I want to ask is . . . You know, what are we? Together, you know, like, what are we doing?" I hesitate, swallowing the lump that's formed in my throat. This man has seen me naked and had me in every position imaginable. Why is it so hard to ask what we are?

"Olivia?"

"Yeah?" I look up again, his eyes crinkling at the corners.

"Are you asking me to be your boyfriend?" He smirks.

Oh god. I'm fifteen again, asking Scott Smith to the Sadie Hawkins dance. Spoiler alert: he said no because he was going with Penny Simmons.

I must pause for too long because he takes my face in his hands and whispers against my lips, "Took you long enough, Killer. I've been telling everyone you're my girlfriend for weeks."

"Who's everyone?"

"You know, Luca, my therapist, Jenny at Squeeze the Day. She asked for an invitation to the wedding, by the way."

"The wedding?"

"Oh yes, did I say I was calling you my girlfriend? I

meant fiancée."

"Austin!" I push away teasingly, but my heart is beating against my chest, screaming, "YES! YES! YES!" *Calm down he hasn't actually asked you.*

"I'm kidding . . . kind of. I told you, I'm just waiting for you to catch up." He drops a kiss on my nose.

I laugh, pushing my hands into his solid chest until he gives way and slumps back onto the couch.

We sit quietly for a minute, and I fail to hide my smile. "So, do you still see this therapist?"

He coughs and looks down; the tops of his ears redden.

"I didn't mean to pry. I was just surprised when you told me about him . . . or her?"

"No, it's not that." He sighs, rubbing his eyes with the tips of his fingers.

"It's just that I think you might know him. He's quite famous, actually."

I don't know any famous psychologists. Except Freud.

"What's his name?"

"Dr. Alfie Adams."

"Oh my god . . . Dr. Angel Adams?"

He rolls his eyes. "Yes, Killer, Dr. Angel Adams. Which, by the way, is a nickname he despises."

"Okay, okay, if ever I meet *Alfie*, I'll be sure to use his given name," I tease.

"Anyway"—he gives me a pointed look—"I call him when I need him, but I have a standing appointment once a week."

Dr. Angel—celebrated psychologist and TV presenter. He helps people on a famous daytime TV show once a week. He's like a qualified agony aunt although I'm not sure I'd ever say that to him. And let's face it, he's absolutely gorgeous. Sharp jawline and dark eyes, he's serious and broody. He looks like he's ready to roll his eyes every time a viewer calls in with a problem, but he's professional and courteous and, honestly, gives great advice.

"I can tell by the pause in our conversation that you are getting dreamy eyes for Dr. Angel." He laughs, honking my nose again.

As much as I try not to, I feel my cheeks redden.

"He really isn't as handsome in real life. And despite being excellent at his job, he's really a boring bastard."

"Is that so?"

"Yes, and I'm much better looking." He winks.

I laugh, throwing my head back. "No doubt in my mind, old man. Alfie, who?" I reach up on my tiptoes to kiss his lips. He palms my ass to assist my reach. Such a gentleman. Can't say I'd get that treatment from Dr. Angel. He'd more likely get me a step stool.

"How did it start with Alfie? Did you tell him everything straight away?"

I let him talk without interruption. His shoulders are bunched up by his ears. His voice isn't smooth like usual; it's hesitant and rough, like just getting the words out is a herculean effort, even though he's already told me the story of what led him to call Alfie in the first place.

"Well, we had our first session, and he said it was a bit of a conflict because we grew up together, but he was intrigued, so he said yes. I told him everything, and I mean *everything*. All the terrible things I'd done that were so unforgivable. Things I could never take back. And after I finished talking, I asked him what I should do."

"What was his advice?"

He smiles now. "He said it sounded like I needed a vacation, a long one."

"A vacation?"

"Yeah, he asked me if it would put me in danger to take an extended vacation from the organization. I thought about it, and I knew that my father wouldn't physically harm me. So that's what I did. Anytime a job was given to me, I'd tell my father no because I was on vacation. Avoiding my father's associate and his wife by running into Squeeze the Day might have been the best thing that's ever happened to me."

"So, she really wasn't your type then?" I tease.

"Nah, how could she be?" His thumb runs up my cheek.

I smile, looking down for a moment.

"So, I ran into Squeeze the Day, and you know the rest. I saw you, the heavens opened, angels sang—"

"Stop it, you goof." I pinch his ribs, and he pulls me onto his chest. I rest my head against his firm chest, feeling how hard his heart is racing.

"I called Alfie that day and told him I'd met you."

"You told him about me?"

"Olivia." He seems bolder now that he doesn't have to look me in the eye, and his voice is steadier. "If I hadn't met you that day . . . Fuck, if I hadn't seen you be so fucking kind and considerate and gentle, I would have gone straight back to work. I would have gritted my teeth and just gotten on with it. You gave me the courage to be better. I wanted to be more like you. A good person that made people feel good."

"You make me feel good."

He strokes my hair, and I nuzzle in closer, aware of how monumental this conversation is.

"I think I fell in love with you that day," he murmurs against my ear.

My heart stops—like a deep breath before the start of a race, before the horses are released and the chaos ensues. My heart kicks back in, galloping against my chest. *In love? In love?*

"You don't have to say anything. I . . . I know this is too soon. Alfie told me not to tell you so soon, but I couldn't wait. You have to know."

My heart is in my throat, choking me. It's blocking my voice box and despite opening my mouth, nothing is coming out. This is where this is heading, right? I know I'm falling for him too. I know I'll be saying the words eventually, but I just never felt I could trust him to reciprocate them. Like this is all some elaborate game, but he's proved time and time again this is real. We're real. I'm going to tell him. I have to let him know, too.

I twist my body around so I'm leaning on my elbow. My free hand feels the warmth of his chest and the thump of his heart. I meet his eyes, and he's smiling softly, nerves clinging to the corner of his lips.

"Austin, I . . ."

Ringing cuts me off, and Austin shifts, grabbing my arms and pulling me off him.

"I have to get this. It's my emergency line."

"Oh, okay." That's not what I thought he was going to say.

He jumps off the couch, answering the phone quickly.

"Yes?" He paces back and forth like a lion locked up at a zoo.

I bite my thumbnail, eager for him to come back to the couch, but the longer he paces, the further we get away from the perfect, vulnerable moment we've just shared. His eyes keep darting toward me as he runs his free hand over his eyes, pinching the bridge of his nose.

"Send the address now. We'll be there."

We'll be there. We.

It hits me square in the chest. My bubble of love and yearning in my chest sinks until it hits my gut. His words penetrate the fragile bubble I've held inside for too long.

Danny. Something's happened to him.

I'm off the couch before he gets off the phone.

"Yes, she's coming. Send me the address, Luca."

He hangs up, turning toward me. He closes the distance between us within a few strides, but something tells me we're further away from each other than we have been in weeks.

"Tell me," I whisper.

"Danny is in hospital."

I wait for him to tell me this is some awful joke. But his eyes tell me he's telling the truth.

"You promised me," I say as a small sob escapes. I draw away from him, and his face falls.

"We should go now," he says as I push past him, heading for the front door.

We don't speak in the car, and despite going over the speed limit, it feels like the longest journey of my life.

"You're bleeding," he says, pulling my hand away from my mouth.

I look down, and he's right. I've chewed my thumb so much that blood is slipping down the knuckle. I put my hand back into my lap, and Austin clenches his fist for a split second before returning to ten and two on the wheel.

Reaching the hospital, I dart inside, not waiting for Austin. I'm focused on getting to my brother, seeing him with my own eyes. It must be bad. Otherwise, Austin would have told me he was okay. But I don't want to hear it from him. I don't want to hear anything from him right now.

Someone must have called ahead because they know who I am when I reach the desk. A nurse calls the doctor over, and he drops everything to speak with me. His eyes dart between me and Austin, who remains quiet behind me. It's now I realize how intimidating he must look. He's tall, broad, and with a reputation for violence. Even without that, he has a presence that commands a room, and he doesn't have to say a word.

The doctor walks us through the hospital quickly; words like "induced coma," "cracked femur," and "fractured eye socket" ring through my ears as bile rises in my throat. The glare of the corridor lights stings my eyes, and the smell of disinfectant sterilizes my lungs as we push past room after room.

We reach a room with the blinds closed and the door shut. The man I'd seen in my basement with Austin all those weeks ago sits slumped out front in the blue plastic hospital chairs. He stands immediately, whispering something to Austin. It pisses me off more than it should.

"You should brace yourself," the doctor warns softly.

He twists the handle, entering the dimly lit room. A

bright line shines in the corner, but the rest of it is almost fluorescent. The beeping of his heart rate monitor is steady, regular, and a comforting sound to hear.

I move past the doctor and a petite blonde nurse who is in the room already. She glances between the doctor and me and presses her lips together in a flat line.

Danny's face is unrecognizable. I'm not even sure how they would know it's him. One side of his face is so swollen; it's like a purple balloon animal has been stuck to his face. Dried blood still clings to his other cheek as if they haven't had time to clean him up yet. A breathing tube hangs limply out of his mouth, his chest inflating and deflating at an unnaturally regular speed. I go to reach for his hand, but the nurse blocks my arm before I can.

"Try the other side, honey." Her voice is warm with a Southern twang I can't quite place. I move around the bed, taking his hand in mine. Tears fall down my cheeks as I sob openly.

All those years I was raising him, barely keeping the lights on just to keep him in school. We'd made it, hadn't we? We'd made it to adulthood, and things were finally starting to go well. We were turning a corner. We weren't just scraping by anymore. We were growing, building.

"Olivia." I hear Austin's deep voice crack behind me.

I can't look at him. I can't. Everything he's done, it's all for nothing because he's broken the only promise that really mattered. He told me Danny would be safe. He told me the business was legitimate. *He told me. He told me. He told me.* His words, his promises. They mean nothing.

He promised.

He told me he was in love with me.

I think I fell in love with you that day.

I couldn't wait. You have to know.

Tension fills the air, and the nurse looks to me to make the next move. I shake my head at her, my eyes pleading, which she reads fluently.

Turning to Austin, the doctor shuffles awkwardly. “It’s family only in the room, I’m afraid.”

“She’s my fiancée,” he says weakly.

He must have thought of the excuse before. Maybe Luca warned him outside that they wouldn’t let anyone who wasn’t family stay. But his voice is limp, like he’s begging me. But I can’t look at him right now.

“I don’t know that man,” I finally say.

“Olivia . . .” he pleads.

“Leave. I don’t know who you are,” I spit out.

“Come on, honey. Time to go,” the nurse says calmly as she guides him from the room by the elbow. Despite her barely coming to his shoulder, he doesn’t put up a fight.

CHAPTER TWENTY-TWO

Austin

"I need an update."

"Sir, I've told you already. You're not family; we can't give you any information."

The warm tone of the southern blonde nurse who led me out of Danny's room is long gone. In her place is an old timer, a black woman who must be in her late fifties and is already sick of my shit. Like I'm not too. I fucking hate myself.

Luca left a few hours ago, returning to the office to attend to the fallout, something I should be doing instead. But I can't leave Olivia here. If I leave, it would be over, and it's not fucking over. Not a chance.

I don't know that man.

It's nothing less than I deserve. But she's the only one who knows me. I've told her things that even Luca doesn't know, that Alfie doesn't know . . . Okay, Alfie might know them. But that's not the point. The point is I've trusted her with everything. And she trusts me, too. She's trusted me to look after her brother. I could have just fired him; I could have let him go, and none of this would have happened. Not that we know what actually happened. Luca is interviewing, *to put it politely.* He's using my dad's old-school tactics on this one. I'm fucking furious, but my usual instinct to fight isn't surfacing. I'm not even running. I'm frozen, like a fucking opossum. This is what I've been reduced to.

Luca is right. I've lost my edge and become soft. And for what? She wants nothing to do with me. I've lost her just as I almost had her.

Austin, I . . .

I'll never know what she was going to say. Was she going to tell me she loved me, too? I was nervous as hell she wouldn't, but I felt it right? I know she felt the same, the looks, the love that radiated from her; she was happy with me. We were happy together. Despite being from different worlds, we were working it out together.

I hear a door open along the corridor where Danny's room is. I've been removed from the seats outside the room, so I've been in the general waiting area for the last twelve hours. I glance up the bright corridor as Olivia shuffles out. Her shoulders are slumped forward, her skin sallow. My beautiful, perfect girl, beaten down by the fluorescent lights and anguish I've caused her. She heads to the counter, where the older nurse is still scowling every time she looks at me. Olivia hasn't seen me yet.

"I need to know what needs to be paid," she says.

Jesus, I don't think she's slept at all. She'll need new clothes, her things. No way I can convince her to go home to rest, but I can bring things here for her.

I send a quick text to Luca with a list of items to pick up from her house. She's already furious with me. What's one more invasion of privacy?

"It's been taken care of, darling. The bill is settled," the nurse says softly.

So she can be nice. Brilliant.

"I don't understand." She shakes her head. Has she eaten anything? Surely the nurses would have brought her some food?

Her head flicks toward me, and I try to hide my face behind my hand like a fucking chump. As if I could look away from her. As if I could hide my six-foot-four-inch body in a waiting room the size of a small café with only four other people in it.

She stares me down. Her tears have gone now. It seems the last twelve hours have hardened Olivia. Now she's all fury.

"How is Danny? They won't tell me anything," I try.

"Why are you here?" Her voice is clipped, uninviting.

"You know why I'm here, Killer."

"Don't call me that," she snaps.

"Oli—"

"No. I need you to leave."

"I can't do that." I shake my head. Fuck, it's dry as fuck in here; my eyes are prickling.

"Why not?" She throws her hands up, her voice rising. The four other people waiting are staring now. Their eyes are on me, trying to work out what's causing the commotion.

"Because I love you, and whether you like it or not, you need me right now. I'm not leaving you. I promised you I wouldn't leave you. Do you remember?"

The nurse puts her hand on her chest, her head tilting slightly.

Olivia shakes her head, and her whole body moves away from me. I'm losing her. I can feel her slipping through my fingers like sand, and the harder I try to grip, the quicker she's falling through my fingers.

"You made a lot of promises, Austin, none of which you can be trusted to keep." The tears fall again, and I can't say which is worse to endure, her tears or her anger.

She turns back to the nurse. "How much did he pay you? I want a record."

The nurse glances at me again, but there's sympathy in her eyes this time.

"Don't look at him. Look at me. He's *my* brother. I don't want that man anywhere near him or paying for anything else. Do you understand me?"

"Yes, miss. I'll have it noted on your brother's record. I'll print the invoice that was paid for you now."

I'm surprised she's so accommodating, but maybe she's

a sucker for Olivia's tears too. She hands her the piece of paper, and Olivia scans down to the fee. Her head snaps back to mine. *Yeah, baby. Paid up.* The American healthcare system is fucked. But I have the money, and there's nothing I'd rather spend it on right now. I want Danny back to full health as soon as possible, not just for him, but for her—and selfishly, for me. If he doesn't get better . . . Fuck, if he dies, then all hope for me and Olivia dies with him.

All that work with Alfie, years of unlearning the things that had been ingrained in me, and I'm still the selfish prick I've always been. It's always about what I can get out of a situation. The realization hits me like the lasers Olivia is trying to blast out of her eyes right now. I'm sure she'd split my skull in two if she could.

"I don't know what happened. But I'm finding out. My best people are on it."

She shakes her head, crumpling the invoice in her clenched fist.

"It's done, Austin. There's nothing you can do that will fix this. We're done."

"No." I shake my head, swallowing hard. "We're not done. This . . . it's fixable, I'm going to fix this."

She strides toward me, her finger jutting into my chest. The masochist in me is just happy she's touching me.

"Do you have a time machine? No, you don't. You can't fix this, you're fucking delusional, and I'm . . . I'm just an idiot who believed you were redeemable."

I recoil. Bile stings up my throat, threatening to spill into my mouth. All this time. All this time I've spent with Alfie. Making better choices, building, rebuilding, rebuilding again. Over and over. The time, the effort, the energy. It's been for nothing. She's gone. Her eyes are dead when they look at me. And I can't even be mad about it. She's right. I'm disgusting. I don't deserve to be anywhere near her, let alone begging for her forgiveness.

Her cheeks are wet, her eyes puffy, her lips part in shock

at what she's just said.

"Austin . . ."

I cut her off before she backtracks because she's right. "There's no redemption for me, Olivia. I know what I am. I'm the villain. I'll always be the villain."

I step back.

"Austin, no. Wait . . ."

I turn and walk out of the waiting room.

I have to accept who I am.

Olivia

Austin left a few hours ago, but the ache hasn't left yet. I'm holding Danny's good hand as tears roll down my cheeks. Eventually the nurse brings a cot in for me to sleep on. She shushes me as I sob, and despite the warmth that radiates from her, I feel colder than ever.

How could I have been so cruel?

I'm furious, of course. Furious that Austin hadn't known this was going to happen, but really, how could he? He's just one man trying to be better. I dragged him into our lives. This is as much my fault as it is his. And really, it doesn't even matter because the real person to blame is Austin's father. I know it in my gut.

The nurse brings in a bag for me, containing some fresh clothes and my phone which I had left in Austin's car.

I shake my head when she asks if there is anyone she should call. Danny and I only have each other. There is no one else to call.

I have a few messages, including some from Jenny at Squeeze the Day.

Jenny: Babe, I've just heard, I'm so sorry. I had no idea.

I jot out a quick reply to let her know Danny is stable and to say thanks.

Me: Hey Jenny, thanks for messaging. I know it's been crazy. Danny is doing okay, though. He has surgery tomorrow morning for his leg, but the doctors are optimistic.

I see three little dots pop up instantly.

Jenny: What happened with Danny??

Me: He's in hospital. What are you talking about?

Jenny: Millie and Travis. They posted another video. They've outed Austin. I had no idea who he was, or I would have told you. I'm so sorry for pushing you toward him.

Shit, fuck, poo bags. What the hell is she talking about?

I quickly jump onto the app. I've been tagged so many times. I'd turned off my notifications recently as it was all getting too much so I hadn't known about the video. Rotating the screen, I pull my thumb to my mouth and bite the skin around my nail. I watch the video, eerily similar to the apology video from weeks ago. Except this time, the looks on Millie and Travis's faces are smug, like they've just found out how to print money out of their ass, and they're going to brag about it to everyone. They're holding hands, sitting close together.

"We'd like to take this opportunity to thank our fans for their patience. We've had a particularly difficult time lately due to one Olivia Daniels. See, the apology video we were *forced* to make a few weeks ago was complete bullshit.

"Olivia has been dating a criminal. Head of an organization called The Unseen that specializes in beating people up so they hand them their money, selling drugs illegally, and now, apparently, forcing any competition to his girlfriend's business into hiding.

"The name of this man, the 'Masked Man' as Olivia has dubbed him, is Austin Black.

"We've had multiple people come to verify this

information to us at great personal risk to themselves. Austin is dangerous and terrifying to work with, we've been told. He's ruthless and will stop at nothing to get his way. And Olivia allows this to happen.

"We're trying to rebuild our businesses. Any support and love you can show us would be greatly appreciated."

The video cuts out, and new streams of tears track down my cheeks.

This can't be happening.

Has Austin seen this?

What will happen to him?

Will his father find out?

Is this why Danny got hurt?

I check the video's upload time: fourteen hours ago. Fourteen hours ago, I was lying on the couch with Austin, asking him to be my boyfriend. His laughing and telling me he'd been calling me his girlfriend for weeks was the happiest I've felt in years. He really does love me. I know he does.

I bring up Austin's contact and press call. It rings only for a few seconds, and then it cuts to voicemail. I huff out a breath. As if, after everything, he's going to reject my call.

Me: Seriously? Too chicken to answer your phone?

He reads it immediately, but no reply comes through.

Maybe I really have pushed him too far this time.

◆ ◆ ◆

It's been two days. Two days since I've pushed Austin away. My brother has had his surgery, and when he's come out of his coma, we've talked about what happened. Eventually, Luca also visits and speaks privately with Danny. I've been hoping Austin would turn up, too, but he hasn't.

Danny knows about the video, which means he's found out about Austin and me. I can't say that hasn't been the most awkward conversation of my life.

So here I am at the brink of potentially losing my business, losing the man I love, and now losing my brother. He's not outright said how pissed off he is, but I can tell. Either he's furious or his pain meds aren't working nearly as well as they should be.

So this has led me to Dr. Alfie Freaking Adams's couch. His real one, not his psychologist one.

I'm curled up with a hot tea, my legs tucked under me as I flip through a book on trauma. Yeah, Dr. Alfie doesn't do light reading. I certainly can't imagine him reading werewolf smut.

"How are you feeling?" he asks, leaning back into his armchair.

Probably the most awkward part of this situation is feeling like I'm constantly in a therapy session. How much should I say? How much should I ask? This man knows Austin better than anyone alive. He holds all my answers.

"I'm angry."

He nods. "Understandable."

We're silent for a few minutes until I can't bear it any longer.

"Have you heard from him?"

"He checks in daily."

Daily?

He must see my expression because he decides to throw me a bone.

"Books like that one"—he points at the huge hardback on my lap—"they can only teach you so much. Some things are only learned by experience, and there's no way, as a therapist or as a partner, that we'll be able to understand someone completely or why they do the things they do. Trauma alters our DNA; it alters our brain chemistry. Undoing that damage takes years, and even then, another traumatic event can slip us right back into those unhealthy coping mechanisms. Austin has almost had two lives. He's killed off one life, or at least, he's tried to. So his new life began two years ago. Would you expect a two-year-old to have the emotional maturity of someone who was thirty-two?

"No, of course not."

He shrugs. "Austin has had to learn how to be human. Honestly, if you think of him as a bit of an alien, in the kindest way possible, it's like he's come to a new planet. Experiencing new things and, importantly, new emotions.

"Austin is well aware of how he wants to treat people. In fact, that's one of the easiest parts of treating him. He's always known how he wants to treat others. Or maybe I should say he knows how he doesn't want to treat people. He works in negatives. He'll see a situation and tell me what he doesn't want to do rather than what he does. But when it comes to his own treatment, how he treats himself, how others treat him . . . he can't fathom being loved or cared for. His previous life was stripped of all affection. There was only competition and brutality. Not just his job. His relationship with his father and his brother are equally problematic. It's only his friendship with Luca where Austin has seen any true loyalty."

I nod. "I just want to help him."

"I know, and you have. You've helped him far more than I have in the last month alone."

I shake my head, hugging the book to my chest.

"But this isn't your responsibility, Olivia. You have your own life and no doubt your own problems, as we saw from that video."

Yes, the video. Which is why I'm here. Dr. Alfie has agreed to house me for my own protection. The deal is that we would be seen together publicly to curb any belief that the "Masked Man" was Austin. We would stand close together, snap a few selfies, and hope that the media would do the rest. Dr. Alfie is enough of a household name that my face would get out there as a potential girlfriend. Luckily for me, it's not often that he's photographed with a woman, so this kind of seems like a bigger deal than it is.

It does mean the comments on my videos have been going wild. Speculation of Dr. Alfie as the "Masked Man" has tripled in the last two days. Comments on my videos and the one posted by Millie and Travis have gone, frankly, nuts.

I've not responded at all, which seems to have incensed Millie and Travis further. They've posted another video, backtracking that they were given the information from a credible source and that it's not their fault that they didn't know the truth.

The fact that the School of Agriculture at Elwood University has announced its collaboration with Austin's vertical farming company "The Unseen" has only discredited their video further. The university's marketing team has really jumped on the hype, too, posting a video of those at the underground farm looking positively confused, dressed as cartoon-like robbers—trying to steal a load of plants. It is pretty genius.

"Are you sure you're meant to tell me this? Don't you have doctor-patient confidentiality?"

"Austin drew up a contract, alleviating me of doctor-patient confidentiality when it comes to you."

"Really? Why?"

"I can't answer that. It would be pure speculation."

His phone rings, and he excuses himself from the room.

I sit for a moment, thinking over what Dr. Alfie has told me. Austin has always been playful and wonderful with his treatment of me, almost hesitant at times. Is that when he stops himself to think about how he really wants to behave? I have so many questions, but how can I ask him if he won't talk to me?

"Your brother is coming over." Alfie's voice interrupts my thoughts. I turn to face him, and I can tell it's bad.

"Should he be out of the hospital yet?" I say, checking my phone. Why wouldn't he have just called me directly?

"That remains to be seen."

"That was Austin, wasn't it?"

"Yes."

Dr. Alfie is kind of cold; he has a tough exterior, but I like that he never hesitates to tell the truth.

"Is he coming too?"

"No," he replies neutrally, taking his seat back on the armchair.

I huff in annoyance, but it's quickly replaced with a sharp stinging in my chest. I hold myself tighter and close my eyes for a moment. Before I know it, the soft throw pillows have lulled me to sleep.

I wake up to the sound of knocking.

A blanket has been placed over me, and I let it fall down as I stand. My muscles ache from the uncomfortable position I took my nap in, but my heart races at the prospect of seeing my brother. I haven't seen him since they told me it was too unsafe for me to stay in the hospital. Apparently, they're still trying to work out what happened to Danny.

Dr. Alfie opens the door and mutters something quietly. I peek over his shoulder and see a short blonde, the nurse from the hospital. No Austin. My brother grimaces when he sees me.

"Hi, Olivia." The nurse smiles softly.

I nod, stepping forward to help Danny through the threshold.

The purple bruises are still so vibrant across his cheek that I have to bite my lip so I don't cry. The swelling has reduced dramatically, so at least it actually looks like him. He sits back into the chair that Luca has lifted over the step into the house and sighs when he's off his foot.

"How are you, Danny?" I ask, wheeling him into the living room. "Do you want to sit on the couch, or are you happy in the chair? Do you need a drink?"

"Livvy, please fucking chill. You're giving me a headache."

I press my lips together tight enough to stop my chin from wobbling. The tears threaten to fall, but I have to keep it together for him.

"What the fuck happened between you and my boss?" he asks.

I dart my eyes toward the hallway, and I can still hear the nurse and Alfie talking.

"I'm not sure I should give you the details."

"Gross, Livvy. Austin? He's old."

I flinch at the sound of his name.

"He's not old. He's thirty-two."

"Right, and you're twenty-four."

"It doesn't matter now, does it? He's ended it."

"Seems like it was the other way around to me," he snides.

"How exactly would you know that?"

He doesn't say anything. Just tuts like he's disappointed.

I lean my elbows on my knees and cover my eyes with the heels of my palms. *Fuck, this is a disaster.*

A small sob spills out, and I hear my brother shift. He can't reach me, but he mutters for me to move toward him. I shuffle, and he puts his good arm around me, the small sob growing into breathless cries. All the hurt of the last few days spills out and for once, it's my brother looking after me and not the other way around.

"If it's any consolation, you were right about him," I sniff.

"Yeah, I tried to tell you. You didn't have to sleep with him," he snarks.

I'm guessing he doesn't know about the kidnapping and the basement, so I keep my mouth shut about that.

"It's more than that, Danny."

"I know. I'm just being a dick. But really? My boss? You hated him."

"I thought he was leading you down a bad path. I thought he was a criminal."

"I told you he wasn't."

"Okay, but you haven't exactly been forthcoming about what your job is, Danny. What was I supposed to think?"

"It was a secret because of the danger of his family. I work in an underground farm. We grow plants for restaurants.

You'd love it; it's all hyper-nutritious."

"I know. I've been there."

He pulls back, and his eyes bug out. He pauses for a moment, then winces. "The crop top . . . in his office. Please tell me that wasn't yours."

"Would you prefer it if it belonged to someone else and he was cheating on me?"

His mouth gapes, and if the situation weren't so dire, I'd probably laugh.

"In his office, Olivia? Damn. I've actually got more respect for you. You're nasty." He laughs.

I shove him, and he winces. "Oops."

Wiping away another tear, I lean into my brother.

We're silent for a moment until he says, "Remember what Mom used to say? If it's meant to be, it'll be."

"Yeah, and if it's not, it's just pushing you toward what is," I reply, smiling a little, the ache easing in my chest.

"The reason I came here today is to tell you it's not safe here right now. Not for you. We've managed to convince Millie and Travis they were wrong, but it's not as simple with Austin's family."

"What about you?"

"I'll be hiding too, recovering until I can get back to it."

"We'll be going together?"

He shakes his head, and another whimper escapes. *Fuck, I need to pull it together.*

"It's up to you where you go. You can choose. I just need to book your flight now."

I hear Alfie shuffle into the room, and as I turn, he's leaning against the doorframe. I don't try to fight it. I can't stay at Dr. Alfie's forever, and despite the concern I feel for my brother, the idea of getting away from this mess makes me feel like I can breathe again.

If I get away, I can always come back. I will come back once everything has calmed down.

"I know where I want to go."

One Week Later—Austin

The crimson color swirls down the sink in a perfect formation. The twang of copper sweeps the air as I watch the blood drain away. The water stings my split knuckles, but I can't be sure the blood that's draining away is my own.

Luca drags the last guy out of the warehouse and into the unmarked van that awaits him outside. He'll be dropped outside my father's front door before dawn. Another message. Another warning. It's not unknown to me that this is exactly what my father wanted. He wanted me back in the fold, back into the business that he'd so carefully molded me to fit into.

But even my father doesn't understand my wrath, the pain of losing something I was so close to having. To belong to someone else entirely. And for that person to be the smartest, most caring, and most beautiful woman on the planet, who saw me not as a monster, but as a person who could bring *her* joy. That is until my father bragged that really he was letting me believe I'd stepped away. And in a way, he was right.

"If you don't know what's happened yet, you're dumber than I thought. Even your fuck-up of a brother could have figured it out. But let me help you out since you're blinded by a wet cunt. I own you. Until my dying breath, I'll own your entire life. You think I didn't know about your pretty little girlfriend, the blogger?"

"It's not a blog, actually," I had spat back.

"Pretty little thing, isn't she? The boys will have their fun with her once I'm through, Austin. That is unless you come back. No more vacation, no more acting like a child. You follow every fucking order I give you. You complete every fucking job. Or that little bitch will be delivered to your fucking doorstep in a body bag chopped up and ready for display."

So, of course, every one of his men has been delivered to him chopped up in a body bag. We've been busy. Not one of them would give him up. I'm not entirely surprised. My reputation has waned in recent years. He isn't wrong that I'd gone soft.

"Boss, that was the last one. He's alone now."

"He'll have new men by tonight." I sigh, drying my hands on a paper towel, blood still flowing from my knuckles.

"I wouldn't be so sure. The rumor mill has been working over time, and they know you're back," Luca says, grinning. He's been all too happy to help me dispose of the men my father has used to hurt Danny, to hurt me. It's been the first time in years that his taste for violence has almost disturbed me. He's fucking blood drunk, powering through the work like it's his life calling.

"I'm not fucking back. I'm finishing this, and then I'm out," I spit back.

"Well, thank god," a deep voice interrupts. "This intervention shouldn't have to last too long then."

I turn to the entrance, and a dark figure stands with the light outside shining brightly behind him. He looks annoyingly ethereal. It's not until he steps into the warehouse that I see him fully. The bastard has a few inches on me; he's broad, filling out his tailored suit to perfection. A lesser man would be jealous, but I'm not a lesser man.

"Ah, Dr. Angel," I goad. "To what do I owe the pleasure?"

"You missed your appointment."

"Who the fuck are you?" Luca shifts, clenching his fists.

"I feel insulted you don't remember me, but then again, you didn't really pay me much attention at school, Luca," Alfie sniffs.

Realization clicks for Luca as his eyes bug out in disbelief.

"Alfie fucking Adams. Fucking hell, you grew at least two feet."

"Unlike you."

"I can fuck you up, college boy. Don't you worry about me."

I roll my eyes. Luca always has something to prove.

Alfie ignores him. Striding toward me, he slaps a hand

on my shoulder, squeezing hard.

"How are you?"

"What the fuck?" Luca mutters.

"A bit busy actually. So if you don't mind," I snip, pushing past him and heading to the doorway he's just walked through. The dingy warehouse seems somehow dirtier with him in it. Like this perfectly crisp white shirt is shining a light on the moldy corners, the cobwebs, on just how low I've fallen in the space of a week.

"It's a relapse, Austin, nothing more. You can start again at any time, but you have to start."

"What the fuck is he talking about, Austin?" Luca spits.

I ignore him, keeping my eyes on the floor. "How is she?" He knows who I'm talking about, even if I can't say her name.

"I wouldn't know. She left a few days ago."

For all I've tried to avoid his eye, it's that sentence that snaps my gaze back to him. I can barely stand to look at him. Having to ask Olivia to pretend to be with Dr. Alfie almost killed me. When I saw the banter on his TV show between the other presenters that Dr. Alfie had a girlfriend, I wanted to throw up.

The plan had worked, but at what cost? Seeing her with him made me hate myself all over again. If only I'd kept Danny safe, none of this would have happened.

"Where is she?"

"She left a note saying you'd know where to find her when you were ready."

Where would she go? I have no idea. We never talked about wanting to live anywhere else. We were in our own little bubble.

I say nothing, and Luca is getting antsy and starting to pace.

"Are you going to stop fighting your father?" Dr. Alfie asks gently.

"She's gone. It's over." I don't answer his question, but in my mind, I do. She's gone, and it's his fault as much as it is mine. I'll punish myself by becoming the man he wants me to be and using it against him.

He sighs, frowning—no doubt racking his big brain on how to convince me to move on. "You didn't start this to win her over, you always thought that was an impossibility. And yet, you started anyway. You did it for you. We can't do all the work for other people, Austin, we have to do the work for ourselves."

"Could you stop?" I pace, back and forth, pointing my finger at him like he's the one that got me in this mess. I know he's not, I know my father betrayed me, I know I had a fucked-up childhood. I know, I know, *I FUCKING KNOW*. "I'm done denying who I am, I was born to be this."

My arms are spread wide, like a ringleader at a circus. Except my circus is some fucked-up house of horrors that would make a great set for the next *Saw* movie.

"How wonderful. You've chosen the easy option." His eyes roll.

My blood-spattered shoes eat up the distance between us, and I shove him hard in the chest.

"You think I chose this? I chose *her.* She was taken from *me.*"

"And by the looks of it, you allowed it to happen. Have you reached out to her? How does the great Austin Black not even know where she is?"

Fuck, this guy is getting on my nerves. Like he has any idea of what it's like to be me.

I can see Luca getting itchy beside me. He's jumping from foot to foot, ready and waiting to pounce. He's like a fucking jackal. I wish he would knock it the fuck off.

The doctor begins to take off his jacket. He folds it carefully over a chair after inspecting it briefly. God forbid he gets it dirty. He undoes the buttons of his crisp white shirt sleeves and begins to roll them up. It kills me, but this is just like a scene out of one of those goddamn romance novels Olivia's been giving me. Corded forearms is all I can fucking think about. My first instinct is to tell her about it so we can laugh together.

"Come on then," he says.

My head shakes in confusion. "Come on then, what?"

"Hit me."

"I'll fucking hit you if one of you doesn't explain what the hell is going on," Luca interjects.

"I'm not going to hit you, doc."

"Hit me. That's what you want, right? Killing all those men wasn't enough, so let's go a few rounds. We're around the same weight and height, and I have the added advantage that I'm not tied to a chair, unlike your previous opponents. So let's get on with it."

"You're fucking crazy. I'm not going to hit you."

"Why not?" He pushes the rolled-up sleeves past his elbows for good measure.

I splutter, throwing my hands up in exasperation. Why is it that even when I'm the fucking boss, no-one ever fucking listens.

"You're not going to hit me, because you're not a villain." He pauses for dramatic effect, picks up his jacket, and heads toward the door.

If I'm not a villain, then why did I force the love of my life out of town, heartbroken and alone?

CHAPTER TWENTY-THREE

Olivia

The ache in my chest relents for a while when I sleep. As my eyes flicker open, I stretch my arms up above my head, arching my back, and it's not until my spine straightens that it hits me all over again.

Austin hasn't come to find me. I've left traces, hiding in the most obvious place, but it's no use. If he wants to find me, he will.

The comments from my channel have been bursting with theories for the last week. Followers postulated that a lovers' quarrel had separated us as my videos of us together dwindled. I've left the remaining ones up; they've proved successful, despite the bitter feeling that aches my throat when I review the analytics. They still think Dr. Alfie is the "Masked Man." My heart breaks for Austin. Knowing him as I do, allowing people to think I belonged to someone else would have been hard to bear.

Luckily, we're not interesting enough that the comments continue for more than a few days. And then it's almost like it never happened, and my heart can't say for sure what's worse.

The air here is stifling. I feel like I've been sitting in a sauna for too long. I'm sweating my tits off, but I'm feeling too floppy to move and do anything about it. *Take me now, sauna gods. Let me just die here.* I'm surprised there's anything left to sweat out. I've cried so much in the last week, I thought I'd need a drip to rehydrate myself, just so I could cry some more.

It wasn't until I saw Danny that the realization hit me square in the chest like someone has been using me for shooting practice. I'd put my brother in danger, the only family I have left. It all began with me. And what I said to Austin . . . it was unforgivable. His face looked like I'd just killed a puppy right in front of his eyes. And I guess I did—our love was the fucking puppy, and I destroyed it in one rageful moment.

We haven't spoken since that night. He told me he was going to be the villain, who he was meant to be. Despite all the work he's done, the hours he's put in with Dr. Alfie, in building his business, in making me feel so cherished, he still thinks he's the villain. This is the most fucked-up situation of my life, and I have no idea how to act, *how to feel*.

And what do I feel? I'm furious. Furious that despite the reputation he has, something like this could have happened. That it was so easy to get to him through me.

He hasn't texted.

He hasn't called.

Austin has left me alone to deal with this, no doubt thinking I'm better off without him, and it's only incensed me more. I don't need someone who thinks they know better than me. I need someone who will love me even when I push back. I need someone who will be there for me despite all odds. Not a man who forces my brother to send me away. He was too much of a coward to do it himself. Danny couldn't even offer an explanation, only that it was life or death and I was the next target. If I left, everyone would be safe. That was the deal.

When I'd called Danny a few times, he'd been improving. The swelling had gone down in his eye, and despite the fact that it was still as purple as the oxalis triangularis I tried in Austin's farm, he looked more like himself. He couldn't walk, could barely breathe from the broken rib, but he was going to be okay. He promised he would come visit me as soon as things had settled down.

He hadn't said much on the phone, no real details. Just vague comments that "people were going to get what was coming to them" or "he's made his bed, now he's got to lie in it." Whoever *he* is. He won't tell me who. At first I'd thought he was talking about Austin, but the one thing my brother isn't sparse on are details about him. He's still gushing about him like he's just been signed with some superhero squad. We haven't talked about the relationship between Austin and me. I know he's still furious about it. He has every right to be. Instead, he asks me if *I'm* okay. He knows enough that my heart is breaking right now. And even though he's mad, he's not vindictive.

So here I am, alone, in a new place and wondering what the fuck to do. I've been given the okay to update my channel as much as I want to. Danny's rerouting it though multiple IP addresses so it can't be traced. All my equipment, including my camera setup, was shipped to me express. It arrived the day after I did.

So I do what I know how. I get to work.

Austin

We've reached a plateau.

My father has run out of men he can convince to work for him, and therefore there are no more left for me to kill. We're at an impasse, a stalemate if you will.

And a plateau is bad for business. A truce is needed on his side. But that's the thing when you take away someone's only reason to be good—I have no incentive for a truce. I have no incentive to do anything except be a fucking menace to him until the day he dies.

So I'm taking this meeting to let him know just that. I'll be here waiting to fuck up every single thing he decides to do. Every deal, fucked. Every investment, fucked. Every time he wants to get his dick wet, well . . . in that case, not fucked. He won't have a single woman touch him ever again. No relief, no pleasure, no fucking desire met.

And it's a small price to pay, for imprisoning me in this life, for what he did to Danny, to Olivia. My girl. Alone and believing that I don't want her when my bones ache at the very memory of her.

My driver pulls up alongside the dock. The lights are bright ahead despite all the workers being home. I'm sure even the security have been let go for this rendezvous. Luca and I step out of the car, doing up the button on my jacket, Luca checks his gun. I'm not carrying a weapon tonight. We have good men with us who've joined us from the old life. They're armed and ready for whatever lies ahead. We stride between container ships, knowing the route like the back of my hand. We don't need to talk; everything has been planned for.

I hear the mutters of low voices and shuffling feet before we turn the corner. My father comes into view, his tall frame and broad build drawing all fields of vision toward him. He's flanked by two shorter men that look like they work out six hours a day. I don't recognize either. Do they know who they're working for and who they're up against? The dumb look on both their faces would suggest not.

"Son." My father beams, arms open like I haven't just killed eleven henchmen.

"John."

His mustache bristles as his nostrils flare. It would have looked quite comical if we weren't in some new-age version of a Western shootout. I can practically hear *The Good, the Bad and the Ugly* in the background. He thinks he's Clint Eastwood and he doesn't realize he's in the wrong century. His time is over. He's obsolete and still clinging to the good old days that no longer exist.

My brother arrives from a container behind my father. His feet come to an abrupt halt once he sees me.

"What are you doing here?" he spits out, gawping between me and dear old dad.

"Hush," my father spits out.

"He's made it clear he's not interested-"

"I said shut your mouth, Augustus!" My father shoves him.

Silence crackles through the air. Luca shuffles from foot to foot as my father and I stand off.

"You've had your fun, Austin. Time to grow up."

"You think that killing the eleven goons you sent to beat up Danny was me having fun?"

"It was actually twelve goons, Austin," Luca interrupts.

I turn to Luca and smirk, spotting a hint of apprehension on his face. "Thank you, Luca. Correction, twelve goons. Not fun. But you didn't give me much of a choice, did you?"

My father's lips flatten, his eyes flitting to Luca for a moment.

"So let me tell *you* how this is going to go. You're going to close up shop, on your terms, because I'm feeling generous."

He laughs, looking around at his two fresh-faced goons, who snicker, too, unaware of how serious I am.

"I warned you what would happen if you didn't come to heel, Austin. That little girlfriend of yours is going to make an excellent centerpiece for when my associates come next week," he sneers, but I lose all ability to hear. All I can see is the blob of red his face distorts into. The dock lights illuminate every contour of his wrinkled face. His white hair is thinning on top; his suit is a little too big. It's almost like me killing twelve of his men has left him a little stressed.

I know he won't lay a finger on Olivia. Not a chance in hell am I going to let that happen.

"We both know you'll be dead long before you get within a hundred miles of her," I say coolly.

He laughs, and his two henchmen laugh too. "You were always soft, you know that? Why do you think I made you an enforcer? You needed toughening up. And thank god I did because you were fucking good at what you did, Austin. You just needed a little push, that's all."

I shake my head. Nothing about me was soft. And

I don't mean that in a self-aggrandizing way. It's meant in a self-deprecating way. I had to learn to be soft. Hardness was ingrained in me. Being tough, violent, aggressive. It was second nature to me two years ago. I had to unlearn that. Alfie taught me how to do it. Olivia showed me why I wanted to in the first place. Soft is used as such an insult, yet all I dream about now is having a soft life. A soft bed. A soft pillow. A soft dream. My hands on Olivia's soft, perfect skin as she curls into me.

"Surprised?" my father continues. "I know what's good for you. If it weren't for me, you'd be miserable."

What the fuck is he talking about? I was fucking miserable working for him. But now I'm not. Well, with the exception of the clusterfuck that was this last week or so. I've never been happier. Despite his intention, he is right. If he hadn't made me an enforcer, I never would have run from that job, I never would have reconnected with Alfie, I never would have hid in Squeeze the Day, I never would have met Olivia, she never would have kidnapped me. The fucked thing is that he's one hundred percent right. He's got the right answer despite doing the wrong calculation. Fuck, that's so annoying.

But do I care? Not really.

"You're right, Dad. You made me who I am. And luckily, I've unlearned a lot of what you taught me. I've met someone who loves me and expects nothing from me. Without you, I never would have met her. So thank you. For the one thing you did right. But this ends now."

"You're damn right it ends now," he spits. "Kill him." He holds my eyes, and I accept that this is happening. My father has ordered my death, and it's the calmest he's looked all night. I hold his gaze as everyone else shifts uncomfortably.

The electric current hums in the air as the crackle of the lights overhead interrupts like a circuit breaker. I can almost hear the waves lap against the concrete. I wonder if he'll throw my body into the port or move me elsewhere.

"Are you deaf? KILL HIM."

The goons stare at each other, wondering who should make the move. My brother steps forward, understanding that he is the one being addressed.

But our father holds out an arm against his chest. August looks to him in confusion, back to me, and then I hear the click of the safety. Even my brother has the decency to gasp.

"I'm sorry, Austin," Luca speaks steadily. I close my eyes and will myself to wake up from this nightmare. Surely not Luca? Luca whom I've known since we were kids. Luca, who broke a guy's nose during my first fight. He's had my back my entire life. I've had his. He left this life with me. We built something together to be proud of.

"Luca, what the fuck are you doing?" I try to remain calm, but the hurt I feel is overwhelming. This guy is more of a brother to me than my actual fucking brother. And even he looks disgusted at this betrayal right now.

Luca moves so he's standing in front of me, by my father's side.

"You weren't coming back, Austin. And I had to do what I had to, to get my old life back."

"I SAVED YOU FROM THIS LIFE!" I bellow.

Fuck Dr. Alfie for opening up my emotions because now I can't fucking control them at all. The hurt of this betrayal has cut me deeper than any wound ever has. I have scars all over my body, knife fights, surgeries, and fist fights that led to split knuckles, split lips, and split eyebrows. There's no part of my body that hasn't suffered from my previous life. And while there's no physical violence in the life I built, you pay the price with your emotions. You learn to care; you learn to love, to trust, to feel something other than shit. So when the ultimate betrayal happens, you're left reeling.

"I NEVER ASKED YOU TO FUCKING SAVE ME!" he screams right back. He's holding the gun to my face. The gun I fucking bought him as a gift. The intricate pattern on the side emulates a gun he saw in a Leonardo di Caprio movie. It is

Catholicism incarnate, and he's always loved the dichotomy of using something so violent in the name of God. Luca's like that —he leans into two halves. I'm learning just how much.

"You never said you were unhappy."

"You've gone soft, Austin. Do you know how fucking pathetic you've been? Running around with that slut who dropped to her knees the second you gave her attention."

"Don't you fucking talk about her like that," I hiss, leaning my forehead into his gun. His lips part in horror. My brother steps forward, and my father sneers.

Silence descends on the docks until the only thing I can hear is the gentle lapping of waves against the concrete. Even the seagulls have the decency to shut up.

"Finish him, and I'll know you're ready," my father interrupts.

My brother snaps his head to face our father. It looks like I'm not the only one who was betrayed tonight. I give him a small consolation smile as he turns back to me, shaking his head. His anguished face tells me everything I need to know. He didn't know I was going to die tonight. He didn't know Luca would betray me, and he had no idea our father had made a deal to let Luca take over.

Luca's hand shakes. I can see the sweat forming on his upper lip. Our last conversation is running through his head. I'm not coming back, and I won't fucking lie now to save myself. Maybe that's stupid. Maybe it's naive. But I won't beg.

I inhale deeply through my nose and close my eyes. The salt air mixes in with diesel and honest-to-god fish guts but I push the stench out of my mind. If I'm going to die, the last thing I see is going to be Olivia laughing maniacally in a field because I've launched a Ghostface mask over my shoulder and tackled her to the ground. I'm going to pepper her face with kisses as she smiles with her whole face. I breathe in again, and I can almost smell her citrus shampoo. I can smell the wildflowers in the field that we ran through. That moment is perfect; she is perfect.

An ear-splitting shot rings out. A flash of white hits my eyes, and then . . . nothing.

Well . . . not nothing.

I assume I am dead for about five seconds when I don't feel my body hit the ground, but then I realize the yelling, multiple shots, and someone getting tackled aren't the sounds of hell. I am still alive.

Either Luca is still a terrible fucking shot, or he wasn't the one to pull the trigger.

I open my eyes, chaos ensuing.

"Don't just stand there, you absolute fucking idiot!" my brother screams at me as he tackles me out of the line of fire. Despite his stocky build and the strength he pummels through my abdomen as he saves me from a flying bullet, I manage to stay on my feet.

Snaps of lights flash across my eyes, disorientating me. The ring in my ear pulses like it's trying to push through me, my head practically vibrating with it. I open my jaw, push my finger in my ear, and try to wiggle. *Fuck, I must have burst my ear drum.*

I force myself back to the present. The two goons standing beside my father have their hands up straight above their heads, and I roll my eyes. They're both shaking, and the one on the left has pissed himself. I've promised myself after the intervention Dr. Alfie gave me that I won't kill again. *Fucking hell. The one on the right is crying.*

Throwing my hands up in exasperation, I yell, "Run away, you morons!"

I shoo them away, and now it's my brother's turn to throw his hands up.

"I promised my therapist I wouldn't kill anymore." I shrug.

"Life-threatening situations might be exempt from that rule, Austin." The deep tones of Alfie fucking Adams ring through my one good ear.

"What the fuck are you doing here?"

"Well, you missed our last two sessions, so I was slightly concerned. I also had a feeling you were going to be ambushed."

"So, you came to a gunfight? Jesus, Alf, we're outnumbered by a fucking lot here. I don't know if I can protect you."

"Is this your boyfriend?" my brother asks. "I thought you were with a woman?"

I'm hoping the ringing in my ear stops soon and just takes my ability to hear away, so I don't have to hear stupid fucking comments like that. He knows full well who Olivia is.

"Augustus, this is Dr. Alfie Adams. He's my therapist."

My brother eyes him up and down. "Got any good drugs?"

"I'm a psychologist, not a psychiatrist, Augustus." It's nice to hear his exasperated tone on someone other than me for a change.

My brother ducks and pulls Alfie down with him as an unknown man rounds the corner and starts shooting. He's squatted low, and before I can move, he grabs my ankle and yanks me down on the concrete just as another shot rings past my ear. I land almost on top of him, and despite sounding a little winded, Augustus is okay.

"Jesus, you're like a fucking concrete slab. Get off me." He shoves me hard in the chest.

I waggle my eyebrows. "I've been working out."

"Gross." He succeeds this time in rolling me away.

"Get your mind out of the gutter, Augustus. I have a personal trainer for a girlfriend."

"Ex-girlfriend," Alfie notes neutrally. If my eyes could shoot daggers, I fucking would. He's lucky I was stupid enough not to bring a weapon.

"She dumped you?" my brother asks, his face looking genuinely concerned.

Wow, are we having a breakthrough? Color me shocked.

He shuffles back against a shipping container that

provides us some shelter from the repeated clunk and clang of bullets hitting metal.

"I don't believe this is the right time for you two to overcome your differences. And you might want to borrow this," Dr. Alfie grits out and hands me a gun from the back of his slacks.

I stare at the loaded weapon in my palm. *Where the hell did he get a damn gun from?*

My brother, too impatient to deal with the crisis of my two worlds colliding, snatches the gun out of my hand and starts shooting.

Alfie and I don't speak for a moment and wait for my brother to give us instructions. One of our guys is hiding behind some crates, using them as cover. The shots are becoming fewer and farther between now. My brother turns around and settles in next to me. His breathing is a little labored, his leg twitching, and I feel the urge to calm him down.

"About your question, she didn't dump me. I . . . I told her to leave. Because of the whole Danny situation." A lump clogs my throat, causing my voice to sound squeaky and unnatural. The words want to go back in; my heart is telling me not to trust him yet. But I want to. I want to believe that my brother is still there. But as it happens, my judgment on whom I can trust is a bit skewed right now. Just wait until I get my hands on Luca.

"Hey, you know I didn't have anything to do with that, right? I had no idea Dad was going to do that."

August's face is sincere, his sharp lines softening. This could be the moment things actually improve for us. If he steps away from the business, I could bring him into mine. Sure, it's legit and not really what he wants to do, but I could help him. We could join forces and really piss our dad off.

I nod as I see Callum ring out another shot. He yells over to someone else behind him. Using his hand to call out to someone up above on top of some shipping containers. *Did he just yell Danny?*

"Callum, we're trying to have a heart-to-heart here. Can you knock it off?" I call out, trying to ease the tension.

"Fuck you, Austin." He laughs, army-crawling toward us. "I'm out of bullets. You got anything?"

I shake my head. "Thank god you got into farming, boss, because you're a terrible fucking gangster, I'll tell you that."

My initial fury is quickly extinguished when I realize how fucking happy I am to hear someone say that.

As the shouts of unknown voices come closer, we begin to crawl to the back of the shipping container we've been leaning on.

"My fucking suit is ruined. Whoever started this fucking gunfight is getting a dry cleaning bill at the very least," my brother moans.

God, he really is a pretentious ass. He's getting shot at, and all he cares about is his dry cleaning bill. The man is worth millions.

"Augustus. Who wears a Tom Ford suit to the docks? You really only have yourself to blame."

The unsettling quiet descends, and I'm not sure if it's safe to come out. I slap Alfie on the shoulder. "Welcome to my world, doc. I bet you're loving your office right about now, aren't you? A nice comfy couch, air conditioning in the summer, heat in the winter, and your beautiful office manager organizing your life for you. None of this chaos."

He grimaces, and finally, I think I might be getting through to him. He needs to pull his head out of his ass and get his girl almost as much as I need to get mine.

"I can't see why you'd want to get out of this life, Austin. I've rather enjoyed myself." He smirks.

I lean against the corrugated metal, wiping the dirt off my pants despite my ass sitting directly in a puddle.

"Are you really out?" Augustus asks.

I hear a few shouts overhead, and Callum gets to his feet. The voice is one of ours, and he goes to investigate.

"Yeah, I'm really out. I told you, I have my own thing going on."

I look around. The dock is usually bustling with workers. The daytime, filled with container ships, no doubt some illegal goods, I'm not completely naive. But at night, it's like the truth comes out. The harsh flood lights shine a light on the grime and dirt, the seediness of it all. The smell of copper permeates the air, and I'm starkly reminded of how much I hate this life.

Even before Olivia abducted me, I had days and days of no violence. Not a single thought that would make me think of murder, or blood, or guns. I was just living this normal life, content with monotony. Then Olivia happened, and despite our unconventional start, it wasn't violent, except for the chloroform and the taser. But that was just foreplay.

I've been hollow for so long. A shell of a man trying to work out how to be human. She fills me up with love and soft kisses, longing and simple desires like coming home to the smell of home cooking. I learned how to cook, learned how to listen. Fuck, I'm so fucking fit right now, it's unreal. She's built my body into a protective force to be reckoned with, not a tool for violence. She's made me into the man I never imagined was possible.

He nods and holds out his hand. I slap mine into it, giving him a shake. Might as well lean into it.

I pull him into a hug, slapping his back, because, of course, *men*.

"I'll help you," he says.

"You will?"

"Yeah, the business is mine. Everything else, the house, the cars, I don't give a shit. But I want the business."

"It's not mine to give, but you'll get no opposition from me. I want my new life back," I say, and I mean it. I've been very upfront about that.

"Fucking hell, Austin. What are you waiting for? Just go get her."

I grin, knowing that's exactly what I plan to do. Danny will tell me where she is. I'll go to her tonight, beg her for forgiveness, tell her I'm hers to do whatever she wants with. I'll love her forever and leave this whole life behind me if that's what she wants.

Callum rounds the corner. His face contorted into a harsh grimace. The gun in his hand is held loosely by his thigh; the fight is over, that's for sure. As I ready myself to stand, to leave and get my girl, he lifts his head and looks me in the eye.

"Your father was shot . . . he's dead."

CHAPTER TWENTY-FOUR

Olivia

"My god, it's actually a bit annoying how good you look in tassels," Nicole says, snapping a few photos.

I laugh, giving her a dip of the cowboy hat she's got me dressed up in.

We're working on a shoot for her upcoming collection. The bright lights are making my eyes burn. And that's not even commenting on the fact that it's so damn hot in here; the thick makeup I'm wearing is practically melting off my face. The lashes are long enough to act as a fan for Nicole, so at least she's keeping cool.

"A few more. Won't be long, then drinks are on me."

"A lot of drinks, please." I jut out my hip and give her a wink. I spot Josh lingering in the background, watching Nicole intently. His ears prick up at the mention of drinks, and I'm sure his hand is still sore from punching out that guy at the bar in L.A..

My heart squeezes at the thought. It was such a perfect day. Austin had been so unexpectedly calm and in control. I was really starting to see a side to him I hadn't realized he has.

Danny is calling me every day, checking in. It's only work-related stuff I can discuss, and there is a lot. I've spent the week devising a new plan for the year: content to create, scheduling follow-up meetings with my contacts from the fitness expo. Which has led me to catch up with Nicole now that I'm in Texas.

We've hung out a few times and gone through some ideas together on where to take our companies. It is actually so helpful to have a friend who also has their own business. We commiserate on bad ideas we've had in the past and the difficulties of owning a small business, especially where customers could be as fickle as social media trends.

I didn't realize how much I missed female company until we started hanging out. And Nicole is one of those people who genuinely feels that happiness shared, is happiness doubled. She's introduced me to her girlfriends and that's where we are heading after we finish up with our promo shoot.

"Okay, perfect. We're all done. I'll edit these tomorrow, and we can go through them together once I've tidied it all up," she says, flicking through the images quickly on her camera. Josh comes up behind her, his eyes flitting across the screen, and gives a grunt of approval. She rolls her eyes at me before letting out a small sigh.

Our phones ding simultaneously, and she whips it from her pocket.

"The girls are out! And oh shitbags, they said there's some out-of-town football team buying them drinks. Let's get going!"

◆ ◆ ◆

Nicole might have the most diverse friendship group I've ever met.

Marianne is the smart one, her cropped shoulder-length hair and tortoise shell-rimmed glasses giving her the ultimate bookish vibe as she sips back on the only wine available in this deadbeat bar. I'm pretty sure when she asked for a wine list, the bartender replied, "Red or white?" The shock on her face said it all as she muttered red, her cheeks flushing.

Blakely starts off the night quiet and reserved, but as

soon as she hits her second drink, she's up on the table dancing and taking over karaoke at every moment she can. Her auburn hair gives the image of flickering flames as she riles up the crowd under the neon lights.

And then there is Nicole, who is the most genuine person I have ever met. She is soaring high with her business, becoming one of the most sought-after brands to work with, and she just wants to bring everyone along for the ride with her. She doesn't have a jealous bone in her body, just pure adoration for her friends with a tendency to take in strays. She tells me after a few drinks that despite knowing Marianne since they were in kindergarten, Blakely is a recent addition to their friendship group. And now there's me—another stray looking for a home.

"That guy has been checking you out for the last twenty minutes." Her eyes dart over to the corner where a tall, broad, dirty-blond-haired man is sitting. His suit is impeccable, styled with a classic Texan bolo tie and a cowboy hat that makes my mouth water.

He tips his hat to me as I catch his eye, but I quickly look away. It's only been three weeks since I left Washington, four weeks since I've spoken to Austin, yet the memory of him lingers on my skin. How could I get a drink with another guy, knowing I could still smell him on my clothes?

"Hey, darlin'," a deep voice murmurs.

I glance up and The Suit has made his way over to our booth and leans comfortably against the partition, towering over me.

Holy moly. This guy is hot.

"Hi there." I smile.

I glance at Nicole, and she fans her face. "She's single!"

"Nicole!" I snap.

"What? You are, technically." She shrugs as Marianne and Blakely snicker into their drinks.

"Ah, technically, doesn't sound all that single." He laughs, holding out his hand. "I'm Levi."

"Hi Levi, I'm Olivia."

"Don't want to be too forward; I can see you're out with your girlfriends. But I was wondering if I could get your number. I'd love to take you out so you can tell me all about what *technically single* means."

Oh, he's charming, not pushy, acknowledging that I'm out with the girls. He's ticking a lot of boxes. And the dimples that keep winking at me are definitely helping his case. I pause for a second before pulling out my phone. It's been four weeks. I live in another state now. What did I have to lose?

"Put your number in my phone, and I'll give you a call."

He takes my phone, typing in his number.

"I texted my number, so I've got yours." He winks. "I'll call you tomorrow, Olivia."

He takes my hand again but this time brings my knuckles to his lips and kisses them gently. I have the urge to fan myself like Nicole. But a second later, he's heading to the door.

I turn to the girls. "Did that just happen?"

"Get it, girl. That guy was hot with a capital H," Blakeley slurs before downing the remainder of her cocktail.

Nicole grins. "He was super hot, Olivia. Are you gonna call him?"

I shake my head. Honestly? No. I could never move on so quickly. Austin still has my heart and it wouldn't be right to go on a date with someone else knowing that.

"I don't think so, but it felt pretty nice to be shown some interest." I wink before I offer to buy everyone a round of drinks to celebrate.

We dance and flirt some more, and it's not until some random cowboy puts his hands on Nicole's hips, grinding against her, that I spot Josh at the bar, gripping his glass so hard I'm surprised it hasn't smashed.

She turns and puts her arms around his neck, and he whispers something in her ear. Her head throws back in laughter, and she lets him twirl her around.

"What are you doing?" I hear Josh yell over the music, gripping her by her elbow. It's not hard enough to hurt, but it's insistent. His eyes are imploring her more than his hand.

"Josh? What are you doing here?"

"Is this your boyfriend?" the cowboy interjects, stepping back an inch.

Nicole raises her eyebrow in question, and Josh splutters. God damn that man. He's dragging her along over and over. Every time I see these two together I can't work out what's happened. Other than the fact it's her brother's best friend. They're clearly in love with each other.

He says nothing, and she rolls her eyes, shifting her body back to the cowboy. "No, he's not."

She drags the cowboy by the hand toward the door, looking back at me and mouthing, "I'll call you," as she skips out the door. The cowboy is holding on to his hat for dear life as poor Josh sinks his drink at the bar.

Blakely loops her arm into mine, and Marianne picks up her purse.

"I just know I'm going to have the worst hangover all day tomorrow and then back to work Monday. Fucking kill me now," Blakely whines. She really does have the worst boss. A super creep if there ever was one.

"You should quit," Marianne says for the hundredth time.

"Sure, Little Miss Four Jobs and Counting. I'll quit my *one* when you quit at least two of yours," she snips back, grinning. Marianne rolls her eyes. She's still a little quiet around us both, but I'm hoping with time, she'll warm up.

I say goodnight to the girls, giving Josh a little pat on the back as I walk out. He gives me a nod before lifting his beer for another pull.

As I'm in my Uber, I check some of the comments on my latest video. Hundreds are still asking where the Masked Man is. I know it's only been a couple of weeks, but I thought they would have relented by now. But truthfully, I want to know, too. I can't stop thinking about Austin. All the promises he has made. He said we would be together; he told me he loved me. I don't know if I'll ever love again or if he'll be stuck in my heart forever. Could I really live a life without him? Knowing how good we can be together, I'm not sure. I want him to choose me. Choose a life together that's on our terms. But if I can't have that, I'll settle for knowing that he doesn't see himself as the villain. I want him to be happy and know how loved he is by so many people.

Pulling up to my new building, I miss the space that my family home offered. I love my new apartment, but a one-bed has significantly less space to live in. I have some dedicated space for my work, but it's a squeeze that I'm adjusting to.

I set up my phone to do a live stream. Something I've never done before. No script, no planning, just enough tequila to give me the nerve and not enough to make me regret this in the morning. At least, I hope not.

I hit record and start talking.

CHAPTER TWENTY-FIVE

Austin

The smooth deep voice of Alfie Adams fills my ear as I answer my phone. He's calm, but quick to the point. "Your girl is breaking the internet, Austin."

"Olivia?"

Fucking hell, if I see a video of her naked, I'm going to quickly forget my no-kill policy.

"Is there anyone else?"

"Of course not," I scoff before heading straight to her channel. *Yes, I have it bookmarked.*

There she sits, just her with a white backdrop. It's a livestream, and my god, she's so beautiful. She's done up like she's going out. Like I don't know already. Callum gave me an update last night that she'd gone to Texas for a business deal, but that was the most I knew about her location. She entered a bar at 8 p.m. with Nicole, the clothing brand owner we met in L.A., along with two other girls named Marianne and Blakely. Marianne is clean, and Blakely has a sealed record from when she was a minor. But she has a stable job and rents her own apartment, so she seems to be on the up and up. Not that I have room to criticize. I did kill eleven men last week. Oh, actually, Luca told me it was twelve. My chest stings at the thought of him.

"I'll give you a minute to watch it. Call me if you want to talk, okay?" Alfie brings me back to the present.

"I'm not going to. I can't."

"It's for you, Austin. She wants you to listen to her."

"How do you know?"

"Well, if you're not the Masked Man she's referring to, then this is going to be awkward."

"Fuck off," I laugh.

"With pleasure. Call me, please."

The phone goes blank, and I hit play, her sweet voice filling my lifeless office.

"Hi, everyone. My name is Olivia, and I run Train with Olivia. I don't do a lot of personal posts; this is my business, after all. But lines got a little blurred when the Masked Man started working with me on my channel."

Fucking hell. She is so fucking brave, even as she plays with her hands; I've never seen a post like this. It's so raw and unfiltered.

"There's been a lot of speculation about our relationship, and as some of you have noticed, there haven't been any posts with him for a few weeks now." She sighs and looks up, blinking rapidly as if to fight her tears back.

"He was my boyfriend, and I . . . something happened. And I was quick to react and place blame. I pushed him away and now that I've moved to another state, I'm realizing that our relationship really is over."

Fuck, fuck, fuck. Why am I watching this?

"Someone gave me their number tonight. He was cute." She laughs. "Really cute."

Let me find a pencil to ram into my eye now and end this torture.

"But I felt nothing. I mean he was super hot and charming and funny."

One more. I can kill one more person, then never again.

"But he wasn't the Masked Man. He didn't make me smile even when he didn't mean to. He didn't surprise me at every turn. I couldn't see myself falling in love with him. Because I am in love. Nothing is going to change how I feel about the Masked Man because even though he's not a perfect person, he's perfect for me. And no cowboy can compete with that.

"So, I guess I'm putting myself out there. My carefully curated and polished workouts will resume tomorrow, but for tonight, I want you to see the real me. I'm just a girl trying to make her way in the world and build something meaningful that I can be proud of. And I want to do that with the man I love by my side. So, Masked Man, if you feel the same, just know that I forgive you, and I hope you can forgive me too. I love you."

The video cuts off abruptly.

She loves me . . .

She knows I'm never going to be perfect, and yet she wants me anyway. How could I ever be worthy of this woman?

I scroll the comments.

What are you waiting for, Masked Man?? Get your girl!

UNMASK UNMASK UNMASK

I thought Dr. Angel A.K.A Alfie Adams is the Masked Man? He's so hot. Not sure why he'd wear a mask though.

Absolutely fucking not. I'm sure Alfie fucking loved reading that one.

I keep reading.

How could anyone leave her? She's so perfect.

Lame. Stick to your workouts.

I push down the instinct to jot down the username for later.

True love does exist.

We need an update!

A knock at my office door pulls me out of my doom-scrolling. I need to book a flight. I need to get to her right fucking now. I'll scour all of Texas if I have to. I need to get rid of this person at the door ASAP.

"What?" I call out, typing in the search box for flights.

Danny walks through the door. His hood is up over his head, and he looks tired. We haven't discussed what has happened in great detail. Other than the fact that Danny had organized a few of the guys to ambush the meeting with my father.

He had hung back, eager to be in the action. I'm pretty sure that blonde nurse at the hospital would have killed him if he were in the thick of it. She sticks to him like cooked pasta to a wall. And honestly, he seems to enjoy the attention. Despite that, his limited movement meant he couldn't be in on the action. While I was having my heart-to-heart with Augustus, he shot and killed our father. I can't say I blame him; the old man nearly killed him. But all Danny cares about is that he threatened Olivia. I can't fault him for that; I would do the same thing.

"Boss."

"Danny."

"I'll make this quick; I know you're busy. I need a week off."

The cojones on this guy. Killed my dad a week ago and now asking for time off. I mean, like I said, I don't blame him but god damn.

I take a deep breath.

I will not run my business like my father did.

I will not run my business like my father did.

"Okay, when do you need the time off?"

"My flight is tomorrow."

Fuck's sake.

"Danny, in a normal company, you have to put in something called a fucking leave request. Then it gets approved. And THEN you book your flights."

He smirks. "Sure, boss. But one, this isn't a normal company. And two, you're in love with my sister, so I figured I'd get some leeway."

I run my hands over my eyes.

"I'm curious. How long have you known?"

"I saw your neck extend from your torso when you were hiding behind the basement door when I came to the house.

You looked like a real creep."

"Jesus."

"That's what I thought. I thought fuck my life, my boss is fucking my sister. But then you were so devastated at the hospital that I knew it was more than that. You sent her away even though it made you miserable."

"I'm not miserable."

Lies. I am.

"Tell that to your fucking face, boss."

"Danny. You're not meant to talk to your boss like that. This is not going to be like my father's operation. We're going to be doing things properly."

"We'll I'd suggest not fucking your employees' relatives then," he quips, grinning.

"That's a good point. We should make a handbook."

Callum enters the room, typing away on his phone. He's swiftly come into my inner circle since the night at the docks. He's shown true loyalty on his end and orchestrated the team like a damn symphony when Luca's betrayal became apparent. It turns out Danny and Callum have been suspicious of Luca for a while. Small comments here and there, sudden needs to take private phone calls when he never used to, disappearing in the middle of the day. All things I had no idea about because I'd taken a relaxed view of work since I found something—or someone, I should say—way more important.

After the team cleaned up the docks, we came back to the office, and Danny explained to me that they'd set up camp at the docks a few hours before. Danny had remained up high, given that he could barely walk. He'd used a rifle to shoot down anyone that was a threat. Turns out, my father pulled out his gun as we were army-crawling away from the fight, and Danny took him out.

Another knock at the door, and Alfie fucking Adams walks right on in.

"I was just popping by to see how you are, Austin."

"He's miserable," Danny and Callum say

simultaneously.

"I'm not fucking miserable!" I bellow, letting my head fall into my hands.

"I presume everyone knows why he's miserable?" Alfie asks.

"Are you really Doctor Angel?" Danny turns to him, eyes wide.

"I prefer Alfie or Dr. Adams," he pouts, still looking gorgeous, the bastard.

"I thought it might have been you that was the Masked Man. A few of the comments on my sister's videos suggested it might be. But I knew she was seeing Austin, so I wasn't convinced."

Alfie glances at me; he doesn't look concerned, but he's assessing my reaction.

"I mean, I wouldn't blame her. Look at you! No wonder they call you Dr. Angel."

"Alright, Danny, that's enough," I say, trying to get a grip of this ambush.

They all look to me; at least, I command some level of respect.

Knock, knock.

God dammit.

Augustus saunters in, sniffing at the others as he does.

"Austin. We need to talk."

"I'm in a meeting," I say, waving my hand at the eclectic group in front of me.

"It's about your girl."

Have they planned this? Am I in some kind of alternate reality where every person I've ever met is going to walk into this office and bring up Olivia? I was about to book my flights before they all interrupted.

The scene of all four of them looks comical. Alfie and Augustus are tall and broad, elbowing each other for space as Danny and Callum shuffle closer to the desk, both only coming up to the taller one's chin. They're small, but they pack a punch when they need to.

Danny hobbles a little. I forget he's still so injured.

"Sit down, Danny."

"Thanks, boss." He's quick to pull up a seat, and his shoulders relax as soon as his ass hits the chair.

"Now. To get this over with, yes, I've watched the video. Yes, I'm the Masked Man. Yes, I'm in love with her. And yes, I'm going to get her back. So if you all don't mind fucking off, that would be wonderful."

"Oh, excellent, because I don't really need a week off. I bought the ticket in your name." Danny hands me a paper.

I scan the ticket quickly, checking the location. My heart somersaults but dips just as quickly when I realize where I'll be sitting.

"Fucking coach, Danny? Couldn't spring for business? You did just kill my father!"

"Boss, you don't pay me enough to buy business flights. And you've been fucking my sister behind my back. I'd call us even."

"That is not even by a long fucking shot."

"You didn't even like your dad!"

"You don't kill people because you don't like them, Danny."

"He threatened Olivia! And he tried to kill me first," he adds as an afterthought.

"Which is the only reason you're still here living, breathing, and giving me shit," I add.

Silence fills the air as the room shuffles awkwardly. I haven't had a chance to talk to Augustus. He knows Danny is off-limits. But I'm not sure how he feels in general about our father's death. I would suggest he talk to Alfie, but I think he'd rather go a more violent route. Maybe I'll take him on an axe-throwing excursion.

"Do you really want someone like me to be with your sister?" I ask Danny as I glance at Alfie.

The doctor rolls his eyes, raising a stark eyebrow at my

self-deprecation.

"We've talked about this, Austin. Olivia knows who you are and wants to be with you," the doctor says softly.

"Boss, you're a good guy. My sister makes her own decisions. Even if I didn't want you to date her, it's none of my fucking business."

I nod and search each of the four sets of eyes looking down on me.

"She's made a few friends, but when she calls me, I can hear how miserable she is. She's heartbroken. She finally had someone taking care of her, and now she's lost that," Danny says.

Augustus perks up next. "I saw how you helped her with her business. You supported her, cared for her, and no offense, you looked like a fucking idiot for her. Thank god you had the good sense to put those stupid masks on, or we'd have been in an even bigger shitstorm. But it's clear you love her, and I think you should go after her."

I nod, looking at Callum next. He's new to this weird wolf pack thing I've got going on, but he might as well lean into it.

"Man, I've never met Olivia. But if she's hot shit like Danny, then I'd say you go for it."

Alfie, Augustus, and I all take turns in looking between Danny and Callum until the tops of Danny's ears turn pink. Well . . . that's a revelation. I wonder if Olivia knows? I wonder if Danny does. But by the way he's smiling so goofily, I guess he's well acquainted with the fact that Callum thinks he's hot shit. And here I was thinking the blonde nurse was more his vibe.

"Are we done with this family therapy session?" August pipes in, seemingly done with this conversation.

"Yes. I'm going to win her back. Is she in Texas permanently?"

Danny grins. "Yeah, boss. She got her apartment set up in Austin."

A smile breaks out on my face. She wants me to make it back to her.

Alfie, Augustus, and Callum leave the room, but Danny stays. He acts as if he's moving slowly because of his injuries, but I know he's delaying because he has more to say.

"I do have a few things I'd like to add."

"I thought you might. Feel free to sit down if your leg is sore," I offer.

"I'll stand for this," he says, bracing himself on his side of my desk. He's almost leering over me in this position and if I didn't know him, I'm man enough to say I'd be a little intimidated.

"I expect you to be fucking loyal to her. You remember what I said about ruining someone's life with the press of a button? I've got the button, and despite my leg being fucked, I can still use my finger. I will fucking press it. Got it?"

"Understood." I shiver. *Fuck, the kid is a little scary.*

"Good. Now can we get back to you being my boss and not some mopey twat that's pining after my sister?"

"This conversation never fucking happened, and if you speak to me like that again, I'll have your tongue stapled to the desk."

"There he is." He grins. "I was starting to worry the old you was completely dead. Now go get my sister . . . Oh, did I forget to mention? That cowboy called her, and she agreed to go on a date with him. Given that you didn't respond to her video, she figured you weren't interested anymore."

"It's been less than twelve hours since she posted it!" I practically screech, jumping out of my seat. *Fuck waiting for tomorrow. I'm getting on a plane right fucking now.*

"Good luck!" he says before hobbling out of my office laughing.

CHAPTER TWENTY-SIX

Austin

That was the longest flight of my life. Despite only being four hours and five excruciating minutes, I've made it. My hair is fucked; I'm pretty sure some snot-nose little kid has been wiping their boogers in it the entire flight. The mother looked everywhere except my eyes when I turned to scowl at her.

But I'm a new man, and not only do I not kill children *—that's always been a no-go,* now everyone is off-limits. So it's *smile and wave* until I see them walking through the terminal, and I trip the little shit up.

Whoopsie. I'm sure Alfie will give me points for trying.

Now I'm sweating my balls off as the driver escorts me to the car. Texas heat really is something else.

As I enter the back of the car, my order is ready and waiting. Thank you, Texas, for the right to carry without a license. The jumped-up little twerp that's on a date with Olivia doesn't need to know I have no intention of using a weapon ever again, but I'll be carrying it to keep her safe for the foreseeable. I check for bullets, taking them all out and putting them in my pocket before tucking the gun under my shirt in my waistband.

Of all the places she could have chosen, she just had to choose Austin, Texas. Not just my namesake, but the place I told her I felt happiest as a kid. Surely she remembers that conversation all those weeks ago in the basement? My heart is pleading with me to believe it's true.

The air conditioning is blasting, and I'm thankful the cool air is keeping me grounded. What if this is a mistake and she's hurt I didn't call her straight away? My heart stammers and questions me the whole ride, warning me that something isn't right. Why would she go on a date so soon after posting the video?

I give the driver the address and lean back into the seat, tapping my fingers on my knee to try and stop my knee from bouncing.

"So, you're heading to the bowling alley?"

"The bowling alley?"

"Yeah, that's the address in the entertainment district you gave me."

"Umm, yes. If that's where the address is, I'll make my own way from there."

I run my hands down my slacks, ironing out the creases —black suit, black shirt, black soul ready to claim what's mine. I may not be a real villain anymore, but it sure is what my girl finds attractive. I'm dressing for her, and I'd bet my ass that this schmuck she's on a date with is nothing like what turns her on. Not some sweet-talking cowboy; she wants someone who can keep up with her. And it just so happens I know I'm the man for the job. The danger from my father is gone. We can be together again. I'm not afraid to grovel and beg, and I am happy to cry in front of her date to make him uncomfortable enough to leave. *Bring it on, cowboy, because these tear ducts are primed and ready.*

I steel myself as we pull up to the Bowlarama. The rainbow of colors strobes through the room, reminding me of a carnival. The sound of the arcade games is already ringing in my ears as I push through the lime-green doors.

My knees wobble as I look down at the garish party-patterned carpet, the swirls making each step feel like I'm on a boat in a rocky sea. As I move forward, my legs double in weight, dragging slowly toward the teenage girl on the desk. My heart is racing, and it occurs to me that I look fucking suspicious as hell.

The realization hits me that I haven't thought this far ahead. This place has fifty fucking lanes. I'm gonna have to walk down every single one. But I should have known I'd spot her in a crowd. Her red sundress falls just above the knee. The straps travel down her shoulders to a sweetheart neckline with the perfect hint of her soft flesh beneath. The daisy embroidery travels up the layered skirt and swishes as she moves. She's perfect, flicking her hair over her shoulder, she's pulling a face at Nicole, the girl from the fitness expo. She looks . . . happy.

I start to back away. I realize she's probably just made that video to appease her followers. She's had to provide some kind of explanation, and at least this way, it garners her some sympathy.

I move swiftly toward the bar area, where I have a clear view of the back of her head. She's settled and despite knowing the group of people for only a few weeks, she seems to be fully in the fold.

I order a beer and tell myself that once I finish it, I'll go over to her. For now, I can just watch her and make sure I know she's happy. Really happy. And then maybe if I feel she's happy enough, I'll leave her be. I won't disrupt what she's built by bringing in my chaos. She deserves that much.

I catch Nicole's eye, and her lips part a little, her eyes darting to Olivia. I shake my head a little, and she skips over. Josh is watching from one of the seats, but his face softens once he sees it's me she's bounding over to see.

"What are you doing sitting over here? Come over," she says, rushing to the point.

"Just having a drink first."

"Liquid courage, I get it. But between you and me, I don't think you need it." She gives me a little wink.

"Is she happy?" I ask, my heart torn, desperately asking

for it to be so and selfishly wanting to be the only one who could make her so. *Fuck, this is why I should leave her be.*

"Yeah, she's happy here. I think she's letting herself live a little now. But she misses you. Even when she's got cute cowboys asking her out." She grins.

"Nicole, please don't tell me any more. I can't fucking bear it."

She grins up at me like a fucking menace. No wonder Josh was pulling his hair out when we met them in L.A..

"Gosh, you're sweet. I'm gonna send her over here, okay? So y'all can have some privacy."

I take a deep breath, steeling myself. At least this gives her the option to ignore me rather than me bombarding her with her new friends.

I watch Nicole whisper into Olivia's ear, and her head snaps up before turning to face me. I give her a small wave and an awkward smile. I used to really hurt people, and now I'm scared of a girl in a sundress. My father would be rolling in his grave if we hadn't cremated him. I'm a second away from accepting my fate, accepting a lifetime of lonely nights, solo workouts, microwave dinners, and a perfectly comfortable bed, which I hate. But then her smile grows. And it's like the heavens have opened.

The disco ball dances colors over her skin in such a way that I'm almost fucking jealous. Her blonde hair is in loose waves, just the way I like. In fact, she's dressed exactly like our first date together. If she weren't running, no, *sprinting* toward me right now, I'd be devastated that she was wearing it for another man.

I open my arms wide, and she leaps into the air, wrapping her legs around my waist and clinging to me like the cutest koala I've ever seen.

I grip her ass with one hand, ensuring that the fabric of her dress isn't flying up and giving the bowling alley perverts a show; the other, I cling to her neck, pulling her against me. Inhaling deeply, I smell her shampoo. Fuck, I've missed this so much. She smells like home. Despite being a gross teenage-filled bowling alley, she's here, and I would set up a tent right now if she wanted. We could live here forever on cheesy fries and watered-down soda.

My eyes start to prick, and I cough, blinking hard to keep the tears at bay. Fuck's sake. Alfie Adams has really turned on the tap and refused to turn it back off again.

"I can't believe you're here," she murmurs against my chest.

She drops her legs down, and once she's on the floor, she peeks up at me through her wet lashes. I'm not the only one with waterworks.

"You are late, though," she teases.

"Late? I thought you were on a date!"

"Yeah," she says sheepishly. "I thought that might get you moving quicker."

Realization hits me. I've been played. Danny lied about the date with the cowboy although I know him giving her his number is true. I shake my head, relief flooding through me.

"I've had a bad influence on you," I murmur.

"Maybe . . . Or maybe I've always been a little bad," she flirts, and the knot deep under my ribs loosens for the first time in weeks. I can finally breathe again.

Before I can respond, she's dragging me over to a group of people, including Nicole and Josh.

"Everyone, this is Austin," she says, plonking down on the hard plastic seat.

The group cautiously mumbles their hellos before the first person, the brunette with shoulder-length hair picks up her ball. I think her name is Marianne from what Luca's told me in his report. Tough crowd. I guess they've heard something about what's happened, although I highly doubt it's the truth. *What is my little Killer up to?* My name is up on the list, ready to bowl, along with everyone else's. They really have been waiting.

I know Nicole and Josh. The redhead must be Blakely.

The only guy I don't recognize is a tall, brown-haired man who is sitting next to Nicole. I glance up at the screen and see the name Mike and realize it's Nicole's brother. That must be why Josh is practically inching away from Nicole in the adjacent seat.

I snake my arm around Olivia and lean down.

"We need to talk, Killer." I keep my voice low in a way that I know makes her squirm. I spot the telltale signs of goosebumps flooding her neck, and I smile.

"Oh, we will. But first, you're going to have to accept your punishment."

Marianne knocks down another two pins, and Olivia is off her chair, whooping horrendously loud.

"Punishment? I like the sound of that." I wink as she parks back down next to me.

"Good. We've got three games to play. I know how much you love group activities and loud noises."

I smile. It's hardly a punishment to be in her presence again, regardless of the circumstances, but if she wants to play this game, I'll play.

"I didn't think *group activities* were your thing either, Killer. But if you really want to share, I'd do it for you."

Her whole body jolts. "Really?"

Her face sinks, and I know we're not playing anymore. I can't drag this out.

"No, Olivia. I was playing. I don't want to share you with anyone. Fuck, I don't want to share you for a game of bowling."

"Three games of bowling," she whispers, and I roll my eyes.

"Yes, two games of bowling."

"Three!" she laughs.

"Three, and then I am literally carrying you out of here. Got it?"

She grins, putting her hand out to shake. Instead, I stand, grab her hand, and pull her in.

"We only seal our deals with kisses, Killer," I whisper

against her lips before pressing mine gently against hers.

Our lips mold together, and I feel her sink against me. Hope springs in my chest, and I finally fully relax until, with brute force, she launches herself at me. Her teeth nip at my bottom lip; her tongue invades my mouth as she tastes me. In an attempt to regain control, I press the flat of my palm against her back, pulling her flush against my chest, but she hitches her leg instead, grinding her perfect pussy against my thigh. Her little whimpers escape her mouth to caress my hardening cock.

"Ah, hem." An irritated tone cuts between us as a wolf whistle from another lane rings through the air.

We break apart. Oh yes, we're in Satan's armpit, the Bowlarama. How could I forget?

"This is a *family-friendly* establishment. Get yourselves under control or get out," a curly-haired twenty-something-year-old manager hisses as our entire party flushes with embarrassment.

"Do you guys need to leave?" Nicole giggles.

"Nicole, don't be improper," her brother snips as Josh rolls his eyes. I'm unsure if it's aimed at us or them. And if it's them, if it's Nicole or Mike.

"No, no, no, we're all good," Olivia says.

"I bet your panties say otherwise, Killer," I whisper so only she can hear.

She flushes beautifully but pretends not to hear.

"My turn!" she announces, bouncing toward the lane. She picks up a bright pink ball and lines herself up against the lane. With a straight arm, she throws the ball hard, slightly off center, and every single pin comes crashing down.

What the hell? My girl is full of surprises.

The girls all woop loudly as the boys slow-clap their appreciation, jaws slightly slack.

"Yes, girl!" Nicole sings loudly before high-fiving Olivia.

She gives me a shimmy before perching next to me, and I stand to take my turn.

After a disastrously poor game on my part, Olivia relents, and she pulls me by the hand away from the group.

"Bowling was really the only activity I could afford to take Danny to do after Mom and Dad died. This kept us both out of trouble. For a while at least." She laughs.

I love that she trusts me enough to still give me tidbits about her growing up.

"Until he met me, you mean."

"Well . . . yes, but I've changed my mind about all of that."

"All of that being the reasons you kidnapped me and held me hostage in your basement." I twirl her hair between my fingers.

"Hostage really does suggest there was a ransom request, which we both know there wasn't." She's right, annoyingly.

I grin down at her, cupping her cheek. Her citrusy shampoo perfectly engulfs her. I want to lean down and take a bite.

She hesitates for a second before lifting her hand up to my face and stroking my beard. It's so familiar I still can't believe I'm not dreaming.

"You kept the beard . . . it looks good."

I run my hand over the stubble. "You like it?"

"Yeah, it suits you, makes you look a little softer."

I nod, smiling, and then we're silent until I can't take anymore. I have to tell her everything. I know Alfie told me to take it easy and give her a chance to catch up, but I can't.

"I'm sorry for Danny. For breaking my promise . . . fuck, I'm sorry I let you go. And I'm sorry it took me so long to get my head out of my ass to make it back to you."

"I know. I forgive you." She strokes my face.

"You do?"

"Yeah, I do."

"Okay, but I hurt you."

"Yes, and I hurt you too. And I'm also sorry."

"You have nothing, fucking nothing, to be sorry for, Olivia. I dragged you into this." She rolls her eyes and steps back. Fuck, it stings.

"It's not for you to decide when I'm ready to forgive you, Austin. That's not how this works. It's not how this is going to work. I decide. I make my own decisions and I make my own choices."

"Okay, well what's your choice then?"

"You're forgiven. I love you, and I want to be with you here. We can start fresh. From what Danny has told me, you can work remotely or you can build a second farm out here, or we can even split our time between here and Seattle. I'll do whatever it takes to be with you, because I choose you, I don't want anyone else. I've met a lot of people this last month or so-"

"Wait," I interrupt, "what do you mean?"

She sighs, softening slightly, allowing me to pull her back in between my legs.

"Yeah Austin, I met a lot of people, I've been asked out a few times. And honestly? I was tempted to say yes sometimes because it meant I might have a chance at getting over you and not feeling so shit all the time."

I groan and lift my chin up to the sky, trying to compose myself, but she ignores me.

"But I didn't feel anything for anyone, so no, I didn't actually go on any dates. No excitement or joy, or spark of attraction. And they were hot, Austin. Like, model hot. Beefcakes that could keep up with me on a workout."

I still can't look at her, but I sigh. "No one can keep up with you on a workout; you're a machine."

She rolls her eyes. "Okay fine, they could *almost* keep up."

I grin finally dipping my head down so I could nuzzle into her neck. *That's my girl.* Now I just need to find out these fuckers' names.

"Are we just going to skip past the fact that I told you I

want you to move here?"

"I'm just reveling in it for a minute."

"Take your time. I've only been waiting for nearly a month."

I tilt her chin up and run my thumb over her cheek. Her lips are so pink and pretty. It's been so long, I never thought I'd be this close to her again.

"Austin?" She frowns.

I smile, kissing her gently. Our lips mold together as I cup her face, my fingers tangling in her hair.

"Olivia Daniels. I'll do whatever you want. If you want me to stay in Seattle for the rest of my life, miserable and alone, I'll do it if it means you are happy without me. I would watch all your fucking videos over and over until I memorize every single one, just so I could keep a part of you with me. So when I hesitate to say I'll move here, it's not because I don't want to. It's because I want this to be your choice, your decision. Coming here wasn't meant to ambush you."

"What's a little ambush between boyfriend and girlfriend?" she whispers before squinting up to the sky to think. "It's almost as forceful as kidnapping someone rather than having a conversation, don't you think?"

I draw her hand to my lips and kiss her knuckles; tears glisten in the corners of her eyes. I continue, "I want you to be the best version of yourself. If that means that I can be with you, I'd be ecstatic, I'd be fucking yelling it from the rooftops and then I'd probably call Alfie and ask him to calm me down. But yeah, I'd move here, I'd do anything for you because you're the love of my life, Olivia. I love you, I'm in love with you. Fuck, for the love of all things holy, tell me your new place has a basement?"

She laughs, throwing her head back before I catch a stray tear falling down her cheek.

"No basement, I'm afraid."

I nod. "Okay . . . I'll get a shovel tomorrow. I'll dig one for you."

“How about you just stay with me?” She kisses my lips, her hands pulling at my shirt.

“In your bed? Outrageous. What would your brother think?”

“Given that he forced your ass down here, I’d say he was cool with it.” Her fingers reach the nape of my neck, and she tugs my hair gently. I pull her in, crushing her body against mine.

“Let’s stop talking about your brother. I wanna see my new room.”

“Does that mean you’re moving in?” She grins.

“I can move in, we can find somewhere new, we can stay in Austin, move back to Seattle, whatever the fuck you want. I’m with you. Wherever you want to be.”

“Let's start in *our* room and see where it takes us.”

“Lead the way, Killer.”

EPILOGUE

"Are you sure you're ready for this?"

"Baby, how many times have I told you? I'm waiting for you to catch up. I've been ready since you tasered me." Austin winks.

We're back in Seattle for the week. It gives us time to catch up with family and Austin has a face-to-face session with Alfie. Which if we're being brutally honest, is mainly them just shooting the shit. But until tonight, we have one final video to do for the year. It's not a workout this time, more of a life update.

The video of me talking directly to the "Masked Man" went viral, my stats went crazy, and my follower count rose by another fifty thousand in a week. The interest in my channel was more than I could have imagined. And now, as well as workout videos, I do lifestyle videos, too. It's nice to talk about health holistically, and it's given me the opportunity to grow, too.

Our life in Austin evolved quickly when Austin permanently relocated. We quickly moved out of the apartment I had rented, and Austin bought a three-bedroom house with a yard and a basement, *of course*. While we're not looking to fill up the rooms just yet, there's space for us to grow our family if we want to. For now, I have my very own studio where I run my videos.

There is a shared office space, which we've decided to split right down the middle. My half is bright colors and fun decorations. A little bit out there, but it's in line with where

I'm moving the business especially now that I'm partnering with Nicole's fun and bright clothing company. Austin's side is styled more in line with the office in Seattle. It's an old money vibe, with a penchant for antiques and hedonism. It's unconventional, but it works and, honestly, looks slightly ridiculous. But I love it. And it helps that when we're both working from home, we're four feet away from encouraging the other to play hooky.

It's December now, and we've been together for eighteen months, minus the little time apart for a month, which we definitely don't count.

We kept Austin's identity a secret for as long as possible until there were one too many articles of Dr. Alfie Adams being my "Masked Man." One online conspiracy theorist even caught Alfie coming out of the house in Texas when he visited six months ago, causing an absolute uproar.

To introduce Austin as Austin, we released a live video introducing him as the "Masked Man," which ended in him growling at some of the comments, stating they were disappointed and whether I had considered Alfie. His growly nature only seemed to help his cause as the comments went wild for his overly protective playful hyperbole. The assumption was that it was his "character" when, in reality, I had to get Alfie to call him and calm him down.

For today, we've decided to begin the video the same as before. This time, the snow makes things a lot harder, and I trip and fall a few times. My heart is beating faster than ever, the cold air taking sharp cuts at my throat and lungs. The plan is that I'm going to pretend to scrape my shoe down the thin layer of skin on his shin before slamming it down on his foot. Then we'll go into a slower explanation.

As scripted, I let him catch me easily, and rather than holding my back against his chest like we practiced, he spins me so I'm standing directly in front of him. I'm laughing, thinking he's forgotten the moves despite practicing fifty times last night. But he's not laughing. He pulls his mask up, but his face is almost ghostlike, even without the plastic Ghostface mask.

My breathing hitches when he drops to one knee.

"Olivia Daniels," he says slowly as if trying to steady himself.

I pull one hand away and hold it to my mouth. The tears have begun already.

"You have brought me so much joy, baby. My whole life was violence and struggle and feeling like I was never enough for anything. I felt like I deserved to be miserable and alone. You taught me how to love, not just you, but myself."

"Austin, you've always known how to love."

He nods gently, but there are tears in his eyes. "There's nothing I can do that will repay you for everything you've given me. But I promise you, I'll spend my whole life loving you, taking care of you, giving you everything you deserve. I'll do anything for you, Killer, but first, will you please, please, marry me?"

I'm nodding; the whole speech, I'm nodding. There is no way in hell I am ever going to say no to this man. This incredible, beautiful, wonderful man that already takes care of me in so many ways. I used to take care of everything for me and Danny; he's relinquished some of that burden. He's given me more than he realizes. A home, a life, *time*. Time to just be a twenty-something-year-old woman with friends, a business, and a life. Time to really appreciate the little things. But most of all, he's shown me truly how it is to be loved. Something I haven't felt since my parents died. I feel complete with him. I feel at home with him.

"Yes. Yes!" I laugh. "There was never going to be another answer."

I kneel down as he pulls out a small, pink velvet box from his pocket. His hands shake a little as he pries open the lid. Inside, an opal sits on a gold band, haloed with ten stunning diamonds. They glisten and sparkle, catching in the tears that cloud my vision.

"Austin, this ring, it's beautiful, it's just like—"

"Your mom's."

He smiles, pulling the ring out of the box and, after kissing it, slipping it onto my ring finger.

"I wanted it to remind you that you deserve love just like your parents. And I'm going to take care of you for the rest of my life, just like you took care of everything after they passed away. I promise you, Olivia, I swear it." His eyes implore mine.

I understand his need to have me believe him. He's completely the opposite of what I initially thought he was, but he still feels the need to prove it every day.

I cradle his face with my shaking hands. "You're a good man, Austin Black. And I've never loved anyone as much as I love you. But I already said yes. You don't need to convince me to marry you. It's a dream come true to be loved by a man like you."

I kiss him softly, tears tracking down my cheeks and mingling with our lips. His tongue licks along the seam of my lips, and I open for him. I smile into his mouth, my only wish being that I could call my parents to tell them. But a flurry of snow whips around us, causing us both to break apart. The still air and blue skies surround us, except for a little tornado spinning around us. As soon as the snow is lifted, the wind stops, and snowflakes flutter back down around us. I know in my heart my parents are here; it's their little sign to say they approve.

He rests his head on mine, taking a few breaths.

"I have two more things for you if it's okay?" he asks, with an edge of anxiousness.

He pulls out a second velvet box. I frown, confused as to why he would bring two rings.

"Firstly, or secondly"—he laughs—"you might not want to wear your engagement ring when you're working out or doing your videos or runs or whatever else you're doing. But I'd love for you to wear something."

He opens the box to a second ring, this time a band of diamonds lined across a gold band. It's stunning in its own way, but not nearly as regal as the one he gave me first.

"They're still diamonds." He laughs. "But I guess they won't catch on to anything as easily."

"You're too generous, Austin. So thoughtful. I love the idea, and I'll absolutely wear at least one at a time. Thank you." I kiss him again, and he smiles, letting out a big breath. His shoulders relax a little, and I laugh at how nervous this big beast of a man is—such a gentle giant.

"And finally. I have this." He pulls out a Ghostface mask that's covered in pink glitter.

I throw my head back and laugh.

"Oh my gosh, I love it. You want me to be the villain?"

"I thought we could team up. Maybe now that you're going to be Mrs. Black, you could be Mrs. Masked Man as well."

"Oh my god, the channel is going to love this. People will eat it up."

"I'll eat you up, Killer," he murmurs against my lips.

"Promise?"

He winks, helping me to my feet. My knees practically shake from a mixture of adrenaline and kneeling in the snow for so long.

We'll announce our engagement in a few weeks, but we'll keep that recording just for us. We do a mock one where Austin offers me the mask on one knee, and we do one shot pretending to kiss through the masks and another where we both lean our heads eerily to the side. We watch them back, and I can't help but jump up and down in excitement. His goofiness and his indulgent nature warm me fully, even out in the snow.

I can't wait to get back to our lives together. Home truly is in Austin now—in more ways than one.

ACKNOWLEDGMENTS

I'm honestly at a loss for words that this book is finished and published. (Yes, published! I hit "upload" and no one stopped me!) I absolutely could not have done this without my husband. He gives me so much—but most importantly, when it comes to writing a book, he gives me time. Time to write, time to rant, time to listen to me read scenes aloud. You made me feel like a real writer long before I believed I was one. I love you more than anything in this world, and I wouldn't ride this chaotic, plot-twisty train with anyone else.

To my family, who I'm really hoping *haven't* read this book —and therefore may not see this acknowledgment (safer for everyone). From my mum and stepdad's confused expressions when I tried to explain the plot, to my sister's early read-through—I love you all, even if you now know way too much about fictional tasering and hostage romance.

To Connor, who has patiently listened to me prattle on about this story for a year: thank you for being the world's most tolerant sounding board. Despite not fully *getting* the romance genre—and despite me ignoring most of your (no offence) wildly sensible plot suggestions—I appreciate you deeply. Especially for not blinking when I said, "So she kidnaps him… but he likes it." Now go buy the book. As previously stated: *you're not getting a free copy*.

To the Facebook book groups—wow. Honestly, you're the only reason I haven't quit Facebook entirely. The BookTok girlies' recs inspired this whole thing. One of you asked for a "reverse kidnapping" trope and, shockingly, the responses were *too few*. So naturally, I took it upon myself to fix that with a story of my own. And that's how Austin and Olivia were born. From here, there are spin-offs galore already brewing. The power of an unhinged book-loving community is real, and without you, this unholy romantic chaos would never have made it to the page. Stay unhinged, girls.

Printed in France by Amazon
Brétigny-sur-Orge, FR

43962257R00201